Snakewoman of Little Egypt

"As Befits a Man" from *The Collected Poems of Langston Hughes* by Langston Hughes,
edited by Arnold Rampersad with David Roessel, Associate Editor,
copyright © 1994 by the Estate of Langston Hughes. Used by permission
of Alfred A. Knopf, a division of Random House, Inc.

"Precious Lord, Take My Hand" words and music by Thomas A. Dorsey © 1938
(Renewed) Warner-Tamerlane Publishing Corp. All rights reserved. Used by
permission of Alfred Publishing Co., Inc.

"Jesus, Won't You Come By Here?" written by Sam Hopkins © 1969 (Renewed 1997)
Tradition Music (BMI)/ Administered by Bug Music. All rights reserved. Used by
permission. *Reprinted by permission of Hal Leonard Corporation.*

"Cake Walk Into Town" by Taj Mahal © 1972 (Renewed 2000) EMI Blackwood
Music Inc. and Big Toots Tunes. All rights controlled and administered by EMI
Blackwood Music Inc. All rights reserved. International copyright secured.
Used by permission. *Reprinted by permission of Hal Leonard Corporation.*

"The Last Thing On My Mind" words and music by Tom Paxton © 1964 (Renewed)
United Artists Music Co. All rights controlled by EMI U Catalog, Inc. (Publishing) and
Alfred Publishing Co., Inc. (Print) All rights reserved. Used by permission of Alfred
Publishing Co., Inc.

Published by Bloomsbury USA, New York

All papers used by Bloomsbury USA are natural, recyclable products made
from wood grown in well-managed forests. The manufacturing processes
conform to the environmental regulations of the country of origin.

LIBRARY OF CONGRESS CATALOGING-IN-PUBLICATION DATA

Hellenga, Robert, 1941–
Snakewoman of Little Egypt / Robert Hellenga.—1st U.S. ed.
    p.   cm.
ISBN 978-1-60819-262-5 (alk. paper)
1. College teachers—Fiction.   2. Illinois—Fiction.   3. Americans—
Africa—Fiction.   4. Domestic fiction.   I. Title.
PS3558.E4753S63   2010
813'.54—dc22

                                                  2010004164

First U.S. Edition 2010

1 3 5 7 9 10 8 6 4 2

Typeset by Westchester Book Group
Printed in the United States of America by Worldcolor Fairfield

Snakewoman
of Little Egypt

A Novel

———◇———

ROBERT HELLENGA

BLOOMSBURY

New York · Berlin · London

I dedicate this book to
Virginia, Rachel, Heather, Caitrine, and Maya.

There are three things which are too wonderful for me, yea, four which I know not: the way of an eagle in the air; the way of a serpent upon a rock; the way of a ship in the midst of the sea; and the way of a man with a maid.

—Proverbs xxx:18–19

1

Rite of Passage

On his fortieth birthday—August 6, 1999—Jackson Carter Jones, associate professor of anthropology at Thomas Ford University in west central Illinois, ate a poached egg for breakfast and then sat outside on the deck. It had rained recently—twice—and the stream, Johnson Creek, which sometimes dried up at the end of the summer, was full. When it was full, it emptied into the Lakota River, which emptied into the Mississippi. He was trying to decide his own fate, take it into his own hands. He took a coin out of his pocket. A quarter. One of the new ones, Pennsylvania, the American eagle replaced by an allegorical female figure. He flipped it. It landed on the glass table top, bounced off onto the plank floor. The dog, a black lab with a little bit of Rottweiler showing in her broad chest, jumped. The coin rolled in a big circle, then a smaller circle, and finally fell through a crack in the deck onto the sand and grit below, where a big groundhog had made his den.

Jackson had Warren's .22, which he'd cleaned the night before. A box of .22 Longs sat next to an empty coffee cup on the table. He was waiting for the groundhog to appear (as he did every morning), but the groundhog was too canny for him. It always outwaited him, or took him by surprise. Took the dog, Maya, by surprise too.

In the old days Warren, the hired man he'd inherited from Claude Michaut, along with the house, had killed the groundhogs in a trap that chopped their heads right off. The trap was still up in the garage, but Jackson didn't know how to set it; and it was dangerous; and he didn't have the strength; and he didn't need the stress. He was still recovering from a bout of Lyme disease. More than a bout. In the last two years he'd been diagnosed with everything from AIDS and the Chinese flu and mad cow disease to giardia, lupus, sleeping sickness, schizophrenia, chronic fatigue syndrome, Parkinson's disease, MS, and White Shaker Dog Syndrome. By the time a doctor in Chicago figured out he had Lyme disease, he was presenting psychotic symptoms—confusion, short-term memory loss, disorientation, inability to recognize his car in the parking lot, religious hallucinations too, and ghosts from the past: his mother, his father, Warren, Claude; Mbuti friends from the Ituri Forest; his girlfriend, Sibaku, and their daughter, whom he'd never seen. Now, on the road to wellness—after a long course of intravenous Ceftriaxone (Rocephin)—the swelling in his joints was minimal and he could walk around without difficulty, once he managed to get out of bed in the morning, and he no longer had to leave written step-by-step instructions on his kitchen table explaining how to get through the day. No more visitors from his past life knocked on the door in his sleep. He was looking forward to the future for the first time in almost two years.

He looked through the cracks between the planks, looked in his pocket for another coin but didn't find one. He could have crawled under the deck. The quarter would have to be there, heads or tails, unless it had gone into the groundhog hole.

Heads meant he should go back to Africa, which still felt like home to him after thirteen years; tails he should get married and settle down right where he was, where he already had a house in the middle of eighty acres of timber, and a garage, with a little apartment over it. The apartment was empty now, since Warren's death. Warren had been a janitor in Davis Hall, which housed the anthropology and philosophy departments, when Claude came to TF. He'd accepted Claude's offer of free rent in exchange for looking after the property. He'd cut up firewood, stacked it, plowed the drive in winter with a little Case tractor with a blade bolted onto the front end, mowed the tall grass in summer and cut down the nettles on the other side of the stream and the poison ivy vines that grew as thick as your arm. He'd killed varmints, shot a deer every year and dressed it for Claude, paid the bills and the real estate taxes when Claude was gone. He'd stayed in the garage apartment even after he became head of custodial services for South Campus, and was living there when Jackson came back from Africa, alone, and discovered that Claude had left the house to him, though there were some legal difficulties because it had been difficult to prove that Claude was dead.

There were rumors, in fact, that Jackson had done away with Claude deep in the heart of the Ituri Forest. The rumors weren't true, of course—Claude had been like a father to Jackson—but it was impossible to stop them, and they created a certain mystique. His colleagues in the department joked about it—"Don't mess with Jackson"—but the important thing was that Warren hadn't believed the rumors; if he had, he might have killed Jackson. Instead he took it on himself to look after Jackson the way he'd looked after Claude.

The prospect of going back to Africa appealed to Jackson. He'd gone to the Congo when it was still Zaire, just as he was about to start his third year in graduate school. Some grant money had appeared out of nowhere, and Claude had tapped him to go along, probably because he spoke French and because he'd done well in Professor Steckley's two-semester Swahili course. Though there were others who had taken the course too and done just as well. Kingwana or "kitchen Swahili," a Bantu language, was the lingua franca in the Congo. The Negroes who lived along the edge of the Forest spoke it, and the polyglot Mbuti spoke it in the villages, though they spoke a dialect of their own among themselves in the Forest. Jackson wouldn't say he'd mastered this difficult dialect, but he'd learned it tolerably well in the four years he'd spent in the Forest. But what had given him the edge over the other graduate students was the fact that he played the harmonica, or the blues harp, at department parties, and Claude had got it into his head that Jackson was an ethnomusicologist who could help him record and preserve the Mbuti music.

Two and a half years after Claude's death Jackson had been arrested outside Étienne Rameau's huge mud mansion at Camp Rameau by two Bantu policemen. They'd been waiting for him to come out of the Forest for two months. Rumors of Claude's death had reached the authorities, and the authorities had done what authorities always do. But suspicion of murder? Assisted suicide, possibly, though Jackson didn't think the charge would have stuck in a court of law, and it hadn't come to that. He'd been taken to the American embassy at Kinshasa. No one wanted an international incident. Claude was not married but had an illegitimate daughter living in Lyon. It was the university—Thomas Ford University—that had wanted to know what had happened to Claude. Had he returned to France without telling anyone? Had something happened to him? No one, it turned out, had been inquiring after Jackson.

By the time Jackson was arrested his visa had long expired and none of his papers were in order. He didn't even have any papers, in fact. Not the kind of papers that the authorities wanted. Though he did manage to bring back Claude's notebooks, which Claude had given to him after Claude's first death in the Forest—before he was dead once and for all, absolutely and completely dead, as the Mbuti put it.

What had happened was, Jackson had gone native. He'd had a taste of something that he didn't think he could live without—ecstasy, or joy, or maybe simply a settled conviction of well-being, of being at home in the universe, of being where he belonged—though this settled conviction was punctuated by periods of incandescent . . . He couldn't find the words. Perhaps Romain Rolland's oceanic feeling, though Freud had regarded this oceanic feeling as a delusion. Had what Jackson experienced been a delusion or an insight? A fantasy or a vision? But it wasn't like that at all, really. And how could an oceanic feeling be incandescent? He could still remember the feeling even if he couldn't name it. His body remembered. His skin remembered the overpowering moist heaviness of the gigantic trees; his eyes remembered the cool shadowy half-light that spooked the Negro villagers; his ears remembered the birdsong and the monkey chatter and the night sounds that might or might not be the cough of a leopard; his nose remembered the smell of the *munu'asulu* leaves used to wrap food to be cooked in the embers of a fire and the sweet body odor of the Mbuti men; his tongue remembered the bitterness of *liko*, brewed from berries and herbs, and the sharp tang of termites—an acquired taste—which provided the Mbuti, as it did our earliest hominid ancestors, with a rich supply of protein.

Living in the Garden of Eden. Not figuratively, but literally. That's what Claude had concluded, and that was what he wanted Jackson to convey to the learned world. But it was a huge job. Jackson would have to decipher Claude's baroque French handwriting, and then he'd have to edit what was essentially a collection of disjointed field notes. And there were other problems. He didn't want to make himself a laughingstock, or damage Claude's legacy.

Claude's reputation rested on a series of authoritative ethnographies, written in French and subsequently translated into all the major European languages, of the various "pygmy" peoples of central and western Africa—the Batwa, the Bayaka, the Bagyeli, and finally, the Bambuti. ("Ba" simply means "people.") But recently Claude's work had come under attack by other anthropologists: for understating serious problems, such as the persecution of old women for being witches or the unequal treatment of women in general, or for treating wife beatings, abuse of animals, and quarrels that escalated into violence in a tone of lighthearted amusement. What would happen now to Claude's legacy if his claim—which he had never published—to have located the Garden of Eden, right on the border between Uganda and the Democratic Republic of the Congo, came to light?

Jackson's own more modest reputation rested on his book *My Life as an Mbuti*, which had drawn the ire of fellow anthropologists. Why? Because Jackson hadn't played by the rules. On the one hand, he'd been too involved with the natives to see them clearly; the book was too subjective. On the other hand, he'd made the cardinal mistake of the old anthropology by assuming that Mbuti culture enacted a set of values and norms and cognitive frameworks and then by reifying conceptually convenient binary oppositions instead of unpacking and problematizing them.

But what really frosted his critics was that *My Life as an Mbuti* had been a national best seller and that in it Jackson had revealed what many anthropologists regarded as a dirty little secret that ought to be kept a secret: he'd slept with the natives. *One* of the natives. Sibaku, daughter of Asumali, the great storyteller, and Makela, who supervised the *elima*.

If you'd asked Jackson who the president of the United States was when he came out of the Forest, he wouldn't have been able to tell you, wouldn't have known that Reagan had defeated Mondale in a landslide, or that Gorbachev was the new leader of the Soviet Union or that Indira Gandhi had been assassinated by one of her bodyguards, or that the *Challenger* had exploded off the coast of Florida after one of the O-ring seals failed at liftoff.

He had applied for a visa to return to Africa shortly after his return to the States—he wanted to see Sibaku, and he wanted to see his daughter—but his request had been denied. He hadn't been able to produce a notarized letter from a host or friend in what was then Zaire, and with Claude dead and Camp Rameau abandoned, he wasn't likely to get one. He'd been persona non grata, and neither the State Department nor Mobutu's government was interested in having him return. But Mobutu's government had been overthrown in 1997 by Laurent-Désiré Kabila and had become the Democratic Republic of the Congo. Kabila, a man with a reputation for burning his critics alive at the stake, was promising reforms, but the borders with Uganda and Rwanda were too unstable. Travel warnings had been issued. A cease-fire had been signed in July between Kabila and the Uganda- and Rwanda-backed rebels, but there was no question of trying to get across the border from Uganda or Rwanda. Or from Sudan. If he got someone to ferry him across the Congo River from the Republic of Congo in the west, where would he be? Five hundred miles from where he wanted to be. He could imagine surviving for a week in the heart of the Forest itself, living on nuts and tubers, mushrooms and honey, but not the five or six weeks it would take to reach the Epulu River, if he could find his way, which was doubtful. Besides, he didn't think he could get from Brazzaville to Stanleyville without papers.

His daughter. He knew it was a daughter because of the last letter he had received from Étienne Rameau, but he didn't know her name. The letter he sent to Étienne to read to Sibaku came back five months later stamped *DÉCÉDÉ*. Étienne, not Sibaku.

He couldn't make contact because none of the Mbuti could read or write, and they didn't have addresses. He couldn't call up a friend, because there were no telephones in the Forest.

He told himself that it was too complicated. But his daughter had come to him in his sleep. In his dreams she looked like her mother. Four feet tall. Bronze. Anthropologists often sleep with the natives, but they never talk about it. It was unprofessional. Regrettable. Always a mistake. That was the official line. But Sibaku had been a *museka*—ready for sex but not yet married—and could sleep with anyone she liked without being reproached, as long as her lover made appropriate gifts to her father, which Jackson was happy to do, presenting the old man with his second-best knife, a C harmonica, and a pocket compass. The Mbuti practiced exogamy, and Jackson was the only one in the whole band who could have married her.

He wasn't worried about his daughter. She'd be taken care of—mothered, fathered, uncled, aunted, cousined, loved. Soon it would be time for her *elima*, time for her to become a woman.

In his dreams she was not unhappy. He didn't have to worry about her. But she worried about him. Was *he* happy? Did *he* have enough to eat? Did the forest where he lived give him what he needed? Did the *molimo* come to wake up the forest where he lived? In his dreams he could hear the *molimo* (grunting, growling, singing, whistling, farting), waking him up just as his alarm went off.

But was getting married in the United States any less complicated than going back to Africa? And would marriage offer what he was looking for? And whom would he marry?

Actually there was no shortage of single women on campus, attractive women his age who'd pursued careers instead of marriage and family, who'd written books and secured grants and received awards and done all sorts of remarkable things, and who were ready to settle into companionable marriages. He'd enjoyed nondangerous liaisons with a number of them, before the Lyme disease, and his old pal Claire Reynolds was bringing another one over tonight. Claire, whom he'd expected to marry back in his early days at TF, had married a priest instead, an Episcopal priest, and had lived the sort of life Jackson had expected to lead himself, at least at the time, in an old balloon-framed Victorian monster with a porte cochere, two children, a dog. Well, he had a dog: Maya. Claire was always fixing him up. She saw her role as looking after Jackson. As an adult might look after a grown-up-but-not-quite-responsible child. She wanted him to live the life she was living and was always inviting him to this or that special service at Grace Episcopal Church.

Jackson didn't mind, didn't mind that she'd invited herself and her priest husband over for supper so that he wouldn't be alone on his birthday. He didn't mind her priest husband, though he was a bit of a dry stick. High church. The sort of priest who might have gone over to Rome if an attractive young woman like Claire hadn't turned to him for spiritual guidance.

Claire was bringing along a friend, someone new in the English department who had the cry of the loons on her answering machine. Jackson should call her, Claire said, just to hear it. But he didn't call. Claire had offered to bring the meal, too, but she thought her friend Pam would be more impressed if Jackson did the cooking, which he would have done anyway, as Claire knew perfectly well.

So, there was Claire's friend in the offing. And there was Warren's niece, Willa Fern. Jackson had promised Warren to look after Willa Fern when she got out of prison. At least to keep an eye on her. And Warren had hinted openly that she'd make a good wife, and that he'd already spoken to her about the possibility of marrying Jackson, though the reason she was in prison was for shooting her husband, and as far as Jackson knew, her husband was still among the living, still her husband, in fact. Warren had hired a lawyer to help her file for a divorce, but then Warren had gotten sick, and the divorce-and-remarriage plan had been put on hold.

Jackson hadn't rejected the idea outright. Willa Fern was a good-looking woman, at least in the framed photo Warren had kept on his desk, and she was neither too old nor too young—mid-thirties—and Jackson had entertained a Pygmalion fantasy in which he played Rex Harrison to her Julie Andrews, or perhaps her Audrey Hepburn.

He heard a sound under the deck. The groundhog. He'd been so quiet for such a long time in his musings that the groundhog must have thought it was safe to go down to the stream. The dog started barking, but instead of going back down in his hole the groundhog made a break for it.

He had a second hole, of course, in the front of the house by the woodpile. Jackson kept filling both holes with a mixture of dirt and clay, only to find them opened up the next time he looked.

The groundhog was scuttling down to the stream. He was halfway down the slope by the time Jackson had him in his sights. Jackson closed one eye, sited on the groundhog, which was turning to look at him. He pulled the trigger, the gun fired, the groundhog scuttled down to the stream.

He took shells out of the .22 and put them back in the box on the table. He put the gun back in its case. He made another small pot of espresso in one of Claude's many espresso pots, a French pot with a spout on it. This one had a little shelf. You put your cup on the little shelf and the coffee came out of the spout and into the cup. If you forgot to put a cup on the shelf, as he sometimes did, the coffee spilled all over the stove and ran down into the burners.

He drove into town. The dog, Maya, riding shotgun.

He stopped at Farm King on the way into town and bought a Have-a-Heart trap. The clerk, who recognized Jackson and called him "professor," suggested pouring antifreeze down the groundhog holes.

"What about the dog?"

"You want to keep the dog away from there for a few days."

"Any other ideas?"

"Get yourself a hose and pour ammonia down the hole. Wait a couple of minutes," she said, "to let the ammonia settle. Then you add a bottle of bleach and get the hell out of there. You don't want to breath that stuff. You know, a lot of housewives get sick that way, mixing ammonia and bleach. They think . . ."

Jackson paid for the Have-a-Heart trap.

"You put some canned peaches in there, you'll get something."

"Thanks."

He put the trap in the back of the truck and stayed on the highway instead of turning on Farm King Road to avoid the smell from the meat processing plant when the wind was from the north; past the prison, then east on Broadway to the Circle at the center of town. It was the most attractive way to approach the town, Colesville, named after Edward Coles, an abolitionist governor who eventually got disgusted with Illinois politics and went back to Philadelphia. Broadway, once you got past Lindon Road, was lined with big houses and big trees, oaks and maples and an occasional elm that had survived the blight. The houses were eccentric, but lovely in new coats of paint. Like the houses in San Francisco, except they weren't all jammed together.

At Cornucopia on East Main Street he bought gorgonzola instead of one of the more expensive French blue cheeses, fresh pasta, French bread. He'd spent a year in France with his parents, when he was twelve, and then he'd gone back on his own for a year of doing nothing in Paris. After a week at the international youth hostel on the rue Trousseau, he and a French girl from Toulouse who was looking for a roommate moved into a little apartment on the rue Stanislas, across from a tanning salon (Centre de Bronzage). They shopped every day at a *fruiterie* on the boulevard du Montparnasse and at the same *charcuterie* that his mother had patronized across from the Métro station. He still shopped every day, at the Hy-Vee in Colesville, and at Cornucopia. It was a way of getting out, giving a shape to the day, being around people, seeing what looked good. He hadn't had much appetite for a while, but it was coming back, and he was able to drink a little beer or wine now without any ill effects.

And there were always good-looking women. Wherever you went. Even in the Hy-Vee. Amazing. So much beauty. Though not like Paris, where the women dressed up even to go to the butcher. His mother had dressed up. His father too. And Suzanne, the woman he'd lived with for almost a year, had dressed up just to look out the window, though she didn't always bother to put on a skirt or pants. She was married now and lived in a big apartment in the ninth arrondissement, across the street from the house where Chopin lived during his love affair with Georges Sand, who had her own house on the same street. Every year Suzanne sent a Christmas letter inviting Jackson to spend the holidays with her and her family in their country place in the Dordogne. And Jackson sent her a Christmas letter inviting her and her family to spend the holidays with him in the woods.

He changed the menu when he saw fresh mussels at the fish counter at the back of the store. Remarkable changes had taken place at the supermarket in the last few years. You could be surprised by fresh mussels, or sea scallops, or wild shrimp, and sometimes even wild salmon. Hoisin sauce was on the shelves, along with Chinese soy sauce, next to the Kikkoman; balsamic vinegar; six or seven kinds of olive oil . . . You could count on radicchio and fennel and arugula in the produce section. He ate well.

He'd eaten well in the Ituri Forest too. His father had warned him that he'd never make it as an anthropologist—because he didn't like yams. And it was true, in a way. Oceania and large chunks of Asia and Africa would have been off-limits. Yams morning noon and night. He couldn't have faced it. The Mbuti ate yams, but theirs was not a yam culture. They lived on mushrooms and wild honey and plants that had no name in English, and roasted duiker, a kind of antelope, and vicious little mouse deer that lived on the river banks. And termites, and sometimes boiled monkey. Occasionally elephant.

When the guests arrived in Claire's new four-door BMW, the dog ran up the ramp to greet them. The house was halfway down a slope. The garage was at the top of the slope. At the bottom of the hill Johnson Creek separated the house from the woods beyond. The ramp was very romantic, but inconvenient. It would have been better to have built the drive right down to the front of the house. Jackson had nailed little pieces of wood on the ramp, which was treacherous when it was icy and you were carrying bottles of wine in paper sacks. The guests stepped on the little pieces of wood even though it wasn't icy.

People spoke of Claude's cabin, but it was really a house—very rustic, but very comfortable. There was a Lopi wood-burning stove in the large living room, which took up most of the first floor and was full of books, but there was a furnace too, and air-conditioning.

Claire gave Jackson a couple of air kisses and introduced him to Pam. "You didn't call her, did you? I mean, just to hear the answering machine?"

"The cry of the loons," Jackson said.

"Why don't you call now?"

"Why would I call her now?" Jackson asked. "She's right here."

Claire invited Pam to admire the kitchen, which Claude had designed himself, turning it into a sort of French farmhouse kitchen, with a large Lacanche stove set back into the wall, old blue and white pottery on the shelves, and terra-cotta tiles on the floor. Copper pots hung from the ceiling, some with tin linings, which Jackson had retired, and some with stainless steel, which he used regularly and which needed polishing.

Pam was wearing a summer dress with a low scooped neckline. Claire was her usual classy self in a pastel sheath dress that would have been suitable for entertaining at the rectory, which she and her priest husband sometimes called the Vicarage—which was beautiful in its own way, with leaded windows on the first two floors and eyebrow windows in the attic. Father Ray, Claire's husband, was independently wealthy. So was Claire. At least her parents were.

"Jackson, if you'd listen to me you'd be able to afford decent wine." She handed Jackson a paper sack with two bottles of wine. Claire had been putting money into dotcom stocks and was trying to get others to join her. Jackson was too stubborn. "Doesn't it bother you to see everybody around you getting rich? It's not too late, you know." And apparently this was the case, because shares kept going up and up and up. Jackson didn't follow the market, but did listen to NPR.

"Get out while you can, Claire," he said. "You'll thank me later. This whole country's gone crazy. It's the South Sea Bubble all over again."

Father Ray came to his wife's defense. "It's different this time."

"It's always 'different,'" Jackson said. He deliberately didn't take the wine out of the sacks until he was in the kitchen. Claire had spent a fortune on two bottles of white Burgundy. "Did you hear about that guy in Atlanta," he said, "who killed nine people and wounded I don't remember how many? He was a day trader."

"He went crazy," Claire said, "because he *lost* money, not because he *made* money."

"I don't want to be around when you lose all your money."

"Jackson won't listen to anyone," Claire explained to Pam. "If he'd listened to me, he'd be a millionaire right now. Or at least a hundred-thousandaire."

She turned to Jackson: "Pam's just taken a course in day trading. She's going to help us all get rich. We're going to form an investment club. Pam will be our guru."

Pam was a poet. She'd taken up day trading to supplement her income, because there's not a lot of money in poetry. She'd gone to a seminar on day trading in Chicago that lasted a full week.

Claire said, "You paid fifteen hundred dollars. Right?"

Pam nodded.

"What did you learn?" Jackson asked.

"Don't hang on to stocks overnight."

"Why's that?"

"Extra risk. You don't need it. Especially when you're starting out."

"What kind of risk?"

"Well, if you go to bed holding on to your shares and they devalue the currency in Brazil, you're in trouble up to here." She indicated her chin. "That's what happened last August. The Dow dropped five hundred points."

"But it came right back up," Father Ray said.

"How do you know what to buy and sell?" Jackson asked.

"You get up in the morning and watch CNBC. You see who the guests are. If they're on CNBC they're not going to be bringing bad news, so you buy those companies.

"You want to get in and out and make a lot of small profits. Everything is liquid, so you can buy at sixty and sell at fifty-nine and an eighth."

"Why would you do that? I mean, why would you sell at a loss?"

"Sorry. You could buy at sixty and sell at sixty and an eighth. Better?"

"If the market goes up . . ." Pam said. "If you make two hundred dollars a day, that's an extra fifty thousand a year."

"Don't be such a stick in the mud," Claire said to Jackson. "Pam says we should invest in ShoppingKart.com. Start with five thousand apiece. You can come up with five thousand, can't you Jackson? You've got nothing to spend your salary on. Unless it's your Save-the-Pygmies fund. Tell them about ShoppingKart.com, Pam."

"ShoppingKart.com's going to be huge. It's going to target the entire American retail grocery market. It's a ten-billion-dollar company."

"What does ShoppingKart.com do?"

"They're reengineering the entire grocery industry. They've got a three-hundred-thirty-thousand-square-foot warehouse in Oakland, and they've signed a deal with Bechtel to build twenty-six more, all over the country. You go on line and make a list. You've got three hundred different vegetables to choose from, three hundred fifty kinds of cheese; seven hundred wine labels. They assemble your order, send it to a docking station, and then it's delivered right to your door. Profit margins of twelve percent. Do you know what the average is for supermarkets?"

No one knew. "Three percent. Three percent!"

"I like to do my own shopping," Jackson said.

Claire was anxious for Jackson to open the wine. He put it off, just to let the anxiety build a little. As if he might not open it until they sat down to eat. Which was the sensible way to do things. Claire headed them toward the kitchen, and a corkscrew.

"This is what anthropologists call magical thinking," Jackson said. "If you wish hard enough for something to happen, it will happen. Like the cargo cults. People think these dotcom guys are some kind of spiritual beings possessing divine powers. Like John Frum."

"I'm wishing that you'd open the wine," Claire said.

Jackson opened Claire's wine. "Is this supposed to breathe, or can we drink it now?"

"Both," Claire said. "Do you have any Campari?"

"No, I don't have any Campari."

Claire laughed. She always asked for a Campari and soda, reminding Jackson of a time when they used to drink Campari and soda all the time.

Pam stooped to admire the view through the kitchen window. "Do we have time for a walk before supper?"

She was looking at eighty acres of timber. Woodlots. Mostly second growth, but a lot of the old trees still standing. White oaks, red oaks. Horse chestnut. Hickories. Kentucky coffee trees, two or three elms that had survived the Dutch elm disease that devastated the campus and the town. There were two cottonwoods at the far end of the property, where the stream ducked under Route 64, and plenty of wild cherry, Osage orange, walnut, hackberry, mulberry.

"You wouldn't want to walk now," Jackson said. "I didn't get the paths cleared this summer. Warren—Warren used to live over the garage—always cleared the paths in the spring with a trimmer mower, but Warren got sick, and then he died. Too much poison ivy, you've got to be careful. Too late to do it now. You've got to watch out for ticks, too."

"Jackson had this marvelous hired man who did everything for him. Plowed the drive, fixed the roof, cleared the paths . . . He inherited him from Claude Michaut. Mr. Pygmy."

Jackson poured olive oil into a large copper saucepan and added some minced garlic. Just before the garlic had started to turn golden, he added a generous splash of white wine.

"He's got a niece," Claire said. "Warren does. In the prison here. Henrietta Hill Correctional Facility—the Hill. He helped her apply to Thomas Ford. Got her a tuition scholarship and left her enough money to pay for everything else. Jackson's supposed to look after her."

Jackson crumbled some gorgonzola onto the salad.

"Have you figured out what to do with her? I mean, is she going to live in a dorm? How old is she? She's about thirty-five, right? Hard to imagine she'd want to live in a dorm with nineteen- to twenty-two-year olds. Of course, after Henrietta Hill, who knows? She could probably teach them a thing or two about group living. What about the church, Ray?" Ray seemed startled. "Can you think of anyone in the congregation who might be willing to take her in?"

"Not off hand, but I suppose we could put a notice in the bulletin."

"She'll need some friends, that's for sure. We can help out there."

"What's she in prison for?"

"She shot her husband, isn't that it?"

"I didn't know that was a crime."

"Very funny, Pamela. But it was more complicated than that, wasn't it Jackson?"

"Much more complicated."

"Her husband forced her to put her arm in a box of rattlesnakes, isn't that right? Forced her at gunpoint."

Pam expressed the appropriate horror. "So she had a good reason to shoot him. Did she get bit?"

Jackson was sorry now that he'd ever told the story to Claire. Like a lot of stories, this one had gotten loose, like a snake, and was probably going to start biting people. Claire had no doubt spread it around the university. *Mea culpa.* "I guess it was too good a story to keep to myself," he said aloud. (Though he'd kept quiet about the Garden of Eden, and about his daughter.)

"She got bit, but I think it wasn't real bad. They got her to the hospital right away."

"Why didn't they put *him* in jail?"

"I don't know. I guess the bite didn't swell up much. Her husband said it might have been their pet raccoon that bit her."

"A box of rattlesnakes? Who's got a box of rattlesnakes?"

Jackson dumped the mussels into the pan, put the top on, and looked at his watch. Soup bowls were stacked on the counter. The loaf of French bread, from the Cornucopia, was on the table.

"Willa Fern's husband, that's who. He's a holiness preacher down in Little Egypt. Southern tip of Illinois, across the Ohio River from Kentucky.

"Is that around here?" Pam asked. Pam was from California.

"Four hundred miles."

"Why does he have a box of rattlesnakes?"

"They handle them during their services."

"Is that legal?"

"Probably not."

Claire poured herself some more wine. "Jackson, I'm going to go with you when you pick that poor woman up at the Henrietta Hill. She's going to need a female friend."

"We'll see."

"There's no 'we'll see' about it. She's going to need some looking after. Imagine, your husband forcing you to put your arm in a box of rattlesnakes. And when you try to defend yourself you get thrown in jail. This country is unbelievable."

Jackson specialized in simple French or French-type dishes. He had both volumes of Julia Child's *Mastering the Art of French Cooking* and a copy of *Larousse Gastronomique* in French, but the only cookbook he used regularly was his first, which he'd bought at Kroch's and Brentano's in Chicago. *The Flavor of France*. A picture on every page (of France, not the food), and no recipe was longer than a half a page. He hadn't given a little intimate dinner in two years, and he was looking forward to the buzz—from the wine, and from the possibility of a strange woman spending the night.

Claire asked Ray to say grace and insisted that they all hold hands. Jackson, sitting across from Father Ray, held hands with Claire and with Pam, ready to disengage his hand before Claire gave it a special little squeeze. Pam's holding strategy was neutral. She had no special message to communicate. No invitation.

He put a side of salmon on the grill so it would cook while they ate their first course, *moules marinières*. One thing he'd learned from Claude was how to give a nice rhythm to a meal by serving two courses of more or less equal weight. The salmon was done by the time he'd cleared the mussel plates, so they picked up the thread of the earlier conversation—ShoppingKart.com—and then Father Ray pointed out that today was not only Jackson's birthday, and not only the anniversary of the bombing of Hiroshima, but also the

Feast of the Transfiguration. There was a connection in Father Ray's mind because his grandfather had been killed at Okinawa in 1945.

"Some churches have started to celebrate the Transfiguration on the Sunday before Lent. It's not a bad idea, actually. It makes a nice transition between Epiphany and Lent. But I don't know. It's always been on August sixth, as long as I can remember."

By the time the conversation turned back to the heat and the humidity, the salmon was flaking nicely. It was beautiful. Jackson served it on large white plates that had room for the salad. A wonderful salad. Spring mix. All kinds of herbs and lettuces in special bags.

"You know what I'm thankful for?" he said. "I'm thankful for the salads in these little bags. It took them a long time to figure out how to get the bags right. Each bag is a miniature biosphere. You have to have a different kind of atmosphere for every kind of salad. You get the wrong kind of ink on the package, bang, your salad is suffocated."

Jackson didn't keep any brandy or cognac around, no hard liquor in the house. So they drank more wine. Jackson had always enjoyed unbuttoned after-dinner talk, but he was thinking of introducing a system of entertaining in which people came over for a good meal and then left right away. That's the way his parents had entertained. Before they'd lived in Paris. But it would be hard to explain this to friends and colleagues when you were inviting them to dinner. *I'd like you to come for dinner, but I want you to leave as soon as we're finished eating.*

Jackson made a pot of espresso. He was afraid to drink any more wine because of the Lyme disease, but Claire kept topping off her glass. Ray tried to slow her down without being too obvious about it, offering to clear her plate and glass. But she was not about to let the glass go. Or the second bottle of white Burgundy, which was still half full.

Later on, in the kitchen, as he was getting some clementines out of the hydrator, he had one of those inevitable refrigerator moments: You stand up and close the refrigerator door, and there she is, someone who wants to know how you *really* are. Someone you've been trying to avoid being alone with. You've been trying to avoid this moment. She's unsteady. Glass in hand, she mouths her words: "You know I still love you, Jackson. Nothing can change that."

Claire was handsome at forty, just starting to look matronly. She wasn't dressing her age, and tonight she'd drunk too much wine and was looking blowsy. Jackson wanted to say that plenty had changed "that." But he didn't say anything, because he remembered Claire. The way she used to be. So young, so full of hope. A different Claire. His first real love. His third, actually, after Sibaku in the Forest, and Suzanne Toulon in Paris. Would she have become a different woman, he wondered, if she hadn't dumped him for Father Ray? And would he have become a different man?

What had happened was, Claire and Jackson had come to Thomas Ford the same year. Both had been rising stars. Jackson had published a popular account of the four plus years he'd spent with the Mbuti, and Claire had an NEA fellowship under her belt. She also had a manuscript and a New York agent. She and Jackson soon became an item. Three years later they were still an item, but Claire's novel, *The Sins of the World*, had been rejected thirty-nine times. Her classmates from the Iowa Writers' Workshop were publishing novels, winning prizes, getting reviewed. Claire's agent dropped her—there were no more publishers left—and Claire had to start submitting it to contests. She was suicidal. Jackson was afraid she'd throw herself off the roof of her building. He told her not to worry, that nobody read novels anyway, but this was her vocation, her calling. She couldn't just walk away from it. She started attending the Episcopal Church—Grace Church, on Broad Street—and she stopped going to bed with Jackson. She needed to be chaste for a while. She turned to Father Ray for spiritual advice, and he told her about God's love and she told Jackson about it. Then the news came. *The Sins of the World* had won the Donner Prize. It didn't matter that no one had ever heard of the Donner Prize. The book would be published. Claire sat on this news for quite a while. Jackson wanted to have a party, offered to throw a party. But Claire thought it was a time to be quiet. Thankful. Prayerful. The romance was over. Claire married Father Ray.

She still came to see him now and then, when Father Ray was out of town or had a vestry meeting, and they'd make love on the big leather sofa in the living room. She thought she was doing him a favor, and he thought he was doing her a favor, and so it was never very satisfactory. But it was better than nothing.

"You don't need to say anything," she mouthed. Putting her finger to her lips. Then out loud: "I'll go with you to pick up Warren's niece—what's her name?"

"Willa Fern."

"You shouldn't have to face that alone."

The clementines were in a mesh sack. Jackson tumbled them into a glass bowl. "Would anyone like an espresso?" he shouted.

2

How I Lost My Faith

S nakewoman" is a nickname I picked up in prison, and I've never revealed it to an outsider, though I've become attached to it in my own mind and in fact have come to think of myself as "Snakewoman."

What happened was that a big rattlesnake got loose in the dining area right after we got moved over from Cell Block A, and there was a general panic. No one ever figured out how it got there because there aren't many snakes around Colesville, which is six hours north of Naqada, my hometown, and even if there were, how would a nine-foot serpent have gotten into the prison? Well, lots of other things got into the prison too, so maybe you shouldn't be surprised. It probably came in on the back of a truck and got into the kitchen from the loading dock. However it got in, it came out of the kitchen and curled up in the dining room outside the double swinging doors. It had trouble getting traction on the waxed floor and became agitated and started to sing, and I couldn't blame it because the cons were all agitated too, standing on chairs and tables and screaming. Though snakes don't have ears and can't hear.

When the warden got there he walked right over to me—I was still sitting in my chair eating my powdered eggs—and asked me would I catch the snake. I could understand that somebody had to do something, and I saw an opportunity.

"I'll catch that snake," I said, "if you'll knock some time off my sentence."

"You know I can't do that," he said. It was hard to hear him because of the screaming. "But I could make your tickets disappear."

A ticket is when you get written up for breaking some rule, but I didn't have any tickets.

"How about if you forget to send my release date to my husband?" I asked. I wasn't afraid of the snake, but I was afraid of my husband. He nodded.

"And you could let my uncle pick me up here at the prison instead of sending me on a bus back to Naqada."

He nodded again. We had a deal.

I was one year into a six-year sentence at the Henrietta Hill Correctional Center. It wasn't too bad. Not the way I'd have chosen to live, but better than the way I'd been living back in Naqada. I needed a time-out from my old life.

It was either a small canebrake rattler, or else a big timber rattler, but it wasn't nine feet, which is what everybody was saying. Probably about four feet, which is big enough. It wouldn't weigh more than three or four pounds. It unwound itself, moving slowly, looking for a hole to crawl into. It didn't want to be there any more than I did. Finally it crawled—it was still having trouble getting traction—under a pallet of canned corn that had been set outside the doors because there wasn't enough room in the storage area behind the kitchen. Big industrial-size cans of corn. I can close my eyes and still see the yellow kernels on the labels. Stacked six feet high. The snake started singing again, louder this time—bRRR bRRR bRRRRRRR.

Everyone was watching me. Black Alice, who'd been giving me a lot of grief. Friends too. Home girls from Little Egypt—that's southern Illinois. There were only a half a dozen of us.

It was January. The snake should have been home asleep in its den. I figured it would be a little slow. Timber rattlers are slow to attack anyway.

I didn't have a snake hook, or a forked stick, but a hook or a stick wouldn't have done me any good unless the snake came out from under the pallet. I got down on the floor and peered under the pallet. I didn't hesitate too long because I didn't want to freeze up. I grabbed it just above the rattle and pulled it out, just like I was going into the box at church and pulling out a snake. I jumped to my feet while the snake was trying to go into a coil. I swung it around my head a few times till it was too dizzy to coil or strike, and then I held it with two hands, one behind the head, one just above the rattle. I walked over to Black Alice, who was not black—they called her Black Alice as in black market. She was from Chicago and had it in for the hillbillies, but she was standing on a table just like everybody else. I asked her did she want to hold the snake. At least touch it. That was all it took. I had no trouble from Alice after that. The guards were up on the tables too. They jumped down and started crowding me, but they were afraid to get too close. I had the power of the serpent.

All my life I'd been taught not to handle a serpent unless it had been prayed over, and unless I was anointed with the Spirit. Well, this serpent hadn't been prayed over, and I sure as hell hadn't been anointed with the Spirit. I was done with the Spirit, in fact, and I was pretty sure the Spirit was done with me. But I felt the power anyway.

Someone started shouting "Praise God." I looked around, but I couldn't see who it was. Probably one of the girls from down home.

I was serving a six-year sentence for shooting my husband, Earl. It was August and hot and Earl and I had been fussing at each other for more than a while. Earl hadn't had a drink in two years, but he had started drinking again and couldn't stop. I was drinking too. He was pastor of the Church of the Burning Bush with Signs Following. Everyone looked up to him, came to him for help. But he had backed up on the Lord. Backed up all the way.

Most of the men in the Church of the Burning Bush backed up on the Lord every now and then, sometimes for a few days, sometimes for three or four years at a time. They'd go on a tear in Paducah or St. Louis, or they might go off and drive a big rig for three of four years, or go out and work in West Virginia where they were still mining coal, or out to the copper mines in Montana, or just disappear. And then they'd repent, get right with God again, and everybody'd welcome them home like prodigal sons.

Well, Earl got himself backed up on the Lord and had to let his friend DX take over pastoring the church. He accused me of going with other men, said I had some kind of sex demon, and to tell the truth, he didn't know the half of it. I was hoping, in a way, that he'd beat me up, but not too bad, just bad enough so I could get a divorce from him, like Eleanor Freeman, who was married to one of Earl's friends from across the river in Kentucky. But it didn't work for Eleanor, and it didn't work for me. Instead Earl said he was going to kill me, which he could have done easily. He was big and strong. He'd been a fighter up in Chicago before he moved back to Middlesboro, over in Kentucky. People would hire him to beat up someone they were afraid to beat up themselves. That sort of thing, but that was before he got saved, before we got married.

We were drinking vodka and orange juice and had worked our

way through most of a bottle. Earl held my arm up behind my back. I tried to run away while he was fooling with the lock on the snake shed, but he never let go. He had a gun, a .22 double load. He forced me into the shed, where he kept about seventy snakes. In aquariums. It was temperature controlled. Air-conditioned. Better than the trailer we lived in. Not just rattlesnakes. We had a black mamba that Earl bought in Middlesboro when he was visiting the church there one time—he came to Naqada from Middlesboro—and lots of copperheads. Once he had a cobra that he traded for. Earl and DX were the only ones that handled it—it would spit right at you—and Punkin Bates, the evangelist, from east Tennessee.

He made me get down on my knees and pray. I was really scared this time. He'd never gone this far before, but it was the liquor talking. He said he was going to see if God would spare me. If I was faithful, I'd be okay, but if I'd been cheating on him again, I'd get serpent bit. I did pray, I prayed hard. And it was the last time I prayed. There was nothing there. Nothing but silence.

He took the top off an aquarium that had a couple of copperheads and an eastern diamondback. Your diamondback is meaner than the local timber rattlers, and this one hadn't been prayed over. He got it from a man at the church in Middlesboro. Traded a bunch of copperheads and a massasauga for it. I told him he could just go ahead and shoot me. That's how down I was. I didn't care. And I'd a lot rather get shot than serpent bit. But he said if I didn't put my arm in the box, he'd force my head down in it and I could take the bite in my eye. So I put my arm in. Nothing happened. Then he started banging on the glass with the butt of his pistol, and the snake bit my thumb.

We went back in the house and Earl put his gun down on the kitchen table and opened the refrigerator to get a glass of milk. I picked up the gun, and when he turned around I waited till he bumped the refrigerator door shut with his butt and then I shot him in the shoulder. I thought about gut-shooting him, letting him bleed out real slow. I was a pretty good shot, but my right arm was starting to swell and I had to shoot left-handed. But he was so close I couldn't miss, and I knocked him right on his can.

I called my cousin Sally, who was married to DX, and Sally—who got serpent bit pretty bad later on when I was on the Hill—called 911. The ambulance had to come from Rosiclare. It took about twenty minutes. The paramedics took us both in the same ambulance. Mine must have been a dry bite, because it didn't swell up too bad and I didn't get real sick, the way I did when I got bit when I was sixteen, and two shots of antivenin was all I got, and Earl got the bullet removed and got all bandaged up. They kept him in the hospital, but they sent me home that night, wheeled me right down to the front door in a wheel chair. I went to Sally's instead of back to the trailer.

Sally was my cousin on my mother's side and my oldest friend. She took after her dad, who was really handsome and who wore sunglasses because he had weak eyes. She was two years older than me: first to handle, first to get bit, first to go with a man, first to get married. She worked as a secretary in the lumberyard in Naqada, and she still handled. This was about five years after I'd gone with DX, but she'd forgiven me—everybody'd forgiven everybody, that was our way. DX stayed at the hospital with Earl. She made up a bed for DX on the sofa for when he got home, and she made me lie down in the bed upstairs and then she lay down next to me like we used to do when we were children and used to spend the night at each other's houses, before we knew anything about loving a man and all the sadness that came with it.

I didn't get to tell my story at the trial. I don't think my own lawyer from the public defender's office believed me, and Earl testified that I'd gotten a snake out of the snake shed and was trying to get it to bite him while he was taking a nap, but it bit me instead, and it wasn't a bad bite anyway—my arm didn't swell up too much and turn black—so why not forget about it. My arm was okay by the time of the trial. And I thought Earl's shoulder was okay too, but he was sitting there with his shoulder all bandaged up.

Afterwards my uncle Warren hired another lawyer, from Newport, to file an appeal, but Warren died while I was still on the Hill, and the appeal was still pending at my release date. The lawyer must have forgotten about it, because I never got any bills.

Apart from Sally, Warren was the only one who stood by me. Sally testified at the trial that Earl had turned the church over to DX because of his drinking, but she hadn't been there when Earl put my arm in the box and when I shot him, so it didn't count as evidence. Uncle Warren put up bail money and took me to St. Louis, and we went to see *An American in Paris* in a revival theater.

Once I got settled on the Hill, the Lord gave me one more chance to come home to him, or maybe it was the other way around. Maybe it was me giving the Lord one more chance. Or maybe I was reluctant to let go. Maybe I was still looking for some kind of explanation. Anyway, I joined a Bible study group in prison. We were a sight—a dozen of us in classroom 4D sitting around a long table, clutching our Bibles, bowing our heads.

I thought I knew my Bible, but what I knew best was what people used to shout in church. Not just the men, the women too. And sometimes I'd be shouting right along with them: "God don't never change." "Don't blame Jesus if you go to hell." "God is talking to you now." "I can feel the spirit covering me."

The woman who taught the study group was from the Methodist church in Colesville. She was a nice woman, round-faced, serious, gentle. And she knew her Bible. She had lessons on God's plan for

your life and on the apostles and on how God created the Garden of
Eden for everyone and how Adam and Eve messed it up by disobey-
ing Him. But there was something about it that didn't ring true,
and it finally dawned on me. I used to think that Earl was a lot like
God. But after studying the Bible I got to thinking that it was the
other way around, that God was a lot like Earl. A kind of a bully.
The kind of guy who will lie and steal and cheat, slap you around.
Look at the Garden. Look what happened to Adam and Eve. "Dis-
obey me, will you? I'll whup your tails till they won't hold shucks."
And what about Jesus himself? What happens to you if you're not
dressed right for a wedding? "Tie him up, throw him into Gehenna."
Gehenna. That's the town dump, but everybody knows it means
Hell, just like the bone pile north of Naqada where they used to
dump the slag before the mines closed down. And look at the way
God jerks Abraham around. "Go sacrifice your only son." You'd
think old Abe would put up a fuss, but he just does what he's told. He
gets everything ready; he's got the knife in his hand. "Ha ha," says
God, "I was just kidding." That's just the sort of thing Earl would
have done if we'd ever had any kids.

That's how I lost my faith. From reading the Bible. But it wasn't
so bad, losing my faith. It was a relief, in fact, not having to worry
about salvation all the time, not having to worry about every little
thing you do because God was watching over your shoulder every
second of every day, waiting for you to fuck up. I may have been in
prison, but I felt like I was finally free.

3

What I Learned in Prison

What I learned in prison was that I didn't need a man to look after me. Not Earl, not God. What I learned in prison was how to do my own time, how to stay out of the mix, how to find a routine that minimized conflict, which was not always possible. Black Alice, the biggest stud-broad in the yard, was keen to be my "dad." But if I was going to *family* with anyone, it wouldn't have been with Black Alice, and Alice left me alone after the rattlesnake episode. In fact, nobody messed with me after that. And I learned how to cook with a coffee can and a stinger. A stinger—that's an immersion heater. With a stinger you can boil water, you can put a piece of tin over the top of the can and fry a piece of meat, but boiling is the easiest. We fixed Chinese on my last night, for my going-away party. Rice, pork, mushrooms. As long as you can boil water you're okay, but without a stinger you're fucked.

And of course I got my GED certificate—fourteen required courses and six electives including two biology courses. Most of the teachers were from the community college, but some of them were retired high school teachers. And they always said they got more respect on the Hill than they did in their regular classrooms.

Life on the Hill could have been worse, a lot worse. I needed a time-out from my old life so I could figure out how to start a new one without Earl or God telling me what to do. I could experiment, shed my inhibitions. Maybe pick up some new ones that might work better. In my old life, I knew what I was doing when I went with another man. I was crossing a line, committing a sin, letting the devil into my body. And I knew what I had to do. I had to repent and get right with God, and then everything would be the way it was before. But I was through repenting. I was going to do what *I* wanted to do, and I had some options. Look at me. Thirty-five years old and full of piss and vinegar. I thought that was how the saying went. Not bad looking. My breasts aren't big enough to have a mysterious shadow in between them, but at least they haven't started to sag. My butt is nice and tight. From behind you might guess seventeen or eighteen. But my face gives me away—it's got some miles on it—and a scar on my neck where I got serpent bit when I was sixteen. That was the only time I ever got bit except when Earl put my arm in the snake box.

I got my official notification two weeks before release. On release day I took care of the paperwork down in R&R—Reception and Release. They had to make sure I was who I said I was: Willa Fern Cochrane. They had to return my property. There wasn't a lot, but I was glad to get the purse back that Warren bought for me in St. Louis while I was waiting for the trial to begin. I got a copy of the original arrest report. I'd done my time and was out on supervised release, but I had my dorm assignment at Thomas Ford: Mary Baker Hall, where I'd be living with eight hundred girls.

Warren loved Professor Jackson Carter Jones, and he loved Thomas Ford University, and he loved me too, though we didn't get to know each other till I was about fourteen and he was in his for-ties. Like a lot of men in the church, he backed up on the Lord and got out of Naqada. But unlike most of them, he didn't come back. Not till my daddy got killed in the mine, and then when I married Earl, and then when I was in trouble for shooting Earl. He took care of expenses and made sure I got everything I needed. And after I was convicted, he got me transferred from Little Muddy, down in Hardin County, to the Hill, and he never missed a visiting day till he got too sick to come anymore. He kept putting money in my ac-count so I could buy cookies and cigarettes, which I could use for cash, till they declared the Hill a "smoke-free campus." I was going to stay at Warren's place, out in the country, till school started. He'd left me some money and his old pickup.

Professor Jones signed me out in R&R. He was a friend of Uncle Warren and I knew quite a bit about him. He was an anthropolo-gist; he wrote a book about the pygmies in Africa—Warren brought me a copy; it was pretty good, pretty funny, pretty amazing, really. Then later he'd been sick with Lyme disease. And he'd been with my uncle when he died. He'd written me a letter saying he'd be there to pick me up and I could stay in Warren's place till school started, because I had to give the prison office an address of where I was going when I got out.

My uncle told me that Professor Jones—Jackson—would look after me and offered to speak to him on my behalf. He told me straight out that if Jackson proposed to me, I ought to marry him, and if he didn't propose to me, I ought to propose to him. *Right!* I didn't want anyone to look after me. I had no intention of getting married again. At least not for a good while. Besides, I was still married to Earl.

August fourteenth. "I'm Jackson," he said, as we walked out into the parking lot. It was a bright sunny day. I looked around. It wasn't

Professor Jones I was worried about; it was Earl. I didn't see his truck. Of course, after six years he might have had a new one, but the warden told me he'd kept his promise and "forgotten" to send Earl my release notification, and I guessed he had. Earl had been writing, but I wouldn't accept his letters, even though I knew it was a struggle for him to put pen to paper. He kept wanting to visit, but he couldn't unless I signed a permission form, and I wouldn't sign the form.

We shook hands, sized each other up.

"I'm Sunny," I said.

"I thought you were Willa Fern."

"I used to be Willa Fern. Now I'm Sunny."

We walked across the parking lot to a bright yellow car, a foreign car. Jackson seemed like a nice man. He was wearing jeans and a white shirt with the sleeves rolled up. So was I. Was this a sign?

There was a woman in the car, in the driver's seat. When the woman saw us, she opened the front door and jumped out. *Where did she come from?*

"Hi," she said, sticking out her hand. "My name is Claire."

She was about my age. Maybe a little older.

"Hi," I said. "My name is Sunny."

She looked at Jackson, then back at me. "I thought your name was Willa Fern."

"It used to be Willa Fern," Jackson said, "but now it's Sunny."

"Is that a nickname you got in . . ." Claire nodded toward the prison.

I shook my head. I didn't know how much this woman knew about me. I figured that Jackson knew quite a bit, that Warren would have told him more than he should have.

"How long have you been 'Sunny'?" she asked.

"About two minutes," I said.

"Wow," Jackson said. "How'd that happen?"

"I just decided," she said, "that from now on I'm going to be happy. I don't care what happens. It's such a beautiful day." I looked around. I'd surprised myself. But I *was* happy. And I was thinking that everyone should spend five or six years in prison. Sort of a transition period. Getting to know your own strengths (and weaknesses). Getting a chance to start over. Like going on a long journey. And because getting out is so wonderful too. I wanted to dance.

I didn't mean to be hostile to Claire. I could see that Claire meant me well. It was crazy to think of Claire as a rival. Warren hadn't said anything about Jackson being married, or having a girlfriend. And what was that to me anyway?

Claire started the car—it was her car. Jackson asked if I wanted to stop for a beer.

"Don't be silly," Claire said. "She doesn't want a beer at eleven o'clock in the morning." She looked at me in her rear-view mirror.

"I'd love a beer," I said. "The stuff they brew in the Hill is pretty rough tasting. But could we go to the cemetery first? It's right across the road. You can see it from the warden's office."

Jackson and Claire fussed at each other like an old married couple. I was surprised to find out that they weren't married at all. Well, Claire was married, but to somebody else. They fussed about stopping for a beer, fussed about the cemetery, fussed about where I was going to stay. And this was before we got out of the prison parking lot.

The cemetery was old and looked like it hadn't been in business for a while. I'd been denied a furlough to go to Uncle Warren's funeral, but the warden had let me watch it from his office—the part at the cemetery. I'd seen Jackson then, in a suit, saying something to a group of about twenty people. I'd always wondered what he said. There'd be plenty of time to ask him later. Warren's grave was on the south side of cemetery, about halfway back. A row of pine trees blocked the view of the Deemer Rubber plant. From the warden's office I'd watched them lowering the coffin into the grave. It was almost worse than my daddy's funeral. There was no stone. Yet. And there was an empty plot next to Warren's.

"That's yours," Jackson said.

"Mine?"

"Warren had two plots. He left everything to you, including the plot."

"What do I want with a cemetery plot?"

"You might need it someday, unless you plan to live forever."

"Jackson, stop it. She's just out of . . ." Claire could never get herself to say "prison." "She's got her whole life ahead of her."

"So does everybody."

We made the circuit of the cemetery and then back onto the highway. We stopped at an old-fashioned bar that still had a Schlitz globe hanging from the ceiling. Like the one in Naqada where Earl and I went the night before I shot him.

"You're paying for the atmosphere," Jackson said.

The bartender, standing at the short leg of the bar, called him "Professor." "Long time no see."

"Three Sam Adamses."

We sat in a booth, Claire and Jackson on one side, me on the other.

"What ever happened to Schlitz?" I asked.

"Jackson has Lyme disease," Claire said. "From a deer tick."

"Warren told me," I said. "About the Lyme disease."

I thought I was competing with Claire for Jackson. And that was true, in a way. But there was another kind of competition: Claire and Jackson were competing for me. For *my* attention! Pretty funny.

"Sunny," Claire said, leaning forward. "My husband and I have a lovely guest room with its own bathroom. You'll have complete privacy. We'd love to have you stay with us until school starts."

"What are you talking about?" Jackson said. "She's going to stay in Warren's place."

"Have you cleaned it up since Warren died?"

"Not exactly. I put all the books on the shelves. I got some new shelves, the folding kind."

" 'Not exactly,' " Claire repeated. "That's just what I mean."

Claire was very good-looking, but a little heavy. Just starting to let herself go, starting to get crow's feet around her eyes and creases running down from her nose to her mouth.

The bartender brought three bottles and three glasses, the old-fashioned kind with a narrow base that opened up like a flower. We poured our beers. Lots of head for me. Not much for Claire. In between for Jackson. We raised our glasses and clinked them.

"I like to think of myself as a man of the people," Jackson said, "but these new beers are a hell of a lot better than the old ones."

"What ever *did* happen to Schlitz?" Claire asked.

"I think they made a mistake," Jackson said, "by aiming at a blue-collar market."

"Grab for all the gusto you can get."

"That was pretty good," I said. "I always liked that."

"But not good enough," Jackson said. "And they changed the formula too. Some of the bottles would have a lot of crap in the bottom after about six months in the warehouse."

"Uncle Warren really loved Thomas Ford," I said. It was the life he wanted me to have. A university life. And he'd made it possible for me. He'd paid my room and board for the first year.

"No one was a bigger booster," Jackson said.

I was trying to guess everyone's feelings. There was some uncomfortable space between us. "This beer tastes mighty good," I said.

"Why did I think you weren't a drinker?" Jackson said.

"It's been a long time. We had home-brew in the slammer," I said, "but I never could get used to it." I made a face.

"I meant because of your background. Your uncle. Back in Naqada. I thought the Church of the Burning Bush would frown upon drinking and smoking."

"Oh, it frowns, but then people get backed up on the Lord. Like Earl. They get backed up on the Lord, go on a tear. Happens all the time."

"So, are you backed up on the Lord?"

"I'd say it's the other way around. I'd say the Lord's backed up on me. We're through, the Lord and me." I pretended to wash my hands.

"Your uncle liked a drink now and then."

"More than now and then," Claire said.

"He got out of Naqada as soon as he could. Signed up with Uncle Sam."

"He thought the world of you, you know," Jackson said. And then: "I'm starting to sound like my father." He laughed.

"How much'd he tell you?"

"Quite a bit."

"That's what I figured. Well, he told me quite a bit about you too, so I guess we're even." I raised my eyebrows into question marks. "He said you'd look after me."

"I'll do what I can."

"You know what I learned in prison?"

"What?"

"I learned that I don't *need* a man to look after me." It felt good to say the words out loud. But I stopped myself before I went into a rant. Was *I* being hostile? Firing a warning shot? I wasn't going to be a flatterer; I was going to be a challenger, but I didn't want to go too far. I stopped to adjust my attitude, like a man adjusting a tie that's too tight. But I couldn't get it quite right.

"How do you feel about going to school with eighteen-year-olds?" Claire asked. "A lot of your classes will be full of freshmen."

"How do I feel about it? Nothing to it, because that's the way I feel myself. About eighteen. Maybe seventeen. Or even sixteen. Like I'm just starting my life all over."

We drove down a long drive that needed a load of gravel. There was a school on the north side of the drive, a field of soy beans on the south. The field was flat as a pancake. Then we drove into the woods and all of a sudden it was like home, like you were up on a knob looking down into a hollow with a stream at the bottom. The house was set halfway down in the hollow. You had to walk down a ramp to get to it, like the ramp at the marina in Naqada. A dog, a medium-size lab, ran up the ramp to greet us, and Jackson introduced us. "Sunny, this is Maya. Maya, this is Sunny. She doesn't do any tricks. Maya, I mean."

The house was beautiful, but it wasn't Warren's house. It was Jackson's. Warren had lived in an apartment over the garage. The dog, Maya, climbed up the stairs behind us. The apartment consisted of one large L-shaped room. A tiny bathroom was hidden by an accordion door. There was a sort of kitchen at one end. I opened one of the drawers in the kitchen and a bunch of baby mice jumped out, jumped right into the air, like popcorn. Claire screamed. The dog went crazy, slapping at the mice with her front paws. Jackson killed most of them with a broom and swept them up into a box. A couple of them disappeared.

"Sorry about that. I've got traps, but I forgot to set them."

"You can't stay here," Claire said, holding her hand over her heart. She repeated her offer of her guest room, and I was tempted.

The mice had given me a start, though I didn't scream like Claire. I pretended that they hadn't bothered me. Like it happened all the time.

"She'll be all right," Jackson said. "She's not afraid of snakes, she won't be afraid of mice. She can always buzz me on the intercom if something happens."

"Like a mouse attack?" Claire said. "You couldn't pay me to stay here." She shuddered.

There was no telephone, but Jackson showed me how to work the little intercom he'd hooked up so he and Warren could talk to each other. It was on a computer table next to Warren's blue and silver Mac. Like the ones we used on the Hill, but newer. You just plugged in the intercom and it went through the electric lines. Jackson pulled out his wallet and handed me four hundred-dollar bills and five twenties. Cash from Warren. I'd never seen so much money in my life. My head started to spin.

"I'll be fine," I said. "But I need to be alone for a while. I've got a lot to think about. I'll be fine," I repeated, and I was.

"You've got to go to the Farmers and Mechanics Bank in the morning," Jackson said. "That's where Warren set up your account."

We packed ourselves down the stairs together. It was noon, but I wasn't hungry. Jackson walked down the ramp to the house, and Claire drove off in her fancy yellow car. The dog appeared from behind the garage, curious. I knelt down and when she came up to me I sniffed her neck, and she sniffed my neck. We were interested in each other. I got into Warren's old truck and drove. It was a full-size GMC half-ton pickup with over a hundred thousand miles on it. It needed new struts and the suspension was shot, but it felt good to drive around with five hundred dollars in my purse. Five hundred twenty, to be exact, because I had twenty dollars from the State of

Illinois. I drove around town, just to get myself oriented, and then I headed out into the countryside. I didn't have a map, but I didn't figure I'd need one. I figured if I went west far enough I'd hit the Mississippi. And I did. The road ran straight through a little town and right into the river. Good thing there was a stop sign. The town was Oquawka and I stopped at a little park to see the grave of Norma Jean, a circus elephant that got struck by lightning. There was a photo of Norma Jean on her monument showing her chained to a tree. Lightning had struck the tree she was chained to and killed her, and they'd buried her on the spot.

At a little grocery store I bought a package of thick-sliced bacon and a dozen eggs. I asked for a six-pack of Sam Adams but had to settle for Miller.

It was dark when I got back to the apartment, which felt lovely and snug and safe, in spite of the mice. It wasn't any too clean, but it was only for a few days. Warren had three cast-iron frying pans: small, medium, and large. I chose the large and cooked six slices of bacon and three eggs. There was a toaster, too, but I'd forgotten to buy bread.

The apartment was small by some standards, but huge compared to my cell. And full of books and magazines. It was exciting. A single unit in the kitchen had a tiny refrigerator, a tiny two-burner stove, and a tiny sink. A tiny hot-water heater was tucked into a closet under the roof in the tiny bathroom. The main room was full of books. Books in German, French, Spanish, Russian, Greek, and Latin. Science books too. Biology. I pulled a large biology textbook off the shelf and leafed through it: cell structure, cell membranes, enzymes, photosynthesis and respiration, cell division—nothing I couldn't handle. I put it on the desk next to the computer. Then I tacked up my GED certificate on the wall over the computer.

I picked up a French book—*Paroles*—to look at while I ate my bacon and eggs. I knew I had to study a foreign language, and I thought it might as well be French. I tried to imagine myself speaking French. I remembered a French song my mother used to sing at New Year's—"La Gui-Année." There had been French people in Little Egypt way back. Whole towns full of French people: Paget, La Chapelle, Beauvais, De Lisle. According to my history teacher, Mr. Broughton, they'd come up the Mississippi or else they'd followed the present route of the Illinois Central. Cahokia and Kaskaskia were French missions. The big bell at Kaskaskia had been a present from the King of France, Louis something-or-other, way before the Liberty Bell in Philadelphia. And Fort de Chartres in Prairie du Rocher was built by the French before the United States was the United States.

The book wasn't really a French book. It was a book about how to learn French. I paged through it, looking at the little conversations and the lists of verbs and parts of speech, till I came to a list of phrases that everyone ought to know. I picked out one that I liked for a kind of motto: *joie de vivre.* I thought that *joie de vivre* was what I was experiencing, even if it was a little scary. I repeated the phrase over and over, out loud, though I wasn't sure how to pronounce it: *joey de viver, joey de viver, joey de viver. Paroles* was all marked up, and so were all the other books. And they had other people's names in them. Lots of them were introductions to this, introductions to that. Like my high school books.

I sat down at the computer and felt around the back for the switch. It was new, but it still took a while to boot up. The picture on the screen took me by surprise. It was a picture of Warren. Back in the woods. Holding a chainsaw in one hand, waving with the other. I didn't recognize him at first. Jackson must have taken it.

I went to bed thinking about Warren, my father's brother. I lay down, but I couldn't sleep. Warren must have been about sixty when I shot Earl. He'd joined the Navy when he was about twenty, to get out of Naqada and see the world. There'd been some trouble in the church, but no one talked about it. I had almost no childhood memories of him. I hadn't seen him in years. I hardly knew him at all. He came to my daddy's funeral. Then to my wedding. And then he showed up and bailed me out of jail in Naqada.

It didn't take me long to figure out he wasn't a professor. Why would a professor be living in a one-room garage apartment? And the books. They were mostly textbooks, like the kind students would leave behind in their dorms when the school year was over. Names in them. All marked up. Physics, calculus, French, German, Spanish, chemistry, biology, Western Civilization. And the stacks of old *New Yorker* magazines had Jackson's name on the mailing labels.

I heard a car pull in the drive, going really slow, as if whoever it was didn't want to make any noise. A car door closed softly. I was tempted to get up and look out, but I didn't. Then the dog started barking. And the owls started hooting. And a baby mouse scurried across the floor on tiny feet. And then I did get up to look out the window. There was no light but the moon and the big yard light by the end of the drive, and the lights sparkling in Jackson's window in the big house down below. There was only one window on the front of the house, except for the window in the door.

Somebody opened the door and let the dog in, and she stopped barking, but the owls kept on calling to each other. Hoo hoo hoo huoaugh, hoo hoo hoo huoaugh. It was strange to be so alone. My first night away from the Hill. I'd wanted to be alone. To be lonely, and I was.

I tried to read one of Warren's books, a western, but I couldn't interest myself in the lives of the people in the book. I wanted to live my own life. I got up and looked out the window again. The lights were still sparkling.

I felt like barking, or hooting, but instead I started to sing. I sang the first verse of "La Gui-Année," which was all I could remember.

> *Bon soir le maître et la maîtresse,*
> *Et tout le monde du logis:*
> *Pour le dernier jour de l'année,*
> *La Gui-Année vous nous devais.*

> *Good evening master and mistress,*
> *And all your household;*
> *On the first day of the year,*
> *You owe us La Gui-Année.*

It was the only French I knew. Except *joey de viver.*

4

Joey de Viver

I woke up in the morning to the sound of the dog barking. Four loud barks, then quiet for a while. Then four more loud barks. Then quiet. I looked out the window. Jackson was throwing a Frisbee to the dog. He was standing down below me on the gravel in front of the garage, throwing the Frisbee down the hill. It went a long way, but the dog managed to catch it every time. She'd bring it back to Jackson, drop it in front of him, and start barking. It took him four barks to pick it up and throw it again. *Joey de viver,* I thought. *Joey de viver.* Whenever the dog stopped to pee, he'd shout, "Big pi-pi girl," and then later, "Big poopy girl." Jackson wore out before the dog did. I could see that his shoulder was hurting him, because he sort of crouched when he threw the Frisbee and didn't let his arm swing out too far. On the way back to the house he turned and looked up at my window. I didn't have any clothes on and I wondered if he could see me through the screen. I didn't think so.

I hadn't bothered to wash Warren's cast-iron frying pan—the big one—the night before, and I didn't wash it in the morning. I just scraped out some of the grease into the garbage and fried up more bacon and eggs, and then a took a shower, all by myself, thinking: *I can do whatever I want to do. I'm free. Joey de viver.*

While I was eating I looked through the mail from TF, which had been coming to me at Warren's address. Jackson had stacked it up on the table. Most of the stuff I threw away without even opening, but I kept the orientation schedule and the information about clubs and intramural athletics—I thought I might sign up for volleyball, which I'd played on the Hill, or maybe badminton. And there was a letter from my roommate—Tiffany, from Winnetka. It began, "Dear Willa Fern . . ." Warren was the only one who called me Willa Fern. I'd always been Fern, and now I was Sunny. Tiffany was planning on bringing a lot of stuffed animals, a TV, stereo, and twenty pairs of shoes. She had a boyfriend who was going to be a junior. Pre-med. She was going to be an entrepreneur. She didn't know what kind of entrepreneur yet, but she knew she wanted to run her own business. Her hobbies were dancing, playing the French horn, and cheerleading. She was looking forward to hearing from me.

What could I say to her?

After I finished eating I turned on the computer and opened a new file. The hard drive was almost empty. Warren had deleted everything except the letters he'd written to me.

Dear Tiffany [I wrote],

I just got out of the prison here—the Henrietta Hill Correctional Institution—and am looking forward to starting at TF. I was in for shooting my husband, but don't worry, he deserved it. When I was your age I'd been married for two years and was working in my husband's bait shop in the Naqada Marina on the Ohio River, selling grubs and night crawlers and stink bait and vacuum-sealed packages of frozen skipjacks. My husband was also the pastor of the Church of the Burning Bush with Signs Following, and that's where we lived our real life, going to church three times a week, handling serpents, going to other serpent-handling churches over in Kentucky and West Virginia and East Tennessee. Building brush arbors for homecomings, and going out in Earl's johnboat, and waiting for children. Waiting and waiting. Earl would nudge me with his elbow and say, "Roll over." And we'd do it, and that would be that. My daddy was killed in an explosion in Number 5, and my mama left right after I got married, and I never saw her again. When we were first married my husband kept rattlesnakes in a box under the bed, and they'd sing (rattle) whenever he was poking me, and then later he built a snake shed. He put a lot of money in that snake shed, and on Friday and Sunday nights we'd cart three or four serpent boxes up to the church, which was in an old DX gas station that used to belong to my cousin Sally's husband, which is how he got his name—DX—after he gave it to the church when the old church on Tomkins Road burned down. And every once in a while someone at the church would get serpent bit. Big news. Everyone would gather around to pray. They'd even pray back the dead sometimes. And someone was always getting taken over by a demon, or backing up on the Lord, and that was exciting too. Folks would support family. Help them through the hard times. Evangelists were always coming through. Punkin Bates, Liston Arnold, Rolly Franklin. You've got to be in the same room with these men to know what they're like. They've got a kind of power over you, especially when they get themselves anointed, and they start talking about Heaven and about how everybody's looking forward to getting there, and singing about it:

Well, I wonder what they're doing in heaven today.
Sin and sorrow all gone away.
Sweet music it flows like a river they say.
Well, I wonder what they're doing there now.

But, Tiffany, what if you get there and there's nothing at all? What if? How do you make sense of a man's life? When that man was your own uncle Warren, who's the only one who stood by you when you were in trouble? And it's the same for everybody. Dead is dead. That's it. I saw my own grave yesterday, right next to my uncle's. They'll put me in a box and throw me in the ground, just like they did my uncle. And there's nothing I can do about it. And there's nothing you can do about it either.

I stopped writing. I knew I couldn't send this letter, but it felt good to write it, and I spent some time imagining Tiffany showing it to her mother. I erased the file without printing it.

There are two main streets in Colesville that run parallel to each other, like railroad tracks—a town main street that's called Main Street, and a university main street, which is called State Street. Coming from the north, the town looks like any town, like Paducah or Evansville. I rounded the circle by the public library on Main Street and went east on Broadway. If you went west on Broadway you came out near the prison.

My first stop was the Farmers & Mechanics Bank, where the bank manager told me I had over eighty thousand dollars in a special account that I didn't have to list on my financial aid application. No wonder he was so polite. I was flabbergasted. I knew Warren had left me some money, but I had no idea it would be anything like this. I was too overwhelmed to think. I'd never even had a checking account before! Just my commissary account on the Hill, where I kept some spending money from Warren. The manager helped me set up a credit card account too.

I walked up and down Main Street letting the fact of all that money sink in. I'd always been poor, but everybody had been poor, especially after the mines closed down. Not dirt poor. Everybody had TVs and cars and boats, but we didn't wear fancy clothes to church. It was a different feeling knowing I could buy anything I saw. At Penny's I bought underwear, a new bra, three pair of jeans, and three men's white shirts. That would do for now. I wasn't sure what I'd need in the dorm, but I did buy one extravagant thing, a beautiful leather briefcase that I saw in the window of the Lafayette Stationery store. I kept walking back and forth trying not to stare. I was carrying my papers in a plastic grocery bag—my TF catalog, my dorm assignment letter, and a campus map. The leather of the briefcase was like a pool of dark water. You could look right down into it, like saddle leather sometimes gets up by the pommel, but soft. It looked old and new at the same time, and it cost a ton of money. I never told anyone how much I paid for it.

I didn't really look at it closely in the store because I didn't want the sales clerk to think I didn't know what I was doing, though if I'd known what I was doing, I'd have looked it over more carefully. But I didn't need to. I just bought it with my new credit card. I wasn't sure what to do with the card. I handed it to the clerk; he put it in a machine; then he had to wait for a phone call saying it was okay, and then I had to sign a piece of paper that came out of a little machine on the counter. As soon as I was out on the street I jammed my plastic grocery sack in the briefcase and walked on down Main Street, past Penny's, back to the bank, and I then turned around and walked back to Warren's truck, admiring myself in the store windows. At a fancy liquor store I bought a fancy bottle of French wine for

Jackson, as a thank-you gift for all his trouble. I put the wine in the bottom of my briefcase.

My first glimpse of the campus took my breath away. It was like looking at another country, another world. I didn't belong here, didn't have a passport. The buildings were big as churches, with towers and spires. I'd been to St. Louis with Warren. I'd been to Paducah and Evansville on school trips, but I'd never seen anything like this. I recognized the Ford Gate from the cover of the catalog, and Coles Circle—half circle, really. It was sort of like the front door of the campus. Straight ahead was Old Main, which housed the administration, and to the left of Old Main was a historical marker marking the site of one of the Lincoln-Douglas debates. I got a cup of coffee at the student union and sat at a table out on Seymour Terrace, which is right on the Lakota River, which runs through the campus, and examined my new briefcase, which had been made using a process that had been used in Italy for several thousand years. It was fashioned out of true Italian skins that had been tanned with vegetable dyes that didn't have anything in them that would harm man or the ecosystem. There was a strap on the outside for an umbrella, and a place to stick your newspaper, and a padded compartment for a laptop computer. Inside there were places for pencils and pens, and a file that opened up like an accordion for different papers, and there was plenty of room for notebooks and books. And a detachable shoulder strap, which I hooked up. I put my papers in the accordion files.

It was like the beginning of any school year. You had your new box of crayons, your pencils, your little tiny pencil sharpener with a blade in it. And you put everything in a satchel. Just like the other kids. But of course we hadn't been just like the other kids. We weren't allowed to go to movies at the Bijou on Phillips Street, and we couldn't watch *The Brady Bunch* and *The Cosby Show* and *Laverne and Shirley* and *Mork and Mindy* unless we went to someone else's house, which didn't happen very often. The other kids were a little bit afraid of us. As if one of us might bring a rattlesnake to school. And one day Timmy Johnson did, because some of the other boys were teasing him because he was afraid of spiders. He threw the snake down on the floor and everybody scattered. They had to wait till Timmy's dad came and caught the snake and took Timmy home and tanned him good.

The table had an umbrella over it, like one of the pictures in the French book, and I pretended for a minute that I was in France. I kept my briefcase on my lap with the strap wound around my wrist. I got out my catalog and flipped through the pages.

I looked around. School wouldn't start for two weeks, but there were people sitting at the tables, under the red umbrellas, enjoying the sun. I studied the women my age. There were a few. They weren't exactly dressed up, but they looked like professors, not students, and their briefcases, lying flat on the pavement next to their chairs, were old and soft.

I located the dorm on the campus map—Sarah Stevenson Hall, where I'd be sharing a room with Tiffany. All the dorms—which were called residence halls—were on the other side of the river, on North Campus, along with the football stadium and the physical plant. There were three bridges across the river, all named after important Illinois politicians: two governors—Thomas Ford and Edward Coles—and Abraham Lincoln. I crossed the river on Coles Bridge, which is a footbridge, carrying my briefcase in one hand, the sack with my new clothes in the other. It felt good to walk after six years on the Hill, where the only place you could walk around was the exercise yard. I stopped on the bridge. The river was flowing so slow it was hard to tell which way it was going. But when I caught sight of the dorm, my heart sank. My *joey de viver* evaporated.

Sarah Stevenson Hall looked like a prison, but bigger. It was huge. I counted six rows of windows. Six stories. The big front doors were locked, but a side door was propped open, though there was a sign saying not to leave the door propped open. The big stand-up ashtray by the door was full of clean sand. I went in. No one was around.

The different floors were called "houses." Tiffany and I were in Adams House on the fourth floor. I climbed a back stairway. The hallway was like a prison too—a long corridor of locked doors. But the lounge was open and the big TV was on. One of the janitors was watching a soap opera. I asked him if he knew my uncle, Warren Rigsby. And he did. He said Warren had looked after Davis Hall before he became head of custodial services for South Campus.

We talked for a while.

"This is like a prison," I said.

"You were out on the Hill, weren't you?" he asked.

I nodded.

"Your uncle told me about you. He was real proud of you."

"For shooting my husband?"

"Yup."

On the fifth floor a crew of upperclassmen was cleaning out the rooms.

The men, or boys—the males—wore jeans and T-shirts with the sleeves rolled up. The females wore T-shirts that said PROPERTY OF THE TF ATHLETIC DEPARTMENT on the front and shorts that said, on the butt, DON'T YOU WISH.

My own room—5A—at the end of the hall had already been cleaned but the door was still open, and it still smelled of Lysol. I sat down on the bare mattress and stared at the lavatory-gray walls and the tiny closets that didn't have any doors on them. Where was Tiffany going to put all her stuffed animals? and her TV? her stereo? and her twenty pairs of shoes. I started to panic. I could feel my blood getting thick. Like when I'd got serpent bit when I was six-teen. Something squeezed me real hard and I had to get out of there.

I stopped at the cemetery on my way home. I had some things to say to Warren, like, "Why did you get me into this, Warren? I don't be-long here with these professor types in their fancy summer dresses and eighteen-year-old girls with PROPERTY OF across their tits and DON'T YOU WISH on their butts. I paid way too much for a stupid brief-case. I don't know any more about life than Tiffany, with her col-lection of stuffed animals. I can't even figure out the difference between the math requirement and the quantitative literacy re-quirement, or between the diversity requirement and the cultural literacy requirement. The only ones that made sense were the sci-ence requirement and the foreign language requirement. I should have gone to the junior college like Mr. Byron said." Mr. Byron taught biology on the Hill. "I can't live in a room with someone named Tiffany who's got twenty pairs of shoes and a shitload of stuffed animals, and a French horn and wants to be an entrepreneur. My room's smaller than my cell on the Hill. What was I thinking? What were *you* thinking? I'm a fish out of water. And why did you lie to me? Why did you pretend to be a professor? Did you think you had to be a big shot to impress me? You didn't have to lie to me. And now here you are at the back of the cemetery, with no flow-ers. And you've even got a place for me right next to you. Me. I may not be ready to go to college, but I'm not ready to die."

You were a fish out of water in Naqada, he said. I could hear his voice inside my head. *You were a fish out of water on the Hill. You'll be a fish out of water at Thomas Ford. You'll always be a fish out of water. Get used to it and stop feeling sorry for yourself. And I never lied to you. I never told you I was a professor. That was your own idea. For Christ's sake, I was the only one who stuck up for you. I came to your wedding. I bailed you out of jail after you shot that jerk of a husband. I drove you down to St. Louis and took you to a French movie:* An American in Paris. *I offered to help you escape to Mexico. I knew a place where nobody would ever find you, but you were more scared of Mexico than you were of prison.*

After you were convicted I pulled some strings to get you transferred from Little Muddy down in Hardin County to the Hill. I came to see you every visiting day. Till I got too sick. I put money in your account so you could buy what you needed. I told you what was going on at the university because I found it interesting. Some faculty members wanting to get rid of the fraternities . . . controversial hiring decisions . . . a new dorm . . . football games, baseball, basketball, women's volleyball. It was all interesting. And those shorts that say DON'T YOU WISH *on the butt. I wish they'd had those when I was working there. It's all interesting.*

"All right, Uncle Warren. I'm sorry. Take it easy."

That's better, he said. *Now tell me what's been happening since I died. You still had two years to go on the Hill."*

"They wouldn't let me out for your funeral," I said, "but the warden let me watch from his office. I could see the little cemetery from his window. I could see someone standing up. Jackson. Talking away. What did he say? I guess I'll have to ask him."

He read a nice poem, one of my favorites. He used to sing it to an old Muddy Waters tune. I don't suppose you know who Muddy Waters was, do you?

"No," I said. "I don't know who Muddy Waters was."

Well you should find out.

"You know, I lost my faith in prison," I said. "I thought it was easy at the time, like taking off a coat that's too warm. But now I don't know what to say. It's like giving the graduation speech as valedictorian. On the Hill, not high school. Did you know I was valedictorian? Top of my class. I didn't know what to say. It was in the exercise room. Everybody was there. The teachers . . . Hard work. That's all I could think of. I'd been the valedictorian and got to make a speech at our graduation. I spent a lot of time working on it, but I couldn't get beyond the obvious. *Hard work will pay off. It really will. If you work hard . . .* I couldn't get beyond this. Maybe I didn't need to. Maybe I really believed it. What my teachers had been telling me in high school. I wouldn't listen. I had the hots for Earl. All the girls did. After Daddy got killed.

"I can't get beyond the obvious now. I guess what I should have said is 'thank you.' For everything you did. And for the money too. But what about a tombstone? You don't have one. We've got to take care of that. What do you want on it?"

But he didn't answer.

"Don't worry," I said. "I'll think of something."

Back home I put my briefcase away—I didn't want Jackson to see it—and took the bottle of wine down to the house. His truck wasn't there, so I knew he wasn't home. But I wanted the wine to be there when he got back.

The door wasn't locked. It wasn't even closed all the way. So I let myself in. I let the dog in too. Maya. It was the most beautiful house I'd ever seen. More beautiful than Mawmaw Tucker's on the bluff by the old lock. Not as fancy, but more comfortable.

The dog was making herself at home. She *was* at home. I knew the dog wouldn't tattle on me. I thought I'd just set the bottle of wine down somewhere. I thought that as long as I was holding the bottle of wine I could always say I'd just stepped inside and was going to put the wine down somewhere.

There was a leather davenport in the big living room, and a chair big enough for two people, and stairs that were wrapped around a stone chimney. A big wood-burning stove with glass doors was vented into the chimney. There were two ceiling fans, and books everywhere. That's why there was only one window in the front of the house. The whole wall was books. I'd never seen so many books. He had more books than the public library in Naqada. The books made me uneasy.

All the windows had shutters with little adjustable slats on them that seemed to warm the beams of yellow light that came into the room. The windows in the back opened onto a deck and then onto the woods. There was a little stream and a bridge over the stream. The bridge had been dislodged, as if it had been lifted up by the stream and set back down crooked. The stream was the bottom of the hollow. The ground rose up on the other side. I couldn't see past the trees. I didn't want to leave this room. I wanted to sit down at the big table—as big as the ones at the library, with drawers on both sides—and read a book.

There was a big kitchen with lots of copper pots and pans hanging from a wrought-iron frame over the table. The fancy dark blue stove—really fancy—had two ovens. Blue and white tiles covered the walls behind the counters. The downstairs bathroom was big too, but there was nothing in the medicine cabinet over the sink. The toilet was running in the bathroom. I lifted the lid of the tank and adjusted the flapper. The huge bathtub, which had some kind of whirlpool hookup, looked inviting.

Upstairs were two big bedrooms, one with the bed made up. Blankets and quilts were stacked on open shelves. The bedrooms ran the width of the house. On one side you could look up the hill at the garage. You could see right into my apartment and I wondered if I could see into Jackson's bedroom from my window. On the other side you looked down at the stream and out into the woods. There were no closets, but there was a big wardrobe built to fit under the slope of the ceiling. I looked in the wardrobe. No sign of any sexy magazines, no vibrators.

The bed wasn't messy, but it wasn't made either. The flannel sheets on top and bottom smelled like they'd been washed recently.

The medicine cabinet in the upstairs bathroom was much smaller than the one downstairs, but it was full of prescription medications. There was a small shower. No tub.

What was I doing? I asked myself. What did I want to know? What did I want to find out about Jackson? What did I *want*?

What I wanted was to live in Warren's little apartment over the garage and not in that prison of a dormitory with Tiffany and her stuffed animals.

I lay down on Jackson's bed. Who was the woman who was here last night? Who drove in with the headlights off? I was betting it was Claire. That's what I was looking for, I realized. Signs of a woman's presence. Clothes. Makeup. Lipstick. But I didn't find anything. Not even a trace of Claire's perfume in the air.

The second bedroom was identical to the first—double bed and another wardrobe—but it was empty except for a locked gun cabinet holding a couple of hunting rifles and a shotgun that hadn't been oiled in a while.

Back downstairs I sat down at the electric piano and played as much as I could remember of "I Got Rhythm" from *An American in Paris*. I looked at the books on the shelves. Most of them were in French, but an English title caught my eye: *Untrodden Fields of Anthropology*. That sounded interesting, and it was. Interesting, but disgusting. It was hard to imagine such things. By Doctor Jacobus X. I almost couldn't look at the chapter titles. "Physical love amongst the Annamites." "The most usual methods of copulation." "Asiatic houses of prostitution." "Dangers of sexual intercourse in Annam." "Perversions of sexual connection in Annam male prostitution." "Usual habits of Annamite sodomites." "Study of the buccal, vulvar, and anal deformities caused by male and female prostitution in the Annamite race." "The Negress and her sexual lust." "The Decoction of 'tight-ening Wood.' " "The hot aubergine." I thought I'd heard about everything there was to hear about sex in prison, but not this, not the hot aubergine. "You cut an aubergine in half and make a groove to hold a man's penis. Then you make a paste out of match tips, small pimentos, peppercorns, cloves and vanilla beans . . ." I was still reading when Jackson came in the front door.

"Find something interesting?" he said.

"I was just going to leave this bottle of wine on the kitchen table and I started looking at the books." I still had my thumb in *Untrodden Fields*. "What's an 'aubergine'?"

"An eggplant."

"Oh." I said. "Look. I'm sorry. I shouldn't have come in when you weren't here."

"Did you find what you were looking for?"

"I wasn't looking *for* anything," I said. "I just wanted to drop off the wine. A kind of thank-you. But it's a beautiful house," I said. "It's the most beautiful house I've ever seen. And so many books."

"A lot of them were Claude's," he said. "Most of them."

Claude was the man who went to Africa with him and gave him the house.

"How could anybody read so many books?" I asked. I handed him the wine. A bottle of Bordeaux. I was glad to hear him pronounce it: Bor*dough*.

"It's all right," he said. "Your uncle always made himself right at home. You might as well do the same."

"I wanted to ask you about my uncle."

"Sit," he said, pointing to a couch.

"I'm not a dog," I said.

He gave me a look of astonishment. "Oh, for Christ's sake. Would you care to sit down? How's that?"

"Sorry," I said. "I've been going through Warren's books. Up in the apartment."

"Do you mind if I do some yoga stretches?" he said. "Lyme disease affects the joints. I try to keep a regular schedule."

"No," I said. "Of course not."

He took his shoes off and stretched out on the floor and started pulling one knee up against his chest. The dog came over and licked his face. He shooed her away.

"He wasn't a professor," I said.

"A professor?"

"I thought he was a professor. I mean, the way he talked about this place. I mean the university, but this house too. He talked about you too. As if you two were friends. Colleagues."

"We *were* friends."

"But he wasn't a professor."

"No."

"I wondered why I couldn't find his name in the catalog."

"Did he tell you he was a professor?

"No. He just let me think it. He said you were an anthropologist."

He nodded.

"We had some anthropologists come to the church once, but they didn't stay long." I laughed.

"We go everywhere," he said. He was still on the floor, doing different stretching exercises. "A lot of cultures are disappearing. Anthropologists try to document them before it's too late. Languages are disappearing faster than wildlife species. There are over three hundred languages with fewer than fifty native speakers. There are over forty languages with only one native speaker left."

"I wouldn't care if *we* disappeared," I said. "I mean the Church of the Burning Bush with Signs Following."

He laughed. "What are the signs?"

"Healing the sick, raising the dead, drinking strychnine, handling serpents, speaking in tongues."

"Quite a list."

"It's from the Bible," I said. "Warren gave me a copy of your book about the pygmies. It's pretty good. Sounds like you had a good time in the Forest."

"The 'Mbuti," he said. "Not 'pygmies,' 'Mbuti.' "

I tried to say it, but it was hard to get the "Mb" sound right.

"You shouldn't feel bad about Warren," Jackson said. "He was a lot of things. You'd be surprised."

"Like what?"

"Well, he was quite a ladies' man."

"Warren? You mean he went with a lot of women?"

"Well, he had a lot of adventures, and he was a good storyteller."

"Like what?"

"After he got out of the Navy," Jackson said, "he hung out in Asia for a few years—Kuala Lumpur, Goa, Sri Lanka; he learned Portuguese; he mined copper in Colorado; an army buddy got him a job at Thomas Ford, and he fell in love with a woman here and bought a house on Prairie Street, not far from the campus, and two cemetery plots. He was putting down roots. But the woman left and he stayed.

"He sold the house," Jackson went on, "but kept the cemetery plots. They're worth quite a bit now that the cemetery's full. That's why there's an empty plot for you."

"Then somebody ought to take better care of it," I said.

"He worked in Buildings and Grounds for ten years and then he was a janitor in Davis Hall for a while before he went over to South Campus. That's how he met Claude. In Davis Hall. They both loved to talk, and Claude offered him the apartment over the garage. Rent free. And Warren took care of the place. He knew how to do things.

"He was a Mason too, and claimed that Old Main was built to the specs of a Masonic Temple. He had Claude convinced, and Claude got him to publish an article in *The Zephyr*. That's our alternative paper. I've got extra copies somewhere."

"You were with him when he died?" I said.

He nodded. "We put up a hospital bed right over against the wall." He pointed his head at the east wall—no windows, but lots of pictures.

"What's it like? Dying? If you're not expecting to go straight up to Heaven, that is."

"I suppose it's different for everybody. I was kind of sick myself."

"What was it like for Uncle Warren?"

"It wasn't too bad. We talked a lot, listened to music. Country blues."

"Muddy Waters?"

"Muddy Waters too, the early stuff."

"They wouldn't let me out for his funeral, you know."

"I didn't know they let people out for funerals."

"Sometimes. It's called 'furlough.' But I watched it from the warden's office. I saw you. At least I think it was you. You were wearing a suit. You made a speech."

He smiled and got up from the floor and sat next to me on the couch.

"I read a poem. Langston Hughes's 'As Befits a Man.' "

> *I don't mind dying*
> *But I want my funeral to be fine;*
> *A row of long tall mamas,*
> *Fannin' and faintin' and cryin'.*

I laughed. "That's pretty funny for a funeral."

"Warren was a funny guy. He used to plop himself down in the

Common Room and say, 'What do you make of these Dead Sea Scrolls?' Or, 'What do you make of this Big Bang theory?' He was interested in everything. And he always knew more about whatever it was than I did."

"And he went with a lot of women?"

"Quite a few."

"That's why there were so many women at the funeral? I could see them, you know."

He laughed.

"I could do Warren's job, you know. Make sure the well gets shocked, check the septic tank, bring in a supply of firewood. I see you've got a splitter in the garage, and a blade for the tractor. I can drive a tractor, keep the drive cleared in the winter. Put a new railing on the ramp. You need some more gravel on the drive too. Fix up the bridge over the creek." I was out of breath, afraid he'd laugh.

"How about shooting a deer in the winter, so we'd have some meat?"

"I could do that."

"Warren's old 30.06 is upstairs in the bedroom closet. All you'd have to do is sit on the deck and wait for a deer to come along."

"Did Warren say anything about me before he died?"

"He talked about you all the time. He wanted me to look after you."

"I don't need anyone to look after me," I said. "But maybe you need someone to look after you." I hoped he wouldn't take this the wrong way, and he didn't.

"I could use someone to look after me," he said. "At least for a while."

5

Meditation

The yoga exercises that Jackson performed every day had been prescribed by Dr. Kali, the internist at Billings Hospital in Chicago who had diagnosed Jackson's Lyme disease. These were simple exercises to relieve pain and muscle spasms, to strengthen damaged joints and tendons and ligaments, to increase range of motion and relieve stiffness. Dr. Kali had demonstrated the different poses in his office without removing his white coat. When he stood on his head—the Sirsasana pose, king of the Asanas, which Jackson had never attempted—two ball-point pens fell out of his jacket pocket. The poses were also intended to calm Jackson's mind, to discourage the visitors from his past life who appeared to him in his dreams and sometimes in waking moments, too, and to ease his neuropsychiatric symptoms, especially his fear that the cylinder-shaped spirochete *Borrelia burgdorferi* that had invaded his central nervous system was not merely adaptable but actually intelligent, capable of advanced survival strategies that would prolong the infection and increase his suffering, and his fear that the universe, which had once seemed full of meaning and purpose, light and beauty, was indifferent to the damage done by *Borrelia burgdorferi*, indifferent in fact to all suffering and to all questions of value.

The yoga exercises had worked, along with alternating courses of doxycycline and erythromycin. He had to acknowledge that the very real advanced survival strategies of *Borrelia burgdorferi* were the result of evolution, not of malevolent design, and once he'd done so, the indifference of the universe no longer seemed to weigh quite so heavily on his mind. It might still be possible, he thought, finishing his stretches and easing into the corpse pose, flat on his back, arms outstretched, palms up, to argue from premises in the indicative to conclusions in the imperative. But how? Not without a "leap." But what kind of leap? From what to what? He waited for his mind to clear, or empty. Surely the answer lay not in logic but in experience, not at the end of the road but at the beginning. Well, not at the beginning, but somewhere between the great apes and the beginnings of cooperative hunting.

But even if his fellow anthropologists—most of them—were right about the Great Leap Forward that took place about fifty thousand years ago—the development of cognitive abilities that distinguish Homo sapiens sapiens from archaic forms of human beings—the problem of consciousness remained exactly where it was. And Jackson did not believe that the neuroscientists would unlock this particular mystery. Imagine a model of the brain that's big enough to walk around in. Like a factory. You'll see gears and wheels and levers, but you won't see a thought. You'll see cells and synapses, but even if you get to the level of electrons and protons, you still won't see a thought. You won't see an idea, you won't see a perception.

He turned his head from side to side to center his spine, and then stretched himself out as though someone were pulling his head away from his feet and his shoulders away from his neck. He breathed deeply and slowly from his abdomen and waited for his mind to clear. The dog, who was always excited—or worried—by the corpse pose, licked his face and neck. He didn't move, because moving only encouraged her. Besides, he liked being touched.

After a few minutes the dog stopped licking him and lay down beside him. He could feel the warm pressure of her back, comforting against his side.

He held the pose for several minutes, but his mind didn't clear. Instead of improving his mental concentration, the pose seemed to stir up the old worries that he thought he'd put aside. He thought about his intention to live a new life, to go back to Africa, or get married; to stop seeing Claire, who'd taken him by surprise the night they picked up Sunny at the prison. He hadn't heard her car in the drive, hadn't seen her headlights flashing through the glass in the door. "You know I still love you," she said, which is what she always said. "I'm just a miserable sinner," she said. And that too was something she always said. "But God will forgive me."

And at the same time Claire was still enthusiastic about Pam. Jackson had taken Pam to dinner once, at Stefano's. She tried to get him to invest in ShoppingKart.com. And he tried to remember one of the poems he used to memorize when he worked out on the stationary bicycle in the fitness center with a copy of *One Hundred Poems for All Seasons* propped up in front of him: "After Apple Picking," for example. "To Autumn." "The Long-Legged Fly," "The Bishop Orders His Tomb." But he could remember only bits and pieces, a line or two here and there. *And have I not Saint Praxed's ear to pray horses for you, and brown Greek manuscripts, and mistresses with great, smooth, marbly limbs?* But Pam had dropped out of the picture. It was Sunny who filled the frame. How funny she was when he had told her to sit. *I'm not a dog.* Her nerve anyway, coming into the house that day. He bet she'd had a good look around before he'd caught her with *Untrodden Fields.* She wasn't just delivering a bottle of wine. What had she been looking *for?* What would *he* look for? He thought: *Nothing she could find in the house would embarrass me. No pornography, unless you count* Untrodden Fields. *No vibrators or toys. Some stuff for Lyme disease, but no Preparation H, no Viagra.* He congratulated himself, but then wondered: *Is this good or bad?*

He was glad to have someone living in Warren's old place, and he was glad that someone was Sunny. She'd been there ten days now, and every morning he could feel her eyes on him when he threw the Frisbee to Maya. He listened for the sound of her truck in the drive in the late afternoon. His heart leaped up whenever she buzzed him on the intercom to ask a question about cooking, or about the computer, or about "lie, lay, lain," or about the orientation schedule. At night he could look out his bedroom window and see her hunched over her computer in her own window.

He bent his knees and pushed himself up to one side and then into a sitting position, the classic Sukhasna, crossing his legs, his feet below his knees, his hands clasped around his knees, his head and body straight. But his mind continued to whirl. He was happy to start teaching again, to be back in the saddle, to feel that beginning-of-term euphoria; but his department chair had pressured him into creating a virtual classroom for his Human Origins course. Jackson wasn't a Luddite, and in fact he thought the virtual classroom was a good idea that would simplify his life in the long run. But not in the short run. Every time someone from the computer center told him, "All you have to do is," his mind closed down. "All you have to do is drag it onto the desktop and double-click"; "All you have to do is open your applications folder and . . ." In his experience it never worked.

He couldn't clear his mind. He'd spent two days with a student helper working on the virtual classroom, downloading slides of the whole fossil record, from *Sahelanthropus tchadensis,* a fossil ape that lived seven million years ago, to Turkana Boy (Homo erectus, about one and a half million years ago), to the first Homo sapiens: Homo sapiens sapiens. Students would be able to drag images from one place to another to create their own hominid phylogeny. Homo habilis, Homo rudolfensis, Homo ergaster, Homo georgicus, Homo erectus, Homo heidelbergensis, Homo neanderthalensis, Homo sapiens (Cro-Magnon), Homo sapiens sapiens. The idea was to make everything accessible on the computer. Everything would be linked to everything else. He moved the "slides" around in his mind. There was plenty of disagreement among the experts; how could students be expected to . . . But wasn't that the point? They didn't have to get it right. They had to experience the thought process . . .

He did his neck exercises, shoulder lifts, eye training, and then began the Salute to the Sun, a flowing series of twelve poses to warm the body and tone the abdominal muscles.

He continued to slide the images around in his mind. Back and forth. Up and down. In and out.

When he'd entered TF as a graduate student, the department of anthropology had been a band of hunter-gatherers—no headman, no chief, no oppressive hierarchy. But now it had evolved into a chiefdom, with a headman—Professor Baker Kimbrough—and a clearly established hierarchy.

He got down on the floor for the Bridge pose—to promote relaxation and reduce stress by strengthening the spine and lower body. He thought about the problem of Claude's field notes, which he could see on the shelves next to his desk if he turned his head slightly to the left. And he thought about his new life: What would it be like? What did he want to happen?

The shutters on the window above his library table were not tightly closed and a thin shaft of sunlight streamed through the crack between the shutters and struck the surface of the desk and then the back of the leather sofa. Jackson spent several minutes studying the motes swirling in the beam of light. *They are everywhere,* he thought. *We inhale them and then exhale them, but we can't see them until they are caught in a beam of light.*

He eased into the final corpse pose, flat on his back, arms at his sides, palms up. He lifted his right foot slightly, tensed his leg and lowered it to the floor. Then he did the same thing with his left leg. Then with his arms, making a fist, tensing the arm, letting it drop back to the floor. He tightened his buttocks, lifted his hips, held them up for a moment, then relaxed. Then his chest, lifting it without lifting his hips or head, then relaxing. The same with his shoulders, hunching them and then letting them drop. He pulled in his arms and willed them to relax. Finally he tucked his chin in and rolled his head back and forth from side to side. He visualized his body, relaxing every part from toes to calves, up to the stomach, the lungs, the jaw, the scalp, his brain. He inhaled, feeling the oxygen flow down to his feet; he exhaled, feeling the tension dissolving. His mind was like the unruffled surface of a deep-water lake. In the center of the lake, in the depths, was his true nature.

His mind was calmer now, but he could still see the beam of light, like the shaft of a spear. He got up from the floor and moved to the library table. He put his finger in the beam of light, moved it back and forth, the way a child will move its finger back and forth through a candle flame.

Then he looked along the beam, through the crack in the shutters. He saw the sun setting behind the wooded hill on the other side of the stream, saw the big oak tree that had once been bent by the Sauk Indians to serve as a trail marker; he saw the stream, meandering toward the Mississippi, and the bridge that had been twisted off the banks by a flash flood the previous spring—two telephone poles that Warren had dragged across the stream with planks nailed across them.

And he was reminded how much time anthropologists spend looking at beams of light instead of along them, worrying about distinctions between witchcraft and sorcery and about different interpretations of initiation rites and burial customs, recording in minute detail the religious practices of different tribes all over the world without advancing beyond the views of Durkheim and Weber, or deconstructing binary oppositions and unpacking dialog practices without shedding light on a single lived experience.

If they hooked the tractor up to the bridge with two chains, attached them to the ends of the two telephone poles, they could pull it back up to the bank.

6

Thursday is Wednesday and
Friday is Thursday

The orientation program was disorienting: what clubs to join, what intramural sports to play, where to park, how to locate your mailbox and get the combination, how to catch the shuttle from North Campus to South Campus, where and when to get your campus photo taken, how to set up your e-mail account. I could handle Black Alice, and I could handle rattlesnakes, but I was still intimidated by these eighteen-year-old girls with their stuffed animals and their green book bags and their PROPERTY OF T-shirts and their DON'T YOU WISH shorts, who wanted to know, at the mandatory sexual counseling session, if you could get AIDS by having oral sex or if you could get pregnant if you did it standing up, or what would happen if you got caught snorting coke in the privacy of your own dorm room, since Edward Coles, the second governor of Illinois, who put a stop to slavery in Illinois, had taken drugs. As Warren said, it was all interesting.

But what I really couldn't understand was why Thursday was going to be Wednesday, and Friday was going to be Thursday.

I asked my faculty advisor, who turned out to be Claire. Claire seemed to know why, but it wasn't something she could put into words.

Claire had already assumed the role of my financial advisor and had talked me into investing twenty thousand dollars of Warren's money in something called ShoppingKart.com, and now I wasn't particularly happy that Claire was going to be my academic advisor as well, especially when Claire told me that she'd pulled some strings, had told the office of the Dean of Students that I'd requested her. She put me in her course in Beginning Fiction Writing, and I wasn't too happy about that, either. And she warned me against Jackson. She thought I should live in the dorm, or there was plenty of room at the rectory. I'd be lonely out in the woods. Jackson was in bad shape. He had Lyme disease. He had enough trouble looking after himself. She reminded me about what I'd said in the bar about what I'd learned in prison: not needing a man to look after me.

"But I don't mind looking after a man," I said, which I could see annoyed Claire. "Besides," I said, "Jackson already warned me about *you*. When he found out your were my advisor."

"About me? What are you talking about?"

"I don't know. It was just sort of a general warning. I still don't understand why Thursday is Wednesday and Friday is Thursday."

"It's got something to do with the science labs. They want to get in an extra lab."

"But I don't see . . ."

"It doesn't matter," she said. "That's just the way things are at universities."

What I learned on my first day of classes was this: I learned that in the beginning—at the time of the Big Bang—everything in the universe was smaller than a grain of rice, smaller than the period at the end of a sentence, smaller than the point of a pin. I learned that the Sun would eventually burn itself out and that even it if didn't, Andromeda and the Milky Way were on a collision course. I learned that the universe was winding down, that the temperature would finally get down to three degrees Kelvin. That's cold. At three degrees Kelvin the molecules stop moving around. Somehow, in between, life happened, and I learned that Evolution, like the Big Bang, is not a theory in the sense of being a hypothesis; it's a theory in the sense of being a law, of being the only way to explain the data, the only way to explain the diversity of life. That it explained everything that used to be explained by God. You didn't need God to explain why we have eyes, which evolved through natural selection acting on small variations. This was Darwin's big idea, Evolution, and it was an even better idea than Copernicus's heliocentric universe, even better than Newton's Laws of Motion or Einstein's $E = mc^2$. It was the best idea anyone had ever had.

And this was in the first ten minutes of my Bio 120 lecture.

I also learned that Homo sapiens is "a tiny new twig on the tree of life." That if you thought of the earth as being formed on January 1, then towards the end of the month you'd see some rocks. Then in August you'd get your eukaryotes. I knew about eukaryotes and prokaryotes because I'd taken biology on the Hill. Then in October you'd find some algae; in November, shellfish and vertebrates. Lights out for the dinosaurs on December 26. Then homo sapiens shows up just before midnight on December 31. Ta-da.

And I learned that broccoli and Brussels sprouts evolved from wild mustard, which seemed like a comedown after the collision of the galaxies and the heat death of the universe and Evolution with a capital E as the cause of everything. Or the explanation of everything. I wasn't sure of the difference.

Professor Cramer, who was six feet six and rather severe looking in his white coat—looking as if he'd just emerged from the lab, and he probably had—had a reputation for being a demanding teacher. He scared us about the heat death of the universe and at the end of the lecture he scared us even more about cutting a class or a lab or missing a field trip or not being prepared for class.

And then he explained why Thursday was Wednesday and Friday was Thursday. The whole thing had been his idea. If everyone pretended that today, Thursday, was Wednesday, then we could pretend that tomorrow was Thursday. Why would we want to do that? So that there would be room in the schedule for a lab in the first week of the semester. If Thursday were really Thursday, then the next day would be Friday, but since all the labs were held on Thursdays . . . This way we'd get in an extra lab.

I thought I understood.

Later that morning I learned how to introduce myself in French 101: *"Je m'appelle Lise. Je viens de Naqada . . ."* *"Vous êtes Jean-Paul."* *"Et vous?"* *"Vous êtes . . ."* *"Enchantée."*

"Lise" was my French name. I picked it because I remembered Leslie Caron was Lise in the only French film I'd ever seen, *An American in Paris.*

We were all stiff and self-conscious, but then Madame Arnot, who was *très chic*, taught us some French gestures, which she demonstrated enthusiastically—the moue, the nose tap, the eye pull. By the end of the class we were milling around pouting, tapping our noses, pulling down the skin under our eyes, zipping our lips, kissing each other on both cheeks (without actually touching our lips to the other person's cheek), shaking hands properly (without pumping our arms up and down), executing the *bof* or Gallic shrug, and saying *Let's get the hell out of here* by holding out one hand and tapping our watches with the fingers of the other hand.

In the afternoon, in my Great Books class, I learned that the stories we tell ourselves about ourselves—*Gilgamesh,* Homer, Herodotus, Thucydides, *The Aeneid*—are the deepest form of knowledge. Deeper than scientific knowledge. I had to think about that one, which I did with a cup of coffee on Seymour Terrace, at a white table with an umbrella over it, like the picture in my French book.

I'd dropped out of high school to marry Earl when I was sixteen, but I'd wised up since then, and I'd been a good student on the Hill. There were a lot of good students. There was a waiting list for almost every class, and you had to toe the line or you were out on your ass. Biology, American Literature, British Literature, American Government, Health, Geometry, Algebra. It took me four years to get through fourteen core courses and six electives. Most of the electives didn't amount to much: Study Skills, Food and Nutrition, and Health Occupations, but I liked Computer Skills and Banking and Finance. If you wanted to know how to declare bankruptcy, you could come to me for help, and I'd download all the forms you'd need from the Internet: your voluntary petition, your individual debtor's statement of compliance, your application to pay a filing fee in installments, your list of principal creditors. Everything you'd need, depending on your circumstances. You wouldn't need a lawyer.

Biology was my favorite, though we didn't have a very sophisticated lab on the Hill—a dozen soapstone lab tables and some old-fashioned optical microscopes.

So, I wasn't a genius, but I had some good bench skills and I figured I was ready for TF.

I spent the rest of the afternoon studying French on Seymour Terrace. I looked through the picture in *Paroles* and imagined I was sitting in an outdoor café in Paris, maybe the one in *An American in Paris*. I'd heard that if you sat in a certain café in Paris long enough, you'd see everybody you ever knew walking by. But I didn't think so. I didn't think I'd see Mawmaw Tucker walking around in Paris in an old-fashioned shirtwaist dress, or Earl with a rattlesnake wrapped around his neck, or DX in his blue overalls and the Greek fisherman's hat that Sally gave him for his birthday years ago. That would be pretty strange. But no stranger than imagining myself sitting in the café.

I liked Madame Arnot, who really was French, but not from Paris. She was very dramatic, but also informal. I liked the way she sat on the edge of her desk with half her butt sticking off the edge, one foot on the floor, playing with a scarf around her neck, making French sound so beautiful. And sexy.

After about an hour I was joined by one of the students from the class, Jean-Paul.

"*Jean-Paul, mademoiselle.*"

"*Enchantée.*"

"*Et vous êtes . . . ?*"

"*Je m'appelle Lise.*"

"*Ah, enchanté.*"

"*D'où venez-vous?*"

"*Je viens de Chicago? Et vous?*"

"*Je viens de Naqada.*"

"*Une belle ville?*"

My choices were: *belle ville, grande ville, petite ville, ville splendide* or *magnifique* or *agréable* or *ordinaire* or *polluée* or *dangereuse.*

I chose "*dangereuse,*" and that was about as far as we could go.

"*Au revoir,*" he said.

"*Au revoir.*"

Now I was three people: At home, in Warren's apartment, I was a thirty-five-year-old ex-con a little worse for the wear. At TF I was an eighteen-year-old freshman; and in French class I was a baby. It was humiliating, but everybody was in the same boat. Except Madame

Arnot, of course. She was beautiful and sophisticated, and she made you want to be that way too.

My Beginning Fiction Writing class met on Friday, which was Thursday. We introduced ourselves and then got right down to business.

"Intentionality is the enemy," Claire said. I liked this. It was just the opposite of what I'd always been taught. But it made sense. Claire made her point by asking us to write a story in fifteen minutes. She had a kitchen timer, which she set on the desk so everyone could see it. I wrote in my four-subject notebook, which I carried in my new briefcase.

"Don't worry," Claire said. "Don't criticize. Just tell me about something that happened to you. Most people are natural storytellers if you just give them a chance. Think about your parents and your grandparents; think about your family stories. Write about the first thing that comes into your mind."

I started to tell about Earl making me stick my arm in the snakebox, but I'd told that story so many times I was getting sick of it, so I just started doing what Claire said to do, and something else popped into my head and took me by surprise. We were in church on a Friday and a woman from across the river in Kentucky started talking in tongues. She was handling and holding fire and drinking strychnine, and nobody thought anything of it, but all of a sudden Earl started shouting that something was wrong with her. She didn't sound right. She was possessed by a demon. She was screaming and hollering and foaming at the mouth, and if you listened real good you could hear different voices. Demons have different voices. One was a real low scary voice, like you'd expect a demon to talk, but another was just like a little girl, and another was like an old woman. There were more than that, but those were the ones I remembered best, and I wanted to keep it simple.

There were three men from the church trying to hold her down, but the demon was too strong and she broke away and tried to run out the door. You could hear the demon talking in her in the low scary voice. "I've got a palace for you. If you just get out the door, you'll be all right. Be all right. Just get out that door." But then Earl started pointing at the door and shouting at the demon to get out, and the demon started cussing him like you never heard. The woman tried to go out the door, but she couldn't, and then she ran to the back of the church and tried to get out the back, but she couldn't go through the door. And Earl kept saying Jesus' name over and over to scare the demon and some men got ahold of her and pulled her down holding Bibles on her and this time she couldn't get away.

And then the little-girl voice started talking, real sweet like at first, but then promising to do anything Earl wanted, talking a lot of real dirty sex talk. Earl told the demon to come out of her and the little girl voice started screaming and crying. Earl kept saying "Come out in the name of Jesus, come out in the name of Jesus, come out in the name of Jesus." And then the demon came out and the voice started coming out of DX, who'd just come into the church and still had his fisherman's hat on, but now it was an old-woman voice. When a demon comes out it's got to go somewhere. It can go into another person, or just go into the air. Earl told it to leave DX alone and go into a dog that was barking outside the church, and DX started flipping around and took off his hat and threw it down on the floor, and the spirit left him and went into the dog, and that poor dog started howling and crying, and the owner . . .

I was just getting to the best part, or the worst part, when the kitchen timer went off. We had thirty seconds to finish our stories, but I had so many things to say I just seized up for that last thirty seconds and didn't set down a word.

If I'd known we were going to have to read our stories out loud

78

I probably wouldn't have written about the demon. Maybe something about Earl singing "Precious Lord" when we were all gathered around the pit head after the explosion that killed my daddy, or going over to Norris Dam in Tennessee with Mama and Daddy and Pawpaw, and Pawpaw telling us it had been Noah's flood, covering up the whole town underneath, all the houses and everything.

The first story that someone read was about a mouse in a music store, listening to the music. The mouse was a Beatles fan and he built a little tiny guitar. The second story was about something called "Skittles," which I couldn't understand because I didn't know that Skittles were a kind of candy. And then I read my story. I had no idea how it was going to affect the other students, but then I could see mouths dropping open, eyes opening wide, everyone looking at me. I didn't know if they liked the story or if they thought I was crazy.

Claire didn't praise or criticize any of the stories, but after class, out in the hallway, she asked me did I have any more stories like this, and I told her I had hundreds, and she asked if I'd ever written any of them down.

"No," I said.

"You should," she said. "You're a natural storyteller."

I wanted to thank her for her vote of confidence, but I said, "You said everyone was a natural storyteller."

"But they don't have stories like yours." She laughed. She offered me her guest room again, but I said I felt right at home in the woods.

"How did that story end?" she asked. "The one you told in class."

"Earl got his shotgun out of the truck, and when he was coming back the dog started snarling, though it was always a nice friendly dog before. Earl had a little bottle of anointing oil in his shirt pocket, and that's what the dog went after. He went right after the oil. Earl knocked him down with the butt of the shotgun and then shot him. Blew him to pieces."

"I've got to sit down," Clair said. "You want some coffee?"

We walked to Seymour Terrace, carrying our briefcases. On the way Claire said, "I can't believe it. But I do believe it. That's what I can't believe!"

"I can't believe it either," I said, "but it's true."

In French we continued to greet each other and inquire about our hometowns in every possible way, and to ask about our family, our friends, our hobbies, our ambitions.

Someone—it was never clear who—had passed out a double-sided, single-spaced Xerox of the kind of French that wasn't taught in school, and these words and phrases, though we weren't sure how to pronounce them, gave an edge to our conversations: *brouter le cresson*, *fumer le cigare*, *ramoner*, *baiser en levrette*: to graze the watercress, to smoke a cigar, to sweep the chimney, to do it dog fashion. Some of the words were the same as in English: *chatte* for "pussy." Others were not so nice: *moule* for cunt. I'd seen mussels at the fish counter at Hy-Vee in a string bag on a bed of ice, next to the catfish, but I hadn't smelled them. *Oignon* for asshole. And you had to be careful to put the right accent on *répétez* when you asked someone to repeat something, which you had to do a lot when you didn't know the language, or you'd be asking them to re-fart.

And then we moved on to the imperfect tense, which I liked because it was so regular. Madame Arnot said you could live your whole life in the present and imperfect tenses. You didn't really need anything else. At least I thought that's what she said.

With a liberal education under my belt, according to the TF catalog, I could be anything I wanted to be. And that's the way I felt at the end of the week. I could become a famous biologist, maybe figure out how you got life out of inanimate matter, like the Miller-Urey experiment in the biology textbook. I could learn to speak French and go to Paris. I could write a book and see it in the window of the University Bookstore or the Co-op on State Street. Maybe I wouldn't do any of these things. I didn't even know how to get through the weekend, which is what I had to do.

In Naqada a weekend meant gearing up for church; on the Hill it meant hanging out and watching a movie in the recreation room. On campus it meant gearing up for a party to which I hadn't been invited. But out at Jackson's it meant hooking the tractor up to the bridge that had been knocked into the stream by a flood and dragging it up to the near bank, which was about six or eight feet above the water, and then renailing the planks—two by eights—that had come loose. And it meant splitting some of the oak and hickory that Warren had cut before he got too sick to work. Jackson and I pulled the splitter out of the garage and hooked it up to the tractor. The wood was stacked at the very back of the property by a funny-looking hill that Jackson said was an Indian burial mound, and we had to take the tractor out to the road and then around to the county highway that I'd taken to Oquawka so we could cross the stream on the highway bridge and come into the property from the back. Jackson hadn't told anyone about the burial mound because he didn't want the State people coming in. He wanted to keep it for himself, for when he retired. He said you could get really lost out here at night because of the mound, which was disorienting. It was a pretty poor thing compared to the mounds at Cahokia, but I didn't say that to Jackson.

The splitter was a serious horizontal splitter, like the one Earl and DX used to split wood for the church, with a six-inch main frame and a two-inch solid steel base plate. I could see that Jackson was uneasy—but not too uneasy—about letting me do most of the heavy lifting, but I liked to work, and once we got the splitter fueled up and topped up with hydraulic oil, we fell into a nice rhythm. Jackson helped me load the logs onto the splitter and then stacked the split wood next to the mound. We'd have to load it into a wagon later on and pull it up to the house with the tractor.

While we worked we talked about our days and swapped stories. I told him about my first biology lab, in which we learned how to use different kinds of microscopes, and he told me about his seminar on hunter-gatherer societies, which included the Mbuti. That was his specialty, because he'd lived with the Mbuti for four years, and he had lots of stories that weren't in the book. He told me about being initiated with the Mbuti boys, and I told him about the first time I handled a serpent, and after that we got into a kind of storytelling competition. He told me about hunting an elephant, and I told him about hunting serpents in the Shawnee National Forest. He told me about an invasion of army ants in the middle of the night, and I told him about Mawmaw Tucker's two sisters coming to Naqada after Mawmaw died and praying her back to life. He told me about Claude dying and how Kachelewa, the elephant hunter, had made him lean over and take Claude's last breath into his own mouth. I told him about Punkin Bates, the evangelist, getting serpent bit and while we were all sitting around praying for him, another serpent came and almost bit him again, but Earl grabbed it by the tail and slammed it down on the floor and broke its neck. And he showed me two tiny black spots on his forehead, about an inch above his nose. His pygmy girlfriend had cut two deep slits with a rusty razor blade and inserted little pieces of graphite from a lead pencil. The black spots, which were still visible, were the marks of a hunter. They meant that he would return to the Forest. The black marks were barely visible, but I could feel them if I ran my fingers over his forehead.

Jackson was really interested in the Church of the Burning Bush. He asked a lot of anthropology-type questions, and wondered if maybe we could go down to Naqada some time, but I told him it was a bad idea. I was thinking about Earl and about what would happen when Earl figured out that I was out of prison, and about what it would be like to go to bed with Jackson. It had been so long I was about to burst. I'd stored up a lot of sex feelings, like the money my mama used to tuck away in an old canister, or the eighty thousand that Warren had tucked away in the bank. I was ready to "sweep the chimney." Or have my chimney swept.

And with Jackson you wouldn't have to do it in the back of a truck. He had a queen-size bed upstairs with a nice firm mattress.

I was thinking that after working shoulder to shoulder as we'd done Jackson would invite me in for a drink, and then for supper, and then into that big queen-size bed. But he didn't, and later that night I heard a car creep into the drive. This time I knew for sure it was Claire. I watched from the window as she walked down the ramp to the house.

About half an hour later I walked down to the house myself—barefoot and quiet as a mouse. I went around to the side window that opened into the living room. I crouched down and peeked through the low window. I could see a light in the kitchen, at the other end of the house, but the living room was dark. I waited a little while to let my eyes get used to the dark. I could make out the wood-burning stove, and then the big leather davenport. Claire was on top of Jackson. If she'd looked up, she would have seen my face in the window. But I didn't think Claire was seeing anything. Her blouse was open, her breasts swinging. I could feel the ground trembling under my feet. I could feel heavy breathing. But the heavy breathing was not Claire; it was the dog, Maya, who'd come up behind me and was sniffing my butt.

I made a noise and jumped up. I thought I was going to faint, and then I was running . . . Maya chased me all the way up to the garage. I stopped at the foot of the stairs to pet her. I held her head in my hands. I bent over and kissed the top of her head. "Good dog, good dog." I didn't know what I was saying.

Up in the apartment I drank some of Warren's whiskey. I was really pissed. I buzzed the intercom, which was on my desk next to the computer. I held my finger down for a full minute. When I let my finger up I could hear someone saying, "Sunny, Sunny, are you all right? Are you all right?"

I wanted to shout *NO,* but I kept my mouth shut.

I was so angry and upset when I got out of bed in the morning that I thought about moving into the dorm. I cooked more bacon and more eggs. I broke the yolk of one of the eggs. I could hear the dog. Her four barks, then quiet as she chased after the stupid Frisbee. I looked out the window and saw Jackson throw the Frisbee. Another hot day. I wondered what the dog was thinking. Wondered what it was like to be a dog. The same routine every day. Jackson takes you out three or four times a day to play Frisbee, and every time you bark with joy. *Joie de vivre.*

I ran my fingers through my hair.

Maya had been spayed. She wouldn't fall in love. Male dogs wouldn't fall in love with her. All this freedom, but she didn't run away. Jackson whistled and she came. *What does she do all morning, when Jackson is gone?*

How was I going to behave toward Jackson? Toward Claire? Was it was too late to change my mind about living in the dorm? Too late to take a different class or get into a different section of Beginning Fiction Writing? How would I explain? And how would I explain buzzing the intercom? I couldn't get the image out of my mind. Claire waving her arms, as if she were conducting a symphony. Her breasts flopping, as if she were possessed by some kind of sex demon.

I directed my anger at Claire. Claire was a married woman. She had no business fucking Jackson.

But then it occurred to me that I was a married woman too. Still married to Earl.

The dog leaped into the air to catch a high throw and almost fell on her back. I started to laugh. *Joie de vivre.* I knew how to pronounce it now. *Joie de vivre.* I was ready to forgive her—forgive Claire. Jackson too.

Almost ready.

The bacon had burned to a crisp and the eggs were solid. I ate them anyway.

That afternoon I went to the public library and got a library card and checked out a book on divorce, on how to do it in Illinois. I was hoping by now that Earl would be glad to be shed of me.

But nothing in life is ever simple. Illinois is not a no-fault state. You've got to have "grounds." I didn't want to get Earl all fired up by listing "attempted murder" as the grounds, so I figured I'd go with "mental or physical cruelty."

What I needed was a Petition for Dissolution of Marriage, a Domestic Relations Cover Sheet, and a Summons. All I had to do was fill out the forms and sign them and file them with the County Clerk of the Court and pay a filing fee. The County Clerk would transmit these documents to the Sheriff's Department in Naqada, and the sheriff would "serve" them on Earl. I shouldn't say this, but it suited me to think about the sheriff knocking on Earl's door with the summons. It was scary too, but I could see the look on his face when the sheriff handed him the papers. He already had two felony counts against him and had to be real careful. Then he'd have thirty days to file an Appearance and Answer. If he didn't file, we'd be divorced automatically.

On Saturday night I went to the French Club movie: *Breathless. À bout de souffle* in French. I sat in on the discussion afterwards. Jean-Paul was there. I felt I didn't understand anything. On the Hill we watched lots of movies, but not like this one. I didn't understand that it was revolutionary; I didn't understand, till the discussion afterwards, that it was poking fun at Hollywood; I didn't understand that it was very self-conscious about being a film; I didn't know enough to appreciate the unusual camera moves; I didn't know what to make of Michel. But Patricia: I understood that Patricia didn't want to be controlled by a man, and I was glad that she turned Michel in to the police to prove that she didn't love him. If there'd been somewhere to turn Jackson in to, I would have done it. Claire too.

What happened was that I confronted Claire during our first story conference. "The sunset stuff works well," Claire was saying about my story. She was reading her comments off her computer screen. "But maybe give Alice a more complex and interesting response. For example, she might come close to pushing Aaron off the catwalk. Or at least think about how satisfying it would be to push him. And I'd like her to understand that the way she behaves now, the way she responds to this disappointment, will shape the person she's going to become. Something like that."

"It would be satisfying, wouldn't it," I said. "Like pushing the buzzer when you were fucking Jackson." I think I surprised myself as much as I surprised Claire.

Claire leaned forward over her desk and put her hands over her face. I was sitting in a chair next to her. I spun her around and pried her hands apart. She was starting to cry.

"I thought we were going to be friends," I said. "Not just teacher and student. I thought that's what you wanted. I wasn't going to say anything, but you stand up there in the classroom and tell us to write out of our deepest values . . ."

"I thought so too," she said. "I'm sorry. I'm so sorry."

I was thinking how I'd been in this same scenario, with Earl hammering away at me. I wanted to laugh, but it wasn't funny.

And then I really did take myself by surprise. I knew all along that I'd get around to forgiving Claire. I just wanted to be sure that she knew I was forgiving her. But now I asked myself, Who was I to forgive Claire? Who was I to be angry in the first place? Who was I to scold her, to disapprove? Did I want to act like God? Besides, my anger hadn't been righteous in the first place. It had been jealous.

"Claire," I said. "I'm the one who should be sorry. And I am sorry. I had no right to push the buzzer, or to throw it in your face this morning."

"I'm forty years old," she said. "I wrote a novel and won a prize, but nobody's ever heard of the prize, and the book is about number two million on Amazon dot-com. It's not even in the university bookstore. It's a good title, though. *The Sins of the World.* You'd think there'd be a lot of books with that title, but there aren't. Mine's the only one. *The Sins of the World,* and I've committed all of them."

"You haven't murdered anyone, have you?"

"Well, all the others."

"Have you borne false witness against your neighbor?"

"Well, I guess I haven't done that either, but all the rest of them, especially coveting my neighbor's husband. You know, Jackson was so good to me when *Sins* got so many rejections, and then I turned around and married Ray. What was I thinking?" She wiped her eyes. "Oh, it's all right. Ray's a good man, and he's good to me too. I shouldn't complain."

Another student was standing in the doorway. It was time for me to go.

"Someone's here," I said.

"Everything is material," Claire said. "For a writer, everything is material."

"I'll remember that," I said.

"But please don't write about this. Please." She looked at my face for an answer.

"Promise."

"And don't say anything to Jackson."

"Not a word," I said.

7

Balanced Reciprocity

One Saturday afternoon in mid-October, the weather crisp and cool after a hot summer and a warm September, they caught the big groundhog that had made his home under Jackson's deck. The dog heard him first and started barking at the kitchen door. Jackson opened the kitchen door and went out on the deck. When he leaned over the railing, he could see the groundhog in the Have-a-Heart trap he'd bought at Farm King. Sunny had been putting canned peaches in the trap. He buzzed her on the intercom. "*Bonjour,*" she said.

"Got the *marmotte d'Amérique,*" he said.

"I guess those peaches did the job," she said. "Be right down. *Au revoir.*"

The groundhog wasn't happy, and they both wore heavy gloves when they lifted the trap onto a plastic sled. They took hold of the rope and pulled the sled up to the drive, and then lifted the trap up into the bed of Warren's truck. Sunny's truck.

On the drive to Oquawka, an old river town twelve miles away, where they were going to release the groundhog far enough away so it wouldn't show up at Jackson's the next day, she put a Taj Mahal CD in the player and sang along: "I had the blues so bad one time it put my face in a permanent frown. Now I'm feelin' so much better I could cakewalk into town."

The groundhog was asleep when they got to Oquawka.

"Like Naqada," Sunny said, looking around. "Seen better days."

They drove through town to the river, the Mississippi, and then turned north and drove along the river till they came to a scenic turnout.

"You'll thank us, Mr. Groundhog. Just be happy Mr. Jackson didn't want me to shoot you." Sunny pulled the hasp on the trap and released the groundhog, who scurried down the bank to the river and then came back up and headed in the other direction in a fast waddle.

They stopped at the Blue Goose for lunch and each had a beer and split a third beer, and then they stopped at a little park on the edge of town to admire the monument to Norma Jean elephant.

Jackson was relieved. The groundhog had really bothered him, gnawing away under the house.

"I want to go on a picnic in the country," Sunny sang, "Mama oh, and stay all day, I don't care but don't do nothing just while my time away."

On the way back she pulled into a motel next to the Schuyler Melon Farm. The Schuyler barn was closed up and the tables were shut away; but the empty stand was still there, with a sign: MELONS: $3 EACH.

"Melons like sandy soil," Jackson explained.

Sunny looked at Jackson. "I don't know if I'm eighteen or thirty-five."

Jackson didn't say anything. He was suddenly aware of the surface of his body, of the joints that still caused trouble, of the deep fatigue that lay below the surface. He was aware of the surface of her body, too, where her blouse lay over her shoulders and over her breasts, the way it was tucked into her jeans, even the pressure of her socks separating the soles of her feet from the soles of her shoes and the ring circling her finger and the watch circling her left wrist that was a little too loose and kept riding up.

"You're not going to turn me down, are you?" she said.

Jackson laughed. "No, I'm not going to turn you down."

"We're going to commit adultery. At least I am."

"Your first time?"

"In this life," she said, leaning over and opening the dash and poking around for something. "You go arrange for a room. I'll pay you later."

They sat next to each other on the edge of the bed, and Jackson thought about Claire. But Sunny wasn't at all like Claire! Sunny was hungry, but she wasn't needy. They didn't take their clothes off for a while. They were feeling shy, or maybe mistaking something else for shyness. Then they started touching, kissing, talking, joking.

Sunny started to unbutton her lumberjack shirt. She said something in French. She sounded, to Jackson, as if she'd been practicing: *"Voulez-vous baiser en levrette?"*

Jackson laughed.

"Did I say something funny?"

"Very funny."

"So what did I say?"

"You asked if I wanted to fuck you like a greyhound bitch."

"What's so funny about that?" She laughed.

"You learn that in your French class?"

"Sort of," she said.

They messed around for a while and then took off their clothes. She handed him a condom. *"Une capote anglaise."*

"An English hood."

"*Baiser en levrette*," she said. "I thought it meant something else." She laughed and turned over and stuck her butt up in the air.

"Maybe it would be better *faire l'amour à la papa*," he said.

"You mean like missionaries?" she said. "I don't want you to be bored."

"Have you been looking at the sex tips in *Cosmopolitan* while you're standing in line in Hy-Vee?"

She laughed again and rolled over on her back and opened her arms. The look on her face was warm and open, as if she already knew all about him.

On the way back Jackson wanted to stop at the McDonald's on the highway, but Sunny wanted to cook something. She'd borrowed one of Jackson's cookbooks—*The Flavor of France*—and had started cooking French up in Warren's apartment.

"I've got a chicken in the refrigerator," Jackson said.

"What more could we ask for?"

"Mushrooms. I've got some mushrooms too. And the bottle of wine you gave me."

"It felt like my whole body was on fire," Sunny said, putting her hand on his leg. "It was like being struck by lightning. It was like a pot of raspberry jam boiling over on the stove."

"You know just what to say to a man," he said.

"I like pulling into the drive," she said. "I like the crunch of the gravel under the wheels."

"You did a good job," he said. She'd graded the drive about a week earlier.

"There's a low spot up ahead that needs more gravel. I should probably put a pipe under it. And that tree." She pointed at a big old oak that had fallen across the fence into Jack Delacort's field. "I can take care of that."

"If there's property damage—the fence—the insurance may cover it. I can get Mason's Tree Service to take it out."

"I like seeing the lights on too, from my window. The woods can be really dark if there's no moon. It's a great place. It's not a cabin, but it's not a regular house either. Maybe some kind of lodge, but not really a lodge either."

"Let me know when you figure out what it is. Claude fixed it up inside like a French country house with that fancy stove in the kitchen, and French tiles and copper pots. He used to give great parties, invite fifty or sixty people."

The dog was waiting for them. If she was annoyed that she hadn't gotten to go along, she didn't show it. She went to Sunny's door, then Jackson's, leaping for joy.

They left the truck outside, next to Jackson's pickup. Jackson liked to see the two pickups side by side. Red and green, Ford and Chevy, six cylinder and eight cylinder.

Sunny came around the truck and waited for Jackson to embrace her, or at least touch her. Which he did. He bent to kiss the top of her head.

"I'm really happy here," she said. "I said I was going to be happy, and I am. But what does it mean?"

"What does what mean—being happy?"

Jackson was wondering the same thing, wondering what it meant, and what it would mean to eat this dinner together, and how pleasant it would be to sit at Claude's French farmhouse table with this woman. He recognized the feelings: endorphins, the chemistry of love. He didn't fight against them. As an anthropologist he was aware of the mating habits of higher primates and familiar with the evolution of sexual dimorphism in animals. But maybe he was a little afraid anyway. Of the mystery of it. He'd been through it enough, too many times, maybe. Always seems different at the beginning. *But love grows old, and waxes cold, and fades away like morning dew.* It was like climbing a mountain he'd climbed before. But this time it really was different. But that was the same too. It was always different.

He kissed her on the lips. The dog tried to push herself between them, as if she wanted to separate them. Jackson put his hand on the dog's head and then on Sunny's bottom. He kissed her again. Because he thought that this was what she wanted. It was what he wanted too.

The pile of firewood was handsome. Over a full cord. It wasn't really cold yet, but he'd build a fire anyway.

Sunny went up to her apartment to change her clothes. When she came back down she was wearing a dark blue turtleneck and a clean pair of jeans. Jackson had a fire going in the wood stove. She looked through *The Flavor of France.* She made herself right at home. She didn't ask where is this, where is that. She just opened cupboards and found what she needed.

Jackson fed the dog and put a tablecloth on the table, which was scored with burns from Claude's Gauloises. He closed the wooden shutters against the dark and opened the bottle of French wine that Sunny had brought earlier—an expensive Bordeaux. Jackson liked wine, and he'd always drunk what Claude drank, but Claude wasn't too fussy. For a Frenchman. At the end of a party he'd pour all the leftover wine into one bottle. Jackson closed his eyes and held Sunny in his imagination, putting together a picture from the sounds she was making—cutting, chopping, using the clicker to light the back burner on the right-hand side, which didn't work properly—and from the sounds she'd made that afternoon, little cries and growls, as if she were in fact a greyhound bitch.

He opened the wine to let it breathe and they each had a beer.

"Do you have any *kir*?" she asked. "That's what they drink in France."

Jackson remembered a lot of things about his stays in France, but he didn't remember drinking *kir*.

"It's crème de cassis with white wine. If you use champagne, it's called a *kir royale*."

"Did you learn that in your French class too?"

"Yes."

"Have you ever tried it?"

"No, but I'd like to."

"We'll have to get some," he said. "Crème de cassis and champagne."

"Chicken Marengo," she said. "It says here that on June fourteenth, eighteen hundred, Napoleon Bonaparte defeated the Austrian army at Marengo, and that his cook made up this recipe for him. To celebrate."

"I think it's supposed to have crawfish," Jackson said.

"What are those, crawdads?"

"And little fried eggs—or just yolks."

"We could use shrimp."

"If we had some shrimp."

The owls were making a ruckus outside the kitchen window.

Sunny was very intense when she cooked. Jackson drank his beer and watched her while he made a salad. She'd pushed up the sleeves of her turtleneck, and she had a pencil stuck through her hair, which had started to curl up behind her right ear, and she was wearing new glasses in fashionable gold frames. The glasses took some of the backwoods out of her. He hadn't noticed them before.

Jackson cut up some bread and went to check the fire. He added two chunks of gorgonzola to the salad while she browned the chicken pieces.

"Intentionality is the enemy," she said. Jackson recognized

Claire's mantra. "You've got to be open to surprises at every stage of the game. Like this afternoon. Were you surprised?"

It had been a long time since Jackson had been so surprised, or since a surprise had come boiling up out of him. It wasn't that he thought he knew everything. It was that he didn't have any idea of what else he wanted to know. Unlike Sunny, who was learning new stuff every day and was too excited to keep it to herself.

"Intentionality is the enemy," she said again. "Leave yourself open for surprises at every step of the way. Don't try to plan everything out. I think that's really true." She paused. "Were you surprised?" she asked again. "This afternoon?"

"I was very surprised. How about you? Did you surprise yourself too?"

"Not exactly. I was just starting to wonder."

"About what?"

She tried to explain in French what she wanted to say, but she couldn't manage it.

"You brought your own *capote anglaise*," Jackson said. "That looks to me like evidence of intentionality."

With the shutters closed, the kitchen was suffused in a warm glow.

It was the end of the fourth full week of the semester. Jackson asked her about her classes, and she told him. She was working on a story for Claire, reading Euripides' *Bacchae* in Great Books, studying the *passé composé* in French. But it was her biology class that was on her mind.

"Professor Cramer's something else," she said. "He doesn't put up with any nonsense. At the beginning of each class he picks a name at random from his class list—there are too many of us for him to know our names—and he interrogates that poor student: If you don't know the answer to the first question, he doesn't ask another student, he just keeps asking you one question after another till you melt down, and then he takes off his glasses and starts shouting 'CAN'T YOU READ?' I've learned to read, believe me."

"Has he interrogated you?"

She nodded. "About the Miller-Urey experiment."

"What's that?"

"This guy—Stanley Miller—wanted to see if he could create life, figure out how it got started, by going back to the way the universe was at the beginning."

"What did he do?"

"He put water and ammonia in a flask with hydrogen and methane gas, and then he boiled it up and zapped it with electricity. Like lightning hitting the earth. He kept doing that and after a week he'd produced a molecular soup containing amino acids. Those are the building blocks of proteins, life itself."

"Two sixteen-year-olds can create life in the back seat of a car."

"I mean out of nothing. Just primal atmosphere. You just keep shooting electricity into it and after a while you get proteins . . . amino acids. You don't need too much equipment. A few flasks. I was thinking maybe we could do that here. In the basement. What do you think?"

"Depends on how complicated it is."

"There's a diagram in my biology text. It doesn't look too hard."

"How do you get the 'atmosphere' into the flask?"

"I don't know," she said. "I'll ask Professor Cramer."

Jackson had helped her fill out the divorce papers and had gone with her to have his lawyer look them over and get them notarized. He was thinking that by the end of the semester—before the end of the semester—she would be free. But out of the blue she said, "I heard from Earl. I got a letter yesterday."

She was standing at the sink with her back to him.

"He's going to contest the divorce. He's coming to Colesville."

And suddenly everything became clear. *Balanced reciprocity,* which is anthropospeak for "tit for tat." She'd given him a gift, her body, and now she expected a fair and tangible return: protection from Earl.

But that wasn't the way it felt. What it felt like was a wave of melancholy sweeping over him, and then leaving him high and dry. He watched her standing at the sink, washing a plate. Scrubbing it. Her left arm pumping. *She was left-handed.* They were both left-handed. He walked up behind her, stood behind her as if they'd been married for years and years and here she was, her hands in the sink, staring out the kitchen window at the propane tank. He put his hands on her shoulders and put his face in her hair and held her, feeling her shoulders work as she scrubbed the plate with a scraper sponge before putting it in the dishwasher.

8

The Garden of Eden

In the third year after Claude's death Jackson and Taphu, a young man from the cohort with whom Jackson had been initiated, went to swim in a hidden pool fed by a secret spring that only Taphu knew about. But as they approached the pool, which was deep into the Forest, more than an hour from the camp, they could hear voices.

"There's someone here," Jackson said, somewhat alarmed.

Taphu laughed.

They came to a clearing where two girls were bathing naked in a shallow pool. Jackson recognized Sibaku and Amina, a beautiful girl who had filed her teeth to sharp points.

"You knew they were here," he said to Taphu.

"Do you like Sibaku?" Taphu asked.

"Of course I do," Jackson said. "Why do you ask?"

The girls had seen them by now but made little effort to cover themselves.

Taphu removed his bark cloth and plunged into the pool. Jackson, who was wearing what was left of a pair of jeans, stayed on the bank. After a few minutes Sibaku called to him. "Aren't you coming in?"

She was a perfectly formed little woman who didn't even come up to his waist.

"Maybe later," he called. He was not exactly shy, but he was uncomfortable. Not sure what was expected, or permitted. He went off to find the spring that fed the pool, which was not far. He drank and filled his water bottle. When he came back, Taphu and Amina were gone. Sibaku was alone, lounging on a rock, her bark cloth and belt on the rock next to her.

"Why did you stay behind?" he asked, trying not to stare.

"Because," she said, "you'd never find your way back by yourself."

On the way back to the camp they came upon Taphu and Amina making love enthusiastically, right next to the path, in a complicated position that Jackson, as an anthropologist, thought he should record. But how? He asked Sibaku if this position had a name, and she laughed and said something to Amina as they walked by, and Amina and Taphu laughed too.

The next night Sibaku came to his hut after a dance. Asumali, Sibaku's father, had brought out a powerful new drum, made out of duiker skin and wood from the devil tree, and the men and women began to dance around the fire in separate circles. When one dance ended, another began, each more complex and frenzied than the last. Jackson danced with the men in the first dance, but then he sat in his three-stick chair and watched. Sibaku, her small breasts and her back beautifully painted, her glowing eyes shadowed with the Mbuti equivalent of kohl, gave him a sassy smile every time she came by, and later that night—after the storm put an end to the dancing—she came to his hut. "I want to sleep here," she said.

She was only thirty-three inches tall. He measured her later with a tape measure that he gave to her father, and he wondered how they'd manage. Other Mbuti wondered too and made lots of jokes outside the hut, jokes which he and Sibaku could hear perfectly well as she was sitting astride him. There was no privacy, and Sibaku threatened to build a new hut apart from the rest if the jokes didn't stop.

A week later the whole band moved to a hunting camp deep in the forest, where they stayed for several months. Sibaku built a hut for the two of them. She cleaned and cooked, and repaired the roof when it was necessary. He took his place with the men in the net hunting, and he managed, with Taphu's help, to kill an antelope and present the skin to Sibaku's father.

Sibaku was five months pregnant when Jackson was arrested at Camp Rameau.

And now, in a way, he had come back to the same place, the beginning of a new life. Standing behind Sunny at the sink he'd experienced a deep longing for a new life. In all his previous relationships, since Sibaku, he'd been guarding himself against this sort of thing, this urgent longing. But when he looked out the window later that night and saw her light—could see her in her window—he opened himself to it. He left his bedroom light on so she could see him. If she wanted to see him. He willed her to look up, to press the buzzer on the intercom, which was on her desk next to the computer. He closed his eyes and counted to sixty. When he opened his eyes, she was still at her window. But the minute he turned out his light and crawled into bed, she buzzed him. "Should I come down?"

"Yes," he said.

At first Jackson was self-conscious about his yoga exercises, about all the antibiotics in the medicine cabinet, about the time it took to get out of bed in the morning, about needing a nap in the afternoon, but she started doing the yoga exercises with him, she helped

101

him get out of bed in the morning, and she lay down with him in the afternoon, unless she was in her bio lab on Thursdays.

He'd come to an understanding with Claire, so the only cloud on the horizon was Earl.

Jackson had broken bread with some strange characters—he'd eaten porcupine with Kachelewa (the renowned elephant hunter) and boiled monkey with Arumba (the renowned singer), he'd drunk the local beer with Chief Mulebaloti (on the way north with Claude to the Mountains of the Moon). Once in Varanasi he'd shared a plate of alloo tikki with the King of the Dead (one of them; there were two). And in the same year he'd attended a banquet held by the Syrian Defense Minister in an underground room with pictures of bare-breasted actresses on the walls, including Marilyn Monroe, Gina Lollabrigida, and Jayne Mansfield.

As an anthropologist he was committed to respecting the belief systems and customs of other cultures. Like Claude, he thought that much of what was wrong with the world today came from a failure to respect others. You didn't have to subscribe to the anthropologist's mantra about cultural relativity to understand that it was important to listen to all the voices in the community.

On the other hand, it seemed to him perfectly obvious that some cultures are better than others. You didn't have to be a genius to see that. Take the Mbuti, for example: no headmen, no chiefs, no rich or poor, no taxes, no war. You worked about four hours a day and spent the rest of the time singing and dancing.

But he was uneasy about Earl. And Sunny's nerves made it worse. He figured that Earl was coming to claim his wife, and that Sunny had claimed him, Jackson, as her white knight.

When she sat down at the piano and started vamping and he joined her on the harmonica, chuffing along and whistling like an old freight train, Earl was there. When they made love after an afternoon nap, Earl was there. When they went to bed at night, Earl was there. When they played pinochle at the kitchen table, Earl was there, reminding them that card games (like gambling and movies and TV) were sinful. Sunny, who'd learned to play in prison, was a quick and aggressive player and studied his face every time she laid down a card or scooped up a trick.

After supper Jackson would look at *L'Avenir*, a French-language newspaper published in Kinshasa that came irregularly. Jackson liked to keep up with the news in the Congo, which was almost all bad, and to explain to Sunny what was going on. Back in June the commander of the Uganda People's Defense Force in the DRC, ignoring the protests of a Congolese liberation movement based in Kisangani, had carved a new "province" of Ituri out of an older province, and ethnic conflict had erupted between the Hema and the Lendu. But nothing was clear, and it was impossible to say how this conflict might affect the Mbuti.

They went to concerts, lectures, plays, French Club movies—all the things that a large university had to offer, all the things that had been forbidden in the Church of the Burning Bush.

But Earl was always there.

Sunny had her own idea of how to prepare for Earl's visit. Jackson tried to talk her out of it. She was sitting on the couch, conjugating irregular verbs out loud, then checking them against the textbook. Jackson was reading an article on Pentecostalism. When he got up to put another log on the fire, she looked up and said, "I want to buy a pistol."

"A pistol? What for?"

"Earl's coming next week."

"Not a good idea." But in fact he thought it was a good idea.

"You don't know Earl."

"Well, buy a pistol."

"I can't."

"Why not?"

"I'm a convicted felon. I can't get a Firearm Owner's ID card. But you must have one—for your rifles. And for the shotgun."

"Why don't you just load up the shotgun and hold on to it while Earl's here?"

"I'd feel better with a pistol."

"There's a reason," he said, "why convicted felons can't get a FOID card."

But this really set her off. "God damn you, don't treat me like a child."

They argued about the pistol for two days. Jackson could see he was up against something stronger than reason. Fear. There was no point in talking about it. In fact he was only pretending to object. He was glad, because he was afraid too.

On the Thursday before Earl was going to arrive they went to a firearms store in Colesville. GUN COLLECTORS was the name painted on a big green sign. It was where Jackson had taken his .22 to have the barrel checked, and Warren's guns and Claude's old .35 to have them appraised.

The guns were in locked cases behind a long counter, and the owner, who sported a biker mustache, was not very helpful.

He showed Sunny a .22-caliber double-action revolver.

"This is the gun I shot Earl with," she said to Jackson. "All you have to do is pick it up and squeeze the trigger."

"Is that what you want?" Jackson asked.

"I think I want something more powerful."

"Who's buying this gun, anyway?" the clerk asked.

"I am," Jackson said.

The clerk went to get another model.

"I don't have a good feeling about this," Jackson said. But he did have a good feeling.

"Don't worry. I know how to use it."

"That's what I'm afraid of."

The clerk brought out a .38-caliber semiautomatic, a Walther PPK.

"That's more like it." She held the gun, turned toward the door, and practiced a draw. "Any draw that sweeps across part of your body, or across anyone else, is not a good draw," she said.

"I'll remember that," Jackson said. He remembered playing cops and robbers as a kid. Practicing dying. Falling down, groaning, thrashing around. Dying with a final dramatic flop.

"It's got plenty of power," the clerk said. "Very reliable."

Jackson handed over his FOID card and his credit card. Sunny wanted to give him cash in the store while the clerk was ringing up the sale.

"For Christ's sake, wait until we get outside."

The pistol cost two hundred fifty dollars.

They bought some police targets, showing a bad guy waving his arms, and every day she practiced. Setting the targets down the hill and shooting from the deck. Jackson tried it too. He was an okay shot with a rifle, but he'd shot a pistol only once, with his grandfather. Sunny gave him tips.

"Keep both eyes open," she said.

"I know that."

"Then do it," she said. "And don't look up at the target. Look *at* the front sight, not *over* it. The target should just be a blur in the background."

"That's what I'm doing."

"Not it's not. You're raising up every time. There's plenty of time to look at the target when you're done shooting. And don't *pull* the trigger. *Squeeze* it."

"Yes, ma'am," he said.

Jackson was listening to NPR when he heard Earl's truck in the drive. Sunny was upstairs. The program was about the shortage of accordion reeds in Madagascar. English missionaries had introduced the accordion back in the early nineteenth century. Jackson turned the radio off.

Their plan was to cook some hamburgers on the grill, treat Earl as a guest. Not serve any alcohol.

He watched Earl walk down the ramp. He was a large man, a prizefighter. He was wearing a tie. That was a good sign. A man wearing a tie wouldn't be about to kill you. He was clean shaven. His shirt collar was too tight, or his neck was too thick. Jackson thought of a wild boar or a hippopotamus.

"You must be Professor Jones." Earl held out his hand. Jackson shook it. *How did Earl know my name?*, Jackson thought. *How did Earl know where I live? Would Sunny's lawyer—my lawyer—have given him my information? Maybe he hired a private eye.*

"I'm looking for my wife."

"Your wife?"

"Yes. Willa Fern Cochrane. She's upstairs. I seen her peekin' out the window."

"Willa Fern. She goes by Sunny now."

"Is that so?"

Jackson nodded. "Ever since she got out of prison."

Earl laughed. "You want to be careful around her. Don't leave your pistol on the table and then turn your back on her to get somethin' out of the refrigerator."

"I don't plan to."

"FERN," Earl shouted. "Get on down here, I got something to say to you."

"I've got a gun, Earl," she called down the stairs.

"You planning to shoot me again?"

"Not if I don't have to."

"What have you got?"

"It's a thirty-eight, but I know how to use it."

"She's been practicing in the woods," Jackson said.

"And she will too," Earl said, aiming his voice up the stairs. "I learned my lesson."

"Why don't we just sit down and see if we can't come to an agreement," Jackson said.

"Sort of like the Jews and the A-rabs."

Jackson heard Sunny's footsteps on the stairs.

Earl looked around. "Nice place you got here. This is the kind of place I'd build if I had the money. Remember Ed Martin," he said to Sunny, who had reached the bottom of the stairs. "Lived up on the river up by Old Shawneetown? He had a place like this."

"It belonged to Claude Michaut," Jackson said, "the anthropologist."

"Some of them come to the church once."

"They study different peoples," Sunny said, "and different cultures. Jackson's one too."

"I know what they is. I just said, some of them come to the church."

"Jackson studied the pygmies in Africa."

"The little people. There was a pygmy come with the circus to Paducah. Wasn't no more than three or four feet high." He held his hand up to show how high.

"You want something to eat?" Jackson asked. "We're grilling some burgers."

Sunny was still holding on to the pistol, sometimes gesturing with it as she described the extent of the woods to Earl, always keeping her distance.

Earl came out on the deck to watch Jackson grill the hamburgers. "You come on down to Naqada," he said, "and we'll catch us some bluefish. Nothing like 'em. Right, Fern?" He called to Sunny, who was still in the kitchen, through the screen door.

"It's 'Sunny,'" she said.

Sunny kept the pistol on her lap while they were eating at the glass-topped table on the deck. Jackson could see the pistol through the glass. She kept one hand on the pistol and picked up her hamburger with the other.

Earl looked uncomfortable in his tie.

Sunny took the pistol with her when she went in to get more napkins. The pistol didn't seem to bother Earl.

"I've been doing some reading," Jackson said. "You've run into some hard times down in Egypt."

"Hard times keeps people in church."

Pentecostalism, Jackson thought—the religion of the disinherited. "Coal mining culture," he said. "Drove out the old agriculture ways. Then coal went under. Marginalization. Embracing customs that keep you apart from mainstream culture."

"What you're sayin' is that Little Egypt is really a part of Appalachia. And it's true. Everybody in Naqada's got family across the river in Kentucky and down in Tennessee and West Virginia. We got the old slave house just off the hard road near Equality. We voted to go with the South in the Civil War." Earl put his hamburger down on his plate. "But that don't make us a bunch of ignorant hillbillies."

"That's not what I'm saying. What I'm saying is that you keep yourselves set apart from mainstream culture."

"If you mean godless people, yes, we do keep ourselves apart. But we got people in the church have gone to college. We got two mechanical engineers and a supermarket manager and a funeral director. We got Jimmy Kay that works over to the bank, and DX's cousin Martha teaches English in high school, and she handles almost every week."

"Tell him about all the people who got bit. Tell him about Bennett Brown."

"Bennett Brown didn't die because he was serpent bit. That's what the sheriff was sayin', but if you look at the video you can see that he had a heart attack. It happened too fast for a serpent bite. They was sayin' he died because he was serpent bit but that was because they wanted to make trouble. When you look at the video you can see that he just keeled right over two seconds after he was bit. That was too quick for a bite. He had a heart attack, that's what it was."

"What about Bennett's wife, Melody? She got bit at a brush arbor across the river, and she died. And what about Ed Banks . . ."

"We don't know what God had in mind. Maybe Melody shouldn't have handled that day. Maybe she wasn't anointed good. Maybe God wanted to show unbelievers that the serpents haven't been doctored up somehow, had their venom sacks taken out. People will believe all kinds of stuff. We just don't know. God don't tell us everything."

"How do you catch the snakes?" Jackson wanted to change the conversation.

"Some guys use a hook or a grabber—like a kind of clamp—but mostly you can step on their neck, right behind the head, and then pick up their tail and just hold it a while and the blood will all go to their head and they'll get real easy to handle. Or you can use a forked stick and pin it behind the head. He pronounced "forked" with two syllables: "fork-èd."

Sunny said, "What about all the people for hundreds and hundreds of years who didn't handle?"

"I reckon the Lord will know what to do with them."

"You think they're going to hell."

"I think I know what God tells *me* to do," he said, turning to Jackson, "and I'm going to do it, and God tells me to handle serpents. I been handling serpents since I started going to church with Gene Morton over in Middlesboro. I *had* to do it, if you know what I mean. It wasn't like I had a choice."

"Of course you had a choice," Sunny said. "Everybody's got a choice."

"Everybody's got a choice of doing God's will or going against it. I done that too, I admit. I been backed up on the Lord more than once. I don't have to tell you. But the Lord has always took me back, like savin' someone from drownding." He stretched out an arm to demonstrate God's reach. "And he's reaching out to you too. Both of you."

Jackson put out clean plates for their salad, which they ate after their hamburgers.

Earl asked if there was any coffee. Jackson got up to make espresso.

"I see she's got you well trained."

Jackson made the coffee in one of Claude's espresso pots. He took out little cups and saucers while he waited for it to brew.

"You got a lot of deer around here?" Earl looked at the little cups.

"Too many. Deer ticks."

"Professor Jones has Lyme disease."

"You know, that's what Doc Weiler said about your cousin Raymond last year, and he went and got himself bit by a big old copperhead. There was a nest of them right outside the door to the church. He got bit and everybody thought it was 'cause he wasn't anointed, and his mama was a-carryin' on like it was the Second Coming. She wanted to call the hospital at Rosiclare, but Raymond said no, and he was feelin' pretty poorly for a day or so, and then after that he was fine. The Lord took away his Lyme disease too, just like that." Earl snapped his fingers.

Jackson poured the coffee.

"I can't take any sugar in mine," Earl said. "Doctor says I'm pre-diabetic, whatever that means."

"It means you've got to cut down on sugar."

"What do you think I just said?"

"Maybe I should try that," Jackson said. "Might be good for Lyme disease."

"Serious. Maybe you should. You know how them honey bee stings can cure arthritis. Old Mammie Carter from the Holler, she swore by it. People couldn't hardly keep her away from their hives."

"What about John Granger, and Charlie Halpern, and Cindy Lofter? Dead, dead, dead. Serpent-bit."

"That was over in Kentucky," Earl said to Sunny.

"What difference does that make?"

"It's hard to explain some things to this woman," Earl said to Jackson. "My wife. She's stubborn as a mule."

"Earl, it's over. You could have just signed the papers I sent you instead of coming all the way up here. I got another set here. Maybe we could settle this while you're up here."

"Did you know that the Israelites and the Canaanites spoke the same language?"

"I never gave it a thought," Sunny said.

"They could talk to each other."

"What's your point, Earl?"

"Sometimes I don't think we're talking the same language. You and me."

Sunny got up to leave, holding the Walther in her left hand.

"You comin' home with me?"

"I'm going upstairs to study." She walked into the living room. Jackson could hear her footsteps on the stairs.

Earl put his head in his hands. Jackson hoped he'd leave, but he stayed put while Jackson cleared the table, rinsed the dishes, put them in the dishwasher. Earl's lips were moving. He was praying.

"I used to argue with God," he said, lifting his head.

"Like Abraham? About Sodom and Gomorrah? Thirty good men? Twenty?"

"More like we would dialogue with each other. Confirm something. I have the gift of prophecy, and sometimes I'm not real eager to deliver the message."

"Would this be one of those times?"

"I've got nothing against you, nor against any human being, but you're living in a situation with my wife, and God can't let me be still about the truth of this situation. I'm the kind of person will share with you whatever you need. If you need food, I will bring it to you. If you need money, I'll give you what I have. But my wife is another thing. God don't look too kindly on adultery, which is what this situation is. Unless you tell me you're living like brother and sister."

Jackson didn't say anything. Earl was standing in the middle of the kitchen. He changed the subject: "You reckon there's anything to this Y2K stuff?"

"I can't get too worked up about it."

"Nineteen ninety-nine. You might want to think about it. Get yourself right with God while you can."

He hadn't changed the subject after all. "You think the end is near?" Jackson said.

"Two thousand. End of the millennium."

"The millennium doesn't end until the end of year two thousand."

"I heard that too. I guess we'll just have to wait and see. No man knows the hour."

Earl was good-looking, well-mannered, polite. You wouldn't expect him to jump up and punch you in the face (or shove your face down into a box of rattlesnakes and copperheads). But at the same time you were aware of considering the possibility. An interesting "anthropological sample," Jackson thought. Not representative, but all he had to go on. He wasn't sure. Maybe there were others like him. A whole church full.

What Jackson had learned from Claude was "disciplined subjectivity." It was seeing yourself through somebody else's eyes. Earl's. Earl was a man with a unified vision of the world. He had a way of filtering out the disconnected information that threatens to overwhelm us.

"Them anthropologists I was telling you about, they come to the church, more than once."

"Salvage anthropology."

" 'Savages'?"

" 'Salvage,' not 'savage.' A lot of cultures are disappearing. Margaret Mead and Gregory Bateson in New Guinea, for example. They had to do everything: learn the language, make a dictionary, write a grammar, make a census, figure out the genealogies and write down the myths, along with trying to understand the political structure."

"Like them pygmies?"

"Exactly. But the pygmies go way back. Theirs is the oldest civilization."

"What about Adam and Eve? You saying Adam and Eve were pygmies?"

Jackson wasn't sure he wanted to have this conversation, but he couldn't think of any other conversation he *did* want to have.

"Yes. In the sense that they were the first people. Older than the Egyptians. The Egyptians held the pygmies in the highest esteem. There's a pygmy right there on one of their oldest monuments. You've got pygmies dancing. It's the oldest civilization in the world. And continuous. It goes back at least forty thousand years, maybe much longer. And now the Negroes who live at the edge of the Forest are chopping down the trees to make plantations."

"But the pygmies," Earl wanted to know, "they live in Africa, right? But the Garden of Eden was in Mesopotamia. 'And the Lord God planted a garden eastward in Eden.'"

Jackson finished putting the dishes in the dishwasher. He wiped off the table with paper towels and went into the living room to fetch Claude's *Atlas historique d'Afrique.* He put some newspaper down on the table, which was still damp, and opened the atlas to the two-page Mercator projection of the earth at the front and proceeded to explain the great African diaspora, a word Claude had always pronounced with the accent on the next-to-last syllable—diaspóra. With his finger he traced the northern route followed by the earliest humans from central Africa, up the Nile Valley. And then the eastern route, either crossing the Red Sea from northeast Africa, or going up the North African coast to Egypt. Then north across the Bering Sea and into the Americas. He didn't take time to explain that this all took place over a period of eighty thousand years or so. He didn't want to get into a chronological argument with Earl, and he didn't bother to explain that sea level had been three hundred feet below what it is today.

"But what about Eden?" Earl asked. "You got your four rivers. 'A river went out of Eden to water the garden; and from thence it was parted, and became into four heads.'"

"Right where I started," Jackson said, putting his finger down on what is now the border between Uganda and the Democratic

Republic of the Congo. "Biological anthropologists (or paleoanthropologists) locate the origins of humankind in the highlands reaching north from the Cape to the Lakes of the Nile."

"That ain't what the Bible says."

"Of course. There's a discrepancy between the Biblical account and the fossil evidence and the accounts of the Arab geographers. But Claude—my teacher—believed that he'd found the explanation for this discrepancy. And it was hard to argue with Claude. Take your four rivers? What are they?"

"You got your Pison," Earl said, "that compasseth all of Havilah; you got the Gihon in Ethiopia, you got the Hiddekel in Assyria. And then you got the Euphrates."

"It's an old problem, Earl. It doesn't make sense geographically. It doesn't match what the Arab geographers knew."

"What don't make sense?"

"Mesopotamia. You don't have enough rivers in Mesopotamia. You've got your Tigris and your Euphrates, all right, both coming down from the mountains up in eastern Turkey. That's two. You need two more. Where are they?"

Jackson paused to let Earl study the map. "But there's a simple solution that involves one assumption. The assumption is that people are inclined to name their own cities and rivers and mountains after older ones. Look at Little Egypt. You have Cairo, Illinois. That's named after Cairo in Egypt. You've got Karnak, that's named after Karnak in Egypt; you've got Thebes, Illinois. That's named after Thebes in Egypt. You have Naqada; that's named after an old Egyptian cemetery. You can see what's happened here. People use the old names for new places."

He opened the atlas to a large map of Africa that folded out.

"The Arab geographers were right when they located the Garden at the source of the Nile, in the Great Lakes region of Central

Africa—right here, see these big lakes. When the book of Genesis was written the legendary rivers of Paradise were confused with the Nile and its tributaries."

"You're saying that God made a mistake, didn't know where he put his own rivers?"

"No, Earl. I'm saying that modern people haven't understood the Bible right. What happened was that when people migrated to Mesopotamia they remembered the names of the rivers from the real Eden and used them to name the rivers there, just like Cairo or Karnak or Thebes or Naqada here. They took the names with them from Africa and used them in Mesopotamia."

"You mean Moses wrote down the old names?"

"All right. Moses. But what's important is this. The Gihon. That's what the Jews called the Nile. Up here, see, where these two rivers come together at Khartoum, the Blue Nile from Ethiopia, and the White Nile from Lake Victoria. That's the Victoria Nile. Then north from Lake Albert. That's your Albertine Nile. All rising out of East Africa, right where the Arab geographers located the Garden. The Egyptians too.

"That's only three rivers."

"The fourth river drained out of Tanganyika—see this big lake here. It drained northward along the African Rift Valley and joined the Albertine Nile. But it was blocked by the Virunga volcanoes. Volcanoes, Earl. You've got volcanoes in Genesis, right?"

"'And ye came near and stood under the mountain; and the mountain burned with fire unto the midst of heaven, with darkness, clouds, and thick darkness. And it came to pass, when ye heard the voice out of the midst of the darkness (for the mountain did burn with fire), that ye came near unto me, even all the heads of your tribes, and your elders.'"

"There aren't any volcanoes in Mesopotamia. Not a one. But look here." Jackson pointed to the Lake District. "Lots of volcanoes. The Virungas. Eight of them. You had eruptions in 1948 and 1958, when Claude was there the first time. There was a major eruption about ten thousand years ago. Gilgamesh refers to it. That's what blocked the river."

How much of what he'd told Earl did Jackson actually believe? He wasn't sure himself. Standing with Claude on the Pavement of Api or sitting with him in an Efé camp on the bank of the Albertine Nile, looking up at the Mountains of the Moon, it was easy to be persuaded that they were in the original Garden. Claude was very persuasive. But back in the States it was easy to be a skeptic. After all, lots of people had claimed to discover the original Garden of Eden. There were lots of rival claims, mostly in Mesopotamia, Anatolia, Bahrain, Iran, even Scotland, and on the Isle of Lewis in the Outer Hebrides. And one staked out in Jackson County, Missouri, by the Latter-Day Saints.

This was why Jackson hadn't published the notebooks. He closed the big atlas and put it away. Earl wanted Sunny home with him. Sunny wanted Earl to sign the divorce petition. Jackson had no idea what was going to happen.

"I can't tell you how many times I drove up here," Earl said when Jackson came back into the kitchen, "but she wouldn't put my name on the list of people who could visit her. And she sent all my letters back. And finally I stopped comin'. Then I run into one of her home girls that just got out, over in Prairie du Rocher, that's how I knew Sunny was out. They was supposed to notify me, the prison was, but they didn't. Now she's livin' here with you."

"Her uncle had a little apartment over the garage. She lived there for a while after she got out, and then she moved in with me."

"Pretty convenient, huh? And what am I supposed to do? As her husband? Just step aside? Do you know what the Bible says about adultery?"

"The Bible's not *pro*-adultery."

" 'If a man be found lying with a woman married to a husband, then they shall both of them die, both the man that lay with the woman and the woman; so shalt thou put away evil from Israel.' "

Jackson took a deep breath. "Nobody's *pro*-adultery, Earl. That's not the underlying issue."

Earl closed his eyes and seemed to be praying again, moving his lips in and out. When his lips stopped moving, he looked up at Jackson. "I'm going to ask you to do somethin' for me."

"I can do that, Earl. But there's got to be some give and take."

"I'm going to ask you to get down on your knees and pray with me and pray for the Lord to show us what's that right thing to do. That's all I'm going to ask. If the Lord wants me to turn around and go back home, then that's what I'll do."

"If I get down on my knees," Jackson said, "will you sign the divorce petition?"

"It don't work that way. There's more than just me involved here. We got to wait on the Lord. Fern ought to be here too. I worry about her. A man tries to walk in the way of the Lord. He does his best. But Satan's always on the lookout. A moment of inattention and he's got his coils wrapped right around you. It don't never do to underestimate the power of Satan. He's the prosecutor, you know. And to accomplish his work he's got the power to place evil on men, the power of darkness.

"Satan darkened her eyes, do you see? Have *you* ever stood outside a house when the woman you love is goin' with another man? You imagine all kinds of things. You think about that man putting his hands all over her body. I never loved a woman like I loved little Fern. And I forgave her for running around on me because I understood it was Satan leading her to do that way. But it tore me up inside, and it tears me up inside when I think about all those times I drove four hundred miles to come up here and they wouldn't let me see her because of a little piece of paper, and all the times I wrote to her and the letters come back unopened. Let me tell you, I prayed hard for Fern, I prayed hard for the Lord to soften her heart."

"I think she's made up her mind, Earl. Maybe you ought to pray for the Lord to help you understand that."

"This isn't the first time she's made up her mind. She went with my best friend, DX. I knew she was going with him because I saw 'em get out of DX's truck and go into the house. I busted DX up pretty good, and then I forgive him and he forgive me. And I forgive Fern too." He paused. "Do you accept the Lord Jesus Christ as your personal savior?"

"No, Earl. I don't."

"I didn't think so."

"I'll walk you out to your truck," Jackson said, and he was relieved when Earl said okay.

When Jackson returned to his office in the morning after lecturing on the "Great Leap Forward," he found a note tacked to his office door telling him to call the hospital. Earl had gone on a tear after leaving Jackson's, had gotten into a fight with some college students and then smashed his truck up on a culvert on Highway 34. He'd given the doctor Jackson's name.

He looked pretty banged up when Jackson arrived.

"What happened?"

"I'm all tore up," Earl said, "just like when they took Fern away. I've been tore up real bad ever since it happened. Handed the church over to Brother DX for almost a year. A bad year. But the Lord picked me up and I came back and started preaching and handling again, and I got the power. God moved on me. There's nothing like it. To feel the Lord's hands upon you, anointing you. I thought I was okay . . ."

"Everything would be a lot simpler," Jackson said, "if you could find it in your heart to cooperate with Sunny. Or Fern. She's not going to ask for her half of the property. She'll stipulate to that. That means she'll agree in writing that you don't have to give her anything."

"Don't talk down to me. I'm not ignorant. I know what 'stipulate' means."

"But look. You haven't seen her for six years."

"She's still my wife. As long as she's alive."

"She's afraid of you, Earl. You forced her to stick her arm in a box of rattlesnakes."

"You believe that?"

"Yes I believe that. Why would she lie about it?"

"That's what she will tell you. But what I will tell you is that she got a snake out of the shed and was trying to get it to bite me while I was taking a nap. And she started hollerin' that she got bit, and I woke up and went out to the kitchen to get me a glass of milk, and she shot me. And then she called her cousin Sally, and Sally come over, and DX, and Sally called the ambulance from Rosiclare.

"Oh, she got bit all right, but I don't know if it was that diamond-back like she said. More likely it was Tricky, that was our pet coon. She told people it was a dry bite, but it was just the coon."

"That's hard to believe."

"Not any harder'n what she told you."

"Look at it this way, Earl. If she's lying about this, telling this story about you, why do you want to hang on to her? Why not let her go? It's over between you."

Earl didn't say anything.

"Are you looking for a sign?"

Earl nodded.

"I think you got one. Loud and clear."

Earl seemed to look inward for a moment. "You mean the accident?"

"That's exactly what I mean."

Earl looked up at Jackson. "I knowed it all along," he said. "But I didn't want to think on it."

"If I bring the papers, Earl, will you sign them?"

"What about my truck?"

"I'll take care of your truck."

"You'll do that for me?"

"I'll do it. I've got a friend on the police force. He'll help me take care of it. I'll have it towed to Bill's Auto Body. They'll put it back together."

"And you was really there? In the Garden?"

"I was there."

"What was is like?"

"It was beautiful, Earl. The river. The mountains. The people; you know, they don't have money, they don't have lawyers, they don't have law courts and banks and government. They don't even know how to make a fire. They carry their fire with them wherever they go. There's no war. They don't kill each other. They don't even kill other people. There's no rich or poor. They don't have to work hard. They trust the Forest to take care of them. They're like the lilies of the field."

"Why don't you go back?"

"I'd like to, but it's complicated."

"I've never been anywhere," Earl said. "Oh, I've been to Chicago and Paducah and St. Louis. Chicago's the farthest I've been from home. It don't seem like much. Does it? For a man my age?"

"Some people travel all the way around the world," Jackson said, "and don't see anything new. Other people never leave their hometown and learn new things every day."

"Bring that piece of paper," Earl said. "I'll take it home and study on it."

9

Fieldwork

He riseth from supper, and laid aside his garments; and took a towel, and girded himself. After that he poureth water into a basin, and began to wash the disciples' feet, and to wipe *them* with the towel wherewith he was girded. Then cometh he to Simon Peter: and Peter saith unto him, Lord, dost thou wash my feet? Jesus answered and said unto him, What I do thou knowest not now; but thou shalt know hereafter. Peter saith unto him, Thou shalt never wash my feet. Jesus answered him, If I wash thee not, thou hast no part with me. Simon Peter saith unto him, Lord, not my feet only, but also *my* hands and *my* head. Jesus saith to him, He that is washed needeth not save to wash *his* feet, but is clean every whit: and ye are clean, but not all. For he knew who should betray him; therefore said he, Ye are not all clean. So after he had washed their feet, and had taken his garments, and was set down again, he said unto them, Know ye what I have done to you? Ye call me Master and Lord: and ye say well; for so I am. If I then, *your* lord and Master, have washed your feet; ye also ought to wash one another's feet. For I have given you an example, that ye should do as I have done to you. —John 13:4–15

"Fieldwork," Claude used to say, "is to anthropology what the blood of the martyrs is to the church." At any gathering of anthropologists, this is the main question: *Where did you do your fieldwork?* The more remote and dangerous the better, of course. But it was getting harder to find "untrodden fields." Naqada, Illinois, was not the Ituri Forest, but it might be worth a monograph, or even an NHI grant. Jackson hadn't published anything in three years, and he couldn't milk any more articles out of the Mbuti, and he wasn't prepared to slog through Claude's notebooks and risk ridicule for claiming to have located the Garden of Eden, so he might as well try his hand at a piece of salvage anthropology at home, a record of a disappearing culture—a straightforward ethnography of the Church of the Burning Bush with Signs Following. How many people in the congregation? How often do they handle snakes? Where do they get the snakes? What kind of jobs? Income? Environment? Kinship? Technology? Economic life? Social life? Political life? Intellectual and artistic life? Religious life? Religious organization? Relationships with other churches?

Sunny was opposed to the trip. Jackson wasn't surprised, but he hadn't expected her to get so worked up. She'd listened from the top of the stairs to the conversation Earl and Jackson had had about the Garden of Eden, but hadn't said anything until Jackson suggested they drive down to Naqada together.

"I didn't know which one of you was crazier," she said. "The 'Garden of Eden'? The 'Mountains of the Moon'? You get Earl all stirred up with your nonsense and now you want to go down there to see people handle serpents and drink strychnine and handle fire, and you want me to go with you? I don't think so. Besides, I've got too much work to do. I'm a college student now. I'm glad you got Earl to sign the divorce papers, but I'm staying away from him. You know he can't marry again as long as I'm alive. Church rules. It's like the Catholics, only they stick to it."

"What's that got to do with anything?"

"Think about it."

"You're serious, aren't you?" he said.

"Damn right."

"Look," he said, "I can see an NHI grant in this. If I don't like the looks of things I won't pursue it, but I've got to do something. I haven't published anything in three years."

"You're on your own," she said.

"Fieldwork," he said. "It's what anthropologists *do*."

She didn't say anything.

"Sunny, don't be like this."

"Like what?"

It was a six-hour drive from Colesville to Naqada, just long enough to make it seem like a journey, a trip, a voyage of discovery—Malinowski on his way to the Trobriand Islands, Margaret Mead off to the island of Ta'u—but Jackson didn't start to feel he was in a different country until he reached Eldorado, where he stopped for a Big Mac and to check his map. There was a picture of George Harrison on the wall by the condiments. Harrison had performed here in 1963, while visiting his sister, five months before the Beatles appeared on the *Ed Sullivan Show*.

He was in coal country now, but most of the spurs that branched out from the center of town, spurs that had serviced the big coal companies, had been turned into bike paths. Open pits had been reclaimed; waste piles, tailings, sedimentation basins were all out of sight. On the way out of town on IL 142 he passed a sign for the Peabody Coal Company.

From Equality, at the edge of the Shawnee National Forest—the southern margin of the Illinois Glacier, which had passed this way more than 200,000 years ago—he drove into rough, unglaciated territory. The trees still held on to their leaves, though it was the end of October, and offered patches of bright color—yellow beeches, red maples and gum trees and dogwoods—against a background of oak and pine. The trees on the secondary roads were so thick he seemed to be driving through a tunnel. He turned on his lights. The towns—Herod, Eichorn, Humm Wye—were little oases of light in the sea of leaves that surrounded him. Until he came to Naqada, on the bank of the Ohio, where—unlike Malinowski or Mead—he had booked a room at the Naqada Inn, an old Italianate Victorian mansion right on a bluff overlooking the river and the marina. He thought of stopping at Earl's Bait & Tackle, in the marina, which he could see from the veranda of the hotel, but decided he needed to rest first.

Jackson didn't speak the new language that anthropologists had borrowed from cultural studies, didn't think in terms of the "anthropological gaze" or "ruling metanarratives." Like Claude, he thought in terms of stories. You talked to people and you listened to them and you let them tell their stories in their own way. Which is what he did with Earl later that afternoon, in a pilot interview on the veranda of the Inn, his little Panasonic tape recorder on the round Adirondack table between them.

Earl's family had come from East Tennessee, on the Clinch River, and had moved to Kentucky after the completion of the Norris Dam, in 1936, which flooded the entire Norris Basin. Earl and his grandfather had visited once when Earl was a boy. They'd rented a boat to do some bass fishing on Norris Lake. When the water was still and the light just right, you could see the houses under the water, and Earl got it confused with Noah's flood.

Earl's stepdaddy had been in the Special Forces and knew a lot
of ways to kill just with his bare hands, and he taught Earl a lot of
tricks, and boxing too. Earl went up to Chicago and fought mainly
in old warehouses.

"I'd fight anybody, it didn't matter, and I usually won. And then
I got older and put on some weight, and I could whup any man alive
just about. I met Joe Louis after a fight over on the south side, and he
gave me some tips. I was doing all right, but I come back to Middlesboro one time, over in Kentucky, just to come home for a while, and
a man named Gene Morton was beatin' on somebody I knew, Jimmly. Little bitty guy. Gene had broke his arm. So I told Jimmly I'd
whup this Gene Morton for him, and he said Gene was comin' over
that night, 'cause Gene was messin' with his wife and he heard her
talkin' to him on the telephone. Somebody must of told Gene that I
was going to whup him 'cause when he got out of his car he had a big
old tire chain wrapped around his arm. Me and Jimmly was sittin'
on the porch, and I said, 'Mr. Morton, I'm agonna whup you.' He
just laught and started unwrapping that tire chain off his arm, but I
got up real close to him so when he swung that chain it come around
me and hit himself in the back of his head, and I whupped him real
good. He kept getting back up, but I wasn't gonna play with him and
I just kept knockin' him back down till Jimmly's wife come out
screamin' she'd called the police, and I see now that the Lord was
watchin' over me 'cause he kept Gene from dyin'. The ambulance
come and took him to Rosiclare, and the police come and took me to
jail. That was my first felony. And about a year later Gene Morton
comes to see me in the prison, over at Roederer, over by La Grange.
I'd been thinking about living right. I knew it was gonna be hard to
give up some of the things I was doing—alcohol, and women, and
fightin'—and when Gene come to forgive me and to talk to me about
livin' right, God moved on me right in the visitors' room and I got

down on my knees and started prayin' too. At first I was trying to make a deal with God. Trying to negotiate. But God wasn't negotiating. It's the same for all of us. We want to negotiate. We want to keep a little bit back from the Lord. Some little corner to call our own where we can keep our secrets. But that's not the way the Lord works. The Lord wants all of you. He wants you to give it all up. That's the only way he can make you whole.

"I was in for three years. When I got out I started going to church with Gene and we've been brothers ever since. He's closer to me than my own brother.

"This was a little church out by Neville Pond, and they handled snakes. Gene showed me in the Bible where it says to handle snakes and I been handling ever since. When Number Five up by Naqada blew up, across the river, Gene, he had a cousin who worked in the mine up there and went to a little church and we went up to help the people there, and that's where I met Fern. Her daddy and about twenty others was down in the mine, and God moved on me to start singin' and preachin', so that's what I did."

"Sunny told me about that."

"You know it breaks my heart ever time I hear you call her that name."

"That's what she calls herself now."

"I know, but it ain't her name." He shrugged. "You think *you* could whup me? 'Cause there been a lot of guys thought they could whup me and found out different. You and me, we're about the same size. What're you, about one eighty? Five eleven? You ever do any boxing? Sparring someone?"

Jackson had done some boxing in college but he didn't think he had a chance against Earl, and he experienced a spurt of shame. He fantasized downing Earl with a karate chop, but he didn't know karate.

But Earl's head was down. His lips were moving. "God is great," he suddenly shouted. "God don't never change. Gloreee. Praise His name." He paused. "*You* don't think God changes, do you?"

"I think that men's ideas about God change."

"That's what I'm thinking too. But God. God himself don't never change?"

"I wouldn't think so."

"Me and Fern was real happy for a good while. I was preaching at the church and we was going to church almost every night for somethin' or other. Then the main services on Friday night and Sunday. And I had the bait shop down in the marina." He nodded toward the marina, a long rectangular Butler building with a low pitched roof. "Still do. You'll see.

"It was good people in the church. Well, you'll see that for yourself. DX and Sally and Mawmaw Tucker and Betty and Jim Thompson and Rob and Doris Hawthorne. We had near a hundred people every Saturday night and the same on Sunday. You could feel the presence of the Lord in the church, you could smell it, like a cloud, like you can smell the river. And then she got tired of livin' right. Maybe it was because she didn't have no kids to occupy her mind. She didn't want to go to church no more. She wanted to party. Then she come home one night with a bottle of vodka and we started drinkin' vodka and orange juice. I hadn't drunk no alcohol since I got out of prison, except two or three times. And then Fern started going with other men. She told me how she was going with all my friends: DX and Sheldon and Tommy Fisher and Daryl Anderson and Cord McAllen. Even old Mr. Thompson.

"I said, 'You do what you want and the Lord'll forgive you, and I'll forgive you too.' And I do forgive her. And I forgive you too."

The service that night began at seven o'clock but didn't really get going until eight. The men greeted each other with holy kisses, on the lips, and the women did the same. Jackson managed to avoid the kisses, the way he avoided the air kisses that had become fashionable at TF. Air kisses in France were one thing, but he didn't care for them at home. Earl introduced him as a friend—as an anthropologist who'd been to the Garden of Eden—and he was greeted warmly. There was plenty to talk about. But where were the snakes?

By eight o'clock about a hundred people had filled the small church, which was in an old DX gas station that DX, Earl's friend, had given to the church after the old church burned down. The pulpit was in the old office space, and the pews in what had been the service bays. Outside, an old Quaker State Oil sign—the kind that was hooked on a frame so it could swing back and forth—had been painted over: THE CHURCH OF THE BURNING BUSH WITH SIGNS FOLLOWING.

Jackson didn't have a camera or he would have taken a picture.

The church was backwoods, but the music setup was professional: Fender amps, high-definition speakers on speaker stands, an eight-channel mixing board, wireless mikes, two twelve-inch monitors. The lead guitarist, tuning a Stratocaster with a triangular metal plate under the pick guard, and the drummer, partly hidden by the pulpit, couldn't have been more than sixteen or seventeen. The bass player, fingering a vintage Gibson with its own small amp and speaker, could have been their father. The woman with straight black hair comping chords at the Yamaha keyboard in the back could have been their mother.

The music started loud and stayed loud. The bass player laid down the rhythm, and the others joined in. The musicians didn't make eye contact with each other, and at first they didn't seem to be playing the same song, or even in the same key. But a communal key eventually emerged and Jackson recognized a mix of commercial bluegrass and country-western using simple twelve- and sixteen-bar blues progressions. He was tempted to get a couple of harps out of his truck, but he decided it was too soon. The church was already full. People were there to be healed, he understood, and to experience God's presence. He was there to observe.

But where were the snakes?

It was October outside but summer inside, too warm despite two electric fans on chrome stands. The music was intense. The first hymn made the windows rattle and the pews shake. Jackson didn't care for "I Wonder What They're Doing in Heaven Today," but they moved on to some great old hymns: "I'll Fly Away" and "Nearer My God to Thee," and "Jesus, Won't You Come By Here," an old Lightning Hopkins song that he'd learned from the movie *Sounder.* He'd rented a VCR and listened to it over and over again until he had learned the song.

The hymns were followed by some preaching. Earl didn't shout and jump up and down, but Jackson felt that Earl was speaking directly to him.

"I want you to remember why we are gathered here tonight, and to remember to keep Jesus at the center of our thoughts. Unbelievers can't see God, they can't see Jesus. If people around here knew that Jesus was here tonight, the walls would be busting out with folks from Naqada and Elizabethtown and Rosiclare, and from Carbondale and Cairo, and from across the river too. But I'm telling you, Jesus is here just the same as you and me are here, and Sister Glenna at the piano, and Brother Lawson number one on the guitar, and Brother Lawson number two on the bass, and Brother Jones here from up north, and these little children with their tambourines, making a joyful noise unto the Lord, because the Lord is joyful. He fills our hearts with joy and takes away the darkness.

"His presence is here. I can feel the Spirit startin' to move on us. Slow at first. But it's startin' to fill this church. The Church of the Burning Bush, where Moses met God."

He elicited some amens and other ejaculations from the congregation.

"The Jews had their holy places. Right here in the world. This world. Places where you could meet God. In the Garden, on Mount Moriah, Mount Sinai or Horeb, the Temple in Jerusalem. The Temple was destroyed by Nebuchadnezzar and it was rebuilt. Then it was destroyed by the Romans. The Jews are still waiting for it to be rebuilt again, but we couldn't wait. We built the temple right here. In this holy place. Like Mount Sinai, or Mount Horeb, where Moses took his father-in-law's flocks. It may be the backside of the desert, but God is here, and he's calling to us just the way he called to Moses. Out of a burning bush. And he isn't calling for a friendly chat, he isn't calling to shoot the breeze. He's got a job for Moses. To lead the Jews out of Egypt. And he's got a job for us.

"God tells Moses to take off his shoes, because it's a holy place. And we're gonna take off our shoes tonight, because this is a holy place."

Ushers started moving to the front of the church with metal bowls, like big dog-food bowls, and pitchers of water. Earl went on preaching.

"And after supper, Jesus girded a towel about Him, took water in a basin and began to wash the disciples' feet."

Jackson had a sinking feeling in his stomach.

"Not everyone believes exactly the same. All right. That's between you and the Lord. I'm not going to judge you if you don't want to do it. But I'm going to tell you what it was like for me the first time I got my feet wet in a pan of water. I wanted to shout for victory. I was filled with the Spirit. It was a great blessing, knowing I was doing what Jesus Christ himself had done, getting down on his knees before his disciples and taking their feet in his hands and washing them. I never done it before I come here. I never done it back in Middlesboro. It was Brother Phillips who started it, and I was scared to death. What was I scared of? I was scared to look foolish. But then I did it, and I got pretty wound up. Praise Jesus' name."

Earl closed his eyes and began to pray silently. And then people started coming up to the front, lining up to have their feet washed and to wash some feet themselves. Taking turns. Men washed men's feet to the left of the pulpit, women washed women's feet to the right.

Jackson was thinking that Victor Turner's classic distinction between ritual and ceremony might be a fruitful approach to clarifying the social dynamics of the service. In a ritual such as baptism, or marriage, or consecration you become a different person. In a ceremony, on the other hand—Memorial Day, Thanksgiving—your status or role is confirmed. When Earl called his name, Jackson was taken by surprise. But not really. He looked up. Earl was looking at him, not giving him a choice. Jackson experienced his own resistance like an inner wall dividing him from the other people in the church. Where were the snakes? He'd rather pick up a rattlesnake than wash Earl's feet, or have Earl wash his feet. But he went up to the front, feeling foolish. He sat down on the front pew and took off his shoes and socks. His laces got tangled, twisted into a knot. *Forty years old and I can't even untie my own shoes.* But the knot came loose. He rolled his pants up and put his feet in the pan of fresh water. The water was cool. About four inches deep. Earl's tough, rough hands on his feet caused him to seize up. His shoulders tensed. But then he felt warmth, maybe even love? Forgiveness? Or maybe a request? Earl soaped up his feet, massaged them. Earl had a towel around his neck, like an athlete in the locker room. He didn't push on any pressure points. Just washed and massaged.

And then it was Jackson's turn. It wasn't clear what the others were doing, but Earl was already barefoot. His pants were rolled up. He put his feet in a pan of fresh water. Jackson knelt in front of him and closed his eyes. He took one foot in both his hands. He massaged and rubbed. He put his fingers between Earl's toes, on his rough heel, on a corn that must have been painful. Earl's third toe was longer than his big toe. *There's a name for this,* Jackson thought, but he couldn't remember what it was. Then the other foot. What message was he sending to Earl? What was he trying to communicate? Earl put his hands on Jackson's head. Enough. Jackson washed more feet. The power of touch created an overwhelming intimacy.

Ritual or ceremony? Writing up his field notes that night, Jackson got out a Gideon Bible from the drawer in the stand next to the bed and looked up the passage that Earl had read that night, John 13:6–20. He realized that the first part of the passage had all the earmarks of ritual: Jesus washes Peter's feet, over Peter's objections, so that Peter may become clean; that is, Peter is transformed, his status is changed. In the second half of the passage Jesus commands the disciples to wash each others' feet to confirm their status as disciples by performing an act of hospitality. This is a ceremony. Jackson's thesis was becoming clear.

Services were held on Friday night and Sunday night. On Saturday night Jackson and Earl had dinner at DX and Sally's. In Colesville, especially in the hospital, Earl had seemed out of his element. Even a little pathetic. Jackson had gotten the better of him. But on his home turf, Earl was a formidable figure, and Jackson had begun to think of him as a kind of shaman, an earlier type of human being, predating the anthropological types produced by capitalism—the Weberian bureaucrat, the disgruntled worker, the dedicated teacher, the devoted husband and father, the impotent intellectual. In the pulpit Earl acted as an intermediary between the natural and the spiritual worlds. On the river and in the forest, he acted as an intermediary between the human and the animal worlds. On the river that morning, sauger fishing above the Smithland Lock and Dam, Earl had told him where to put his line down, and more often than not he'd come up with a fish. Walking in the woods that afternoon—in the Shawnee National Forest—Earl would stop and point to a pile of leaves snagged around the root of a tree, and Jackson would look and see nothing but the leaves and the root of the tree, until Earl would poke at the pile with a stick and reveal a timber rattler. It was the tail end of the great snake migration, he explained. Every spring thousands of snakes, frogs, toads, lizards, and turtles leave their dens beneath the outcroppings of the Shawnee Hills and head for the swamps and bogs in the bottomlands. And every fall, they head back to hibernate for the winter. "Over by Carbondale," he said, "they even close one of the roads in the LaRue-Pine Hills from the first of September to the last of October. Too many snakes getting killed. They close it in the spring too."

Sunny's cousin Sally sautéed four nice sauger that Earl had cleaned. She cooked them the way Jackson's grandfather had cooked walleyes—in bread crumbs and Lawry's lemon pepper—and served them with coleslaw and macaroni and cheese. And coffee. DX drank Coca-Cola; Earl and Sally drank coffee; Jackson drank a 7-Up.

After supper they sat on the porch until it got dark. It was chilly, but no one suggested going in. It was a clear night and from the porch they had a good view of the southern sky. "Seek him that maketh the seven stars and Orion," Earl said, and DX went into the house to get a two-headed snake he'd caught a week before. The snake had been crossing the road on its way to winter quarters in the river bluffs.

"That serpent ain't been prayed over," Sally said. "You got no business handling it tonight."

The snake was in a wooden box with a screen over the top. On the side of the box someone had carved JESUS SAVES.

"I call 'em Moloch and Belzebub," DX said, setting the box down on the floor. "They pretty much work together, but Belzebub does most of the feeding."

Jackson was thinking that this man had been Sunny's lover. Once upon a time. All three of them, in fact, had enjoyed her favors. Earl he could understand, but not DX. Maybe she just wanted someone she wasn't afraid of.

"Let's pray over it right now," Earl said.

"I don't know," Sally said.

But Earl started to pray. And DX and Sally joined in. It was a wordless prayer, but when Jackson closed his eyes and listened, he could hear words fluttering in the air all around him, like moths around a candle. Certain words fluttered by again and again, words from another language. He could feel something tugging at him, but he resisted, as a man might resist a sexual urge. Sally took his hand. She was a beautiful woman, and Jackson wondered why DX would ever fool around with anyone else, even Sunny. Her fingers burned his and he pulled his hand away, but she took his hand again, and he could feel something in him yielding. But then, just as suddenly as they had started, they stopped, and Sally resumed her knitting. Earl, who was sitting in a rocking chair back in the shadows, got up and went over to the snakebox. He knelt over the snakebox, opened the latch on the front, reached in, and took out the snake. He went back to his chair, holding the snake against his chest. The snake raised its heads up and looked Earl in the face. Earl stroked it with one hand. He scratched the top of one head, then the other. He stroked the neck, running his finger back and forth where the neck split into two. The snake gave a few sharp rattles and then settled down. Earl held the snake against his body to keep it warm.

They sat in the darkness for a while, listening to the night sounds, the end-of-October sounds, and then Earl said, "What I been thinking on is what we don't understand about dyin'. It ain't easy. It ain't pretty. It ain't just going to sleep and flying away and leaving your old body behind. I know that's the way we talk. And we sing that old hymn 'I'll Fly Away.' We sung it last night. But that ain't the way it was for Jesus. When he washed the disciples' feet he knew he was going to die, and he didn't want to. When he was dying on the cross, it was his body was suffering. So bad he thought the Father had betrayed him at the end. But then he come back. His father hadn't betrayed him after all. And when he come back, he come back in his body. He didn't come back like a ghost or a spirit. It was his body. Doubting Thomas had to stick his finger in the wounds. His wounds were part of his story, do you see? His story was written on his body. God didn't want him to fly away and leave his body behind, and he don't want us to leave our bodies behind. Our stories are written in our bodies. You can't leave that out of the big picture. Look at that little scar on Fern's neck where she got bit when she was sixteen. That's a story inscribed on her body. And look at me. I been bit thirty times. My stories are inscribed on my body. That's what the Bible's trying to proclaim—the resurrection of the body."

" 'Inscribed on her body,' " Jackson said. "You're starting to sound like an anthropologist." He looked down at his own hands, thinking, *Earl's an interesting guy. Too bad he doesn't have a sense of humor.*

But maybe he did. "Come on over here," Earl said. But Jackson shook his head.

"You know you want to hold him," Earl said. "You know it. I know it. DX and Sally know it." All three of them were watching him. They were all smiling.

"I'd better get back to the hotel," Jackson said.

Earl laughed. "Next time."

In the truck Earl turned the heater on. "You know you want to hold him," he said again. And he was right. Jackson did want to hold the snake. He could feel his hands cupping. But he had other business to take care of.

"Earl, did you think about the divorce petition?"

Earl didn't say anything for about a mile. "Them papers you was wantin'? They's in the glove compartment. All signed and notarized."

Jackson opened the glove compartment. The papers were in an envelope underneath a pocket knife, a pair of pliers, a flashlight.

"That envelope," Earl said. "That's the papers."

"Thanks, Earl." Jackson didn't open the envelope.

The cab of the truck was warm. Earl turned off the heater.

"DX thinks he can get a lot of money for that snake," Earl said. "What do you think?"

"I haven't got any idea," Jackson said. "Do zoos pay good money for something like that?"

"I don't know," Earl said.

In the hotel parking lot Earl kept his hands on the steering wheel and looked straight ahead at the sign on the lawn: Naqada Inn. "I done my part," he said. "Now you got to do yours."

Jackson was alarmed. "What do you want me to do? I took care of your truck, didn't I?"

"You did, and I thank you, but now I want you to pray with me."

"Here?"

"Unless you want me to come up to your room."

"Here is fine."

Earl bowed his head. His lips began to move in and out again. Jackson closed his eyes and bowed his head. The truck was still running and some of the exhaust was leaking into the cab.

"Lord," Earl said after a long two or three minutes of silence, "look after this man, and look after little Fern. Turn their hearts back to you. Spare them at the last day as a man spareth his own son that serveth him."

Jackson folded the envelope and stuck it into the pocket of his windbreaker. "Thanks, Earl," he said, opening the door and sliding out of the truck.

10

A Faustian Moment

The divorce was final. The road had opened up before them. They could move ahead, cross the border into new territory. It was possible to imagine a future. But Jackson didn't want to look too far into the future. He was too interested in what was going on all around him. It was Sunny that was going on all around him, clearing out dead trees, putting a culvert under a low spot in the drive, painting the kitchen. She was strong, physically strong, and her strength communicated itself to him, drew forth from him an opposing counter force. He stopped taking doxycycline. His yoga exercises become easier. It was easier to get out of bed in the morning. And she had a gift for creating beauty wherever she went. The house, which was on the gloomy side, soon became bright and cheerful. A few flowers from the grocery store on the kitchen table and a few more in a vase in the upstairs bathroom. A potted aspidistra on the landing, an avocado seed (supported by toothpicks in a glass of water) starting to sprout in the window over the sink, a new lamp for the big library table in the living room, three-way light bulbs in the floor lamps, an enameled humidifier to sit on the wood stove, wicker hampers for dirty clothes. He didn't have to work at loving her, or pleasing her. He didn't have to work at being interesting, because she was interested in everything: the fossil record, the Peloponnesian war, Camus's *L'Étranger*, and, especially, in biology, in the theory of evolution, which seemed to her to explain everything, including Earl and the Church of the Burning Bush—evolutionary dead ends, like the hybrid eel or the soccer kangaroo.

This was the only issue that divided them. She could not, or would not, understand why he insisted on making two more trips to Naqada in November. Each time he invited her to go with him and each time she not only refused; she begged him not to go. "Why can't you transcribe Claude's notebooks or write another book about the pygmies? I don't understand." What she didn't, or didn't want, to understand was that for Jackson the Church of the Burning Bush with Signs Following provided a professional opportunity too good to be passed up. Other anthropologists had been there before him, to be sure, but they'd been looking *at* the beam of light instead of *along* it. Jackson wanted to look *along* the beam, and he thought he was in a good position to do so, because he wasn't afraid, because Naqada took him back to the times he'd spent with his grandparents in Kendallville, Indiana, while his parents were off in Iraq or Syria, took him back to hymns on Sunday mornings and prayer meetings and church suppers with ham and split-pea soup and scalloped potatoes, which he'd never cared for, but which now appealed to him. He was even starting to like yams, the way Mawmaw Tucker fixed them—roasted and sliced into thick rounds. No brown sugar. Vinegar. It was good people, as Earl put it. Warm, friendly, ready to help each other in hard times.

On the second of these trips he took along half a dozen harmonicas, and when the lead guitarist, Phil Stone, invited him to sit in, he stepped up to one of the vocal mics. He held back at first, but not for long. The harp is the least intellectual of instruments. (And cheapest!) You breathe through it, in and out. It's the closest instrument to the human voice. It becomes your mouth, your voice. And you can play between the notes of the piano. You can wail like an old freight train. You can howl and waiver and cry like a woman in pain. You can grab your audience by the ears, which is what he did. And later that night he touched DX's two-headed snake with the back of his fingers and then jerked his hand back. It was like touching an electric fence, which he used to do with Steve Decker in Kendallville, when he stayed with his grandparents during the summer. Steve lived on a farm a mile down the road from Jackson's grandfather's grain elevator, and they used to shoot the cows in the field with BB guns, until Steve's father caught them and made them currycomb the cows as if they were horses.

"You're too stubborn and unreasonable," Sunny told him when he told her about playing the harp in the service.

"You're the one who's stubborn and unreasonable. This is my vocation."

On the second of these trips, right after Thanksgiving, Jackson put his hand around the middle of the snake, which was lying flat against Earl's chest. The snake thrummed in his hand, like a powerful erection, a superhuman erection.

"You feel that?" Earl asked.

Jackson nodded.

"That's somethin', ain't it?"

"It's something, all right," Jackson said, reluctant to let go.

The snake turned its two heads to look at Jackson. The yellow eyes caught the lamplight, glittered like diamonds.

"It's like looking into the depths of hell," Earl said.

Jackson took a deep breath.

"You want to hold him?" Earl asked.

Jackson let go. "No, no," he said, "that's all right."

No one was quite sure how "Little Egypt" got its name. Perhaps the Mississippi River recalled the Nile in the minds of the first settlers, and the mysterious Indian mounds at Cahokia suggested the pyramids, and perhaps the ruins of this ancient native American civilization strengthened the association with Egypt. Perhaps settlers from the north who traveled in wagon trains to buy grain during bad winters or droughts recalled the ancient Israelites traveling to Egypt to buy grain. But Jackson put his money on John Bagley, a Baptist missionary who came to convert the Indians and the French settlers after the Revolutionary War. It was Bagley who first called the gently sloping highlands and fertile bottoms the "Land of Goshen," the land the pharaoh had given to Joseph's brothers after they came to Egypt.

Naqada itself was beautiful, situated on a bluff overlooking the Ohio River. It wasn't exactly prospering, but it wasn't falling apart either. You couldn't get a drink in a restaurant, but there was a row of taverns on the road down by the river, north of the marina.

On these visits Jackson interviewed as many people as he could. He didn't bother to position himself as a white male ethnographer; he didn't set out to challenge the masculinist bias that underlay the strict codes and traditional models of interviewing; he didn't think of himself as producing subjectivities; and he didn't worry about the instability of knowledge claims that characterize post-structural and postmodern modes of research. He simply asked a few questions at the beginning of each interview, and then let people talk without trying to control the interview. Everyone had a sackful of stories, stories about the coal mines and the feldspar mines over in Rosiclare, stories about the river, stories about the timber companies that had decimated the hills; stories about hard times and good times; and stories about the church: healing the sick, raising the dead, handling fire, drinking strychnine, handling serpents, speaking in tongues. Many had grown up in the church and had known from early childhood that they wanted to handle. They looked forward to turning twelve—when they'd be allowed up in the front of the church with the serpents—the way other kids look forward to turning sixteen so they can get a driver's license or twenty-one so they can drink legally. Others came to it late in life.

What he wanted to know was not how many members were in the congregation, not how often they handled, not where they got the snakes. What he wanted to know was why. Though in a sense he already knew, had known ever since he put his hand around DX's two-headed snake.

At the American Anthropological Association meetings in Chicago at the end of the month, he asked everyone he knew: Why? And he got all kinds of answers: materialist, structuralist, functionalist, structural-functionalist, cultural-materialist. But none of his colleagues had washed Earl's feet or wrapped his, or her, fingers around DX's two-headed snake.

He drove back to Colesville instead of staying for the banquet at the Hilton. Sunny was not at home, and he was asleep by the time she got back and crawled into bed beside him. Not really awake, he lay behind her with his hand on her hip. They hadn't sorted through all their feelings for each other yet, hadn't put them into words.

In the morning he thought it was the dog licking his face, but it was Sunny. She was kneeling over him, naked despite the cold. The room was still dark. He looked at the clock. It said 4:30. The bottom of the red "3" was burned out so that it looked like a backward "F."

"*Veux-tu me baiser en levrette?*" she said, which is what she always said, whatever she wanted, because she liked to say it. But in the morning it took him a little while to loosen up his joints, and so she climbed on top of him. The dog woke up and stuck her head over the edge of the bed. Jackson stroked her head, Maya's head, and after a couple of minutes she lay back down again.

Don't leave your pistol on the table and turn your back on her while you're getting' something outta the refrigerator.

He looked up at Sunny. Earl had given him new eyes: Sunny was tough, frightening, dangerous. He didn't really believe Earl's story—that Sunny had gotten a snake out of the snake shed and was trying to get it to bite him while he was taking a nap—but he could *imagine* her getting a rattlesnake out of the snake shed and holding it up against Earl's neck. Look at the way she'd kept one hand on the pistol in her lap while they were eating when Earl came up the first time. If Earl had tried to leap across the table and grab her, he'd have been dead meat in two seconds. He could imagine her not wanting to live right and "going with" Earl's friend DX and a lot of other men. Maybe even Cramer, her bio prof, who had won teaching awards and who'd been voted the "most desirable professor" by the girls in two different sororities, and whose evolutionary explanations of everything from A to Z she seemed to have adopted.

He reached up and pulled her down on top of him so that their mouths joined.

Later, in the kitchen, he boiled water to poach eggs. He turned on NPR. And turned it off again after learning that in Utah eight teenagers taking part in a wilderness program for troubled youths had beaten one counselor and tied another to a tree and fled into the desert. They'd all been rounded up within days and seven of the eight had accepted plea bargains.

He looked out the window at Sunny, who was sitting on the deck with a rifle, waiting for a deer. She'd put on some of Jackson's long

SNAKEWOMAN OF LITTLE EGYPT

underwear this morning. He'd watched her put it on. It was too big and sagged in the back like the loose folds of a cow's butt. Through the window he could see her sitting at the glass-top table. Warren's homemade hunting knife was on the table, and some rope, a hide tag, and a plastic bag for the liver and heart.

He took two plates of bacon and poached eggs out to the deck and Sunny kept the rifle, Warren's old 30.06, on her lap. Jackson salted and peppered her eggs for her and added a few drops of Tabasco. They ate in silence. Warren's Winchester .35 was in the kitchen. The scope was out of line. There was no scope on the 30.06, but she said she didn't need one. They'd cleaned and oiled both rifles the night before.

Jackson cleared the table. He rinsed the plates in the sink before putting them in the dishwasher. A bit of egg white stuck on the bottom of the saucepan. He scraped it off and then heated up milk in the pan while he made coffee in a French press pot, added hot milk and some sugar. Maya kept banging her tail against the wall, eager to go out.

He took a pitcher of café au lait out to Sunny, being careful not to let the door slam or let Maya out, though the deer didn't pay much attention to Maya and Maya didn't pay much attention to the deer.

Jackson's feelings about deer had changed since he'd contracted Lyme disease, which probably came from a tick from a deer he'd shot himself, right after Warren died. Kill them all! Wipe them out. A menace. Two people in the county got West Nile Virus and there was a panic. *West Nile.* Egyptian. Foreign. Arab. But Lyme disease, which affects a hundred times as many people? That's Lyme, Connecticut. How could anything bad come out of Lyme, Connecticut?

He turned NPR back on as he did the dishes. The shot took him by surprise.

Out on the deck, he could see the deer lying on its side on the other side of the stream. Its legs were not moving.

"Good shot," he said.

It was a young buck and would make good eating. And all of a sudden he thought of himself as the deer. Killed in an instant. Wiped out. He was overwhelmed. All doubts resolved. He could see everything clearly. Sunny, Earl, Cramer. It was a perfect moment to die, a Faustian moment: *Du bist so schön.* He would have been happy to have time stop. But it didn't, and after a moment he no longer saw everything clearly, and he couldn't remember what it was that he had seen so clearly. It had all happened too fast.

They drank their café au lait and went to field-dress the deer. Dark blood was running out of the deer's mouth, but Sunny checked for signs of chest movement. The eyes were glazed. She touched one of them with a stick. No response. "Earl had one kick him once," she said. "Almost broke his leg."

"If you were a Neanderthal," Jackson says, "you'd have had to get up close and personal to kill this poor devil, and you'd have had to use a flake knife to cut him open and scrape the hide."

She unloaded the rifle and put the shells in her pocket. She notched the date, antler points, and sex on the kill tag with the tip of her knife and wired the tag to the lower jaw. Then she turned to Jackson and grunted. "Ugh ugh ugh."

"Neanderthals couldn't talk," he said, "but they could communicate."

"Ugh ugh ugh."

"Hunting is one candidate for the development of human consciousness," he said. "It requires cooperation, strategizing."

"You're thinking about your pygmies," she said, "with fifteen or twenty people holding a net."

"Mbuti," he said. They rolled the deer over and he held back the paunch while she cut it open from breast bone to anus.

She tied off the bladder so it wouldn't spill piss all over. "He should have taken a leak earlier," she said.

Jackson looked away as she severed the base of the penis and testicles and pulled them out and held them up.

"The Chinese eat penises," he said. "Bulls' penises. You can buy them in the market. An aphrodisiac. You have to clean out the urinary tract or it will taste like piss."

"You know this from experience? I mean your experience as an anthropologist?"

"From the *National Geographic*."

"Cramer says that snakes have two penises. Hemipene."

"Two? Why would they need two?"

"An extra one, just in case."

"Good for them."

She held up the penis. "You can eat this one if you want, but count me out."

She cut out the anus and tied off the intestine. She pinched off the bladder and slowly cut it free with one hand and pulled it out with the other.

"Did you know that modern human beings and Neanderthals lived side by side for over forty thousand years? Two different twigs on the bush of life."

"Like African and Indian elephants?"

"Not exactly. But sort of."

"Can Indian and African elephants interbreed?"

"No, and neither could Neanderthals and Homo sapiens sapiens."

"How do you know?"

"DNA evidence." He paused. "Actually, the DNA evidence isn't conclusive. A lot of people think they did. Interbreed. It's a big controversy."

She cut out the heart and held it in her hands. Jackson opened up the plastic bag and she dropped it in. They rolled the buck on its side and the entrails rolled out onto the ground. Sunny cut them free from the back of the deer and then cut through the esophagus and the blood vessels near the diaphragm. When she'd cleaned out the body cavity they dragged the carcass out on a plastic toboggan, almost tipping it into the stream when they went across the bridge. They hauled it up to Sunny's truck and then went into the house and showered, checking each others' bodies for tiny deer ticks.

Images of the buck filled Jackson's imagination, like early morning light—the buck, the woods, the top of Sunny's head, her fingers curved around the handle of the heavy balanced knife, the bare branches of the big horse chestnut where they'd field-dressed the deer. The spiky leaves of the red and white oaks were sprayed onto his retinas. He kept rubbing his eyes.

"The Neanderthals were the first hominids to bury their dead," Jackson said, when they had stepped out of the shower.

"I thought they were cavemen," Sunny said.

"They were. They were a dead end. But they must have had some sense of . . . something."

"Maybe we're a dead end too," she said.

They drank another cup of coffee and drove in to the locker plant and left the deer to be butchered.

11

Shopping with Claire

I needed something to wear to the big millennium party, and when Claire proposed a shopping trip to Chicago, just before Christmas, I said yes. Exams were over, and I knew I'd done well on all of them. I'd spent the end of the term conjugating irregular verbs, reviewing biology labs, putting together my short story portfolio, reviewing Western Civ notes. I needed a break before I started working on my hot-snake certificate.

We took the seven-o'clock train, the Illinois Zephyr, that would get us to Chicago by ten thirty. We were going to spend the night at Claire's parents' place on the north side. Claire was eager to trade confidences, girl talk. She was going to write a novel, she said. She didn't know what she was going to write about. Not yet. She'd had an affair with a professor of astrophysics a couple of years earlier and she thought she might write about that. Or she might write a woman's extreme adventure novel. In any case, she wanted to stay up in the apartment over the garage for the winter break. She'd already talked to her husband about it.

"What about the mice?" I asked.

"I was hoping you could help me. Maybe set some traps when we get back. You could help me with the novel too. You've got a lot of stories. Maybe I'll write about someone like you."

"Like me?!"

"Why not? I could start with the snakebox story."

What could I say?

"It's a great story," Claire said. "I'm going to write two thousand words a day," she said, "for twenty-seven days. That's fifty-four thousand words. Two thousand words a day. I'm going to follow my own advice and write without stopping."

"Intentionality is the enemy," I said.

I let Claire's words wash over me, along with the noise of the train. It had snowed during the night, and the fields were white as clean sheets. We didn't get snow like this in Naqada. We settled down to read. Claire had her *Wall Street Journal.* I had a copy of Stanley Miller's original paper that Cramer had photocopied for me.

We were bound together by our interest in Jackson and by our substantial investments in ShoppingKart.com, which we'd invested in against the advice of Claire's broker. This was another subject I didn't want to think about, but Claire was reading the *Wall Street Journal* and relaying the bad news. In the four months since we'd bought the stock, ShoppingKart.com had burned through almost half a billion dollars without showing a profit. Today, Claire noted, it was down three points. The twenty thousand dollars of Uncle Warren's money that I'd invested had been worth almost thirty thousand at the end of November, but now it was worth about fifteen thousand.

"Don't worry," Claire said, "Pam says that this is what most Internet companies do at first. Besides, ShoppingKart-dot-com's not like most Internet companies. It's got a business plan and a path to profitability. And anyway," she said, perhaps reading my thoughts, "you've got plenty of money. Spend some of it. Treat yourself. We'll start at Marshall Field's."

I bit my tongue and studied Claire as the train rocked back and forth. I didn't know what to think about Claire. Was she a pathetic figure, or was she a brave spirit, making the best of things? She had lots of energy, plans, lots of plans, including plans for me, and she looked smashing in a striped coat dress and a white silk blouse and knee-high boots.

And what about me? Was I a pathetic figure or a brave spirit in my black slacks and an old blue blazer? My dressiest outfit. I bit my tongue again at the thought. No more ShoppingKart.coms, I was sure of that, but I was happy in spite of ShoppingKart.com. I was living with a man who spoke French with me at the dinner table—for the first fifteen minutes—and never made fun of me, a man who didn't frighten me, a man who understood my body and didn't beat it, a man who didn't want to know where I was every minute, a man who didn't have to win every argument. Though I couldn't stop him from going to Naqada. He may have been a professional anthropologist, but I didn't think he knew what he was getting into.

The Stanley Miller article from *Science* magazine wasn't even two pages long, and the general idea wasn't that hard to understand, and the diagram of the apparatus wasn't as clear as the one Cramer had sketched for me on a napkin in Seymour Union back in the middle of December, just before the end of the term. Professor Cramer had come to my table during the last lab of the semester. We'd been examining a flatworm *(Dugesia)* under the dissecting microscope, shining a bright light on it, feeding it pieces of liver and cat food, touching it with a probe, and my lab partner and I were waiting for Laura Gridley, one of the lab assistants, to check our drawings of a series of prepared slides of different planaria to make sure we'd labeled them correctly. We were watching Laura, whose flaming red curls were held back by a scarf, stroll down our row of soapstone tables and turn at the end as if she were modeling her lab coat, which (unlike the lab coats of the other assistants) was open at the top and flared at the waist, when suddenly Cramer appeared out of nowhere and started looking over our drawings. He made a correction on one of my drawings, with a pencil, and asked if he could speak to me after the lab. He'd wait for me outside. My eighteen-year-old lab partner, Molly Christiansen, was stunned.

Walking across campus, Cramer—everyone called him "Cramer"—and I talked about how what you saw through a microscope was always messier than the diagrams in the textbook. Over coffee in Seymour Union, he explained his "translocation" project. He needed someone who wasn't afraid of rattlesnakes. He had two other grad students lined up, but they were in fact afraid. He was worried about them. He needed someone he could count on.

"What makes you think I'm not afraid of rattlesnakes?" I asked.

"A little bird told me," he said.

Claire, I thought. I should never have told that story to Claire. But then, why not?

In the fall, Cramer went on, a local farmer had discovered a relict population of rattlesnakes on one of his woodlots and had called the biology department. He wanted the snakes out of there. If the bio department wanted them, they were welcome to them. Otherwise he was going to dynamite the den. Which was illegal. Cramer could have gotten an injunction, but what was the point? He'd wanted the snakes, he'd scrambled to get the money, and now the funding was in place for a five-year study

"You'll find timber rattlesnakes—*Crotalus horridus horridus*— in thirty-one states," he said. "You'll find them along the upper

Mississippi in southeast Minnesota and southwest Wisconsin, and in the Mississippi River Valley, where you come from. But you won't find *Crotalus horridus horridus* in central Illinois, which is why this relict population is important in the herp community."

He wanted to capture the snakes when they came out of hibernation in the spring and translocate them to a new denning area. This was the exciting part. Rattlesnakes always went back to the same dens. How would they choose a new den? We'd implant them with radio transmitters and follow each snake. Cramer had no idea how many snakes there were.

"Could be any number, I said. "And you've got to figure on other kinds of snakes too. Maybe twenty, thirty. We used to catch them in winter. Down in Egypt they don't always hibernate. They just kind of snooze."

We had a second cup of coffee and I asked him about the Miller-Urey experiment. Could you do it in the basement?

"No way. Too dangerous. You've got hydrogen, you've got ammonia. You could have a bad explosion."

"It doesn't sound too hard in the book."

Cramer sketched the apparatus on a napkin. "You've got your gases mixed with water here, in this big flask at the bottom. Hydrogen, ammonia, water, methane. You've got to be very careful."

"How do you get the gases in the flask with the water?"

"You pump the air out of the flask to create a vacuum, and then you hook up your hydrogen or whatever to this valve at the top and open the valve." He added a hookup for a vacuum pump to the sketch on the napkin.

I nodded.

"You heat this up and it goes up to this big flask at the top and hooked up to electrodes. You turn on the juice and it zaps the mixture."

"That's your lightning, right?"

He nodded. "The gases are forced down this tube on the left into a cooling condenser. Then the liquid that's left runs down to the bottom. You open this valve and you're ready to sort out what you've got with a paper chromatogram. I believe there's a graph in the original paper."

"And you wind up with amino acids?"

"Right. You've got some other stuff too, but the amino acids are what got everybody excited. Organic compounds—the building blocks of life—coming out of nonorganic matter."

"Pretty amazing."

"But don't try it at home, okay?"

I said I wouldn't.

"For a while everyone thought that Miller had a great experiment but that he got the composition of the original atmosphere of the earth wrong. The geologists wanted life to begin in volcanic gases, but they were forgetting that if the earth is formed out of chondrites—stony meteorites—slightly different gases are going to evolve. No one did the calculations to predict the earth's early atmosphere. Now they're using computer codes for chemical equilibrium to analyze what happens when the minerals in meteorites are heated up and start to react with each other . . ."

He suddenly interrupted himself. "Sorry. I've been gassing on."

"It's all right," I said.

"Miller just had a stroke," he said. "Last month. He's in a nursing home. He should have gotten a Nobel Prize. Harold Urey didn't put his name on the paper because he already had a Nobel Prize and he wanted Miller to get one."

"That was very nice of him. Did he get one?"

"Nope. I'll send you a copy of the paper. I think it was in *Science*, fifty-three or fifty-four."

"I'd like that."

"What are you taking next term?"

"Bio two-thirty."

"What else?"

"French one o two. Western Civ two. Fiction Workshop."

"You had some chemistry?"

I shook my head. "I had a chemistry course in high school, but they didn't offer it on the Hill."

"Drop one of your other classes," he said. "You need General Chem. Sign up for Debra Hamilton's section."

I had to laugh. "You're very serious."

"Sorry. Look, come back to the office with me. I can give you some stuff to look at for your hot-snake certificate. We'll get started on the training program during the break. There'll be a lot of paper-work too."

We sat in Cramer's small office in George Davis Hall, across from my biology lab, for an hour, going over the requirements for my hot-snake certificate and talking about the evolution of snakes from lab-yrinthodonts, which means that the enamel on their teeth is folded in on itself, like a labyrinth. I didn't understand everything, but I understood that as far as Cramer was concerned science has revealed a universe more wonderful and fantastic than anything you can read about in the Bible or in Greek mythology. You didn't have to look up at the night sky to see this universe. You could see it in the Miller-Urey experiment—the building blocks of life arising out of hydrogen. You could see it in the lab, looking at a lowly flatworm under a dissecting microscope, or you could see it in the tooth of a snake. I was standing on the threshold of this world. Right where I wanted to be.

But I was standing on the threshold of Claire's world too.

In Claire's world we took a cab from Union Station to Marshall Field's. A first for me. The cab. Marshall Field's too. It wasn't what it used to be, Claire said, when she was a girl, when it had defined Chicago as an international city.

When I'd gone to a big city, which wasn't often, it had been Paducah or Evansville, except when I went to St. Louis with Warren while I was waiting to go on trial, when we saw *An American in Paris*, which I knew now had been shot on a sound stage at the MGM studio in Los Angeles. Except for a few establishing shots.

We walked up and down State Street looking at the Christmas displays in the big windows, and then down a side street over to Wabash Avenue, under the El tracks. I tried not to act *too* unsophisticated, but Field's was overwhelming, a world in itself.

We had coffee on the third floor where we could look at the big Christmas tree in the Walnut Room. Children were lined up to speak to a fat Santa, and I thought for a minute that Claire had forgotten that she was a forty-year-old woman and that she was going to get in the line. She remembered coming as a child and hadn't lost her enthusiasm. She reminded me, just a little, of the dog playing with the Frisbee. *Joie de vivre.*

In the elevator we ran into an old friend of Claire's, who asked how her writing was going, and then on the ninth floor, we ran into Jean-Paul from my French class. "Jean-Paul," I shouted. He didn't look up and I thought maybe I'd been mistaken, but it turned out he hadn't recognized himself in French, though he was wearing his beret. He was with his mother and his younger sister and I was really pleased to see a familiar face. "*Enchanté*," he said. "*Enchantée*," I replied.

We picked out a basic wardrobe on the ninth floor, which was very pricey, but not as pricey as the 28 Shop, which had a private elevator entrance at 28 East Washington. Claire's advice was to get a few *really good* things, and the saleswoman, who also recognized Claire and asked about her writing, agreed with her. Everything was an investment. A winter coat was an investment. A suit was an investment. A black dress was an investment. So was a white shirt and a good black leather purse and black leather pumps, and a sweater set and on and on.

"A suit," I said, "what would I do with a suit?"

But Claire couldn't understand the point of the question. "A suit is like a coat of armor," she explained. "You wear it to protect yourself. Or to attack, depending."

I tried on a couple of suits and confronted myself in the triple mirrors outside the dressing room.

"A suit is more than the sum of its parts," Claire said. "You can match the jacket and the skirt up with different items and wear them separately. It can be the foundation of your basic wardrobe. Once you've invested in a good basic wardrobe you can update it each season—a new scarf, a new pair of shoes, a new purse.

"I can't recognize myself in a suit," I said.

"That's because you still need to define your personal style," the saleswoman said. "Your 'look.'"

"Do you want to attract attention or deflect it?" Claire asked. *Good question.* "Do you want to stand out or fit in?" *Good question.*

"Do I really *need* a 'look'?"

"Everybody needs a look," Claire said. "You don't have to be Audrey Hepburn to need a 'look.' Besides, you've got a 'look' whether you want to or not. Everybody's got a look."

I had never seen Audrey Hepburn in a movie, but I knew who she was, and I'd read an article about her "look" in one of the magazines at the checkout counter at Hy-Vee. Any woman could achieve this look by flipping out her hair, buying large glasses, and wearing little sleeveless dresses. Hmm.

Claire had a look: subdued elegance. My French teacher had a look: flashy. Some of the students in my French class had a look. (Some didn't.) Jean-Paul had an existential look. Cramer had an L. L. Bean look. My Western Civ prof, Professor Henry, had a rumpled professorial look. Jackson? I didn't think Jackson had a look, at least not one I could put a name on. At home he sometimes wore a safari jacket, but he had an Italian suit too and a Bruno Magli leather jacket.

My look in Naqada had been long house dresses; on the Hill it had been a medium blue jumpsuit, and at TF it was jeans and a man's shirt. "You're dressing fifteen years too young," Claire said. "You and your clothes are speaking different languages." And maybe she was right, maybe it was time to branch out a little. I had an unfocused idea of what I wanted, but I couldn't explain it to Claire and the saleswoman.

After a struggle over the suit, which I didn't buy, I got into the swing of things and started spending all the money I'd saved by *not* buying a suit. Like Earl saving money by buying a johnboat instead of a fancy bass boat and figuring he'd saved the difference. But to be fair, Earl was not interested in possessions. But I was, at least at the moment. Claire thought that the fitted sexy clothes I was drawn to were too risky, so we compromised. Back to investments: A little black Audrey Hepburn dress was an investment. A cashmere sweater was an investment. A strappy dress was an investment because I could wear it under a tailored jacket. A small Balenciaga bag was an investment. A pair of Ferragamo heels was an investment. And it always paid to buy quality.

Claire arranged for the dresses, skirts, blouses, sweaters, purse, and shoes to be sent to her parents on the north side, along with Claire's leather suitcase and my canvas duffle bag. We ate, unencumbered, at a deli on the seventh floor. "We just need a few more things," Claire said, "which we'll find on Rush Street. I'm going to treat you to some lingerie."

Claire asked the cab to let us out in front of the John Hancock building, on Michigan Avenue, so she could point out her father's office, on the thirtieth floor; the former site of the Playboy offices a block to the north; and Water Tower Place, across the street to the south. But I couldn't take it in. I'd never spent so much money in my life. I didn't want to look in another shop window.

We walked over to Rush Street, which runs on a diagonal, to a shop called Département Féminin that specialized in slightly naughty underwear, which Claire called lingerie. Claire was going to treat me. I'd never seen anything like Rush Street. We could have gone to a nude dancing show in the middle of the afternoon. Therewere nightclubs and sex shops and restaurants. The women on the street could have been Playboy bunnies. Some of them were, Claire said. She'd had a Playboy bunny for a babysitter when she was little.

I had to admit that the thought of wearing French satin panties under a pair of old jeans was exciting, like having a naughty secret. I grew up in a world where underwear didn't matter and was not discussed. But it wasn't underwear that caught my attention. It was the dress in the window. It was what I'd been looking for all day without knowing it. The tag said CAMI–CACHE-COEUR–SKIRT.

"That's it," I said. "That's what I'll wear to the party."

"Restrain yourself," Claire said, shaking her head. "You can't possibly wear something like that to the party."

"Why not?"

"It's a summer dress. You can't wear a summer dress on New Year's Eve."

"What difference does it make?"

Once again, Claire couldn't understand the question.

The woman who waited on us explained, in a strong French accent: Chicago winter weather was so depressing; she wanted it to be spring; so she put a summer dress in the window. Her long curly hair was held back from her shoulders by a curved tortoiseshell comb.

Claire wasn't buying it: "That means it was left over from *last* spring."

The woman shrugged.

I said something to her in French: *"Je le veux."* I want it.

"Of course you do," the woman said, and then switched to French. I couldn't follow her very well, maybe not at all, but I'd cut Claire off at the pass. It took me a while to grasp that a *cami–cache-coeur–skirt* was not one thing but three separate items: a white spaghetti-strap camisole, a wraparound blouse, and a pale putty-colored skirt.

"On peut porter cela pour le New Year's Eve?*"*

"Le réveillon du nouvel an. Mais oui."

"See," I said to Claire. "I know this upsets you, but it's what I want to do."

Claire started to argue but apparently thought better of it.

I tried on all three pieces and this time I thought I recognized the sexy, vibrant person in the mirror. I bought the camisole, the *cache-coeur*, and the putty-colored skirt, and some scarves, which the French woman showed me how to tie in different ways, and something called a *débardeur*, which is a kind of tank top. Claire treated me to some sexy panties and a lace teddy, and we were finished.

Claire's parents lived on Bellevue Place just around the corner from Département Féminin, in a four-story townhouse. Elegant. I'd never seen anything like it. Gray brick with black shutters. Ivy growing around the windows. A big curved window in the front full of plants the size of trees. A wrought-iron fence enclosed a tiny yard. The huge wooden door looked like the door to a castle.

Claire's mother answered the door. She was smaller than Claire, but she had the same big eyes, the same chestnut hair, the same subdued elegance. There was nothing subdued about her greeting, though, and I soon felt right at home as we opened the packages from Marshall Field's and reviewed the day's shopping—though not at home enough to model the clothes from Département Féminin.

By the time I'd packed the clothes back in their boxes, I was feeling a little queasy and was glad to have a room of my own so I could lie down for a bit. Claire and I took our bags up in an elevator. An elevator right in their front hall. I felt sick to my stomach. I *was* sick to my stomach.

I dozed off for a while and then Claire and Claire's mother and I walked down to the Oak Street Beach—past Ann Landers' apartment in a high-rise at the end of the street. We walked along the edge of the water. The buildings along the Outer Drive were spectacular. Where did all the money come from? And Lake Michigan, another first for me, was spectacular too. It was good to walk with Claire and her mother, talk girl talk, or woman talk. But it was Claire's father who understood me better than the women.

"It's not too late to take all this stuff back," he said at dinner. He was a large man, a senior partner in a law firm. His name was Konrad.

"Why on earth would she want to do that?" Claire's mother asked. "She's bought some lovely clothes."

Konrad laughed. "Buyer's remorse. Happens to everyone. Used to happen to you all the time. Besides, she's taken a beating in ShoppingKart-dot-com. You too," he said, turning to Claire.

"Daddy," Claire protested.

Buyer's remorse. I breathed a sigh of relief. I was glad there was a name for what I was going through. I started to feel better right away.

That night Claire came to my room in her nightgown. I slept in the nude. I kept the sheet up over me. Claire lay down beside me.

"Do you want to return the clothes?" she asked. "It's okay if you do. My mom can take them back if you don't want to. She knows everyone at Field's. In the women's department. It wouldn't be a problem. And we could walk back to Département Féminin in the morning. We'd still have time to catch the train."

I turned on my side so I was facing Claire. "I like your parents," I said, truthfully. "You're lucky."

"I feel like a little girl when I'm home," she said. "Safe."

"And at TF?"

"I have to be a grown-up."

"It's all right, Claire."

"You've been my student all semester, Sunny, and I've been your teacher. But now I think it's the other way around. I think you're the teacher and I'm the student. You have all these great stories, about your husband shoving your arm in a box of rattlesnakes, about shooting him, about casting out demons, being in prison, and raising that woman's daughter from the dead, and that evangelist getting bit and dying and then the people in the church telling the police it was a heart attack. What have *I* got? A nice house and a priest husband and two kids who spend all their time in front of the TV."

"*I* didn't raise anyone from the dead," I said.

"But you were there."

"You've published a novel."

"Yeah, and nobody read it."

"What about your affair with the astrophysicist?"

"I've got that too, but it's nothing to brag about."

"Write about the collision of the Milky Way and Andromeda, or the heat death of the universe."

She laughed.

"Everything is material, Claire. That's what you told us over and over in class." *Everything is material. Intentionality is the enemy. Be open to surprises at every stage of the way. Write shitty first drafts. There are only two stories: someone goes on a journey; or someone comes to town. "Araby" and "Cathedral."* I was running out of advice. Claire's advice. "This trip is material," I said. " 'What was your agenda? What did you want to happen? What obstacles did you encounter? Was it a success or a failure? Why did you want me to come with you? What did you want to happen? What did you learn? Did anything take you by surprise? Did you discover something you really care about?' You made it sound easy in class."

"*This* is what I wanted to happen, Sunny. I wanted you to be my friend. I wanted you to be my sister."

Now I was taken by surprise. Really taken by surprise.

Claire turned over on her other side and I snuggled up behind her and put my arm over her, and we went to sleep that way, and when I woke up in the morning, Claire was gone.

12

A French Christmas

On Christmas Eve Jackson drove home from his office in the early afternoon. It had snowed the night before. Not too much. Just right. Snow plows had cleared and salted the roads. The sun was out. Jackson put on a pair of clip-on sunglasses he kept in the dash.

The thesis that had emerged spontaneously from his field notes was "managed ecstasy." Think of the festivals of Dionysus, or of Demeter, think of Mardi Gras, think of the dance of the *molimo* among the Mbuti, think of all the indigenous communal rites and festivals—in the Caribbean, in Africa, in Hawaii, all over the globe—that Christian missionaries had been at such pains to suppress. Think of Christmas. Think of the early Christian church itself. There was no rational reason to join the church in the first century. Why subject yourself to ridicule, alienation, even persecution? You joined because you'd experienced something: ecstasy. And ecstasy was what the Church of the Burning Bush was about. Not sexual ecstasy—though Jackson thought of Sibaku, bathing in the river; of Suzanne leaning out the window on the rue Stanislas wearing her blazer over a white blouse but no pants; of Sunny growling with pleasure as she approached a climax and whispering nonsense in French—but something larger, something that Freud was never able to acknowledge: collective ecstasy, stepping outside of one's self into a larger whole. The people in the Church of the Burning Bush had come to this experience the hard way, out of a rural culture that had been marginalized in the modern world, and the church, like the ancient festivals, offered them a sacred space—however irrational and even misguided—in which it was safe to explore ecstatic experience. It was impossible to imagine them sitting quietly in their pews, like Episcopalians.

He stopped at Bertrand's Cellar on State Street for a bottle of crème de cassis and a bottle of champagne. Expensive, but it was Christmas Eve. He was thinking about cutting a Christmas tree but Sunny had objected. She had no objection to shopping, no objection to presents. She'd just spent a small fortune in Chicago with Claire. But she wanted a secular Christmas.

His present for her was a trip to Paris. In June. He had the non-refundable tickets—direct flights from O'Hare to Orly—in an envelope in his briefcase. They would stay in the residential hotel on the rue de Lille where he'd lived with his parents. They'd go to Suzanne's country place in the Dordogne and visit the excavations at Abri Pataud. He'd propose to her in the Café Anglais. There was a picture of it in the Time-Life *Classic French Cooking*. They'd hit the tourist spots, of course. The Eiffel Tower, the Louvre, Montmartre, Les Deux Magots. They'd walk along the Seine, take coffee at one of the bars near the Hôtel de Ville, where he'd skated with his parents, and spend an afternoon in the Grande Galerie de l'Évolution in the natural history museum. But they'd also go to special places that Suzanne had shown him: the Square d'Orléans, the garden at the

Musée de la Vie Romantique, or the Irish Cultural Center (the Centre Culturel Irlandais).

She'd cleared the drive, which always drifted over when the wind was from the north, a second time. The sensation of entering a magic realm came over him, as it often did, as he entered the woods, where the snow had not drifted, and where a woman he loved was waiting for him in the valley below, which she called a bottom.

Jackson had never gotten over Christmas. He still experienced the special sense of time that anthropologists recognize as sacred time. Like sacred places—Mount Moriah, Saint Peter's, Half Dome in Yosemite, the sequoias, the Mountains of the Moon. Traces of sacred time still resonated in popular commercial culture: the "magic" of Christmas. But there was a deeper resonance too, the experience of time unfolding not just as one damn thing after another, but as a cycle of observances or festivals anchored in the cycle of the seasons. Among the Mbuti—no calendar, no winter, no snow. But he'd still felt Christmas in his bones, meshing with one of the irregular Mbuti festivals.

He could smell wood smoke. Sunny had built a fire. She was out in front, filling the wheelbarrow with logs from the woodpile. She tossed a log into the wheelbarrow and waved exuberantly. Maya, who was watching her, turned her head to look at Jackson, and what Jackson thought at that moment was that they should go to Paris that night and get married in Paris. Why wait until June? Or go tomorrow. Saturday. They could fly to Paris on Christmas day and get married at the Mairie on Monday. He'd call the travel agent, and he'd call Suzanne tonight. He looked at his watch. Three o'clock. It would be nine o'clock in France. Although there was probably a residency requirement. They could go for two weeks, three. The second semester at TF didn't begin until the end of January. Almost the end.

It was three o'clock. The sun was still shining, but the snow was not melting. It was too cold. He helped Sunny with the logs and followed her as she pushed the wheelbarrow around the deck to the back of the house. She'd stacked up enough wood for a week.

Inside the house was nice and warm. Sunny added a couple of logs to the wood stove and checked the humidifier. The ceiling fans were going, pulling warm air up to the ceiling and forcing it down the outside walls.

"Let's go to Paris," he said. "Tomorrow. I'll call the travel agent. They're still open. We can go tomorrow. Stay for three weeks. We can stay at Suzanne's apartment. They'll be at their country place in the Dordogne."

She laughed. "What about the millennium party? You've invited thirty people to a party a week from Saturday."

"We'll cancel. People will understand."

"What about a passport?"

"You don't have a passport?"

"No, why would I have a passport?"

"You can get a passport in one day at the passport office in Chicago."

"And I've got to start work on my hot-snake certificate."

He could see that she was right, that he'd gone temporarily insane. "Then let's put up a Christmas tree," he said.

"Now I see what this is all about!"

"Forget Christianity," he said. "Think of it as a midwinter festival, a Saturnalia, a celebration of the harvest, the introduction of agriculture. Restoring the mythical golden age. Propitiating the threatening forces of winter."

"Okay," she said. "We won't go to Paris, and you can have a Christmas tree."

He didn't mention the tickets in his briefcase. When he closed the shutters over his desk, he was aware of a beam of light, the same beam of light he'd seen back in September. But weaker. But you could see it. You could see the dust motes if you looked carefully.

He ran his finger through the beam and then he looked out through the crack between the shutters.

"Look at this," he said.

Sunny looked.

"Do you see it? The beam of light."

"Barely."

"You see all the dust motes?"

"I see them. Barely."

"But you can see them?"

"All right, I can see them."

"You're looking *at* the beam, right?"

"Right."

"Now come over here. Look along the beam. Between the crack in the shutters?"

She looked.

"What do you see?"

"What do you think I see? I see outside."

"But what exactly."

"I see a lot of finches and nuthatches, and chickadees at your squirrel-proof bird feeder. I see a woodpecker, I see two cardinals on the railing. And beyond that, the stream, the bridge, the woods."

"That's the difference between looking *at* Christmas and looking *along* Christmas. When you look *at* it, you see a lot of old pagan customs that have been cobbled together with Christianity and the modern advertising industry."

"And when you look *along* it?"

"When you look *along* it? You get a glimpse of the ecstatic core that lay at the heart of the ancient religions."

"The *magic* of Christmas? 'Frosty the Snowman'? 'Rudolph the Red-Nosed Reindeer'?"

"Frosty and Rudolph too," he said.

They cut a Scotch pine from a stand of evergreens at the very back of the property, which bordered on a cornfield. To the south of the evergreens was the old Indian burial mound.

"I'm saving it to dig in my old age," Jackson said. "I don't want the state archeologists getting involved."

"How do you know it's an Indian burial mound?"

"Just look at it."

"Looks to me like an old wood pile that somebody abandoned a long time ago."

Jackson laughed. He was lying on the ground under the Scotch pine, sawing through the trunk with a curved pruning saw. "My dad hated Scotch pines," he said. "The needles are too sharp. There's too much sap. My mother liked them because they didn't drop their needles." Jackson looked up at the sky. "In another fifteen minutes it'll be dark," he said. "We could get lost."

"Yeah."

"This Indian burial mound can be disorienting."

"Yeah."

"One night we had a molimo party," he said, "and everybody came out here, and we couldn't find our way back."

"Yeah," she said. "How about Maya? Did she get lost too?"

When Maya heard her name she jumped up on Sunny.

They dragged the tree together. They were both wearing gloves, but the needles pricked through the gloves.

Jackson set it up in a new kind of stand that could be adjusted to hold the tree up straight no matter how crooked it was. That is, once you had the tree locked into the stand, you could adjust it any way

169

you wanted. He'd used it only once, before he got sick. It was not a very nicely shaped tree, and it was pokey and sticky. But it was a tree, and once they got it on the stand, it stood up straight.

Sunny modeled her new clothes while Jackson put the lights and the ornaments on the tree, coming down the stairs in her little black Audrey Hepburn dress, then in her beige sweater and slacks, then in her new lightweight blue blazer for spring over a white T-shirt and pair of Calvin Klein boot-cut jeans, and finally in a checked blazer for winter, a striped shirt, brown bag and matching shoes. She modeled the French scarves from Département Féminin, the opaque black stockings, the T-shirts, the tight-fitting strapless bra, a French teddy—everything except the cami–*cache-coeur* outfit and the putty-colored skirt, which she was saving for the party.

By the time she came down in her Egyptian cotton pajamas and warm slippers, he had the lights and ornaments on the tree and was in the kitchen, fixing omelets.

The Flavor of France was open on the kitchen table to a Christmas Eve menu in the back of the book. "This is what we should have had," Sunny said, saying everything in French: *huîtres, Estouffat de Noël à la Gasconne avec des pommes de terre à la vapeur, salade de mâche, Camembert, et Crêpes Grandgousier* for dessert."

"Next year," Jackson said.

After supper they were going to watch a French film about a drunk who wants to be a circus performer and a painter who's going blind, but on a sudden impulse Jackson got his parents' old slide projector out of the basement and brought up several boxes of his mother's slides. He and Sunny were both a little tipsy.

The slides were in trays. Thirty slides per tray. All labeled by Jackson's mother in her neat handwriting. In special slide boxes.

Jackson hadn't looked at them since his mother's death. Since long before that. None of his cousins had wanted them, and he hadn't really wanted them either, at the time, but now he was glad he hadn't thrown them out.

There were several boxes, each containing a dozen trays of thirty slides. It took him a while to find what he was looking for. PARIS 1971–72. He'd been twelve years old. After the initial shock of going to a French school, the Collège Saint-Denis, it had been the happiest time of his life. And, he thought, in his parents' lives. His father had been a visiting professor at the École Pratique des Hautes Études.

His mother had taken the slides, and she'd labeled each one with a fine-nibbed pen in her neat handwriting.

The bulb was burned out, but there was an extra one in the projector case. When he put it in, a powerful beam of light lit up the wall above the piano. He could see the beam itself, full of dust motes, like the shaft of light he'd watched that afternoon, but more powerful. He put in the first slide. He could still see the beam, but when he looked at the wall, he could see himself, a younger self, standing between his parents in front of the residential hotel on the rue de Lille, not far from the large office that his father shared with the editor of the *Revue d'assyriologie*, whose book was being published by the University of Chicago Press and who had arranged his father's visit. He looked at the beam of light again, and then at the screen. He ran his finger through the beam. He looked up. Sunny was watching him.

"You ready?" he said.

"Any time you are," she said. She thrust both hands in the beam of light and a black bunny appeared on the screen, blocking the image of him and his parents. And then a black dog that looked like Maya, and then a flying bird. An then a couple kissing.

"Where'd you learn to do that?"

"Vacation Bible school," she said.

"Not the last one?"

She shook her head. "Not the last one." She laughed. "Let's get this over with."

He looked at her to make sure she was joking and advanced the tray to the next slide.

His mother, who had taken a year off from her job as a librarian at the University of Chicago's Regenstein Library, had busied herself with small things in Paris. She loved shopping in the small markets. Stopping for a coffee at the café. Stopping to chat with the woman at the *boulangerie* and the men at the different butcher shops, for pork, beef, horse, who offered free advice. She loved the apartment with its little terrace overlooking the street. She took pictures of everything: the café, the bistro where they ate twice a week; the Cave Rue Fabert on the rue Fabert where the proprietor let Jackson help him seal wine bottles with wax; the dead stuffed rats in the window of a shop that sold rat traps near Les Halles.

There was a slide of Jackson with Claude Lévi-Strauss, a former director of the École, shortly before Lévi-Strauss was elected to the Académie Française. Slides of him with the concierge, on the carousel in the Luxembourg Gardens, at the puppet show at the Théâtre du Grand-Guignol. There were slides of students in the courtyard of the Sorbonne, wrapped in long university scarves; slides of the Christmas lights on the Champs-Élysées: and one of the three of them, taken by a stranger on Christmas Eve, ice skating at the Hôtel de Ville. Jackson between his parents, holding their hands, unsteady on his rented skates.

"Did you have to speak French at dinner?" Sunny asked.

"Yes. It was hard at first—hard for me—but then it got easier."

He got out his *Guide Bleu* and located the residence hotel on the foldout map. On the rue de Lille.

Later, after he'd been graduated from the University of Chicago, Jackson had taken a year off and gone back to Paris. He hadn't taken a camera because he hadn't wanted to look like a tourist, but later he'd regretted it. He had a picture, somewhere, of the apartment he had shared with Suzanne Toulon on the rue Stanislas, not far from the residential hotel. By this time his parents had divorced. It wasn't a bitter divorce. It was amicable. They'd simply gone their separate ways. One day they were married, the next day they weren't. His father stayed in the apartment in Hyde Park and continued to work on the Assyrian dictionary at the Oriental Institute. His mother got a job as a reference librarian at the Blackstone branch of the Chicago Public Library on South Lake Park. She moved into a small apartment on Fullerton, near the Church of Our Savior, which she attended for the rest of her life. Neither remarried. And what Jackson wondered, as he followed Sunny up the stairs, was what his parents saw when they looked back on that time in Paris. Would they have recognized the handsome couple in the slides of them skating in front of the Hôtel de Ville or sitting at a bistro table, holding hands, or standing at the flower stall at the Métro stop at Place Maubert? And he wondered if from a distance of twenty years he would recognize the forty-year-old professor sitting on the edge of the bed, eager as a young man, and the beautiful woman sitting next to him, pulling off her jeans.

13

Millennium Party

I was excited on the night of the party—my first time appearing in public as Jackson's . . . What? Mistress? Friend? Lover? Significant other? Who cared? Nobody. I was excited nonetheless.

Despite my protests Jackson had invited my professors: Madame Arnot; Cramer; Professor Henry, who taught Western Civ. I'd refused to convey the invitations in person, but Jackson had called them.

I was the hostess. Jackson didn't seem to understand my fears. "It's a potluck, that's all, just like a church supper." Jackson and I had fixed a large cassoulet, with venison and venison sausage, which had taken all day, and cooked a venison roast on the grill. A dozen wine bottles stood at attention on the kitchen table. Two cases of beer were keeping cold on the deck. Jackson said that people would bring lots of stuff. I pictured casseroles, fried chicken, meatloaf, catfish.

We'd built a huge bonfire down by the stream. I kept looking at it from different windows.

I didn't put on my outfit till after the first guests had arrived. When I did, it seemed to emit light, like the bonfire. The light washed over me. I could feel the earth turning beneath my feet.

Everyone brought food and wine and hard liquor too, and everyone was having a good time. It really was like a church supper, but with better food. Claude's big French table was loaded down with shrimp, pasta salads, guacamole, cheeses, all arranged around the big cassoulet, which we had cooked in a terra-cotta pot. Claire had put her special New York Chocolate Cheesecake out on the deck to keep cold.

Everyone was very agreeable. Not just agreeable, but making it clear that they were happy to be here and not somewhere else. And these were the people Earl would consign to Hell.

Even the good-natured argument about when one millennium ended and another began didn't upset the apple cart. I listened with pleasure. Cramer maintained that the old millennium wasn't over till the year 2000 had been completed. "When are you ten years old? At the *end* of your tenth year, not at the beginning."

"In China," someone said, "you're one year old the day you're born."

I didn't see how it made a difference.

"A millennium is a thousand years," Claire said, agreeing with Cramer. "A thousand years won't be up—completed, finished—until the *end* of the year 2000."

Someone else said, "But there was no year zero."

Cramer was getting annoyed. "Stephen Jay Gould made that point on television the other night," he said, "but so what? Of course there was no zero. There's no zero year in a human life. You go from zero to one, and at the end of your first year, you're one year old."

Claire, who had already moved into the apartment over the garage to work on her novel, had to leave because her husband was celebrating a special New Year's Eve mass at nine o'clock. "I'll be back," she said. "Ray's coming too."

I walked her out to her car. "That argument about the millennium," I said, "makes about as much sense as the debate about which way to put the roll of toilet paper."

"Which way is that?"

"Either way. Who cares?"

"A lot of people care. Just read Ann Landers. But you must be freezing in that outfit," Claire said. "You better get back inside."

"Feels good," I said.

"You want to go to church with me? I'll bring you back afterward."

I shook my head and laughed.

I tried to avoid my professors, but didn't have much luck. They seemed to be drawn to me, as if I were a magnet. Maybe it was because I'd gotten A's in all my courses and was radiating excitement. Or just maybe it was because I was wearing my spaghetti-strap camisole under my *cache-coeur* wraparound blouse. And my putty-colored skirt.

But maybe not.

I didn't want to have to speak French to Madame Arnot, but what could I do? "*Enchantée*," I said.

"*Bonsoir*," she said.

"*Bonsoir*," I said.

"*Quel joli ensemble. Très chic.* But it's for spring, non?"

I was the first time I'd heard her speak English.

"I'm tired of the winter weather," I said. "I wanted to make a statement."

"*Vous Américains!*" she said. "*Quelle idée.*"

"*Pourquis pas?*" I said. "*Amusez-vous bien!*"

"*A plus.*" She laughed.

Professor Henry hadn't come to the party, but I had to talk to Cramer. I was a little afraid of him, though we'd already started working together in the herp lab, and I'd already joined ASIH— the American Society of Ichthyologists and Herpetologists—as a student member, and he'd invited me to go to the annual meetings in Baja California, in June. Laura Gridley, a graduate student who'd been one of the lab assistants in Bio 120 and who'd be in the training program, would be going too.

The training program was required by the Federal Animal Welfare Act. There were Public Health Policy and USDA regulations governing just about everything: waste disposal, feeding, housing, and so on. Every member of the team—which included Laura Gridley and Frank Benson—would have to be familiar with animal welfare laws, and especially with the special procedures for handling venomous snakes: what to do in case of escape or envenomation, whom to call, what to report, what hospitals had the CroFab antivenin used to treat all envenomations by pit vipers (water moccasins, rattlesnakes, copperheads). We would have to master a complicated system of record keeping—how to keep a real-time inventory for each specimen, how to maintain a cage-card notification system for the Office of Research Compliance. Cramer had ordered new equipment—hooks and tongs, the plastic cages—and we were going to practice on the two old timber rattlers in the lab. These snakes were left over from someone else's experiment. They'd been hanging around for ages. If they hadn't had their venom sacs removed, the lab would have had all sort of restrictions.

I'd forgotten about my outfit till Cramer commented on it.

"Do you like it?" I said. "It's French."

"I've never seen anything like it."

"Is that good?"

"I'm not sure. It looks like somebody else's idea of who you are."

"Maybe it's just not your idea." I was annoyed.

"That dress," he said, "is totally wrong for you. It's false. Like everything French. Phony, artificial. A tease. Like pornography. Sex coming out of your head instead of out of your body. You don't need a dress like that. You're a blue jeans girl. Woman. A pickup truck woman. Natural. Unaffected. Down to earth. You're a herpetologist, not a French whore. You don't need a dress like that. Is *that* who you think you are? A French whore?" He laughed, but I didn't think it was funny. It wasn't the first time I'd been called a whore, but it was the first time I'd been called a herpetologist.

"Who do you think bought and paid for the dress?" I asked. My only comeback. It was weak.

"If I had to guess I'd say Jackson. I'd say it was a Christmas present from Jackson."

"Well, it wasn't."

"Sorry."

"Well, shit," I said. "I'm sorry I asked for your opinion."

I went into the kitchen and when no one was looking poured some red wine down my front so that I had a good excuse to change my clothes. Upstairs, looking in the mirror on the closet door, I was mortified. *Somebody else's idea of who I am.*

By the time Jackson found me, sitting on the edge of the bed, I'd settled back into my old self, in jeans and a turtleneck.

"What happened?"

"I spilled some wine down my front," I said.

"We need you to play the piano," he said. I could hear a guitar. The singing was about to begin.

Claire came in as I was coming down the stairs. Ben Wagner was picking out "Amazing Grace" on a twelve-string guitar. He was what Jackson called a real band in a box.

I sat down at the electric Yamaha.

Jackson had his harps in a belt around his waist. I'd given him six new Lee Oskars for Christmas and he'd taken them all apart and tinkered with the reeds.

The music was familiar—the only music we all had in common. "Just a Closer Walk with Thee," "Precious Lord, Take My Hand," "The Old Ship Of Zion," and "When the Roll Is Called Up Yonder." I didn't really feel like playing hymns, but I knew they'd annoy Cramer, who'd devoted most of one lecture to the adaptive value of illusions like religion.

> *When the roll (when the roll)*
> *Is called up yonder,*
> *When the roll (when the roll)*
> *Is called up yonder,*
> *When the ro-oh-oh-oh-ll is called up YON—der,*
> *When the roll is called up yonder I'll be there.*

Cramer wasn't a singer, but Claire, who'd come back to the party with Father Ray, had a beautiful alto voice and sang the "when-the-roll" echoes. I turned up the volume on the electronic piano, and we made so much noise that the owls started calling, as if they were joining the singing. Or protesting. Someone opened a door so we could hear them better, and Maya went out.

I was amazed at Jackson's harp playing. We'd played together a few times, but this was different. I realized that he'd just been backing me up.

I tried to teach everyone "La Gui-Année" and got some help from Madame Arnot:

> *Bon soir le maître et la maîtresse,*
> *Et tout le monde du logis:*

Pour le dernier jour de l'année,
La Gui-Année vous nous devais.

When the singing died down Claire went out on the deck to get her chocolate cheese cake. The next minute she was back inside, furious: "The dog ate the cheesecake."

The cheesecake was out on the deck. I'd told her to put it out there, thinking she'd put it on the table. But we'd carried the table inside, so she'd put it on the floor. Maya had poked her nose through the foil covering.

Jackson reacted quickly and picked up the phone to call the vet. "Chocolate is poison for dogs," he shouted. But he was only pretending to call. I could see he had his finger on the button. Pretty soon he had Claire apologizing for poisoning Maya.

"You can't eat that," Claire said, when Jackson started to take the foil off the cheesecake.

"Why not?"

Maya had made a hole in the foil but hadn't managed to eat much of the cheesecake. Jackson cut around the hole in the center and served small pieces of cheesecake on paper plates. It was delicious.

After another round of singing, some people started to leave. Coats and a few children were brought down from the bedrooms upstairs. About a dozen of us settled down in the living room with a bottle of Irish whiskey. Jackson put more wood on the fire and filled the cast-iron humidifier on top of the wood stove. Some water splashed on the stovetop and sizzled. At eleven thirty the phone rang. It was for me.

It was Earl. He was worried about me. He was worried about the end of the millennium, about the end of the world. I tried to explain to him that the new millennium wouldn't really start for another year. He wouldn't believe me, and I was too tipsy to explain it very well. "Earl, Sweetie, that's nice that you're worried about me, but I don't want you to worry. I'll be okay."

"Let me talk to Jackson," he said.

I handed the phone to Jackson and listened while he explained to Earl, in language that Earl could understand, why it was impossible to predict the Second Coming. *No man knows the hour,* he kept saying. Christ himself didn't know. *He'll come like a thief in the night.*

"It's my ex-husband." I had to shout to make myself heard. "He thinks the world's going to end at midnight. It's going to happen tonight." I looked at my watch, but I could barely read it. "What time is it?"

"Eleven forty-two."

"We've still got eighteen minutes."

"Eighteen minutes."

"It's been two thousand in Greenwich for five hours already," somebody said.

"All the computers are going to crash," I said. "The government will have to shut down. Businesses won't function. It's going to set the stage for the Antichrist. First world government, then the Antichrist."

"What are we supposed to do?"

"He wants me to pray. We could all pray. Somebody pass the whiskey!"

Laughter.

Jackson lit a Coleman lantern, one of the big ones with two mantles, and turned out the electric lights. Mellow. The bottle of Irish whiskey was making its rounds. It was time for ghost stories, and I had some good ones, but Cramer started in on Y2K. *What if? What if?*

It was Cramer who scared the pants off everybody, I suppose because he spoke with the authority of a scientist: What if the computers *do* crash? The planes *are* grounded? Credit cards *don't* work? Emergency communications break down? Power fails? Telephones don't work? Tax records are unavailable? Military defense systems go down? No traffic lights?

"How long could we last without electricity?" someone asked. "That's the real question."

"Jackson's okay out here," Claire said. "At least he's got plenty of wood, and plenty of food. And he's got these nice Coleman lanterns."

"What about water?" Cramer asked. "How do you get your water?"

"Well."

"Pump."

"Electric pump?"

Jackson nodded.

"Got a generator?"

"Nope."

"What about the stream?" Madame Arnot asked. "There's a stream in the back, *n'est-ce pas*?"

"Would you drink that?" Cramer asked. "All the runoff from the soybean fields? Phosphorus, sulfur, herbicides? You wouldn't last long."

"You could boil it."

"Wouldn't take care of the herbicides."

"Well," Jackson asked, "what are we supposed to do?"

"How long do you want to plan for? Two weeks? Two months? A year? Two years?"

"How about two months."

"You can bring up water from the stream to flush the toilet, but you're going to need sixty gallons of water per person just for drinking and cooking. And you're going to need food."

"I've probably got enough beer and wine for a month."

It was like the ghost stories folks used to tell back home. But scarier.

"The United States has six thousand electrical generating units," Cramer said, "twelve thousand major substations, and half a million miles of bulk transmission lines. Thousands of low-voltage transformers are linked together in a grid. There's a lot of built-in redundancy and a lot of fail-safe mechanisms, but there are still problems. In 1965. In 1977. You probably remember 1996. A million and a half phones out; people stuck in elevators for hours, half a million customers without power in California."

"I was on the subway in San Francisco," Madame Arnot said.

"The grid is controlled regionally by computers in a hundred separate control centers. If these computers fail . . ." He shrugged. "And what are you going to do for money? Have you got enough cash? There's going to be a massive run on grocery stores. They won't be able to restock. The inventory management systems will be down. And you won't have your freezer or your refrigerator. You'll need bottled water and powdered milk. You'll need to stock up on canned goods. But it will be too late."

It was 11:54.

"Let's get back to Jackson, here. He's got Coleman lamps. Already burning. Let's say he stockpiles. But his neighbors don't. How long do you think it'll be before they show up on his doorstep? Then what's he going to do?"

"I've got a pistol," I said, "and Jackson's got a .22 and a 30.06 and a .35 and a shotgun."

"Two thousand is a leap year."

"So? What's that got to do with the price of tea in China?"

"I wondered if that made a difference."

Cramer was distracted. "The problem is that the computer will read 'zero zero' as 'nineteen hundred.' That's what will screw everything up. It doesn't matter about the millennium. Besides, two thousand is not a leap year."

"A year is a leap year if it's divisible by four, unless it's divisible by a hundred."

"Yes, but there's an exception to that. If it's divisible by *four* hundred, then it *is* a leap year."

Another argument broke out, like the argument about toilet paper in Ann Landers.

Jackson didn't have a television, but we turned on the radio and listened to a countdown on the local NPR station.

It had been midnight in London since six o'clock, midnight in New York for an hour. No reports of plane crashes or power outages. It wouldn't be midnight in California for another two hours. If anything were going to trigger the end of the world, that would be it. California. But most of us were satisfied that nothing bad was going to happen.

Cramer's crack about my dress still rankled, but I made room for him on the piano bench as we sang "Auld Lang Syne," and then another argument broke out: about the correct pronunciation of "Syne." Should it be "sine" or "zine"?

Nothing was settled that night. Not the actual starting point for the new millennium; not the proper position for toilet paper rolls; nor the correct pronunciation of "syne." But we had a good time. Jackson hooked up his eight-track digital tape recorder and we sang some more and he recorded "The Old Ship of Zion." Jackson played the piano this time and led the singing. After a few verses he asked us to add the name of someone dear to us, and I put in Warren's name.

> *It has carried dear old Warren,*
> *It has carried dear old Warren,*

It has carried dear old Warren,
Get on board, Children, get on board.

I thought of Earl, too. I could see him standing at his old desk in the church office, talking on his old-fashioned dial phone. Worried about the Second Coming. The millennium. Calling me up to warn me.

It *was* just like home, sort of. Talking about the apocalypse. Singing the old hymns. Arguing over Jesus' Name vs. Trinity. Friendly and not so friendly arguments over scriptural texts.

Things hadn't always been so bad between Earl and me. He showed up in Naqada the day after Daddy was killed, Daddy and twenty-seven others, in an explosion in Occidental Number Five. The whole town was gathered around the pit head. Nobody knew what had happened and the company officials were saying that the mine had just been inspected by the state and there hadn't been any violations found. The president of the UMWA was there, and the Secretary of the Interior, and they were trying to calm everybody, and then Earl walked through the crowd up to the pit head and started to sing "Precious Lord, take my hand," and everybody got real quiet, and pretty soon everybody started to sing:

Precious Lord, take my hand,
Lead me on, help me stand,
I am weak, I am tired, I am worn.
Through the storm, through the night,
Lead me on to the light,
Precious Lord, take my hand, lead me home.

And then he started to preach, and you might have thought it was Jesus himself come to lead us home.

It took three days to get all the bodies out. Daddy's was one of the last. There wasn't much left of him, but enough to tell. What happened was methane gas had accumulated in part of the mine that should have been sealed off. The State of Illinois hadn't found any violations, but the federal inspectors had cited more than thirty violations.

Earl was helping everyone, including Mama and me. The bodies were taken to the junior high school, which they used as a morgue. All the bodies were burnt pretty bad. Earl went with us.

Number Five was one of the biggest shaft mines in the world and one of the best mechanized. But that didn't help Daddy.

Earl was everywhere. He and his friend Gene had come up from Middlesboro, over in Kentucky, where there was a big serpent-handling church, when he heard about the mine disaster. And just stayed. Stayed at a motel for a few days and then moved in with DX, who was engaged to my cousin Sally. DX was trying to hold the church together—the Church of the Burning Bush with Signs Following—but he didn't have the gift of preaching like Earl and he was having trouble and was glad to let Earl start preaching. I was taken just as hard as everyone else in the congregation. Earl was tall and handsome in a funny way. Or maybe ugly in a funny way. Like the picture of Abe Lincoln in the hallway at the high school. You got used to it, and after a while it became handsome.

He had a wonderful voice that filled the whole church, proclaiming immortality and the victory over Death and Sin, and made me think of Elvis. We weren't allowed to listen to Elvis. But I'd heard him at my friend Tilly's house. Tilly didn't belong to the Church of the Burning Bush, and my parents didn't like me going to her house after school, but sometimes I did anyway. To listen to her old records.

There was always competition to invite Earl to dinner. That was our way. And, of course, there was competition among the unmarried women, though this wasn't the sort of thing anyone said openly—not through hypocrisy, but through a kind of breeding, good taste.

My mama didn't know what to do with herself with Daddy dead and buried, and she was glad to turn me over to Earl. I was fourteen at the time, and sixteen when we finally got married.

14

A Snake Is a Snake

It was the end of winter break, the beginning of a new semester. Jackson had just come back from Naqada and was upstairs taking a shower. Claire was sitting at the kitchen table, looking at the pictures in *The Flavor of France.* I was fixing *poule au riz* —chicken and rice. As I added two egg yolks to the top of a double boiler, I was suddenly overwhelmed with a sense of well-being, a sense that the answers to life's big questions had fallen into my lap. From Madame Arnot in French 101 I'd learned that life is a party and that it's okay to be sexy and sophisticated and to drink kir royale and to fuck like a Greyhound bitch. From Professor Henry in Great Books I'd learned that life is a journey (Gilgamesh, Odysseus, Aeneas) and that you can't expect any help from the gods along the way. Just the opposite, in fact. From Claire in English 207 I'd learned that life is a story and that intentionality is the enemy. From Cramer in Biology 120 I'd learned that we are a part of the universe, not separate from it, that we share the room, that taking turns is important. And from Jackson?

The kitchen was warm and smelled of chicken stock and wine and onions. I could imagine spending the rest of my life in this kitchen, but was this what I *really* wanted to do? That was one big question that hadn't fallen into my lap. One of these days Jackson was going to propose, seriously, and I didn't know what I was going to say. I wouldn't know till he did it, and then I'd surprise myself one way or the other. But I wasn't going to Paris with Jackson. I was going to the ASIH conference in California with Cramer.

"The stock is simmering," I said. "What am I supposed to do now?"

Claire looked at *The Flavor of France.* "Beat the egg yolks and then start adding the stock. Strain it first."

"I've already strained it."

"The stock's got to be hot but not boiling."

"It's hot."

"Add the stock slowly and stir it with a whisk until it begins to thicken and then add a tablespoon of butter."

I whisked the egg yolks with a wire whisk and started to add the hot stock, a little bit at a time. I kept whisking, watching the stock to see if it was starting to thicken. It wasn't.

Claire wanted to open the champagne, but I told her to wait till Jackson came down.

Claire had spent every day of the semester break, from Christmas to late January, including Sundays, up in the apartment, writing two thousand words a day. She'd finished a sixty-thousand word novel. Or a sixty-thousand word manuscript, and she too seemed to be filled with a sense of well-being. The novel was not going to be about her affair with the astrophysics professor; it was going to be a woman's extreme adventure novel, but she hadn't shown me anything she'd written. Whenever she got stuck, I'd feed her another snake story or give her some of her own advice: intentionality is the enemy; write without stopping; be open to surprises at every step of the way.

She was leaving in the morning, Monday morning, to go back to her family. Her first class wasn't till Tuesday, so she still had Monday to prepare. She'd brought a bottle of expensive champagne, which was sweating on the table next to a bottle of crème de cassis.

Jackson came into the kitchen, his wet hair combed straight back. I was poking at the chicken. "Rice," he said, looking into the copper pot on the stove. "One of the great mysteries of agriculture."

"I thought that was corn," I said.

"Corn too. Another one of the great mysteries of agriculture."

"What about wine?"

"Wine too. Mysteries everywhere."

"What about millet?"

"I don't know about millet."

Claire poured a little crème de cassis into three wine glasses. She opened the champagne and filled the glasses. I took a sip. It was *sooo* good. We drank to Claire's manuscript, and to my hot-snake certificate, which was propped up in the center of the table, and to Jackson's NHI proposal, about which he was very excited.

"Earl's an interesting guy," Jackson said. "Too bad he doesn't have a sense of humor."

There was no point in bringing up my opposition to his trips to Naqada, so I bit my tongue. I spread the rice out on a platter and put the chicken pieces on top and spooned the sauce, which had finally thickened, slightly, over them directly from the double boiler.

"*Bon appétit*," Jackson said.

"*Bon appétit*," I said, automatically.

"His pal DX has a two-headed snake. Rattlesnake. He read in

Time magazine that there're only about twenty two-headed snakes in the world. He thinks he could get a lot of money for it."

"Jackson," I said, "if you're going to tell me you handled that snake, I don't want to hear about it."

"Moloch and Beelzebub. Those are the two heads. Earl handled it. He held it right up against his chest and scratched the two heads. Moloch and Beelzebub."

"You didn't handle it, did you?"

"I just touched it. Put my fingers around it. It was fantastic. Like putting your hand on a powerful erection, a superhuman erection. It's really something. I didn't want to let go. It's really something."

"How many powerful erections have you held in your hand?" Claire asked.

"Just one. Well, the same one, I mean. The same one more than once. Well, not the same one, actually."

"It's all right, Jackson," Claire said. "We know what you mean."

"It's really something, all right," I said. "It's a rattlesnake. You've got no business messing with it. What if you got bit?"

"Then I guess it would be up to the Lord."

"Jackson, don't talk like that. It's not funny. You're supposed to be a scientist, not a snake handler."

"Just kidding. But when it turned both heads to look at me, the eyes caught the light from the stars. They glittered like diamonds. Earl said it was like looking into the depths of hell, but I didn't want to let go."

"You going to put that in your NHI proposal?"

"No." He laughed. "But I see you've got your hot-snake certification, so I don't see why you don't want me to have a little fun."

The framed certificate was on the table. Jackson picked it up and looked at it.

TRAINING CERTIFICATION FOR WORK WITH
VENOMOUS SNAKES AT THOMAS FORD UNIVERSITY

I have taken the base module of the online training for personnel involved in animal care. I have read the Procedures for working with snakes compiled in the red binder in Buehl Laboratory (or the copy immediately outside Buehl Laboratory), and have read the policies described above. I have also been trained by Dr. Cramer to work with venomous snakes and to handle a snake-bite emergency according to the procedures described in the red book.

Approved by: Eldon Cramer   Trainee: Willa Fern Cochrane

Date: January 24, 2000   Date: January 24, 2000

Buehl Laboratory was the name Cramer had come up with for our basement snake lab. Victor Buehl had taught biology for forty years at TR. Cramer put up a picture of him next to the door. A distinguished man with a pointed white beard.

I served the chicken and Claire refilled our glasses with champagne, and we ate. I had tried, several times, to talk seriously to Jackson about what he was doing in Naqada, but it was as if there were something he did not want to grasp, and he always retreated behind a wall of jokey humor.

"Jackson," I said. "What Cramer and I are doing—and Frank and Laura—is science, it's not getting your kicks by touching rattlesnakes. We're studying rattlesnakes scientifically. We're going to catch the snakes in the den that Cramer's located and bring them into the lab and put radio transmitters in them and take them to a new denning area. Snakes go back to the same den every year. Nobody knows what the impact of translocation will be—releasing them in a new denning area. It's a big deal for Cramer, a big opportunity."

Supper was over. "Why don't we do the dishes?" Claire said. "Maybe Jackson could make some espresso in his new pot."

I had given Jackson a new espresso pot for Christmas. It had a special valve that held the steam down till the pressure reached a certain point. Then the steam would explode through a filter and form a light *crema* or foam on the top of the coffee. It was delicious. Jackson loved it. And so did I. But it was temperamental. Sometimes it didn't produce *crema*. Sometimes it leaked out the sides. But when it worked, it worked beautifully. And when we were working at the library table and I'd offer to make a pot, he'd hold up his cup of regular coffee and say, "Good idea. I'll have a cup of coffee while I'm having a cup of coffee."

After supper we sat in the living room at the big library table, which had room for everyone—it was at least eight feet long—with plenty of room for books, papers, computers. Jackson added a couple of logs to the fire in the wood stove. Claire was writing by hand, with a green-and-black-striped fountain pen, in a special notebook with detachable pages. She'd filled four notebooks since Christmas. Jackson was typing up his field notes on his laptop.

The last thing on Cramer's agenda—though it was not part of the IACUC (Institutional Animal Care and Use Committee) training program—was a drawing assignment. Laura, Frank, and I were each supposed to draw one of the two old rattlers that we'd practiced on with the new snake hooks and clamps that Cramer had bought. How hard could it be? The snakes were old and tired and just wanted to sleep. They didn't move around.

"A pencil is the best eye," Cramer said. "Just draw what you see."

All semester in Bio 120 I'd been drawing what I saw through different microscopes—losing specimens when switching from high power to low power and then finding them again.

But drawing a snake was harder than I thought. I was never any good at drawing, but a snake is just a hose with a head on it. And that's what my first drawings looked like—hoses with small football-shaped heads.

Cramer laughed. He had put each of the two old rattlers in an aquarium on one of the soapstone lab tables, and we spent the rest of the day making one drawing after another. Cramer would reappear every hour or so and look at our drawings. "Keep looking," he'd say. But we didn't know what we were looking *for*.

I left the lab at four that afternoon and went to an art supply store on State Street and got a book on how to draw animals. I bought some drawing pencils and some shading pens while I was at it.

That night Jackson suggested taking a photo of my snake and then tracing it. Or drawing a grid on the glass of the cage. Claire said she thought Cramer'd gotten the idea from an essay about Louis Agassiz that showed up all the time in English composition textbooks.

My drawing book was full of good advice: Draw what you see, not what you *think* you see. Don't think snake (or lion or elephant or dog or cat), think shapes, distances, contours. Think angular, rounded, sharp, intricate. Look for negative spaces.

I spent another day drawing my snake, and I thought I'd mastered it, but Cramer wasn't satisfied. "Keep looking."

That night—the second night of the drawing project—Claire brought an English composition book with the Agassiz essay. It was about a fish, not a snake. It was written by a student at Harvard who'd told Agassiz he wanted to be a naturalist. Agassiz had given the student a fish to draw (a fish preserved in alcohol) and had given him a hard time, just as Cramer was giving us a hard time, even though Laura and Frank were Rembrandts compared to me. *Keep looking.* But at least I had the idea. I knew what he was looking *for*. I was looking for information. And the next day I kept looking till I seemed to be seeing the snake for the first time and managed to get a drawing that satisfied Cramer.

And now, sitting at the library table with nothing else to do, I tried to draw the snake from memory. Claire was writing furiously with her fountain pen. Whenever she got stuck, I'd remind her that intentionality is the enemy. Jackson paused from time to time to ask questions that were really intended to convey information. Did I know this? Did I know that? Did I know that in ancient Mesopotamia the world was often depicted as a tree with a pair of intertwined snakes? And that the same snake reappears in the Garden of Eden, and later in the caduceus, borne by Hermes in Greek mythology? Did I know that in all ancient cultures—European, African, American, Asian, Australian—the snake, because it sheds its skin, came to symbolize resurrection or immortality? Did I know that the Greek demigod Aesculapius once killed a snake and saw another snake enter the house with some herbs in its mouth and bring the dead snake back to life? Did I know about the sky serpent of Persia, and the Sumerian salt water serpent, Tiamat, and the Phoenician serpent god, Basilisk? Did I know that in Egypt the cobra represented the goddess of life? That the world's oldest ritual, over seventy thousand years ago in the Tsodilo Hills in Botswana, involved the worship of snakes, and that according to the San creation myth humankind descended from the python? Did I know that Tore, the god of the Ituri Forest, was guarded by a giant snake?

My answer to these questions was always the same: No.

How about the Near Eastern serpent goddess Anat, sister of Baal? Now there was a name I knew. Baal. "He had a pissing contest with Yahweh, and lost, right?" Here was something Jackson didn't know.

All I had to oppose this mythological knowledge was my taxonomy. Instead of drawing my inner snake, I wrote out the taxonomy on my drawing pad with a Kimberly 4B pencil:

> Kingdom: Animalia
> Phylum: Chordata
> Subphylum: Vertebrata
> Class: Reptilia
> Subclass: Diapsida
> Order: Squamata
> Suborder: Serpentes
> Family: Crotalidae (pit vipers)
> Genus: Crotalus
> Species: horridus
> Subspecies: horridus

I closed my eyes for a moment, and when I did, I could see the snake in my imagination: the dark dorsal bands, like upside-down V's, on the yellow-black-brown body, and the flat triangular shape of the head, and the thermal-sensitive pits between eyes and nostrils, the elliptical pupils, the rough appearance created by the petal-like scales; the blotches in different hues, from dark brown to light yellow, that merge with the laterals to form cross bands toward the tail, the dark dots on the cream-colored belly, the irregular dark spots on a white background around the vent, the rows of strongly keeled scales that bordered the dorsal hexagons; I could count the rows of scales between the V-shaped bands and the number of scales in each row. I didn't have to squeeze these images out of my brain, like toothpaste out of a tube. They were just there—not encrusted by mythology, not overlaid with my own childhood memories; neither devil nor god. Just the thing itself. *Crotalus horridus horridus.* My hand moved by itself, and the snake emerged out of nowhere—or rather out of a mess of shapes, blank spaces, patterns, distances, contours, relationships, angles, curves—and revealed itself on the page. My sense of well-being, which had been seriously upset, was restored. But I didn't say anything, because I didn't want to get into an argument.

15

Everyone Is Going to Paris

Jackson couldn't believe it: Sunny couldn't or wouldn't go to Paris in June. She refused to cooperate with his fantasy, refused to play the role he'd scripted for her in his little drama. She was going to the ASIH meetings in Mexico.

"I'm sorry," she said. "I should have told you sooner. I didn't realize there was a conflict at first."

It was a Saturday morning in February, three weeks into the semester. Jackson's NHI proposal was due in one week. He and Sunny were sitting at the library table, piles of books between them. It was fiercely cold out and the wind was blowing hard, and even though it was ten o'clock it was so dark out they kept the shutters closed. The lamplight made her hair look like straw. She'd pulled it back into a ponytail. Like a high school girl.

He didn't know how to react. He'd been dealt a body blow. "I've told Suzanne we're coming."

"You'll have to cash in the tickets and tell Suzanne we'll come some other time. You've got plenty of time. You've got three months."

"They're nonrefundable. The tickets."

"I'm sorry, Jackson, I've already signed up for the meetings."

"You'll still need to get your passport."

"Why would I need a passport to go to California?"

"It's in Mexico. Baja California is in Mexico."

"Mexico?"

"You want me to show you on a map?" She didn't believe him. He got out the *National Geographic Road Atlas.* There it was, a long ragged strip attached to the bottom of California, connected to mainland Mexico by a smaller strip that ran under Arizona.

"How could I be so stupid?"

"Ignorant, maybe, but not stupid."

"Thanks."

"Is Cramer going?"

"Yes, Cramer is going."

"Are any other students going?"

"I don't know. Laura is going."

Jackson knew better than to get into a fight. He could tell by the way she held herself that this was a done deal.

"I've already sent in my registration fee."

"Not taking any chances, are you?"

"What's that supposed to mean?"

"I was going to propose to you in Paris."

"I think we should talk about this later."

"I'll propose to you right now. Will you marry me?"

"Don't be ridiculous."

"What's ridiculous? We're living here like man and wife. Husband and wife."

"I don't need a man to look after me."

"I'm not so sure about that. You think Baja California is in California? And what about ShoppingKart-dot-com?"

"What *about* ShoppingKart-dot-com?"

"It's been hemorrhaging money. It's down to three and a half to-day. If it goes any lower they'll stop listing it on the New York Stock Exchange. If you'd listened to me . . ."

"You've been following it, haven't you, just so you could hold it over my head. I'm not going to talk about ShoppingKart-dot-com."

"I've been listening to NPR," he said.

Sunny fixed bacon and eggs for her lunch.

Jackson ate a sandwich. They didn't speak. They kept the radio on though the reception was terrible.

Maya was puzzled. Jackson put on his heavy coat and took her out to play Frisbee. She'd learned to take the Frisbee first to Jackson, then to Sunny, who usually came out with Jackson. The wind tore at the Frisbee and slapped it to the ground. Maya stopped each time she picked it up and looked toward the front door, expecting Sunny. Jackson had to shout at her. They were both hoping that Sunny would come out and play, the way she usually did. But it didn't happen.

Jackson was the first to apologize. The silence between them was intolerable. He was afraid she'd move her things back up to the apartment over the garage. He couldn't hold out any longer. He wanted to grab on to her, pull her back, keep her from slipping away, but what he said was, "I'm sorry, I was out of line. I should have asked you *before* I bought the tickets." He was already afraid, afraid of losing her, afraid that he'd lost her already.

Sunny apologized too. "I should have told you as soon as I realized there was a conflict, but I knew you'd be upset. I'm upset too, but this is something I have to do. It's a good career move."

"It's all right," Jackson said. "I'll go by myself." And at the time that seemed like a good plan. It was the only plan he could think of.

As an anthropologist Jackson understood jealousy as a solution to the problem of the uncertainty of paternity—an evolutionary adaptation that promoted reproductive success. Jealous males introduce more genes into the gene pool than males who are indifferent to the infidelity of their mates. It made sense, from an evolutionary point of view, for the Yap husbands of Micronesia, or the Toba-Batak husbands of Sumatra, to kill their wives and lovers if they caught them in the act of adultery. Texas husbands too. As an anthropologist he did not find it surprising that sexual jealousy is a leading cause of homicide in many parts of the world. But this was to stand outside the experience, to look *at* the beam of light. Now he was standing inside the experience, looking *along* the beam of light. He didn't like what he saw. He told himself that his marriage proposal had been ridiculous. He told himself that he was glad Sunny had been more level-headed. He told himself that jealousy was inappropriate, that Sunny had made a professional decision, not taken a lover. But he didn't believe it himself, and he knew, not as an anthropologist but as a man, why cuckolds are subject to ridicule and loss of social status. He felt slightly ridiculous himself, humiliated, and he was aware of the physical symptoms of jealousy—sensitive skin, edginess—as if he'd drunk too much coffee too fast. He didn't know what to do with his fantasies: holding hands with Sunny in the Luxembourg Gardens, proposing to her in the Café Anglais. He'd assumed that she wanted what he wanted, that her desires would be molded by his own. Better to admit that he'd mistaken the intimacy they'd shared in the kitchen and in the bedroom, and in the living room too, and out in the woods, for love.

He did the only thing he knew how to do: He retreated into his work, his NHI proposal, which was due on March 1: "Managed Ecstasy: An Ethnography of the Church of the Burning Bush with Signs Following."

Marxists and Freudians offered alternate explanations, as they did for everything. According to the Marxists the Pentecostal movement should be understood as a response to hard economic times. Industrialization had transformed rural Appalachian society. Railroads made mining and logging possible on a grand scale. Capitalist owners of coal and timber companies had bought up huge tracts of land from unsuspecting farmers, who were reduced from independent yeoman to laborers. Missionaries from the traditional denominations—Methodist, Presbyterian, Baptist— legitimated the exploitation. The holiness churches grew up as a kind of resistance movement, developing practices that set them apart from the secular world as a way of preserving their identity.

In the Freudian version of the story repressed sexuality was evident at every turn, tension between a pleasure-prohibiting religious culture—an overdeveloped superego—and the demands of the id, projected onto the eroticized Serpent. The preachers tended to be psychopathic personalities who enjoyed baiting authority figures—the police, the law, God himself; risk takers who believed themselves to be exempt from the iron laws of nature—from the heat of the fire, from the toxic effects of strychnine and rattlesnake venom.

As an anthropologist, Jackson found these explanations too reductionist. He proposed linking the practice of snake handling to the snake cults of Africa and the ancient Near East, and to the snake dance of the Hopi. In all the Old World stories, the snake comes to bring a message of immortality, but the message is, through some mischance, perverted and immortality is lost. There's even good reason to believe that in the earliest versions of the stories the serpent is none other than the original creator God.

He also placed the Church of the Burning Bush with Signs Following squarely in the tradition of ecstatic religion going back to the worship of Dionysus, of the mother goddess Demeter at Eleusis. To tarantism, and Mardi Gras, and rock festivals. To early Christianity, which was experiential rather than dogmatic, which depended on certain experiences, such as glossolalia. What Plutarch had said about the initiation at Eleusis held for early Christianity. The pilgrims were transformed not by something they learned but by something they experienced. Something that had disappeared almost entirely from mainstream religion.

Jackson's NHI proposal was completed in plenty of time. The deadline was Wednesday, March 1. He'd had it ready to go on the previous Friday, but instead of spending a couple of hours at the Xerox machine, cranking out copies, he had to file his proposal electronically. All NHI proposals, starting in year 2000, had to be filed electronically to comply with the new Federal Financial Assistance Management Improvement Act of 1999, also known as Public Law 106–107.

Jackson called the NHI help desk. He begged them to let him submit a paper proposal—or submit his proposal as an attachment—but he got nowhere.

It wasn't possible simply to submit the proposal as a document attached to an e-mail. You had to use special software, which had to be downloaded electronically, and then, if you used a Macintosh computer, you had to download special software in order to use the special software that you'd already downloaded. And you had to be registered. The TF grants officer was tearing his hair. TF had in fact registered. The registration had been confirmed more than once by the business office. There were a lot of complicated passwords that the grants officer had printed out for anyone submitting a proposal, but on Tuesday Jackson's user name and password were repeatedly refused. By whom? It wasn't clear.

It turned out that Jackson's proposal had not been properly authorized by the university comptroller, despite the fact that TF had registered with the NHI months earlier.

On Monday the comptroller tried to register Jackson but couldn't do it without a special PIN number. She called the NHI help desk. The person didn't know how to locate the PIN number, but did know that it would take ten days to get a new one.

The comptroller spent the afternoon on the phone, with Jackson at her elbow, looking through file folders and listening at the same time. She eventually came up with the elusive PIN number and was able to register Jackson as a user.

On Tuesday it turned out that Jackson didn't have the right version of Adobe Acrobat on his computer. He could fill out certain necessary forms on his office computer, but he couldn't save them, so he had to transfer all his files into an updated version of Adobe on a computer in the grants office.

At four o'clock on Tuesday afternoon he pushed the "send" button on the computer in the grants office and received a "submission successful" message, which was cause for celebration, but by five o'clock various error messages had arrived via e-mail: His proposal failed to include the credentials for the Senior/Key Person Profile component. He would have to start all over, using a different NHI Web site for Corrected Proposals. He would also need a Common User ID.

The NHI help desk in Washington was closed, and he got nothing but automated responses to his e-mails telling him not to respond to this response.

He went over the error messages with the grants officer. It turned out that he needed to type his own name in all capital letters on the cover sheet for the proposal.

On Wednesday morning he called NHI and learned that the

Senior/Key Person was his department chair, Baker Kimbrough. He added Baker Kimbrough's vital statistics and re-entered his proposal (sixteen separate files) on the Web site for Corrected Proposals—with his name typed in all capital letters. He and the grants officer had made more than sixty calls to the NHI help desk and had received as many e-mails.

At three o'clock on Wednesday afternoon he pushed "send" again on the computer in the grants office and received a "submission successful" message. He waited until four. No more error messages. He thanked the grants officer and went back to Davis Hall and sat down in the Common Room. He wasn't ready to go home. He and Sunny continued to live together as before, continued to cook dinner together and work together in the living room after dinner, but they didn't talk about Paris.

The only other person in the Common Room was a colleague in Philosophy whom Jackson had dubbed "the philosopher king," or, eventually, the "PK."

"You still going to Paris?" the PK asked, looking up from the book he was reading.

Jackson nodded.

"You and Sunny?"

"Going alone," Jackson said. "She's off to a herpetology conference in Mexico."

"Hunh."

There was no need to explain further.

"*Everyone* is going to Paris," the PK said. "Wittgenstein. Imagine a world where everyone was trying to get to Paris. It doesn't matter what they're doing right now. Their goal is to get to Paris."

"I want to get to Paris," Jackson said. "But most people have other things on their minds."

"Excuse me," the PK said. "I had it wrong. What Wittgenstein really said was, 'Everyone is *really* going to Paris.' It's a heuristic, you see. It doesn't matter whether or not they are consciously aware that what they're *really* doing is preparing to go to Paris. The point is, it makes *you* look at the world in a totally different way."

Various people entered the Common Room: Angela Shepherd, the chair of Philosophy; Paul Molson from the dean's office popped in, looking for someone who wasn't there, and then popped out again; more philosophers appeared; a couple of anthropologists. At every entrance the PK gave Jackson a meaningful look and mouthed *Paris.* The TF grants officer who had helped Jackson came in looking for Jackson. Jackson imagined all of them bound for Paris.

Paris, Jackson thought. But he held up his hand to ward off bad news from the grants officer: "Don't tell me . . ."

"No," the grants officer said. "It's all right. I just got a confirmation e-mail from NHI. I thought you'd want to know."

"Thanks," Jackson. "I don't think I'm up for another battle."

Everyone was interested in Jackson's experience with the NHI, which Jackson turned into a humorous adventure, though he was still somewhat shaken.

The coffee and the stories ran out at the same time, five o'clock. It was time to go home, and everyone left except Jackson, who was remembering how Warren used to show up at five o'clock and plop himself down in one of the comfortable chairs with a story about the winter of '71, when the snow drifted up over the windows on the first floor and the power had been out for three days, or with a question about the greenhouse effect or the situation in the Middle East. And you'd soon find out that he knew more about whatever it was than you did.

It was dark when he got home. And bitter cold. Snow from the empty fields had drifted across the drive and he thought for a minute he wasn't going to make it. He opened the window so he could tell if Sunny'd built a fire. He could smell the wood smoke before he could see the house.

Outwardly things were the same. There were no more quarrels. They were making love regularly. But inwardly he could feel her pulling away from him. Maybe not pulling. But drifting away from the shore, letting the current carry her. There was open water between them. He thought she could still hear him calling. But he couldn't hear her calling back.

16

Translocation

Jackson was angry at first, when I told him that I couldn't go to Paris. I didn't blame him—I'd have been pissed too—but there was no way I was going to change my mind. But then he apologized. He thought it was a good idea, that going to a conference would be good for my academic career. I was relieved. I knew how disappointed he was and I'd been prepared for a scene, or a bigger scene. I was disappointed too. I wanted to go to Paris, but I also wanted Jackson to put up more of a fight, to storm around a little more. It was Claire who really laid into me. I'd never seen Claire so mad, not even when Maya got into her New York chocolate cheesecake at the millennium party. "What the fuck do you think you're doing? You fucking whore. How could you do this to Jackson after all he's done for you? You're like one of those female rattlesnakes you told us about that won't breed unless you've got two males in the cage with you, with two penises each."

"Not two penises," I said. "Hemipene. The male reproductive organ is bilobed . . ."

"Jesus Christ," she said. "What next?"

And so on. No one had ever talked to me like this, not even Earl. I didn't try to defend myself. I just sat there, at a table in Seymour Union, and took it. The funny thing was, Claire wasn't shouting, she was talking in a low husky voice so she wouldn't make a scene. But it wasn't funny. I felt bad. Was I really like a female snake that needed two males in a cage with her, each with two hemipene?

I went down to the cemetery, but Warren wasn't any more sympathetic than Claire. *You don't need a man to look after you? You need a man to whup your tail like Earl done. God damn it anyway. You got a good man who loves you and you don't treat him no better than you treated your jerk of a husband. Don't come back here till you get this nonsense out of your head.*

Crotalus horridus horridus eats mice, shrews, chipmunks, squirrels, rabbits, bats, and also birds, bird eggs, other snakes, and amphibians and in turn is eaten by badgers, hawks, king snakes and racers, and hogs. The major threat to the long-term survival is habitat degradation and destruction; and rattlesnake roundups, like the ones in Texas, where thousands of snakes are slaughtered every year; and the commercial skin and live pet trade (boot companies in Texas and Tennessee); and the meat trade; and the novelty trade (stuffed and mounted snakes, jewelry, watchbands, and the like).

It was a big project. Cramer had been preparing all winter, scrambling around for funding. In Little Egypt rattlesnakes tend to snooze through the winter without actually hibernating, but up north they aggregate in the fall (like gypsies) and spend the winter together in dens below the frost line, sleeping in each other's arms, so to speak. They're vulnerable because if a farmer or rattlesnake hunter discovers the den, he can dynamite it—though dynamiting is illegal—or remove so many snakes that the colony is no longer viable. They emerge in the spring and mate in early summer before dispersing. But how do they choose a den in the first place? Some dens have been occupied since the beginning of time (as far as anyone knows). Other apparently ideal den sites remain empty. How far do rattlesnakes travel in the summer? How do they find their way back to their den? What would happen if you moved (translocated) an entire colony to a site that already had an existing colony? To a site where there was no existing colony? Would the snakes disperse, or would they stay together? The translocation of snakes has received very little systematic scientific attention. That's why Cramer was so excited. I was excited too.

Cramer's plan was to capture the snakes as soon as we had a spell of warm weather—capture them when they were just waking up, before they became active in April and started wandering all over the place. He wanted to release them in a suitable denning area on state-owned land before the end of April. So we still had six to eight weeks to prepare and two weeks to implant the radio transmitters. We'd have the snakes in captivity for a month at most, and we had to set up a serpentarium or hot-snake lab in a storage area in the basement, the only place we could find with running water and enough room for the forty Neodesha escape-proof cages with triple latches on glass doors that could be locked, and two big soapstone tables and cabinets for the surgical equipment. The cages couldn't be stacked, so special shelves had to be built to hold them, and the room had to be rewired for forty individual heaters, one in each cage, and it had to be snake-proofed. Cramer was a fanatic on safety protocols. There are only three things to remember, he said, over and over: one, security; two, security; three, security. All the vents and ducts required special snake-proof grates; the doors required special seals, and so on. "If someone gets bit and drops dead, I don't want the snake to be able to get out of the room."

No one was to enter the lab who wasn't certified. The list of those permitted to enter was not a long one: Cramer, Laura, Frank, and I, two local veterinarians; and two other biology professors. The three biology professors were the only ones with keys.

The setup was very different from the Church of the Burning Bush. At the church a certain amount of effort went into keeping children away from the snakes, but snakeboxes were left lying around, and if a snake got loose it was no big deal. Someone would pick it up and put it back in its box. But if a snake were to get loose in the lab it would be a major emergency. There were procedures to be followed. These were posted on the inside of the door and on the outside of the door. If you were going to be working with a hot snake, you had to put up a sign on the outside of the door. And so on. Emergency telephone numbers were posted.

By mid-March the lab was ready and we'd completed mountains of paperwork to comply with Illinois Administrative Code, Title 17: Conservation. Cramer's five-year radio-telemetry translocation project didn't really fit one of their categories, but in the end they made it fit: It would bring together the overlapping disciplines of population ecology and genetics, behavioral biology, conservation biology, and speciation—enough research agendas to keep graduate students busy for years.

We made our move on the last Saturday in March, when the temperatures got up into the seventies. Jackson wanted to go too, but Cramer had said no. Jackson hadn't been trained, hadn't practiced with them, he wasn't part of the team. Sorry.

We assembled at eight o'clock in the parking lot on the west side of Buehl Hall. Cramer got there first in a TF truck with a crew cab. He had brought moose-hide boots and heavy gloves for everyone. He'd also brought a pair of small shovels to open up the den. The shovels, and the newness of everything, especially the moose-hide boots, made me suspect that Cramer had figured out how to hunt rattlesnakes by reading a book. All the equipment in the back of the pickup—hooks and grabbers and tongs—was brand new, including my own favorite snake-handling tool, which I'd made out of a butterfly net. You could attach a canvas snake sack to the frame of the net. You couldn't scoop up a snake, but you could persuade it to crawl in the sack.

And think about it. There were only two rattlesnakes in the herp lab at TF, and their venom sacs had been removed, so they were no longer "hot," and besides, they were too old to put up any kind of resistance to being picked up with a hook. We might as well have been practicing with rubber snakes. And Cramer was planning to dig up the den with a couple of little shovels. It would take a week and a day. I'd brought a little bottle of gasoline and a fifty-foot plastic tube—just in case. The smell of gasoline would roust the snakes.

Laura and Frank soon joined us in Frank's old VW, the kind that looked like a bug. Laura, who had tucked her curls into a straw hat, as if we were going on a picnic, had brought her own fashionable boots and protested when Cramer insisted she wear the moose-hide ones. Frank had brought a new camera and took a lot of pictures, mostly of Laura.

We drove past fields that would soon be planted with corn and soybeans through some backcountry that had never been farmed—about as deep into the country as you can get in central Illinois. I had driven around a lot, exploring, and still didn't know where we were, but if you looked in Jackson's *Illinois County Atlas* you'd see a wide-open area about fifteen miles south of town with no roads. You'd see a network of streams, and an old abandoned railroad that used to run from Stockwell to Hardin Springs, and an old railroad grade coming out of Homecroft. That's where the snakes had to be.

Laura had discovered that I was also going to the ASIH meetings, and she wasn't too happy about it. She would be giving a paper in one of the sessions for graduate students, but she didn't see any reason for me to go, since I was only a lowly freshman and she was about to embark on her Ph.D. dissertation. She was also unhappy about sitting in the back seat with Frank, while I rode shotgun, and she kept leaning forward to discuss, with Cramer, the problem of settling her dissertation topic: she'd been planning to work on the phylogeography of North American rat snakes using mitochondrial DNA, but now she was wondering if it would be a good idea to switch to rattlesnakes.

I countered with some rattlesnake stories.

Frank, I thought, was basically a decent guy, but he was in love with Laura and nothing he did seemed to please her. He was a nervous type and reminded me of my cousin Raymond, who'd gotten bit by a copperhead once that cured him of Lyme disease. At least that's what Earl said. Frank was trim and fit from running five miles every morning before breakfast, but he kept chewing on one strand of his long black hair. His dissertation was on population genetics; he worked with fruit flies, whose reproductive cycle is only seven to eleven days. I figured he'd volunteered for the rattlesnake hunt in order to be with Laura.

We passed the house of the farmer who'd discovered the snakes in the first place and kept going on County Road N and turned off on a dirt track, an old access road, that stopped in the middle of nowhere. We left the truck and walked into the woods half a mile to the den. We'd have to carry the snakes back to the truck, each snake in its own canvas sack. Back in Naqada we just put them in a big garbage can and hauled the can out of the woods, but Cramer had nixed this idea because he was afraid the snakes would smother.

We lugged all our sacks and hooks and grabbers into the woods, following Cramer single file, not talking. We had a snake-bite kit, in case of an emergency, though according to Cramer traditional remedies were contraindicated: mouth suction, incising the bite across the fang marks, tourniquets, applying ice. Not good. But the kit contained a vacuum extractor that would work if you used it right away. And St. Francis Hospital in Colesville had agreed to maintain an adequate supply of CroFab antivenin.

We didn't see much animal life except squirrels, fox squirrels and gray squirrels, which Cramer said almost never shared the same territory. What was going on? Another dissertation topic.

We followed Cramer along a creek that hadn't had time to straighten itself out. He went right to the den, on a little bluff that rose up about twenty yards from the creek—a long way to carry the snakes.

As we set out equipment down at the den site, about ten or twelve deer gave us a quick look and disappeared into the woods.

It was chilly, but we'd worked up a sweat by the time we got to the den and we unbuttoned our coats. Cramer pulled out a hip flask of whiskey and passed it around.

"Now what?" Frank shifted back and forth on his feet, as if he had to go to the bathroom. He passed on the whiskey. Laura took a swig and handed the flask to me. I hadn't tasted whiskey since I left Naqada. Jackson never kept any around, just beer and wine, and a supply of crème de cassis. It probably wasn't a good idea, but I swigged anyway.

We got our gear laid out, and Cramer reminded us to be careful with the hooks, to lift the snakes in the center. If you grab a snake too high up and jerk it around you can break its neck, which sometimes happened in church, where the snake's death would be attributed to the power of the Lord. Cramer knew a lot, but I had a feeling he'd never actually hunted rattlesnakes before.

I let Cramer and Frank dig for a while. They were trying to dig under the rocky ledge. It was hard going, even with the new shovels with pointed tips like a spade and serrated blades. It would have taken forever to open up the den the way they were going at it. After about fifteen minutes I took out my coil of plastic tubing and poked it down one of the holes into the den till I couldn't poke it any further. I put my ear at the end of the tube. Nothing. I tried another hole. Nothing. Then a third hole. This time I could hear some singing. "They're down there," I said. I took my little bottle of gasoline from my coat pocket and poured a few drops into the end of the tube. Cramer made disapproving noises, but it was pretty clear by now that we'd never open up the den with the shovels. I blew on the end of the tube, sending gasoline fumes into the den. You can kill the snakes that way if you use too much gasoline, but Cramer didn't know that. And then we waited. Now *I* was nervous. Impatient. But after about ten minutes we saw our first two rattlers. They stuck their heads out of two different holes and looked around. It didn't take long for more snakes to emerge. I congratulated myself, since no one else was interested in doing it for me.

Most of the snakes were groggy, and the easiest thing would have been just to pick them up by their necks—gently—and drop them in the sacks, but protocol demanded that we use the hooks.

Most of the snakes were about three feet. Some of the younger ones were smaller. The largest one, about four feet, was wide awake and looked annoyed.

The whole thing, actually, was pretty wonderful. Not many people have seen what we saw: about thirty specimens of *Crotalus horridus horridus* all in one place. They're smaller than your eastern diamondback, and not as feisty. There were some flashy rat snakes too, which often den with timber rattlers, but the timbers were beautiful in their own modest ground colors, basic browns and greens and yellows. It was an astonishing sight, and I was glad that Frank had brought his camera.

We faced each other—snakes and humans—like two football teams facing each other across the line of scrimmage, waiting for the referee to blow his whistle, or for the quarterback to call the play. But no one moved. Not for a long time. I didn't know what the others were thinking, but I was thinking of a verse from the Bible: "There are three things which are too wonderful for me, yea, four which I know not: the way of an eagle in the air; the way of a serpent upon a rock; the way of a ship in the midst of the sea; and the way of a man with a maid."

And I was thinking that someone had better do something. I attached one of the sacks to my butterfly-net frame and decided to face the four-foot snake that had lifted up its yellow head and was staring right at me with its lidless eyes. Earl would have pinned him with a forked stick. But you can hurt a snake that way, especially a big one. He'll twist and turn and maybe break his neck. Or her neck.

I took a deep breath. The muscles in my arm were twitching. My heart was pounding. My feet and arms were tingling. I had my hook in one hand and my net in the other, and the snake and I faced each other like a couple of Roman gladiators. I was the one with the net and the three-pronged stick. Or maybe like two lovers who've taken all their clothes off for the first time and are sizing each other up.

I wanted to get the hook under its middle, a little toward the front, but when I touched him with the hook he exploded and went into a defensive coil, his rattle singing.

I moved toward him, staying out of striking range. About two feet. I distracted him with the net, holding it over his head. Snakes can't strike up, which is why deer and horses can trample them so easily. Earl would sometimes wave a hankie over a snake and then reach down and scratch it right on top of its head. It would have been an impressive trick, but I decided against it.

I kept touching the snake with the hook, and every time I touched him, he struck, leaving gobs of yellow-orange venom on the hook itself and on the handle. I kept doing this to wear him down, and after a dozen strikes, he straightened out and started to head into the woods. I dropped the net and managed to get the hook under his middle and lift him up. He was heavy, probably about four pounds. Four pounds may not seem like much, but four pounds of twisting rattlesnake on the end of a stick will wear your arms out pretty fast.

"Hand me the sack" I barked. Nobody moved. I barked again: "The net. Somebody hold the net under him." Finally Cramer held up the net. I tried to maneuver the snake tail first into the sack, but he kept swinging his head around to look at me. I twisted the hook one last time to slide him into the net, but he straightened out his neck, in a kind of clumsy strike, and glided over the edge of the net, his head sticking straight out into midair. I worked him back till most of the weight was over the sack. I lowered the hook suddenly and the snake disappeared into the sack.

I was hardly conscious of what had been happening. The other snakes were slowly coming to life. Some were singing. I put the net on the ground and blocked the snake with the handle of the hook while I unsnapped the net from the frame. I folded the top of the bag over and fastened it. The handle of the hook was still thick with venom.

We had our first rattlesnake. I was wild with excitement, which I did my best to conceal. This was better than being anointed.

There was venom on the net and on the sack as well as on the handle of the hook. I cleaned both sack, net, and hook with water from the stream, while Cramer passed the whiskey around again.

I could feel the power surging through me, not from being

anointed, but from being in touch with something. What? A snake is just a snake, but still . . . I was psyched up.

Cramer suddenly moved into action, ordering everyone around, handing out equipment, wading in with his new tongs, forgetting his own advice about not stressing the snakes. I held the net for him and we bagged snakes two, three, and four. But too late for Cramer. I'd already established who was in charge.

The whiskey was hot and strong in my stomach.

By noon we'd bagged thirty-two snakes, including two gravid females. I could see each snake in detail, as though I were looking through a special magnifying lens that allowed me to register the number of rattles and scales over the forehead and at other key places without actually counting. I blew a little more gasoline into the den and a couple more snakes emerged. Cramer and I watched as Frank and Laura bagged them. A third snake—large, active, wide awake—crawled into the woods, moving slowly. I followed with my hook till we encountered a ground squirrel. I expected the squirrel to back off, but instead it stood up its rear paws, almost on tiptoe, and waved its tail back and forth. I'd seen this happen once or twice in Naqada, when we were hunting snakes. The hairs on the squirrel's tail were erect, like a cat that's been struck by lightning in a comic strip. The squirrel had probably been protecting its pups. In any case the snake backed off. We watched for a few minutes. Cramer was very interested. I hooked the snake and Laura bagged it.

It took half an hour to carry the bagged snakes back to the truck, and another half hour to get back to the new serpentarium. We spent the rest of the day getting the snakes into their new crates and labeling them. It was the end of a big day. I was tired, but my body was radiating heat and energy, and as I was about to lock the cage holding the big rattlesnake that had given me such a hard time at the beginning, I slid open the glass door and put my hand around the snake just to feel its strength. Like one of Jackson's powerful erections! It only took four or five seconds, but I think Cramer noticed, because he looked at me over the tops of his glasses.

"I'm having a little trouble with this door," I said. "It sticks."

He could have made an issue out of it, but he let it go.

The crates looked like rows of computer monitors lined up on their new shelves.

The next day we would start checking the snakes for mites and parasites. Ideally the snakes should be quarantined for at least a month, but we were going to turn them loose in two weeks if we could get the transmitters implanted, and if the weather cooperated.

In the parking lot outside Buehl Hall we were reluctant to say good-bye. It had been an adventure, and we'd bonded, though in a funny way. Funny like the Shakespeare play where everybody gets mixed up. Frank wanted Laura to go for a drink; Laura didn't want to leave me behind with Cramer. But Frank was impatient to leave and dragged Laura off with him in his VW. I was glad that they'd both bagged several snakes despite Frank's obvious fear.

There was a tiny bit of whiskey left in the flask, and standing by the TF truck, Cramer and I finished it. It was a good feeling, warm and dangerous. I wasn't surprised when Cramer put an arm around me. I thought he was going to bend over and kiss me, and he did. I almost exploded. He smelled of snake—musky and meaty. I knew I'd crossed a line, but it was a line I'd crossed before, and I was a little bit sad rather than worried. I thought I could draw another line around this kiss and keep it separate from the rest of my life.

That night Jackson and I drank beer while I cooked two small steaks on the French stove—*Steak au poivre*—and then we drank a little red wine with the steaks. I drank just enough to maintain my high. After we finished the dishes I went upstairs and put on my French outfit. I wanted to discover whose version of myself I was going to be. I hadn't washed it, and it was wrinkled and still had the red wine stains down the front. I doubted if they'd ever come out. My small breasts looked nice and firm in the spaghetti-strap camisole. I admired myself in the mirror over Jackson's big chestnut dresser. I don't think I've ever been so aroused. The dress was like the magic girdle I read about in Western Civ. Not a girdle girdle but some kind of a belt that you fastened under your breasts. More like a bra than a belt. Hera, the queen of the gods, borrows it from Aphrodite, the goddess of love, when she wants to seduce her husband. All you have to do is put it on and you are irresistible. That's the way I felt. Irresistible to myself too, even though I hadn't taken a shower, and when I put my hands up to my nose I could smell snake and gasoline and whiskey (and maybe Cramer too). My body was trembling, just the way it had when I'd confronted the big snake. My mind was spinning, my heart pounding, my feet and hands tingling, my stomach churning.

"Jackson," I called. "Come up here. I want to show you something."

He took his time, made me wait.

Then on the stairs. I felt each step like a smart sassy slap on the ass.

At the top of the stairs we confronted each other in a rush of fear and of pleasure. I could hear my own bones singing, like a rattle-snake's rattle. I could feel my stomach coiling, and below my stomach, something ready to strike.

"I wondered what happened to that outfit," Jackson said, looking me up and down. "But I was afraid to ask."

"You look ten times better than you did when I got here," I said. "You look like you're full of life." I could already feel his hands on me. I unfastened the *cache-coeur* and the little putty-colored skirt and then pulled the cami over my head, like a snake shedding its skin. I could feel my blood thickening. I was turning into DX's two-headed snake, into a powerful erection that would pulse under this man's touch. I was Snakewoman, I was the python in the San cave in the Tsodilo Hills, and when we embraced we turned into the ancient Mesopotamian tree of life. His kisses were like blood and salt.

But afterwards, when he turned to me and asked, "What just happened?" I didn't say anything about the snakes.

"What just happened?" I had to think. "My heart started beating faster," I said, "and my breathing got faster too, and I tightened all my muscles, and my nipples got hard, and my clit swelled up and my pelvic area got engorged with blood, and I had about fifteen muscle contractions, and then my body got rigid, and then it relaxed. Why? What do *you* think happened?"

"You took me inside you," he said, "and devoured my seed when I was most vulnerable, and you were most triumphant. I explored your dark continent at my own risk. You lured me on. But because I survived the encounter, you will now share your great riches and power with me, because you love me."

It wasn't really funny, but I started to laugh. "Is that what *really* happened?"

"That's what really happened," he said.

I thought maybe he was right.

There were no more Cramer kisses, no brushings up against each other, no secret glances—just the kind of intimacy that comes from working closely together in a crowded lab. Four of us working together, collecting blood and fecal samples, and tissue samples that would have to be stained, sectioned, and sequenced in order to determine genetic variability.

Cramer did the first surgical implants himself. I had to admire him. He hadn't done it before, but he didn't flinch. During the first one he was on a speakerphone with a woman from the University of Florida.

"Maneuver the snake head-first into the plastic tube," the voice said. "Head first. Just hold the body and slide it up into the tube." The voice was talking to me. The snake felt like a pulsing penis in my hand. It twisted and turned till the anesthetic flowing through the tube took effect.

Cramer made an incision towards the lower third of the snake and placed the transmitter itself under the ribcage and tied it to a rib, and then he slid the flexible antenna between the skin and the pink flesh along the ribcage and stitched the snake up.

Forty minutes. We were all sweating.

I took the snake out of the tube and put it in its Neodesha cage and triple-locked the door. C.h.h.1. *Crotalus horridus horridus* 1. All the vital signs seemed to be okay.

We thought of giving the snakes names: Slinky, Creepy, Crawly. But then we ran out of names, and Cramer vetoed a plan to name them after biology professors.

We did two more implants that afternoon and then called it a day.

It took a week to insert all the transmitters and to weigh and measure the snakes and check them thoroughly for mites. Cramer taught Laura and Frank and me how to insert the transmitters.

Before releasing them in a new denning area we had to wait for the weather to warm up again after a cold snap. We wanted to get them to their new home before they started to shed. Once they're shedding, you can't handle them without damaging the skin.

17

Fleecing the Lord

Jackson managed to convince himself that Sunny was doing the right thing and did his best to support and encourage her—locating material on Baja California and La Paz, where the conference was going to be held, and ordering a book about snakes in Baja. He looked at his mother's slides again, several times, letting the slides transport him back into that world where he could be eleven years old again. He'd visit his old school, have dinner with Suzanne and her husband and children, he'd walk along the Seine, eat at the Café de Flore. His clothes were packed. His tickets were in his briefcase with his passport. He was going to fly from Peoria to O'Hare instead of driving.

But the moment Sunny left—Cramer picked her up in a TF car on Tuesday morning at three o'clock for the drive up to O'Hare—he went to pieces. His joints swelled up, and by first light he couldn't recognize his own truck in the drive when he looked out the bedroom window, he couldn't sleep, he could hardly get out of bed, he couldn't tell right from left, couldn't tell the front door from the

back door, couldn't tie his shoes. And all the time he felt that someone was right behind him, a presence, but he couldn't be bothered to
turn his head. So, he thought, this is what love is really like. He took
two big sky-blue capsules of doxycycline, which he had trouble
swallowing. He stayed in bed on Tuesday, and Wednesday too, getting up only to take more doxycycline and to feed Maya and let her
out. On Thursday morning—his flight was not until one o'clock—he
felt better. He threw some clothes and his *Guide Bleu* into a suitcase,
gathered up his tickets and passport, and dropped Maya off at
Claire's. Claire took one look at him and told him he wasn't going
anywhere. We'll get you to a doctor and then you'll stay right here.
But he wouldn't listen to her. Her voice seemed to come to him from
a long way away, and while she was explaining things to her husband, in his study, he got in the car and headed for the airport in
Peoria, but instead of taking the airport exit, he kept going, heading
south on 155, picking up I55 at Lincoln. Six hours later he was in
Naqada, parked in front of the Naqada Inn. He was in bad shape.

Gladys Rose, who ran the hotel, gave him his regular room, the
Winterthur Room on the second floor, overlooking the river.

"You don't look good," she said.

"Just tired," he said. "It's a long drive."

He closed the heavy velvet drapes and sat down on the edge of the
big double bed and watched the dust motes suspended in the beam
of light that sliced through the narrow opening where the drapes
failed to come together. He sat down at the desk and started to write
a letter to Sunny, tried to explain, again, the difference between
looking *at* the beam of light and looking *along* it, but his head wasn't
clear and he didn't think he was getting it right, so he tried to explain his feelings. Jealousy, of course. Which he wanted to conceal
or at least soften. It was a matter of principle. But what principle?
What did he want to say? He was writing with a blue ball-point pen

on a piece of glossy motel stationery with the name of the hotel—The Naqada Inn—at the top. The main thing: He wanted to leave the door open. Maybe he was jumping to conclusions. About Sunny and Cramer. He didn't realize he was writing in French until he couldn't remember the word for *drape.*

He pushed the chair back and stood up to walk to the bed. His knees were swollen. He grabbed the back of the chair and used it as a walker. He was disoriented, worse than on his first night in the Forest with Claude, his first night of the real fieldwork—for which he'd been preparing himself ever since Anthropology 101 at the University of Chicago—and he was unnerved by every stimulus. What am I doing here? He could see the folly of anthropology, the folly of seeing "through" everything. It was like having X-ray vision. If you could see through *every*thing, you wouldn't be able to see *any*thing. He thought he could smell kerosene, though it was summer, hot outside, and the room was air-conditioned.

When he woke up, Earl was sitting on the edge of the bed. "I brought you some sassafras tea," Earl said. "Mrs. Rose called me."

Jackson swallowed some tea. It tasted like root beer.

"Isn't sassafras illegal?" Jackson asked. "A carcinogen?"

"This here is homemade," Earl said. He'd already asked DX to round up some of the women from the church to come and pray over Jackson. Jackson didn't have the strength to object. Didn't want to object.

Later the women from the church came to his room. Their warmth and kindness took him back to his childhood. This was what they knew how to do. These were the women you could count on for help, the women who knew what to do when someone died, or when there was an accident at the mill or the grain elevator. Women he could picture at a church supper in the Methodist church in Kendallville, where his grandparents worshipped.

The women told stories about healing.

"If the Lord can handle snakebite," Jackson asked, "why not a broken collarbone?"

There was quite a bit of controversy over this matter. The women offered examples and counter examples. They knew their Bibles—Saint Paul getting serpent bit in Malta, Jesus healing the sick, raising the dead too. Lazarus, and the little girl . . . And they had examples from their own experience.

"But was the person really dead?" Jackson asked.

"Absolutely."

Earl came back in the evening, bringing Mawmaw Tucker. They did a lot of praying, touching, laying on of hands. Earl and DX too. It was unnerving to see grown men on their knees.

The visit by Mawmaw Tucker was regarded as quite an honor. She placed her hands on his head, over his face, and he could feel the swelling in his knees going down. Her drooping lower lip was moist and reflected the light.

"You was in the Garden," she said.

Ordinary reality seemed to recede. Jackson seemed to be looking down on himself, and on Earl and DX and Mawmaw Tucker and the other women, as if he were floating above them. They began to talk, not to each other, but individually. Babblings. Ejaculations. Murmurings. But measured, pulsating phrases of equal length, every pulse beginning with a heavy stress that faded away in a kind of trochaic rhythm. As an anthropologist Jackson thought immediately of shamanistic spirit possession—in the Zar cult of Ethiopia, or among the Lapps and the Yakut, or among the Ke'let, when the spirit enters the shaman's body, or the Semang, who chant to invoke the *cenoi*, who then speak to the shamans and through them.

But Jackson was also inside the experience, and from the inside—looking along the beam of light instead of at it—the talking became a kind of music, a kind of chanting. He seemed to see things as if he were a child seeing them for the first time, as if he were looking out the window at the river, waiting, or as if he were waiting with his grandparents for a glimpse of the Twin Cities 400, the bright yellow train that ran from Chicago to Minneapolis. They'd driven up—he and his grandparents—to Muskegon and taken the ferry to Milwaukee and they were waiting in a park for the train to appear. He tried to put the experience into words, but he was like a child who hasn't learned to talk, who could only cry out. And then the words came, in a strange language. He could explain every-thing. But only for a moment, or a few moments. Then Mawmaw Tucker took her hands off his head, just as the train was streaming by below them, and his daughter was waving from the last window of the last car.

"I was there too," she said. Taking him by surprise. "It's hard to explain." Her eyes were moist. "Them mountains was just like you said. And the rivers too."

He didn't have to tell her that he wanted her to put her hands back on his head. She already knew what he wanted. He closed his eyes and focused on her touch.

"When you were dead?" he asked.

"Ummm."

When he opened his eyes and looked up into her face, he saw a young woman looking down on him.

"How old were you?"

"I was only twenty-four."

"That was a long time ago."

"During the war," she said. "My husband was killed in the Phil-ippines. I keeled right over when they come with the news. His plane went down. They never found it."

"I'm sorry," he said.

227

"It's all right. My sisters come from across the river and took care of me."

Jackson had more questions, but there was a knocking on the door and the door opened. It was Mrs. Rose. "The doctor's here," she said. "You're going to have to leave. This is a hotel, not a church."

Mawmaw Tucker rose up. She was a large heavy-set woman in a wide gray dress the color of winter sky. "Is that Dr. Arnold?" she asked.

The doctor stepped into the room, a middle-aged man with a thick mustache that covered his upper lip.

Mawmaw Tucker approached the doctor. "Dr. Arnold," she said "this man needs to be prayed over more than he needs whatever you're sellin'."

"Mrs. Tucker," the doctor said, "I know you and I don't see eye to eye, but if you put your mind to it you might remember wanting to see me when you had that appendicitis, and if I put my mind to it, I think I might remember three or four other visits . . ."

"You take care of your business here as quick as you can and then kindly leave us be."

The doctor asked Jackson a few questions and got him back on his doxycycline. He held one of the big blue and white pills up for everyone to admire. Jackson swallowed it with the remains of his sassafras tea.

"Give him something to eat," Mawmaw Tucker said when the doctor had gone. "He's hungry. Tell Mrs. Rose to bring him some soup."

And he *was* hungry. And Mrs. Rose did bring him some soup.

The next day he was feeling better. He was tired, and his joints ached. But not so bad. Earl picked him up at the hotel and they drove down several hairpin turns to the marina in Naqada, where Earl kept his boat.

The air was warm, heavy with fish stink. "The river's rising," Earl said, smacking a mosquito on his forehead, leaving a spot of blood. "This is good if it don't get too high. It gets too high, them fish hide off in the swamps where you can't find 'em."

Jackson didn't care. He liked fishing with Earl and DX in Earl's flat-bottomed johnboat with its square prow and a big Evinrude motor on the stern and four outriggers, two on each side. Jackson's grandfather had had a rowboat, which he kept over at Little Long Lake, where they fished for bluegills and crappie. And he'd fished in the Seine once with his father, with rented tackle, but they hadn't caught any fish.

As they rounded a bend in the river, south of Naqada, Earl told DX to get out the bait. "I sometimes wonder if Jesus was a fisherman," he said, looking at Jackson. "He picked fishermen for his disciples, but the Bible don't say anything about Jesus himself fishing. You ever think about that?"

"Fishers of men," Jackson said. "I will make you fishers of men."

"That's me too. I'm a fisher of men."

"And I'm a fish?"

"That's the idea. When you're sick like this, you got to ask God to heal you. Look at how much better you are already. When you got here you couldn't hardly move. Now look at you. Walking around. Just with the women asking God to heal you . . . You're feeling better, right?"

Jackson nodded.

"You can see it plain as day. But you still ain't right with the Lord, and you know what I'm talking about."

Jackson didn't say anything.

"Now she's done you like she done me. Ain't that what you told me last night, or don't you remember? That's what's making you sick."

"It's the Lyme disease," Jackson said. "Stress makes it act up."

"You got to get this settled in your mind, one way or the other. Maybe put a fleece out on the Lord. Like Gideon. So you'll know what to do. Maybe stand up and confront this man, and maybe whup Fern's tail. Or walk away from it, like I done."

"Gideon?"

"It was Gideon that saved Israel from the Midianites. He was down to three hundred men, and so he put a fleece out on the Lord. A fleece, you know. Wool. From a sheep. He put the fleece out on the ground and said that if the dew came only on the fleece and the ground around it was dry, then he'd know that God was going to save Israel by his hand. And that's what happened. The fleece was wet and the ground was dry. Then he done it the other way too, so the fleece was dry and the ground was wet. That was a sign from God. Like when I drove up to Colesville the first time to see Sunny at the prison. My truck needed a new head gasket. Where was I going to get the money? I put a fleece out on the Lord. I said, 'Lord, if you want me to make this trip, give me the money I need to fix that head gasket.' And the next day DX and a couple men from the church got a portable hoist and come over and they pulled the gasket right out in the front yard. That was the Lord showing me that I was meant to make the trip."

"So what am I supposed to do?"

Earl laughed. "If we get us a big blue cat," he said, "maybe that'll be the sign you're looking for."

"Winter's the best time for big blue cats," DX said.

"June is good too," Earl said. Earl explained everything. The Smithland Pool was formed by water backed up from the lock and dam on the Illinois side of the river, across from Smithland, Kentucky, all the way up to Uniontown, Kentucky, at the confluence of the Wabash and the Ohio. There used to be a lock and dam at

Naqada, but it was no longer necessary. The Smithland Pool holds
one hundred fifty kinds of fish. You've got to go upstream past Old
Shawneetown to catch sauger, but they were going for blue cats
today. "Guy over in Indiana caught one a hundred and four pounds
last year. Your blue cats are mean and tough, real fighters, like me.
Biggest one I ever caught was eighty-two pounds. Now I want to get
me one over a hundred. We're looking for deep water on an outside
turn."

The current seemed pretty fast to Jackson. He put his hand over
the side of the boat and trailed his fingers through the water.

"They like the bends, but there's hundreds of them on the river
and you got to find the right one. Your blue cats love the current.
They sit right in it all day long. I suppose it's like takin' a shower
for them."

Earl's depth finder showed they were in forty feet of water.

"We're looking for holes," he said. "Sixty, eighty feet deep."

Earl found a suitable spot and put down the anchor. They used
small shad with their tails cut off for bait, and fresh dead skipjacks
vacuum sealed from Earl's shop. Earl rigged up four big bait casting
rods on the outriggers, gave one to Jackson, and kept one himself.
One of the rods dipped down almost at once and Earl reeled in what
looked like a big fish to Jackson. A ten-pound blue cat, which Earl
threw back.

After half an hour they pulled in the anchor, reeled in the baits,
and tried another spot, in ninety feet of water. They weren't trolling—
just drifting. There was nothing to do but wait, like waiting for an idea
to come to you. It's out of your hands. *This is my fleece.* A sign. Something getting through to him from the other side. The world speaking to him. The Mbuti were the least superstitious people in the
world. Nonetheless, they spoke to the Forest, and the Forest spoke
to them. He thought of his old relationship with Claire. She'd ask

him what she should do, A or B, and if he said A, she might choose A, but then again, she might choose B. But she'd *know*.

The pole on one of the outriggers slammed down. Earl nodded at DX. "Hand the pole to Jackson. This here's the fish he's been waiting for." He turned to Jackson. "This here's your fish." DX lifted the pole out of the outrigger and handed it to Jackson. The fish put up a tremendous fight. Jackson had always thought catfish were sluggish, like suckers, but the fish pulled the boat downstream. Jackson forgot the swelling in his joints, in his shoulders, felt his own strength filling him as he reeled in the fish, letting out some line every now and then, Earl coaching him. "Reel him in. Give him some line. Don't pull too hard. Keep the tip of your rod up." Jackson was excited, and so was Earl. He forgot all about Lyme disease and arthritis. But the drag was set too tight. When he tried to adjust it, he released it unintentionally and the line shot out and went slack, but he managed to get it back on at about fifty pounds. They allowed the fish to drag the boat downriver until it tired and they got right on top of it and waited for it to surface.

The fish was still fighting when Earl hooked it with the gaff. It was the biggest fish Jackson had ever seen, except for the sturgeon his grandfather's friend Swede had caught in Lake Michigan. Earl put the fish on the scales. It weighed almost fifty pounds. He jiggled the scale until it did read fifty pounds. The fish had pulled them almost five hundred yards upstream.

What did it mean? Jackson wondered. They'd never specified what a fifty-pound fish would signify.

They were back at Earl's bait shop, in the marina. "A lot of fishermen," Earl said, "release big catfish—anything over twenty pounds. Too much trouble to clean. But I like the big ones. You can cut yourself a lot of nice steaks."

Earl put on a yellow rain slicker to clean the fish. With his fillet knife he put the blade through the bottom lip of the fish, then put a rope through the hole, tied a loop, and hoisted the fish up over a tree, as if he were dressing out a deer.

Outside was a sort of scaffolding for stringing up big fish and a wooden table for cleaning. The floor was covered with scales and bits of fish.

Once Earl had the fish hoisted up, the gills lay about eye level. He cut the tail off and let it bleed for five minutes. He was proud of his sharp knife. "Just runnin' the shadow across your finger'll make it bleed."

He cut the skin below the gills and used a fish skinner—a device that looked sort of like a fancy cheese slicer—to take off most of the skin. He cut the belly open and pulled out the guts.

He filleted the fish as he went along, and put the fillets in a picnic cooler with ice water.

"Some people put salt in the water," he said, "but that just makes 'em tough."

He gave some of the fillets to DX. "Tell Sally to cook these up," he said. "We'll be over about five o'clock."

18

Brush Arbor

He that believeth and is baptized shall be saved; but he that believeth not shall be damned. And these signs shall follow them that believe; In my name shall they cast out devils; they shall speak with new tongues; They shall take up serpents; and if they drink any deadly thing, it shall not hurt them; they shall lay hands on the sick, and they shall recover.
—Mark 16:16–18

The brush arbor meeting, which was going to be held in a woodlot belonging to an Amish farmer on the Kentucky side of the river, was a kind of homecoming that would draw people from Kentucky, Alabama, West Virginia, and East Tennessee. Preachers from holiness churches around Appalachia would preach, but the main attraction would be the traveling evangelist Punkin Bates.

Jackson armed himself with a couple of harps he always carried in the glove compartment of his truck. Earl put a chainsaw in the back of the truck and they left Naqada early on Sunday morning to help set up the arbor. They crossed the river on a ferry at Cave In Rock, an old pirate hangout. The pirates used to put out a sign at the mouth of the cave saying WOMEN AND WHISKEY, and when unsuspecting riverboat men stopped to enjoy themselves, the pirates would rob them. And kill them.

At the brush arbor site, four trees, forming a square, had been cut off about twelve feet above the ground. Men with chainsaws were clearing everything inside the square. When the square was cleared, the men improvised a roof, nailing poles across the top and spreading brush out on top of the poles.

More people started arriving about noon, spreading out food on plank-and-sawhorse tables. Earl was busy with the other preachers. Dogs and children chased each other. Snakeboxes, many of them beautifully carved, were placed near a makeshift pulpit in the arbor. Many had signs on them: JESUS SAVES or DON'T BLAME JESUS IF YOU GO TO HELL. Jackson felt a little uncomfortable and was glad when a caravan from the Church of the Burning Bush arrived: about thirty familiar faces, including DX and Sally and Mawmaw Tucker. Some of the men greeted him with a holy kiss.

Jackson was tired but in good spirits. He had regained some of his anthropological detachment, but he wasn't sure what had happened to him in his room at the hotel. He couldn't put a name on it, and he couldn't make sense of the gathering unfolding in front of him: clan, tribe, or chiefdom? None of the categories made sense. There was no central authority, no clear hierarchy, no one in charge, no headman.

He helped gather wood for a big bonfire and he helped the musicians

set up next to the pulpit, using car batteries to power the electric guitars and amps as well as some additional electric lights strung
above the pulpit.

In the afternoon small groups read their Bibles together, and occasionally someone would shout, "God don't never change." Jackson wondered about this preoccupation—probably a desire for
stability, something permanent behind the unstable facade of sense
experience. Like Platonic forms. Many of these people had lived
through astonishing changes. Computers, the closing of the mines,
the Internet, the impeachment of a sitting president, the breakup
of the Soviet Union. Mawmaw Tucker, probably the oldest, had been
born in the twenties.

Some of the men had stashed their snakes in bushel baskets or
cardboard boxes while they cleaned their snakeboxes. Musicians
riffed through hymns. The guitarist, Sunny's cousin Phil Stone,
was from the group that played in the Church of the Burning Bush
in Naqada. Jackson enjoyed playing with him and was looking forward to the music.

The service, like most holiness services, started a little bit at a
time. The musicians tuned up and did a last-minute sound check.
People wandered around the arbor, which was not big enough to
hold the crowd. Children darted in and out. A few people danced.
Some of the women raised their hands above their heads and slapped
and shouted "Hallelujah" and "God don't never change."

The musicians played a hymn that Jackson didn't recognize, but
nobody sang. They were waiting. Phil motioned to Jackson and they
played "Jesus, Won't You Come By Here." Jackson stepped up to the
microphone and sang. He'd taught Phil to skip a beat at the end of
the first four lines and add an extra beat after the chorus, just the
way Lightning Hopkins plays it in *Sounder.*

Now it is a needin' time, right
Now, it is a needin' time,
Now it is a needin'
time
Jesus won't you come by here, oh
Jesus won't you come by here.
Jesus won't you come by
here.

Soon other voices joined in, improvising verses, bending the melody the way the Mbuti did when they sang to wake up the Forest, their voices as high and clear as birdsong, as deep and resonant as a canyon. No one was bothered by the missing beat at the end of the verse or the extra beat at the end of the chorus. They took several breaks and Jackson filled in the holes left by the guitar. He held his A harp between his thumb and first finger and a D harp between the first and middle fingers, and when Phil modulated from E to A and the other musicians followed, he switched harps and played an obbligato way up above the melody, just as high as the harp could reach, holding onto the final A while Phil drew out the ending with some fancy finger work until Jackson's breath was gone and he started to get dizzy. They looked at each other and started to laugh. How could this simple song be so moving?

Earl stepped up to the microphone and began to preach. He was nervous and kept saying "heh." "God is not moving," he shouted. "Heh. We got to open our hearts and invite the Holy Spirit. Heh. Satan's in control tonight. Heh. We got to take aholt. Heh. We got to start praising Jesus. Heh."

Some women started to dance, rocking back and forth.

"We're fixin' to welcome the Power, heh."

"The power." Some men shouted back.

"We're gonna make Satan shed some big ole tears. Heh."

Earl paced back and forth and little by little the Spirit started to move, to cover the congregation.

The musicians played "The Old Rugged Cross," and people started to sing. The music was so loud you could hardly hear them.

Several other preachers took turns winding up the congregation, which responded with little outbursts that blended in with the words streaming from the pulpit. Jackson looked and listened, trying to distinguish between ecstatic vocalizations and states of dissociation, between self-authenticating spirit possession and hysterical frenzy.

When Punkin Bates came up to take his turn at the pulpit, the congregation suddenly became quiet. The sermon he preached was dark. Damnation. Hellfire. He scolded the congregation.

"You know what happens if you don't take Jesus into your hearts. You know. You know."

"Bring it on," someone shouted.

Punkin did a little dance. He mopped his face and paused to comb his hair.

"You know where this whole country's going. You know. You know. Are we going along for the ride?"

"NO."

"Or are we holding onto the cross?"

"The cross."

He told the parable of the wedding, returning repeatedly to Jesus' hard words: "Bind him and throw him into Gehenna. Gehenna. You know Gehenna. It's like a bone pile behind a mine. Bind him and throw him into Gehenna. Into Hell. Everlasting fire. That's Jesus himself talking, folks. Are you listening? Bind him and throw him into Gehenna.

"Some folks say that Jesus is real nice. But let me tell you, folks. Jesus ain't nice. That ain't the word for Jesus. 'Bind him and throw him into Gehenna.' And you know why? Because the man wasn't ready. He wasn't prepared. He was like the foolish virgins that didn't fill their lamps with oil. Are we like those foolish virgins? No man knows the hour. Christ could come tonight. Before I finish preaching. No man knows the hour. Are we ready?

"Sometimes you can see the spirit in the church, like a blue cloud. Do you hear me? I don't see nothing tonight. Just a bunch of sinners. 'Bind him and throw him into Gehenna.'

"You may have heard about that doctor over in Louisville. He was a specialist in internal medicine and cardiovascular disease. One of the top men, top specialists. And he was an atheist. He didn't believe in God at all. Thought the world just sort of fell together like a bunch of junk in your backyard getting knocked around in a storm and turning into a new Cadillac. He was a good doctor, and he saved a man's life that was dead. And when the man come back, he was screaming; he was terrified. Then something would go wrong and he'd go back again, and the doctor would revive him again. His face had an expression of sheer horror. He was sweating and trembling. And do you know why? I'll tell you why. Because he'd been in Hell. He'd seen it with his own eyes. And that doctor knew he was telling the truth just from the look of horror on that man's face. The man begged him not to let him go back down there. And that doctor said that anyone who had seen and heard this man would know that Hell is real. That doctor became a Christian.

"The Bible warns of a place called Hell. It warns us a hundred sixty-two times. And seventy of those warnings were uttered by Lord Jesus Christ."

People started to weep, and it seemed to Jackson that Punkin was spiraling down into Hell himself. Punkin threw himself down on the floor. He got up on his knees and raised his hands up in the air and cried out.

Then someone shouted, "Tell 'em about the good news."

This happened twice. It was like Mahalia Jackson telling Martin Luther King to tell the people at the Lincoln Memorial about his dream. She had to tell him twice.

Punkin began to modulate. "Did you think I forgot the good news? Well, if you did, then you don't know me very well. If you did, you ain't heard me preach before." He jumped up and down and ran to the back of the arbor.

"I'm beginning to feel the Spirit cover me," he shouted. "How about you? God don't never change. You know it. I know it. Let's shout it. GOD DON'T NEVER CHANGE."

The spirit was moving on the people, and the people were speaking in tongues and dancing. Jackson soon lost whatever was left of his anthropological detachment, his professional inclination to distinguish between different types of ecstatic utterances. He'd been reluctant to dance with the Mbuti. But he'd gotten over it, and everyone had laughed at him, but it hadn't mattered. He'd become a good dancer. An okay dancer. He caught Earl's eye as he started to dance. He wasn't sure at what moment he knew he was going to handle, but he could feel his hands starting to draw up, starting to tingle, as if he were about to pat Sunny's bottom. His whole body started to tingle. Growing warm. He could feel the rotation of the earth and the heavens. Colors looked different. He could feel the spirit covering him. Looking at things from the inside, looking *along* the beam.

He watched with mounting excitement as Punkin Bates opened a snakebox and grabbed a handful of copperheads in one hand and a rattler in the other. Jackson had been told to expect this signature move. Punkin hugged the copperheads to his chest and held the rattlesnake up in front of his face and looked into its eyes. "It's like looking straight into Hell," he shouted. "You can see what that man saw before the doctor brought him back."

The snakes moved but didn't try to coil. Punkin flung them around his neck and over his shoulders and picked up a rattlesnake from a different box, an eastern diamondback. Then he picked up another handful of copperheads.

Earl went to one of the boxes and took out a medium-size timber rattler, made his way through the dancers, and offered it to Jackson. Jackson shook his head. He wanted to handle DX's two-headed snake. He laughed. He imagined handing a snake to Sir James Frazer, or Radcliffe-Brown, or to Margaret Mead or Bronislaw Malinowski, or Clifford Geertz or Lévi-Strauss, or even Claude. Imagined them turning away in fear.

Punkin Bates held his snakes to his chest and then threw them down and walked on them in his stocking feet. His wife had been serpent bit and died. His brother too. Others followed Punkin's lead. First the men, then the women.

The snakes couldn't hear the music, which was getting louder and louder, but they could surely feel the vibrations. Everyone wanted to handle DX's two-headed snake. DX took it out of the box and handed it to Punkin, who wrapped it around his neck. "PRAISE THE LORD," he shouted, staring into the eyes of the snake, first one head then the other.

Jackson could feel the anointing becoming more intense.

Earl handed him a small copperhead, and again Jackson shook his head. The two men stood and looked at each other, but it wasn't a staring contest. It was more like two lovers. Or two musicians about to play a duet. Earl understood.

Earl put his copperhead around his neck and got the two-headed timber rattler from Punkin and carried it to Jackson. Jackson had no idea how much it would weigh. It was about three feet long and he put his fingers around it as he'd done on the porch at DX's. The snake lifted its head. Jackson looked into its eyes. He held it in both hands. It weighed about four pounds. Earl was standing in front of him. The musicians were playing "The Old Rugged Cross" again.

The snake felt clean and smooth, like a woman's silk nightgown. But he was aware of the keeled edges of the scales as the snake moved through his hands. He tried to throw it over his shoulders, the way Punkin had done, but the snake resisted. At first. Then it allowed Jackson to wrap it around his neck. Jackson looked into the eyes again. The pits, the infrared sensors, were right in front of his face.

Jackson seemed to be looking down on the scene, just as he had felt himself looking down on the small band gathered in the hotel room when he'd been sick. He could see the top of his head, the snake draped around his shoulders, its two heads next to each other. Dancing. Singing. Speaking in tongues. But he couldn't hear anything. It was like watching television with the sound turned off, or as if he were a snake and didn't have any ears.

Mawmaw Tucker made her way to the pulpit, using her walker. She made her way to the front of the church. The band played "The Blind Man Stood in the Road and Cried." Jackson thought there were more words, but they just sang the same verse over and over.

> *The blind man stood in the road and cried;*
> *The blind man stood in the road and cried;*
> *Cryin' o-o-o-oh Lord, don't turn your back on me;*
> *The blind man stood in the road and cried.*

Mawmaw Tucker started to sway back and forth, holding on to her walker. "Cryin' o-o-o-oh Lord, don't turn your back on me." The band played louder and louder, and the singers laid harmonies on top of harmonies. Mawmaw Tucker danced without her walker, graceful as some large animals can be graceful. She was the locus of power, Jackson realized. Not Punkin Bates. Not Earl. None of the others. She carried with her the sense not of the mystery, but of the mystery behind the mystery, whatever was beyond explanation. She'd been dead and her sisters had prayed her back to life, and then she had prayed others back to life, called them back.

She danced back to the pulpit, put her walker to one side, and picked up a fruit jar filled with a colorless liquid. The music stopped completely. Jackson didn't realize it was strychnine until she said in a loud voice, "I mixed it up myself. And I mixed it strong. You can see the feathers."

"Feathers," he knew, were undiluted crystals of strychnine.

"Praise Jesus," she shouted. She held the jar out toward the congregation and then brought it to her lips. "Praise the Lord," she shouted.

She drank it down, and Jackson was brought back to anthropological mode. He could understand the emotional kick you'd get from handling the snakes. He could understand it in every fiber of his being. He was experiencing it from within. But why would anyone drink strychnine? It didn't make any sense. "If they drink any deadly thing, it shall not hurt them." Mark 16:18. There had to be more to it than *that*. One more thing to investigate if his NHI proposal was accepted.

He was thinking about the proposal as he lifted the two-headed snake off his neck and shoulders. He felt a sharp sting in his finger, like a paper cut. He could see a drop of blood. He touched it with the first finger of his right hand. It took him a few second to realize that he'd been bitten. He wasn't frightened. Not at first. Earl and DX had seen it too and were at his side asking if he wanted medical attention. According to Sunny this was the accepted protocol. Jackson said "No," which was also part of the accepted protocol. He felt indestructible. Nothing could harm him. Certainly not a paper cut.

But two minutes later he was in agony. Four minutes later his legs were starting to go numb. He collapsed on the floor. His finger was bleeding and starting to turn black and swell. Ten minutes later the whole finger was black. His arm was turning black and blowing up like a balloon. His face was swelling up. He was vomiting and shitting. Sally came up to him, looked into his face and screamed. He passed out for a minute and then came back. Four men carried him to Earl's truck. His finger was blistering. He couldn't stand to have anyone touch his arm. Earl cut off the sleeve because of the swelling. His arm had turned dark red. The skin was rupturing. He was weak, giddy, collapsed, confused, frightened. He was hemorrhaging from the mouth and the nose. He was pissing blood.

The ferry at Cave In Rock wasn't running this late and they had to drive north to the bridge at Old Shawneetown and then south to Naqada. Three men crowded into the cab. Jackson thought they were taking him to the hospital, but when he woke up Earl and DX were getting him out of the cab in front of Earl's trailer. He'd said he didn't want medical attention, but that was before the bite really took hold. Now he was unable to talk. Or scream. He was thinking about the man in Hell.

When he wakes, he's sitting with the men outside the elima *house. His daughter is in the house with Sibaku and the women. The door is guarded by young women holding whips made out of brambles. Any young man who tries to force his way into the house will have to deal with these young women, and will not get through unscathed. Though he may get through. If he does, he will flirt with the young women waiting who are being initiated. The initiation itself is secret.*

The men have built a fire and are singing. Jackson has only one harmonica left. Some have broken reeds; others he has given away. The Mbuti love the chugging train sounds, and the faraway whistle, though they have never seen or heard a train.

His daughter and two others are being initiated, and like most Mbuti initiations there are rules that have to be followed, but if they aren't followed exactly, it doesn't really matter. The Mbuti love ceremonies, but they don't worry about sticking to the proper procedures, don't worry about initiating Jackson with a cohort of young men half his age, don't worry that sometimes the molimo the young men bring back from its secret hiding place in the depths of the Forest is an old plastic drain pipe instead of a beautifully carved wooden trumpet, don't worry if the women sing the molimo songs that are supposedly known only to the men.

Suddenly three young women erupt out of the hut, the initiates, and take off running, pursued by the young women who have been guarding the hut. They disappear into the Forest. They are pursued in turn by the young men. Jackson can't follow them.

19

ASIH

We flew American Airlines from Chicago to Mexico City and AeroMexico from Mexico City to Manuel Márquez de León International Airport in La Paz. It was my first flight, and I tried to conceal my excitement, my inexperience, as we boarded the plane and crammed our coats and carry-ons into the overhead luggage bins. I'd made the mistake of telling everyone that I'd thought Baja California was in California, and I didn't think Laura was ever going to let me forget it. "Off to California," she said, ushering me into the window seat so she could sit between Cramer and me. She was beautifully turned out, as always, in a dazzling lime-green dress and matching scarf, big sunglasses pushed up on her head. Cramer took the aisle because of his long legs. I didn't mind. I'd been to the airport in Paducah before. With Earl. Just to look around and watch a plane come in every now and then. But this was the real thing. I wanted to see what was going on.

I could see that no one else was paying attention to the flight attendant's carefully choreographed routine about safety instructions.

I wasn't paying much attention either, and I closed my eyes as the plane took off and didn't open them again till I was sure we were in the air. Things were growing smaller. I recognized Chicago from pictures and from my shopping trip with Claire—the Sears Tower, the Hancock building, the lake, which was on our right as we circled around, and which soon disappeared as we headed west and then south. Pretty soon Chicago itself disappeared.

While Laura was talking to Cramer about the paper on rat snakes she was going to deliver at the conference, I went through the stuff in the seat pocket in front of me: an American Airlines brochure that showed our route to Mexico City—we should cross the Mississippi north of St. Louis—and a catalog advertising more things than you could imagine. All kinds of electronic gadgets, money clips, exercise machines, a storage system that fit under the bed, a cigar humidifier, ice buckets, martini shakers, a globe that opened up to reveal a minibar inside, a magnetic wine accelerator ("10 seconds ages drink 10 years, 3 minutes ages drink 20 years") for only $39.99, flasks bearing the logos of professional football teams, automatic plant waterers (would Jackson remember to water the plants?). Titanium knives, a germ-eliminating knife block for $89.95, a laser comb to promote hair growth for $495, various hair-removal devices, a uHarmony massage chair for almost four thousand dollars, another massage chair that squeezed your calves and feet. And then, at the end, "Successories." Inspirational wall plaques for executive offices—pictures of flowers, trees, storms, waves, birds: "Caught in mid-flight, its wings blurred in motion, a majestic bald eagle propels its mighty form through the air. The motivational quote affirms that those who achieve greatness do so by taking risks."

When I closed my eyes again I could hear a lot of voices—my mother's, Earl's, Warren's, Jackson's. They were all saying the same thing: "What do you think you're doing?" And I had to remind myself.

What I thought I was doing was asserting my independence. The truth is, I hadn't really wanted to go to Paris. In fact, I was sick of Paris before I even got there. I was tired of trying to speak French at dinner every single night, even if it was only for fifteen minutes, and my second-semester French teacher, Monsieur Boucher, couldn't have been more different from Madame Arnot. No more fun and games. According to Monsieur Boucher, the primary French emotions were *angst, nausée,* and *ennui!* And we were reading parts of a novel by Albert Camus, pronounced "Camoo," that demonstrated them all. *L'Étranger.* The stranger, Meursault, wasn't the sort of Frenchman I'd been imagining. Or was the Arab the "stranger"?

And then there were the books on France that Jackson had given me for Christmas: *French or Foe?, Almost French, Unleash Your Inner Gaul,* all of which gave me the strong impression that the French weren't very nice—that the customer is always wrong; that if you go to a fancy restaurant the waiters will try to intimidate you; that people will make fun of you if you try to speak French. And I didn't want to meet Jackson's old girlfriend, who'd arranged an apartment for us, and had invited us to their country place in something called the Dordogne. She was probably the woman described in the books: short skirts, tailored jackets, a padded push-up bra, casual chic, creamy skin. I didn't think my *French outfit* would be a match for Suzanne. And what I really wanted before dinner on Friday night, after a long week, was a Sam Adams, not a *kir,* not even a *kir royale.* But the real reason I didn't go to Paris was that I was afraid Jackson was going to propose to me in Paris, maybe in the Café Anglais, and I thought that if that happened in Paris, I'd be trapped, like the poor groundhog we carted over to Oquawaka on the day we stopped at the Starlight Motel, or like the snakes we'd captured back in March.

Laura complained about the food, but I thought it was pretty amazing that they managed to serve a hot meal and give you some choices—chicken or vegetable lasagna—at thirty thousand feet up in the air. But I didn't say so. Laura complained about the lines at the lavatory. But I thought this was amazing too. Taking a dump at thirty thousand feet in the air.

"Are you nervous?" I asked Laura when Cramer got up to go to the john.

"About what?"

"About giving your paper?"

Laura shook her head. "What could go wrong? It's not like you have to memorize it. You just read it and look up once in a while."

"In front of a lot of people."

"The more people the better. It's when there are only a handful of people . . . Besides, what can they do to you?"

"Ask embarrassing questions."

"How about you?" she asked.

"What should I be nervous about?"

"All the students are going to have to sing mariachi songs at the dinner on the last night."

"What's a mariachi song?"

Laura explained—violins, trumpets, three kinds of guitars, fancy costumes—but I couldn't form a clear picture of what the students would be expected to do. I decided to worry about the mariachi singing later.

I looked out the window for a while. It was one o'clock. We'd crossed the Mississippi a long time ago and were probably over Arkansas or Texas. The flight to Mexico City was four and a half hours.

Then a three-hour layover in Mexico City, and then a one-and-a-half-hour flight to La Paz.

A movie started to play on several big screens suspended from the cabin roof. People were putting on headphones. I closed my eyes and played my own movie in my head, just letting things happen. It was the same old stuff. Jackson's pygmy girlfriend. Hardly three feet tall. Hard to imagine. Him on top. Her on top. I couldn't get much out of him about her. Or his French girlfriend. All dressed up, leaning out the window and chatting with people without her pants on. And Cramer. I liked Cramer because he was so hard-edged. "Intentionality is the enemy," Claire used to say, and it might have been Cramer's motto too. He was determined to root *intentionality* out of our understanding of science. You don't need *intentionality* to explain the human eye, or to explain why Andromeda and the Milky Way are going to collide, followed by the heat death of the universe, or even to explain the human mind, which hasn't been designed like some kind of computer program. It's a biological entity that's been cobbled together by evolution over millions of years.

But what kind of intentionality was taking us to La Paz? I was thinking about the scene that would unfold in the hotel in La Paz. In my imagination I was wearing my French outfit that had started all the trouble. I'd had it cleaned and you could hardly see the wine stains. I thought it would give Cramer a poke in the eye with a sharp stick. I was excited, but I was melancholy too. I knew, from Madame Arnot, about *post coitum triste*, but this was *pre-coitum triste*—a kind of philosophical melancholy at the way things were working themselves out. I was sad for Laura, could almost feel her disappointment when she discovered that she wouldn't be sharing her bed with Cramer. But Laura was young. Not eighteen, but not thirty-five either. Late twenties, I thought. She was working on her Ph.D. She'd be fine. She'd survive. And I was sad for Jackson—going to Paris by

himself. But he'd have a good time. He'd drink *kir* every night before dinner and eat at the bistro on boulevard Saint-Germain. Not
the famous bistro where Hemingway used to eat, a different one.
That's why he liked it. Suzanne had told him it was still there. I
could imagine them sitting together . . . I was sad for myself too,
and I had to remind myself that there was no divine plan here, not
for me; no hand of Fate. Just my own choices. I'd made my bed and
now I was going to lie in it. I dozed off, and when I woke up we were
over Mexico City, which was surrounded by mountains.

The airport was crowded. Everyone was smoking. Baked goods were
on sale everywhere: pies, cakes. It was better than a church bake
sale. We stopped at the AeroMexico office to locate our boarding
gate. Laura spoke Spanish. I'd been studying French, but I'd never
realized before what it would be like to be someplace where you
didn't speak the language. I hung onto my beautiful, expensive
briefcase for dear life, as if I expected someone to grab it out of my
hand. It held my ticket, my new passport, and a copy of *L'Étranger*.
There were no lines at the gate, just a scrimmage to get on the plane.
Cramer and I followed Laura, who was easy to keep track of in her
lime-green dress. I was now about five years old, and Cramer, who
didn't speak Spanish either, was not much older.

Laura negotiated us through the airport in La Paz and got us into
a taxi that took us to Hotel Araiza, the site for the herps meetings.
We registered, got our nametags and a schedule of meetings, or sessions (as they were called). We had rooms on separate floors. I sat in
my room and tried to relax. It was my first time in a hotel too, except
the time with Warren in St. Louis.

There was a reception in the lobby of our hotel. There was lots of
good food spread out on long tables—typical Mexican food, or what
I thought of as typical, and lots more. Lots of seafood. And it was

okay to drink beer as an *apero*. I had a Negra Modelo and then a glass of wine.

We put two tables together and ate outside with a dozen herpetologists. Everyone wanted to go on a whale-sighting trip, but it turned out to be the wrong time of year. The whales had gone north in March. You'd think a bunch of biologists would have known that. But they were herpetologists, not ichthyologists, or mammologists, and some people did go looking for whale *sharks*. The ichthyologists were meeting in a different hotel. We drank margaritas and pitchers of beer and ate platters of seafood. By ten o'clock I was stuffed and tired. Laura was sticking close to Cramer.

In my room, alone, I realized I'd had too much to drink. I got tired of waiting for Cramer and went out for a walk on the beach. *Paz* means "peace." I walked along the Malecón, which means "street by the sea." The sidewalk was wide. I sat and watched the sea. Another first. Teenagers cruised the broad street.

There would be chances to scuba dive, snorkel. I'd never done either of these things, though I could swim all right. Maybe I'd try.

At a white gazebo in the Malecón Plaza musicians played trumpets, violins, guitars, and great big fat guitars. I thought this might be mariachi music, but I wasn't sure.

I saw Cramer and Laura walking together but they didn't see me. I thought for a minute that I'd been mistaken all along. That I was the "cover" for Laura instead of the other way around. But I was too tired to care. No, not tired. I was relieved. I was taken by surprise. I'd had too much to drink, but I could see clearly. I'd made an important discovery. I went back to the hotel and lay down on the bed.

But just as I was falling off to sleep, there was a knock on the door. Cramer. I hadn't been mistaken after all. But it was Laura.

Laura was upset because Cramer was meeting somebody else.

She didn't know who. She'd thought he'd invited her to the conference because . . . She burst into tears.

"You're a Ph.D. candidate in biology," I said.

Laura nodded her head.

"So I shouldn't have to explain this to you."

"Explain what? Why this scientific conference is just a big fuck fest? It's disgusting. If I report this to the dean, Cramer will be in deep shit. He'll lose his job."

"Is that what you want to happen?"

"This whole place is nothing but a big whorehouse. Everybody's gearing up for an orgy. It's disgusting. These people are in heat. You can smell it."

"How old are you, Laura?"

"Twenty-five."

"When was the first time you got laid?"

"None of your fucking business."

"Right. And if Cramer gets laid, it's none of *your* fucking business. Besides, it's not a big deal. A man and a woman go to bed together. So? Their brains get saturated with certain neurotransmitters, and hey bingo."

"Phenylethylamine and dopamine," she said.

"What?"

"Those are the neurotransmitters." She was still crying, sitting upright on the bed, not bothering to wipe away her tears.

"It's human nature," I said. "You're a biologist? You know that people, or animals, who really want to get laid pump more genes into the gene pool than people, or animals, who don't. After a while you're left with a lot of people who really want to get laid. That's where we are now. That's what you want too, isn't it? It's what everybody wants? But no one wants to admit it. Well, some people admit it. I admit it. And you should admit it too before you start laying down the law."

"I'm not an animal."

"You haven't been paying attention."

I got some toilet paper from the bathroom. Laura's eyeliner was smudged. Her eyes were like big hollows. I handed it to Laura. "Come over here and lie down."

I patted the bed. She lay down, and I started to rub her back. I was reasonably pleased with myself. "In France," I said, "people have *petits aventures. Petits aventures* are part of the fabric of French life. It's what everybody wants. Well, almost everybody. Deep down." I was thinking of the explanations of French sex in the books Jackson had given me for Christmas.

"So, you think we should be more like the French?"

"I don't know what I think, Laura." And I didn't.

Laura was asleep by the time Cramer knocked on the door. We went up to Cramer's room, two floors up. We took the stairs.

"Ms. Cochrane," he said, closing the door behind him. He stood in front of the window, solemn, as if he were about to deliver a lecture. "This isn't a game for me," he said. "I don't make a habit of bedding my students. I've never done it before, in fact."

"I wish you'd told me sooner," I said, laughing. "Are you sure you want to do it now?"

"You're strong, you know. Or maybe you don't. Like a big rattlesnake. And you're not afraid of anything."

"Well, I'm not afraid of rattlesnakes."

"And you're not afraid of me."

"Why would I be afraid of you?"

He laughed. "I'm the village atheist. I scare a lot of people. They agree with me in theory, but they still go to church. They're afraid to fly without a net."

I patted the bed and he sat down beside me. I asked him if he was nervous and he nodded.

"It's all right," I said. I could feel the balance of power shifting.

"We share the same values," he said. "You combine all the qualities I admire . . ."

"In a woman." I finished the sentence for him.

"Honesty," he said, "intelligence, scientific curiosity, backwoods sassiness . . ."

I put my hand over his mouth and pushed him down on the bed because I was afraid of what he was going to say. I hadn't wanted Jackson to propose to me in Paris, and I didn't want Cramer to declare his love in a hotel room in La Paz.

I had a great time at the conference, which lasted a week. I went to a lot of sessions, including Cramer's and Laura's, and heard some really interesting papers on rattlesnakes. I learned that new techniques in molecular biology were going to give us a more complete picture of snake evolution in spite of the patchy and incomplete fossil record. I learned that the "burrowing ancestors" theory of snake evolution had come under attack. I learned that many types of squirrels are resistant to rattlesnake venom and that by isolating and synthesizing venom-neutralizing proteins in their blood, biomedical researchers were developing a new antivenin effective against the numerous species of rattlesnake, including *Crotalus horridus horridus.* I learned that certain California ground squirrels will chew up a rattlesnake's skin and smear it on their fur to mask their scent from predators.

At the end of this particular session I asked a question about the squirrel-rattlesnake confrontation I'd witnessed when we were catching the snakes we were going to translocate. I thought everyone would look at me and shake their heads as if to say *What a stupid question,* but I didn't care. The speaker, Aaron Matthews from the University of California at Davis, said the behavior was called "flagging" and was not very well understood. The squirrel, which was immune to rattlesnake venom, was probably protecting its pups, which were not immune, but it wasn't clear why "flagging" seemed to deter rattlesnakes.

At the banquet on the last night I was a little nervous about the mariachi singing, which was going to follow the speeches. Laura had gotten over her funk. Her paper on rat snakes had been very well received, and because of her excellent Spanish, the leader of the mariachi band had put her in charge of rehearsing the students. She divided us up into two groups, those who knew Spanish and those who didn't. The sheet music was in Spanish and Laura improvised translations of the choruses. I had to admire her. Her Spanish was perfect, at least as far as I could tell, and she managed to help everyone in such a nice way that you didn't realize you were being corrected. There were a lot of "la la la's" and "ba ba ba's," which both groups sang. Then several verses in Spanish, and then the rest of us, the non-Spanish speakers, would sing our parts by ourselves.

The food was good. I started to imagine Jackson in Paris, but at the same time I was also thinking I was where I wanted to be. It was amazing how much fun people were having. Even during the speeches at the banquet before the singing. I usually tuned out speeches, just the way I learned to tune out sermons. There were resolutions honoring the recently dead and resolutions honoring the volunteers who kept ASIH functioning; there were resolutions condemning various ecological atrocities and resolutions on standardizing the common names of new species; a resolution allowing underage students to drink alcohol at all future ASIH meetings; a resolution proposing that the first letter of common names of fishes and snakes be capitalized in accordance with the *Little, Brown Handbook*.

The old guys in charge weren't exactly stand-up comedians, but they didn't seem to have any sense of self-importance. I liked that, and for the rest of the evening I didn't have any sense of self-importance either, and when it came time to sing, I didn't hold back. There were "la la la" and "ba ba ba" choruses and some verses in Spanish and in English, and then we sang the first verse again in English:

> *I'm a strong-headed steed, no one can reach me,*
> *I'm a little naive in love, perhaps you could teach me,*
> *I see that you're lonely, and your heart could use mending,*
> *And I don't believe in unhappy endings.*

That night Laura went off to a party with the mariachi band. Cramer and I went back to the hotel. I hadn't worn my cami *cache-coeur* outfit for him, and I was still wondering what version of myself I wanted to be, wondering how my own version of myself would differ from Jackson's. From Cramer's. These were deep questions. I'd been hoping I could settle them in bed, but it didn't work out that way. Maybe it never does.

Afterwards we walked along the Malecón, where I'd walked by myself the night we'd arrived. We walked past the cafés and the restaurants and looked at the bay and the sailboats and yachts. It was after midnight, but the musicians were still playing in Malecón Plaza. We stopped to listen, and I thought that this trip had taught me what I needed to know, even though I couldn't understand the words.

I couldn't understand the words, but I could understand the songs. I didn't need Laura to translate. Longing, lost love, the difficulties of love. Joy. Sadness. *Post coitum triste.*

We sat on a bench and looked at the water, which glowed as if there were little candles under the surface. We took our shoes off and waded in up to our knees, soaking our clothes. I was imagining Jackson in Paris. Walking along the Seine with Suzanne. They were speaking French, but I couldn't hear what they were saying.

"Bioluminescent dinoflagellates," Cramer explained. "Single-celled algae. They absorb light during the day and then give it off slowly at night."

20

Under Arrest

When I got back to the house on Tuesday morning—after several delays—there was a phone message from DX saying Jackson had been serpent bit by DX's two-headed snake. And it was like looking along the beam of light that Jackson was always talking about. My heart started kicking me in the chest. Hard kicks.

I called DX right away. "Jackson's in Paris," I said.

But he wasn't in Paris. He was in Earl's trailer. I called Earl and told him to get Jackson to a hospital.

"He don't want medical attention."

"Earl, get him to the hospital."

"The Lord'll look after him."

I called the small hospital in Rosiclare and told them a man had been serpent bit and needed help right away. I gave them Earl's address and directions. They had only ten vials of antivenin, probably not enough for a serious bite. I thought of Paducah or Evansville, but they probably wouldn't cross the state line. Memorial Hospital in Carbondale was about sixty miles from Naqada. Good roads. Plenty of experience with antivenin. He could need up to thirty vials. I called Cramer and he came to the hospital in Colesville and signed for me to pick up some antivenin. He offered to go with me, but I said no.

Six hours later I was in Naqada. But Jackson wasn't in the hospital. The ambulance had come back empty. Jackson was still at Earl's. Earl had sent the paramedics away. The trailer and yard were full of people, drinking coffee and praying. Serpent bites were social occasions. Jackson was stretched out on the bed in the back of the double-wide. The bed that Earl and I had shared for thirteen years. Earl followed me into the room. "He don't want no medical attention," he said.

I rushed to the bed. He was unconscious. His arm was black, swollen to three times its normal size. It was enormous, as big as his thigh, and hard as a rock. The skin was breaking open from the pressure.

I picked up the phone from a stand next to the bed and started to dial 911, but Earl slapped the phone out of my hand. I was glad I'd brought the pistol.

"Earl, we've got to get him to a hospital."

"I told you, Fern, he don't want no medical attention. You don't believe me, you ask DX or Sally or Mawmaw Tucker."

I started to argue and then thought better of it. I started to back out of the room. "Earl, I've got to go to the bathroom."

"You can hold it a while longer. I got some things to say."

"This is crazy, Earl. You'll never get away with it."

"There's nothing to get away with. It's all up to the Lord now."

"Earl, how could you send the ambulance away?"

"Sit down. You're not going anywhere till you hear what I got to say."

"God damn it, Earl. I've got to pee."

"There's no call to talk like that. You didn't learn that from me. No, I reckon you learned that kind of talkin' up north."

"He thought you were his friend."

"I am his friend and I never gave him no reason to doubt it. He come to me wantin' to handle that two-headed snake while you was off with another man."

"He's going to die, Earl, if we don't get him to a hospital."

"I reckon it's up to the Lord. Or have you backed up on the Lord so hard you can't see nothing plain?"

"Say what you want to say and let's get on to the next thing."

"What I got to say is that I'm your husband. Nothing you can do about that. You get down on your knees and witness the truth that I just said and you can call any dang one you want."

"We're divorced, Earl. It's all legal."

"Not in the eyes of the Lord it ain't legal. You think that piece of paper that the lawyers fussed up makes one bit of difference to the Lord?"

"Earl, I've got to go."

"All right, go then."

I took my purse into the bathroom, which was not much bigger than the toilet on the airplane, except it had a little shower with a plastic shower curtain with yellow flowers on it. The curtain was new. I really did have to go. I sat on the toilet and took the pistol out of my purse. The toilet paper roll was on backward so the paper was hanging down against the wall. And it hit me: This was my old home. I'd sat on this toilet hundreds of times. Thousands. Three four five times a day for thirteen years. I'd washed my hair in the tiny shower. And now Jackson was in my bed. The bed I'd shared with Earl. I couldn't remember my first night with Earl. I'd blacked it all out. But I remembered how Earl used to stand outside the bathroom when I was in it. He was standing outside the door right now. The door didn't close tight. It didn't lock. It never did lock right. Was Earl still dreaming about getting a big bass boat and setting up as a charter fisherman? Was he still preaching three or four times a week?

What I understood now that I hadn't understood then was that in some way this would always be my home, just like every place you've ever lived will always be your home.

My hands shook as I took the roll of toilet paper off the roller to turn it around. I dropped the roller on the linoleum. I put the toilet paper back on the roller. I had some trouble fitting it back into the slot.

I still hadn't peed. I had to calm down. I could sense Earl standing right outside the thin sliding door. I checked the pistol, trying not to make any noise. I held the barrel against my forehead. It was cool.

I flushed the toilet and checked the chamber, hoping the noise of the flush would cover the sound. The safety was off. I could have shot him right through the door, but that wasn't what I wanted to do. I finally let go, wiped myself, and pulled up my panties, which I hadn't changed since the flight back from La Paz. I was very tired. I turned on the tap and splashed water on my face. There was rust in the basin. Brown stain, but the floor was pretty clean around the toilet. I was worried about opening the door with Earl standing right outside. The hallway in the trailer was very narrow, not much room to maneuver. I remembered a story from the *Reader's Digest* about a polar bear. A man who lived alone up in the Arctic was sleeping when a polar bear climbed in his window. The man ran into the closet where he kept his guns. There was no room to lower his rifle . . . I didn't want to shoot Earl. I wanted to talk to him.

I listened at the door. Earl was praying out loud. I couldn't make out the words, but he was probably praying for my soul. Mumbling, murmuring, low voice. Then the tone changed. He was talking to someone. He moved away from the door. I slid the door open quickly and stepped into the hall. Earl turned and looked, registered the gun. He was so big he almost filled the hallway.

"Earl," I said, pointing the gun at him. He smiled. "Let me call the hospital."

"You gonna shoot me again?"

I nodded. "I will if you don't let me use the phone."

"He said he don't want medical attention. You can ask DX; you can ask Sally. You can ask Mawmaw Tucker. I askt him straight out did he want medical assistance, and he said no." DX was standing right behind him.

"He didn't know what he was in for. He was out of his mind."

"Because he was putting his trust in the Lord?"

"Don't come any closer, Earl. I'll shoot."

"Bullet ain't gonna do me no harm. You know why? 'Cause I feel the anointing. My whole body is anointed."

"It put you right down last time."

"I was backed up on the Lord. I wasn't anointed."

He took another step.

I took one step backwards, then another. I didn't want to shoot him, but I didn't want him to get close enough to slap the pistol out of my hand.

"One more step, Earl, and that's it."

"Besides, you don't want to go back to prison, do you? You shoot me again, they'll put you away for a long time this time. Rest of your life, and you won't have Uncle Warren to get you transferred out of Little Muddy. The rest of your life. It's a long time. Not as long as eternity, and when you're dead, you'll be wishin' you was back in Little Muddy. You hear about that doctor in Paducah was bringing a man back from the dead? The man come back screaming, knew he'd been in Hell. Wasn't any doubt about it. The doctor knew it too. He was a convicted atheist, but not no more."

I heard a noise. I was afraid someone was coming up behind me, but it was Earl, tapping on the wall to distract me.

I thought of Meursault shooting the Arab that we'd read about in French 102. There was no reason to shoot the Arab, there was no reason for anything. Maybe the intensity of the sun. Nothing more. I was losing focus.

I backed up as far as I could, all the way into the bedroom. Earl took another step and tried to slap the pistol out of my hand, the way he'd slapped the phone out of my hand earlier. I shot him. I didn't aim at his heart, I didn't aim at anything. I just closed my eyes and pulled the trigger. But that's where the bullet hit him. In the heart. He collapsed on the floor. People in the kitchen started to scream.

Earl was lying on the bedroom floor, his mouth open, a black hole in his chest. DX was standing beside me. I sat down on the bed next to Jackson. His arm as big around as his thigh. Black. Hand the size of a baseball glove. A coma, that's what happens right at the end.

"You've got to call the hospital," I said to DX. But DX looked like he was going to faint.

"You can't touch him," he croaked. "This is a crime scene."

"You've been watchin' too much television," I said. I waved the pistol at him.

I picked up the phone and called 911. "There's a man's been ser-pent bit," I said, "and another's been shot."

People were crowding into the trailer, plugging up the narrow hallway, wanting to know what had happened.

"Earl's dead," DX kept saying. "Earl's dead."

"Out," I yelled. "Everybody get out." I kept yelling till people backed out of the hallway and went outside.

I waited for the ambulance at the kitchen table. A woman I'd never seen before kept trying to tell me a long story about sitting up all night with someone who'd been serpent bit and was dead but they didn't know it. I could hear voices outside, people praying, trying to pray Earl back to life. Mawmaw Tucker was there. I could hear her voice, rising above the others and then falling below them. I hadn't wanted to kill Earl; I'd just wanted to stop him, and I was hoping that Mawmaw Tucker would call him back, like she called her sister back, like she got called back herself, like Jesus calling Jairus' daughter back. And wondering would Earl be hungry like that little girl: "Give her something to eat," someone says. Jesus himself. A woman came into the kitchen and I thought maybe she was going to get something for Earl to eat, but she wanted some anointing oil. I showed her where Earl kept it in a cupboard over the sink. They were still praying—just getting started—when the ambulance came, two ambulances. The paramedics from the first ambulance had trouble getting through the crowd to get Jackson on a stretcher. The paramedics from the second ambulance were still arguing with DX and Mawmaw Tucker about taking Earl when we left. I followed the first ambulance to the little hospital in Rosiclare.

They wheeled Jackson into the emergency room at the little hospital in Rosiclare. I had the antivenin from Colesville in a cooler, but it was pretty late in the game, and the doctor who looked like he was about twenty was reading up on snakebite.

Jackson received ten vials of crotalidae polyvalent immune fab (ovine) antivenin and then five more vials.

"He's going to need a fasciotomy," the doctor said, putting his book face down on a counter. "Someone's going to have to cut open his arm to relieve the pressure. We're going to have to get him to Carbondale. He may make it as long as he's not allergic to the horse proteins in the antivenin."

I rode with Jackson in the ambulance to the American Legion baseball field, where the helicopter landed, and then in the helicopter. It wasn't till I was in the hospital in Carbondale that the Naqada County sheriff's officers caught up with me.

I was in the room with Jackson and the doctor who was going to do the fasciotomy. Jackson would be lucky to keep the arm. The duty nurse came in. Someone wanted to see me. It was the police. I was under arrest.

"I can't leave now," I said to the sheriff's officers. But of course I didn't have a choice.

I was driven back to the jail in Naqada in the back of a police car with metal bars protecting the two officers in the front seat. I didn't know either of the officers, but I knew their parents. They were curious about the snakes, about the church.

"I could be in Paris," I said. "I could have gone to Paris with my boyfriend."

In my own mind I was completely justified in shooting Earl and had nothing to worry about, legally, but I knew enough not to answer any questions. I'd been in the Naqada County jail before. I could look out the window and see the row of two-story brick buildings that lined Main Street, down to the Baptist church on the corner of Main and Forest. I tried to hold myself together and not panic, but I knew I couldn't face prison again. That part of my life was over. I had a chunk of Uncle Warren's money left, in spite of the collapse of ShoppingKart.com, but not enough to get the kind of lawyer I was going to need to get me off. And Uncle Warren was dead and Jackson was the closest thing to being dead. If I hadn't lost my faith, I'd have started praying and singing hymns, like Paul and Silas in jail in Rome. Only I was pretty sure an angel wasn't going to come and knock down the walls. Instead I started going over my rattlesnake taxonomy. I didn't have a pencil or pen so I couldn't write it down. But I had a notebook in my head, and I wrote it down on that, the way I used to do on a piece of paper. Kingdom: Animalia, Phylum: Chordata, and so on.

A snake is a snake, not an avatar of the devil. The two-headed snake had simply done what rattlesnakes do by their nature. It wasn't a punishment or a judgment. Well, maybe a judgment on Jackson's lack of common sense.

It was Tuesday night, almost midnight.

In the morning I thought of calling Cramer, but I called Claire instead.

21

Carmina Burana

I didn't need the high-priced lawyer Claire had hired—a partner in her father's law firm—to explain that homicide is the most life-altering criminal charge you can face. In Illinois, the minimum sentence is twenty years. If you use a firearm, it's forty-five years—mandatory. Forty-five years.

"What's going to happen?" That's what I wanted to know. I tried to remember what had happened the first time I shot Earl, but it was all a blur.

"If the state goes to the grand jury," Ms. Potaczek—Stella—said, "the prosecution doesn't have to present exculpatory evidence; we won't be able to cross-examine witnesses; you won't get a warning about self-incrimination; and I won't be able to advise you in the courtroom." She paused to let this sink in. "But my guess is that the state will hold a preliminary hearing before a judge."

We were sitting in an office in the John Hancock building in Chicago, with a view of Lake Michigan. Stella and Claire and I sat in mismatched chairs at a little round table. Jackson was still in

Memorial Hospital in Carbondale. Stella, according to Claire's father, was a top-notch criminal attorney who'd been passed over for several judicial appointments.

Stella would need to know, she said, everything that had happened. Every word Earl had said. Every word I had said; everything about my relationship with Earl; everything about the first trial. She was especially interested in the first trial, in fact, and made a note to herself to get the records, transcripts. She would need to know about the divorce proceedings.

We were drinking tea rather than coffee, which Stella poured out of an old-fashioned brown teapot. On a big desk, behind Stella, sat a bowl of fruit. I wanted an apple, but I didn't want to ask. It was a desk that two people would sit at, facing each other. There was a set of drawers on each side, and I imagined sitting across from Jackson at this desk.

"Claire's father told me to ask you about a necessity defense."

Stella laughed. "He's not a criminal lawyer, but he's always keen on a necessity defense. Did he tell you the story about the soldiers and the natives in the jungle?"

I nodded.

Claire and I had spent the night with Claire's parents on Bellevue Place. Claire's parents went to quite a bit of trouble to make me feel at home, but I could see they were uncomfortable. Claire's father spent most of his time cooking a coho salmon on a big outdoor gas grill. He'd caught it himself, in Lake Michigan, which was stocked every year with coho and lake trout. He preferred the coho. It was a huge fish, and Claire's mother busied herself in the kitchen, making a delicious sauce with butter and lemon, but I didn't have much of an appetite. No one said a word about the shooting or about the upcoming trial except Claire's father, in his study after dinner.

The story he told went like this: "You're in the jungle in South

America and you come to a clearing where a group of soldiers are about to execute ten innocent natives. The captain of the soldiers offers his pistol to you and says, here, you kill one of these men and I'll let the other nine go free. You figure it's better for nine of the ten to go free than for all of them to be killed, so you shoot one of them. The nine natives disappear into the jungle in one direction; the captain and his men disappear into the jungle in the other. Suddenly a helicopter lands in the clearing. Argentinean police pour out and put you under arrest. How do you plead?"

"She had to kill one man to save nine others, right?" Claire said. "She didn't have a choice."

"Let Sunny answer," Stella said.

"Right," I said. "But you know what I would have done, now that I think of it?"

"What?"

"I'd have shot the captain."

"Good choice," Stella said.

By the end of the June I'd been arraigned before a judge in Allensboro, and then bound over for trial. Peter Franklin, Stella's "local council," had come to the first appearance and arranged bail—and he knew the judge. The trial would be held in October in Allensboro.

The judge figured I'd never make bail, which was set at $500,000, but Claire came up with fifty thousand dollars without batting an eye, and the two of us went back to Carbondale and stayed at the Holiday Inn till Jackson was released from Memorial Hospital in the middle of July. He'd had his arm closed up with a skin graft from his leg. He'd had a fasciotomy and four surgeries to clean out the dead tissue from his arm, then the skin graft. He would need several months of physical therapy before he could use his hand normally. We drove back home in Claire's BMW. Claire hired the cousin of someone who worked at the Holiday Inn to drive my truck back to Colesville and then take a bus home. The weather continued very hot and humid, the way it was, according to Jackson, in the Ituri Forest.

Claire never wavered in her support. "You did the right thing. The man was trying to kill Jackson and he was attacking you. You didn't have any choice." And Jackson too. Jackson let me take care of him without fussing too much about it, though I could see it made him uneasy. He was eager to help with my expenses, but I told him we'd think about that later, that Claire was helping me and that I still had quite a bit of Warren's money left.

"You saved my life," he said the night we got back to the woods, after Claire had left. "I can never repay you."

"Does that bother you?" I asked.

"A little."

I was putting clean sheets on the bed. Jackson was sitting in an old armchair with broken springs, his feet up on a small table.

"It shouldn't," I said.

"When something bad like this happens in the Forest," he said, "they call out the *molimo*. Maybe that's what we should do." And he told me about the *molimo*, which is a trumpet made out of a beautifully carved wooden tube—or it can be a plastic drainpipe—and the young men run around with it making a lot of noise and scaring everybody in the camp. The women all stay in their huts and pretend not to know what's going on. It can sound like a leopard growling or an elephant trumpeting, or an owl hooting. Sometimes it just makes loud farting noises. He tried to make some *molimo* noises, but he was too tired. "They want to wake up the Forest because the Forest looks after them, takes care of all their needs. If there's trouble, they need to remind the Forest to do its job."

I smoothed the sheets, put on clean pillowcases, and helped

Jackson back into bed. Something stopped me from saying "I love you," though I did love him. Maybe it was that something was gnawing away inside me, like a tapeworm, and not the kind of tapeworm that could be drawn out of you by Mawmaw Tucker's pumpkinseed tea. I tried to tell Jackson what it was like—not guilt, not remorse, not anger, not panic, not fear, not dread. It was all these things, but it was something more too. But I couldn't get whatever it was into words. And there were a lot of other things to think on. Like staying out of jail.

I sat with Jackson for a few minutes till he went to sleep, and then I kissed him good-night.

Three things kept me going: the trips to Chicago to meet with Stella so she could figure out how to keep me out of jail; looking after Jackson—taking care of all the things he couldn't do with one arm, like brushing the dog's teeth with the poultry-flavored tooth paste that I'd used for a whole week when I first moved in with him; and monitoring the rattlesnakes that we'd released back in April. There's nothing like hunting rattlesnakes to concentrate your attention. The sun was hot and we all followed Laura's example and wore straw hats. The antennas we carried could pick up signals at a distance of five hundred meters, so you could get within a few feet of the snakes. You hold your antenna and walk in the direction of increasingly loud beeps, but sometimes the transmitters failed, or were set wrong, and sometimes the signal would bounce around on a rock formation, and it could still be hard to spot a snake even when you were right on top of it. We tried to locate each snake once a day, and then use a GPS system to record its location. We'd usually finish before noon.

It took my mind off the trial. At least when I was closing in on a snake. Frank and Laura never mentioned the shooting, but they made an extra effort to be nice to me, sympathetic, as if I was sick with some terrible disease and maybe wasn't going to get better. But Cramer came right out and asked me what had happened, and I told him. We were in the lab, just the two of us, entering the day's data into a computer that had been set up on one of the lab tables. He was standing behind me, reading the slips, and I was doing the typing. He said I'd done the right thing and asked did I need anything, and I told him that Jackson and Claire were helping with expenses and that I still had some money left from my uncle Warren. I tried to tell him about the tapeworm, gnawing away inside me.

"Tapeworms," he said, "always require an intermediate herbivore host before they reach their final carnivore host. If we knew when hominids first became their final hosts, we'd know when our ancestors started eating animal flesh as their regular diet."

"Cramer," I said, "I know you like to understand everything in evolutionary terms, but how does this information apply in my case? What's the evolutionary lesson here? Where do these feelings come from? What purpose do they serve?"

"Sorry," he said. He put his hands on my shoulders. It was the first time he'd touched me since the ASIH conference. "Have you thought about counseling? Like a police officer after killing someone, even when it was what they called a 'good' shoot."

"I don't think there is any such thing as a 'good' shoot," I said.

"You're a good friend," he said. "I don't have to watch what I say around you. And I hope you don't have to watch what you say around me."

"Thanks," I said. He was right. But neither one of us had anything more to say that day.

Afternoons it was too hot to do anything except take our clothes off and lie next to each other on the sofa bed in the living room, under the ceiling fan. Jackson kept a flannel sheet on the bed to absorb the sweat, and sometimes he'd put another flannel sheet over me and rub my back with his good hand.

But I was still afraid. I was dragging a weight around. I was putting off living till after the trial. It was hard to focus. I couldn't see things up close.

There was no rain. The stream dried up.

On Saturday nights we listened to *A Prairie Home Companion*.

Jackson rented a TV and a VCR and in the evenings we watched movies. We watched English-language movies and Jackson would fall asleep. We seldom got to the end of a film.

One morning Jackson's petrified finger—the one that had been bitten—which he wrapped with a towel when we made love, came off in the towel. We went to the hospital. The doctor in the emergency room gave him some antibiotic ointment to keep on the stump, or whatever you'd call the place where a finger comes off, and we buried the finger on the other side of the stream, way in the back, by the Indian burial mound. I dug the grave myself because Jackson couldn't handle a shovel with only one arm, though his left arm was getting better with the help of stretching exercises. He'd barely been able to move his fingers when we came back from Carbondale, but by the end of the summer he'd regained most of his strength. He was always squeezing a rubber ball.

After I'd buried the finger, I took the shovel and stuck it into the base of the Indian burial mound. Jackson tried to stop me, but I kept digging. "I was right," I said. "It's nothing but an old woodpile that's collapsed in on itself."

I'd been on the edge of panic most of the summer, but I didn't really fall over the edge till classes began at the end of August. I'd already declared a biology major and Cramer had signed me up for Biology 210 (a methods course), General Chemistry II, French Conversation, and another Great Books class to complete my Humanities requirement. But I didn't bother to register. I was sinking fast, drawing back into myself the way I'd learned to do when Earl went on a tear. I couldn't face the world, couldn't face the crowds of young, healthy, innocent boys and girls charging around the campus in backpacks. The train pulled out of the station without me. I was left standing on the platform, like someone in one of Jackson's old blues songs.

I'd saved Jackson's life and now he had to do for me like I'd done for him. We hadn't talked about it much. Maybe there wasn't that much to say. What did Jesus say to Lazarus? Or to that little girl he raised from the dead? Jairus' daughter? Not much. *Take off his graveclothes. Give her something to eat.* I don't mean that Jackson was ever *really* dead, any more than Lazarus or Jairus' daughter. But still, it was like Mawmaw Tucker praying someone back to life—her sister Hannah, who'd been bit by a big copperhead, and Jubilie Harris, who died of cancer right after my daddy was killed when Number 5 blew up. I didn't know either of them very well, but everyone said they were different after they came back, said they were almost transparent. You could almost look *through* them. As if they hadn't come all the way back. I felt that way about Jackson. As if he hadn't come all the way back. Part of him was still in another world.

And of course there was more to it. Not only had I saved his life, I'd put my own life at risk, and he wanted to help in any way he could. And he did help. He gave me twenty thousand dollars to help pay for the lawyer, though it wasn't necessary. And he sat up with me when I was too scared to go to sleep, and he did research on the necessity defense, and checked out the credentials of Peter Franklin, Stella's local counsel. He searched the Web for stories about women who had killed their husbands. A woman in Tennessee, for example, had shot her husband in the back with a shotgun while he was sleeping, and she got only five months in jail and two months in a mental institution. A woman in California had stabbed her husband a hundred and ninety times and was acquitted because her lawyer established a long history of abuse.

He was always kind to me because he was a kind person. And he was kind to Cramer too, invited him to come out, got him interested in maybe using the woods as a field station for students to do research. And he was kind to Claire. He read the manuscript she was working on and encouraged her when she got discouraged.

At the end of September we drove down to Allensboro for a pretrial conference with Peter Franklin and his assistant, Julie. Peter was wearing a three-piece suit with his tie pulled down. He'd gone to law school with Stella at the University of Michigan and said his job was to open the mail and pass it on to Stella without reading it, but he handled a lot of complicated paperwork for us and went over the kinds of questions I'd be asked by the prosecutor, because I was determined to take the stand. Nobody wanted me to take the stand. Everybody said it was a mistake. But I wasn't going through another trial without telling my story.

But what if it was a mistake?

And then all of a sudden it was fall. The temperature dropped. Fall melancholy hit. It's more powerful up north than down in Egypt. The maples turned bright red and yellow. I brought a wheelbarrow full of logs from the woodpile to the deck and we built the first fire of the season, and then Jackson worked on transcribing Claude's notes, which were stacked up on the library table. When he went to bed, I stayed up looking at the cartoons in old *New Yorkers*, and when I knew he was asleep, I closed the dampers on the wood stove and got in the truck and started out the driveway. The corn had been harvested and the fields along the drive were bare, nothing but stubble. My foot was unsteady on the clutch and the truck bucked all the way down the drive and kept bucking till I sped up on the highway. I couldn't face forty-five years. I thought I'd turn right at the first crossroads and head for Oquawka, where the elephant was buried—get up to ninety miles per hour and drive through town right into the river. It was after midnight, there wouldn't be anyone around. But I kept going straight. I opened the windows and cold air filled the cab. An orange rolled around on the floor on the passenger's side. I kicked at it and almost went off the road. I went past Broadway and kept going till I came to the bar we'd gone to on the day I got out of prison. I stopped and had a Sam Adams and watched the twirling Schlitz globe. The bar was full of men, but no one offered to buy me a drink. I drank a second beer, paid up, and drove back to the cemetery. I wanted to have a chat with Warren. It had been a long time, and I hadn't gotten the tombstone I'd promised him.

There were no lights in the cemetery, and the moon was hidden by clouds, but the lights from the prison parking lot provided some visibility once I'd shut my headlights off. I stepped up to the grave.

"Warren," I said, "I've done it again. I shot Earl."

Is that all?

"This time he's dead."

Then he won't be botherin' you no more.

"That's what I keep telling myself, but what am I going to do now? I didn't mind it on the Hill. I really didn't. I was free from Earl. Then I got free from God. But I can't go back. I can't do it again."

You should marry Jackson.

"I couldn't do that to him. Not after what I've done."

Warren didn't say anything.

"Warren, what's it like being dead? I think I'd rather be dead, lying right here next to you, than go back to prison. Forty-five years. How'd they get that number? Forty-five? Probably some committee. Couldn't settle on forty or fifty."

I could see the prison from the cemetery, could see the window in the warden's office where I'd watched Warren's funeral. All the windows were dark, but there were lots of lights in the parking lot.

"The warden was a good man," I said. "There were lots of good people on the Hill. But I can't go back, I can't go back, I can't go back. Besides, they'll probably send me somewhere else anyway, Joliet, or back to Little Muddy. It'd be like having another MRI scan, like that time Earl hurt my shoulder. It was like being in a coffin. I got through it once. I thought it'd take about two minutes, but it was more like twenty. I had to hang on to keep from losing it, to keep from screaming. The banging was driving me crazy, like someone pounding on my coffin. I suppose being dead's like that too."

It's not like that, Warren said.

"What is it like?"

It's not like anything.

"Jesus, Warren. You know what some of the girls used to do on the Hill. They used to make dominoes out of old bread and play dominoes. One of the girls kept a rat as a pet. They used to drink the cleaning fluid to make them hallucinate.

"At the second pretrial conference the State's Attorney offered second-degree murder. I'd be out in ten years. I said I was tempted. I thought my lawyer, Stella, would say, 'Don't be ridiculous.' That was when I talked to her on the phone. But she just said, 'It's your call.' Like she didn't think I was going to get off. This is my goddamn lawyer from Chicago. It's going to take all the money you left me and then some just to pay her bill. I had to sign a legal contract for twenty-five thousand dollars, and Claire said that was cheap.

"Maybe I should have taken it. Maybe it's not too late. Do you think I should have taken it? Ten years instead of forty-five? Or do you think I should drive to Oquawka. Get going about ninety and drive right through town and into the river? What do you think? Off a cliff would be better.

"And what does the State's Attorney have against me? He's my age, for Christ's sake. Why is *he* so keen to put me in prison?

"I know, I know. He's just doing his job. But why so passionate? I didn't shoot *him*.

"I've got a thousand questions I should have asked. The State's Attorney wants to use Earl's sworn testimony from the first trial. Isn't that double jeopardy? Stella says he can't do it unless I take the stand. But if I take the stand, then he can ask me about it. But if I don't take the stand, I won't get to tell my story. That's what got everything fucked up the first time. I didn't get to tell my story.

"You think I should take the plea bargain?"

No. Of course not.

I wasn't sure if that was Warren's voice or my own.

"What'll I do in prison?"

You'll have to go back to cooking with a stinger.

"Fuck you, Warren. That's not funny."

Sorry. A bad joke. I was trying to bring some humor to the situation. But Jackson'll stick by you.

"I know he will, like he's knocked me up and is doing the right thing. I should have married him when he asked me. I should call him."

I looked around for a pay phone, I wanted to call him, but there were no pay phones in the cemetery. None in the prison parking lot across the road.

"What do you want on your tombstone, Warren?"

I want something that tells the truth. I was thinking of a line from the Langston Hughes poem that Jackson read at the funeral.

"What's the truth, Warren?"

But then I thought of something else: "It don't matter now that in a million years nothing we do now is going to matter."

I had to think about this for a while. "So it doesn't matter what I do? Nothing matters?"

That's not what I said. Think about it.

I thought about it on the way home till the truck started bucking again. I'd burned out the clutch. I couldn't get it into fourth gear. I made it to the intersection by the grain elevator, then I couldn't get it into third gear. I stopped at the end of the drive, before turning in, to wait for a truck to pass, and then I couldn't get it into second gear, so I drove down the drive in first. I'd have to call someone in the morning and have it towed. Shit.

I didn't think things could get any worse, but they did. I stayed in bed most of the time, didn't keep track of what day it was. I was suffering, and the tapeworm was gnawing away inside me, and part of me wanted Jackson to suffer too, wanted everyone to suffer. But another part of me knew this was crazy and I was afraid of dragging him down into the hole with me. I couldn't do it anyway because he held on to me, refused to be dragged down, and he was stronger than I was. It was easier to make Claire suffer. She'd sit on the edge of my bed and read parts of her novel, but I wouldn't listen. Or she'd tell me about some of the student stories in her Beginning Fiction Writing class. She tried to get me to see a psychologist at the university, but I wouldn't go. Couldn't go.

Sometimes in the evening Jackson would build a fire in the wood stove, and sometimes I'd come down and lie on the sofa while he worked at his table.

Something he was transcribing would remind him of a story, something he'd done with Claude, or with his pygmy girlfriend, who was only thirty-three inches tall, and I wondered how they made love.

One time he was looking for antelope with Sibaku's brother, and they went all the way to the center of the forest where the god Tore lived, a place that was guarded by a great snake. But he didn't see the snake.

Listening to these stories, I felt safe in the big chair, a quilt pulled over me. But then it would get real quiet and you could hear the owls, and Jackson said that for the Mbuti the owl was the bird of death, just like it was back home, and that some of the hunters would throw burning logs in the direction of the owl to drive it away.

He kept coming back to the *molimo*. He wanted to wake up the Forest, and I think that's why, in the middle of October, he dragged me to a performance of *Carmina Burana*—Latin popular songs—in Kresge Recital Hall. I didn't want to go, but I went, and I found something I'd been looking for without even knowing it, something that put everything I was feeling into words for me, words and music. Especially the "In the Tavern" section. It was more than a little bit scary, this appetite for physical life. Eating and drinking and fucking. Not worrying about salvation, or about a homicide trial. I didn't know a word of Latin, but I didn't need the translations in the program to understand the songs: *Estuans interius, ira vehementi* . . . It was as if suddenly everything had a name, all the things that were gnawing away inside me. Like the singer, I was burning with violent anger; my heart was made of ashes; I was carried along like a ship without a helmsman; I looked for people as miserable as me; my heart was a heavy burden; but it was still fun to joke around, and fucking was sweeter than honey, better than salvation.

But there was love too, and beauty. A young girl stood in a red dress. If anyone touched it, it rustled. *Eia*. She stood like a little rose. Her face glowed. Her mouth was like a flower. The soprano sang it several times and every time it was more beautiful. I was that girl too.

But it was the big copper drums that woke up the Forest and broke my heart wide open. I'd never seen or heard anything like them before. Jackson called them kettle drums, because they looked like big kettles. Why so many? There were five of them. Were they all the same? Did you tune them? Why was the drummer, a distinguished silver-haired man, always bending over and tapping them? What were the knobs for? What wonderful sounds they made!

Jackson knew the kettle drum player, who had retired from the Detroit Symphony and come back to his hometown to teach part-time and play in the Colesville Symphony, and for my birthday, Tuesday, October 26, about three weeks before the trial, he gave me a kettle drum lesson, except they aren't called kettle drums. They're called "timpani." And Professor De Vries, Paul, was not a kettle drum player but a "timpanist." But this I learned later. Jackson blindfolded me and drove me into town. I knew every turn on the way into town, to campus. I could visualize: Farm King Road to Western Avenue; past Burger King, McDonald's, Hy-Vee, the Hawthorne Garage, the Amoco station; then left on Broadway. West on Broadway to Cole Circle, past the Circle and into the campus; but I got turned around as Jackson searched for a parking place. Jackson walked me into a building, but I didn't know which one. I was still blindfolded when Professor De Vries, the timpanist, who'd been waiting for us, played a drum roll that sounded like thunder. I tore the blindfold off and Professor De Vries, Paul—a man in his sixties, trim, distinguished, silver hair, glasses with dark frames and round lenses that looked too small for his face—gave me a lesson right then and there in the rehearsal hall in the Fine Arts Center. I wanted to start banging away, but Paul treated me as if I were a serious student, and I didn't get to make a sound till he'd shown me how to stand, and how to hold the mallets. He recommended the French grip, with the thumb on top of the mallet. "Relax relax relax," he kept saying. "Now: palms facing each other, thumbs up, mallet shafts parallel to each other about six to eight inches apart. Ready? Strokes straight up and down. Don't slice the head. You want the mallet to rebound back to your starting position."

I held my breath and brought the left mallet down on the beat spot, about a third of the way into the drum. The mallet jumped back at me with a life of its own. Then the right mallet. The same thing happened. The mallets had lives of their own. All you had to do was hang on and apply a little pressure now and then. It was like sex when it's really good. The room was filled with a big sound that kept getting bigger and bigger. I don't know how big it would have gotten if Paul hadn't physically stopped me, standing behind me and putting his hands on my arms.

"How much does a timpani cost?" I asked.

"'Timpanum,'" Jackson said.

Paul laughed. "'Timpanum' is grammatically correct, but no one says 'timpanum.' It's always 'timpani.' And a good set will run you seven or eight thousand, minimum."

"Oh," I said. "You don't need just one?"

He laughed again. "You could start with just one, but it wouldn't be very satisfactory. You could play only five notes."

ShoppingKart.com had closed its doors in June. I had lost twenty thousand dollars, and I'd had to pay Stella's big retainer, and that was just for starters. Plus I had three more years of school to pay for. On the other hand, if I went to prison . . . But there was no orchestra on the Hill. No *Carmina Burana.*

Paul showed me a sheet of music. I didn't know how to read music, but I could see that the lowest notes were played on the thirty-two-inch timpani, the middle notes on the twenty-six-inch, and the highest on the twenty-four-inch. You could play five different notes on each timpani by pressing on a pedal. I thought it might be a way to stay strong, a way to beat back the emotions that were battering me.

We had continued to monitor the snakes till they'd gone into hibernation after the cold snap at the end of September. They hadn't run away, or crawled away, which is what Cramer had been afraid of, and everyone on the team was glad that they were safely snugged away in their new hibernaculum, which is a fancy word for "den." I was still working for Cramer, entering the data we'd collected onto the computer. Frank had gone back to his fruit flies, and Laura had decided to stick with the mitochondrial DNA of rat snakes.

At home Jackson and I continued to work in the living room, in front of the wood stove. It was a big room, but it was crowded because the table took up a lot of space, and because I had rented a pair of fiberglass timpani at Thompson's Music for a hundred dollars a month. Paul De Vries went with me to pick them out. He showed me how to check to make sure the bowls were round and the bearing edge flat. Copper bowls would have been better, but they cost twice as much. I rented a thirty-two-inch, for the bass, and a twenty-three-inch for the higher notes. That meant leaving out some notes in the middle, but I didn't want to spend another fifty bucks a month for a third timpani. I would have given Mr. Thompson's men a bottle of scotch, but there was no scotch in the house when they came, so I gave them a bottle of crème de cassis. I wanted to put the timpani out on the deck, but they looked at me as if I were crazy. A thirty-two-inch timpani won't fit through a standard doorway unless you remove the leg assembly and turn it on its side. They're very awkward. You need a professional instrument mover. Besides, you couldn't possibly keep them outside.

The timpani came with tuning gauges, but Paul insisted that I learn to hear the fundamental pitch of each timpani by tapping the head very lightly with a mallet and adjusting the tension till the drum began to resonate. "You want to draw the sound out of the drum," he said, "not beat it into it." He also gave me a short course in cleaning and lubrication. "They're machines," he said, "systems of levers and cams and fulcrums that transfer energy from one place to another. Don't be afraid of them. A few drops of oil into these oil holes and in the pedal assembly, that's all you need, every six weeks or so, and a little grease on the ends of the tension rods and on the end of the master turning screw. Just don't get any grease or oil on the surface where the cam and roller interface, or between the pawl and the ratchet." He pointed out all these components as he went along. The pawl was a little hinged device mounted on the frame beneath the copper drum that fit into the notch of the ratchet to keep it from slipping backward when you increased the tension with the pedal. "Later on," he said, "we'll take them apart and I'll show you how to replace the heads, though you won't need to do that unless you get a set of your own."

I tried to do most of my practicing when Jackson was gone, working on my strokes (legato, staccato, roll), working on getting a consistent sound, controlling the length of the sustain by placing my fingertips on the playing zone of the head, which took more coordination than I could muster at first but which eventually would become (Paul assured me) second nature.

Jackson and I ate simply, like monks or nuns—lots of soup, lots of eggs, lots of bread and cheese—did the dishes together, fed the wood stove, took a nap after lunch, went for a walk in the late afternoon.

One afternoon Jackson brought along a small spade because he still couldn't believe that his mound was nothing but an old woodpile. We took turns digging for half an hour and didn't find anything except decayed wood. I put my arms around him and held him tight, so we couldn't look into each other's eyes. It felt safer that way. "I love you," I said, and he said he loved me too, and I started to laugh and cry at the same time because I knew that if I went to prison, he would be the one who showed up on visiting days, knew that whatever obstacles lay before us, we would confront them together, head on. I loved Jackson with my whole heart, and I think he loved me too. No more evasions and half-truths. Ever.

Paul bought a copy of the score for the percussion parts for *Carmina Burana* for me. Carl Orff had used five timpani. I had only two that I rented and a third one that Jackson chipped in for. And so I made do. Paul worked out a simplified version for me that required only three drums, and every evening just before bed I'd put on a CD of *Carmina Burana* and crank up the volume and play along and sometimes Jackson would sing the words. I'd start with "In taberna quando sumus," though the pedaling in the middle of each verse was more than I'd be able to manage without a lot more slow practice. Then I'd move on to track 24, "Blanziflor et Helena," with its heavy single-note hammer blows, and then swing into the repetition of "O Fortuna," letting the mallets pull the big bass notes out of the drums, going a little crazy at the last verse, like a big storm breaking, and something would break inside me too, every single night. Luck and virtue are against me. There's nothing but pain and exhaustion. So pluck the strings; bad luck brings down the strong man. Everyone weep with me. O Fortune, as variable as the moon, always changing, waxing and waning. Hateful life oppresses and then comforts, melting poverty and power like ice.

22

The Trial

Jackson and Claire and I, and Stella and her law clerk, Julie Anderson, stayed at the Arbor Bed and Breakfast, which advertised itself as a finely appointed Arts and Crafts bungalow that revealed some of the traditional values of the Craftsman era, including tongue-and-groove yellow pine and a Mission oak staircase. It was located about a mile from the courthouse, which was on a hill above the town flats. Peter Franklin, who joined us for dinner, explained that the jail and sheriff's residence used to be located in the uppermost level of the courthouse where the prisoners took their exercise along a narrow, open-air roof walk.

In theory I was presumed innocent and didn't have to prove a thing, but that's not the way it felt—not after the preliminary hearing back in July, not after the pretrial conference in September, not now. If felt as if everything for the trial was already scripted—the cast of characters, the props—as if we were putting on a play. There would be no surprises. Except for the ending. The charge was first-degree murder, meaning that the prosecution was going to argue that I'd brought an illegal weapon with me from Colesville with the intention of shooting Earl. Second-degree murder wasn't going to be an option—an easy out for the jury. Nor was the felony charge for possessing an illegal weapon. It was going to be all or nothing.

Jury selection was going to begin on Monday morning. We spent Sunday in the lobby of the Arbor. We ordered takeout from a Thai restaurant and watched TV while we played Scrabble. Stella was an avid player with a huge vocabulary. She bingoed out three or four times a game and she won every game. Later I learned that Stella was a nationally ranked player and that she scheduled her vacation travel around Scrabble tournaments. I couldn't concentrate. Couldn't make any words out of the tiles on my little tray, couldn't see beyond cat, hat, bat . . .

On Monday morning I ate breakfast in the dining room with Stella, Julie, and Peter. Peter had already filled Stella in about Judge Macklin, but now he reminded her that Judge Macklin didn't want the attorneys to leave the lectern and approach the jury or wander around the front of the courtroom.

Stella's dream jury, she said, would consist of women my age who'd had some experience of being slapped around by men like Earl. Her nightmare jury would consist of men like Earl. After two days of *voir dire*—which I thought meant "to see to say" in French but actually meant "to tell the truth"—we had a jury of my peers. Not a dream jury, but not a nightmare jury either. Nine women and three men. No snake handlers! At first they looked like such ordinary nice people that I told myself they couldn't possibly want to send me away for forty-five years. Later on they looked like the most extraordinary people I'd ever seen, and I told myself they couldn't possibly want to send me away for forty-five years.

The small courtroom had not been full during *voir dire*, but on

Wednesday morning there were about a hundred people, including a couple of sketch artists intent on my profile—because cameras were not allowed—and a dozen reporters in the first row behind the prosecution, and the court reporter with a funny little one-legged steno machine. Judge Macklin appeared from behind the bench, and the bailiff commanded us to rise, which we did. Department Twelve of the superior court was now in session, the Honorable Elizabeth Macklin presiding. The bailiff told us be seated.

The judge spent most of the morning laying down the ground rules for the jury: They were not to discuss the case with anyone, not to read about it in the papers, not to watch accounts of it on the evening news. She explained the procedures in broad terms and made it clear that she did not expect any surprises.

The State's Attorney or prosecutor didn't get to make his opening statement until well after lunch. Some of the people in the courtroom may have been a little drowsy, but he had *my* full attention. He looked like a man trying to present an image of authority and good will, but he also looked nervous. He thanked the jury and expressed his appreciation for the important work they had undertaken. The prosecution, he said, represented the people of the State of Illinois, but the prosecution also represented the victim . . .

Stella was on her feet with an objection. "Improper argument."

The judge agreed. "Tell us about the evidence you're going to present."

"Yes, Your Honor." The prosecutor then told a simple story about a woman who had shot her husband at close range with a Walther PPK. She'd shot and killed him in his own home. He approached the jury and spoke slowly and clearly, shaking his head as if to wonder how such a thing could have happened, how someone could commit such a brutal murder. Judge Macklin scolded him back to the lectern.

"The evidence will show," he went on, "that she persuaded her lover, a man not her husband, to buy the Walther PPK for her on October fourth, nineteen ninety-nine, at Gun Collectors in Colesville, Illinois. The evidence will show that the defendant could not buy the gun herself because she was a convicted felon and could not obtain a FOID card—that's a Firearm Owner's Identification (FOID) card. It will show that on June twentieth, two thousand, when she drove from Colesville to Naqada, she carried this illegal firearm concealed in her purse and that she used it to fatally shoot her husband in his own home."

The victim, he went on, was a man of faith, a minister, a man well loved in the church, and so on. There was more, but that was the gist of it.

In her opening statement Stella said that she was sure that the jurors knew that in an ordinary criminal trial the burden of proof was on the prosecution, that the prosecution had to prove beyond reasonable doubt that I had committed the crime of which he or she was accused. But this wasn't going to be an ordinary criminal trial, and "reasonable doubt" wasn't the issue. The state wasn't going to have any trouble proving that I had shot my *former* husband. The issue was whether or not I was *justified* in shooting my former husband, and she went on to explain the different justifications for the use of force listed in Article Seven of the Illinois Penal Code, starting with "self-defense," which she was sure everyone on the jury was familiar with, and ending with section 7-1: "Use of force in defense of a person."

"The evidence will show," she said, "that on the night of June twentieth, Ms. Cochrane—Sunny—was not only defending herself against her former husband, she was defending another person, a person whose life was being willfully endangered by her former husband, Mr. Earl Cochrane.

"The law makes it perfectly clear that 'A person is justified in the use of force against another when and to the extent that he reasonably believes that such conduct is necessary to defend himself or another against such other's imminent use of unlawful force. However, he is justified in the use of force which is intended or likely to cause death or great bodily harm only if he reasonably believes that such force is necessary to prevent imminent death or great bodily harm to himself or another, or the commission of a forcible felony.' "

The law leaves a lot of room for interpretation. Did I "reasonably believe" that I was defending Jackson against "the imminent use of unlawful force"? How would anybody know what I "reasonably believed"? I wasn't sure myself. Was Earl engaged in "the imminent use of unlawful force"? Was Jackson's death "imminent"? Was Earl engaged in committing a "forcible felony" at the time I shot him?

Stella went on to tell a story about a woman who'd had good reason to fear her husband—her *former* husband—a snake-handling preacher with a long history of violence, including two felony counts; a woman who had shot this man after he'd forced her at gunpoint to put her arm in a box of rattlesnakes; a woman who had spent her time in prison studying history and biology and mathematics and world literature; a woman who was presently enrolled in a prestigious university; a woman who had been forced to shoot her *former* husband again when he forcibly prevented her from calling for medical assistance for her fiancé, who'd been bitten by a rattlesnake, and who would have died if she hadn't intervened.

When Stella was finished with her opening statement, the prosecutor called the police photographer to verify half a dozen photographs of Earl lying in a pool of blood on the floor of his trailer. Yes, the photographer said, he had been there, he had taken the pictures, this is what it had looked like. Stella objected to what she called a "dog and pony show" and offered to stipulate that the victim was dead. Besides, she'd agreed to three photos at the evidentiary hearing, not six. The judge told the prosecutor to stick to the three photos that had been agreed upon, which were then entered as evidence—People's Exhibit 1—and passed around to the members of the jury.

If I'd been looking for signs, which I was determined not to do, this little courtroom battle would have been a small one.

The prosecutor called a ballistics expert who established beyond all reasonable doubt that the 85 to 100-grain bullet that had killed Earl had been fired from the Walther PPK that had been in police custody since the shooting. The gun, which had a yellow tag on it, was introduced as People's Exhibit 2. Stella had offered to stipulate that the Walther PPK in police custody was indeed the weapon that had killed Mr. Cochrane, but the prosecutor, she explained, wanted to put on his dog and pony show.

Stella declined to cross-examine, but she reminded the court that she was presenting an affirmative defense and did not intend to challenge the "facts" laid out by the prosecution.

The second prosecution witness was the owner of Gun Collectors in Colesville, whose ridiculous mustache looked like a horseshoe had been stitched onto his face. He kept tugging on it as he told the court that he had sold the Walther PPK to Mr. Jackson Jones, but that the defendant had offered to pay Mr. Jones for the pistol right in the shop.

The prosecutor asked the owner of the gun shop to identify both Jackson and me, which he did.

Stella declined to cross-examine.

Don't ask me how it happened, but by the time the prosecutor finished with the gun-shop owner, it was time to quit for the day.

During that first day of testimony, there was so much going on in the courtroom, so much to think about, that I remained relatively calm, but that night, eating Thai food again and watching *Seinfeld* reruns and playing Scrabble in the lobby of the Arbor, I started to panic. It started with Scrabble. I couldn't come up with a single word. I couldn't read the tiles on my little Scrabble rack. I turned in all my tiles and took more, but I still couldn't read them. My thoughts were like brambles tearing at the inside of my head; I started to sweat; my hands started to tremble and I couldn't hold on to my tiles; I couldn't catch my breath; I felt like I was choking. I was convinced I was going to die.

Stella stopped the game. "She's having a panic attack," she said. "Jackson, put your arm around her. Don't grab her, just let her lean on you."

Stella turned off the TV and we sat in silence for about half an hour, and then I was okay again, more or less. I watched another *Seinfeld* rerun, one I'd already seen in prison, while the others finished the game. I went to bed early and Jackson and Claire stayed in my room till I went to sleep. As I was drifting off I thought, I should have brought my timpani. I could have set them up my room. It was big enough. *O fortuna, velut luna, statu variabilis.*

The state called DX Wilson in the morning. He was brought in from the witness room by the bailiff. He took the stand and swore to tell the truth and nothing but the truth. He was the closest thing the prosecution had to an eyewitness, and was definitely their most important witness. He'd been out in the hallway when I shot Earl and was the first one to come into the bedroom. And he'd been on the scene when I shot Earl the first time. And he'd known both of us for years. Now that Earl was gone, DX was preaching and trying to hold the church together, but Sally said he was having a hard time and they were thinking of moving over to Middlesboro.

DX was the first man I'd gone with after I married Earl, and it made me sick to my stomach to see him raise his hand and swear to tell the truth and nothing but the truth so help him God.

It had happened like this. I'd stopped to see my cousin Sally one day, but Sally was gone, and DX and I got to fooling around and couldn't stop. We fooled around every chance we got after that, and I went kind of crazy. So crazy that one day after church, after we'd been going together for a while, I told DX, "Let's stop pretending and tell everybody we're in love," and DX's face went as gray as the cement in the cement plant where he worked, and if I were going to thank God for something, it would be that DX was either too smart (unlikely) or to scared to do it, or I might be on trial for shooting DX. I was seventeen years old at the time.

As it was, Earl caught us and almost killed DX, broke his jaw so bad it had to be wired shut for two weeks, and beat the tar out of me. And then he forgave me and blamed everything on a sex demon. And I thought maybe he was right. At least I got down on my knees and prayed with him to get right with the Lord. And then I was all right for a while.

DX got right with the Lord in the hospital and when he got out he went over to Earl's and the two of them went out behind the trailer by an old stump where Earl used to go when he wanted to settle something with the Lord and started praying, even though DX's jaw was still wired shut—I watched them from the kitchen window— and pretty soon they were best friends. That was the way Earl did things.

DX was younger than Earl. Smaller, thinner, softer than Earl. Nicer than Earl. He'd take over the church when Earl backed up on the Lord, but he didn't have Earl's fire. He'd just sort of hold things together till Earl got right with God again.

I stayed with DX and Sally during the first trial, but DX and I never fooled around again. And look at him now. His narrow face looked the way it had back when I wanted to tell everyone we were in love. Like wet cement.

The point of DX's testimony—the prosecutor's point—was that nothing out of the ordinary had happened till I showed up with a pistol. Jackson had come down to the church to have a look-see and maybe poke some fun at everybody, and pretty soon he'd got involved, taking part in church activities—more than he'd let on to me—footwashing, speaking in tongues, playing the mouth harp. No one was ever forced or even encouraged to handle serpents. "He took a liking to my two-headed serpent," DX said, "Moloch and Belzebub is what I call the two heads, when he and Earl was havin' a sup with Sally and me."

The prosecutor asked DX to describe the relationship between Mr. Cochrane and Professor Jones.

"They was getting to be good friends. They washed each other's feet, like I said. And they went fishin' out on the river and walking out in the Shawnee National Forest. The last time I went along too. Fishin'. There wasn't no trouble."

"Could you tell us what happened on Professor Jones's last visit?"

"He was in pretty bad shape when he come down here on Thursday. He couldn't hardly walk. His girlfriend had gone off to Mexico with another man and . . ."

Stella objected. "Hearsay."

"Sustained.

"He was pretty broken up about it . . ."

Stella objected again. "Hearsay."

The judge told DX to stick to what he'd observed himself and not to say anything about what he'd heard from others. "Mrs. Rose from the Naqada Inn called Earl, and Earl went over there, and then he come and got me and we went over to the Rose where he was. Professor Jones. A lot of women from the church come over too, to pray over him. Mawmaw Tucker come. Everybody prayed over him real hard and he got to feelin' better. Next day we went fishin', him and Earl and me, and Professor Jones caught a real nice blue cat.

"At supper that night Sally, my wife, fried up some cat fillets, or maybe it was sauger, and afterwards Jackson—Professor Jones— touched the snake when Earl was holding it. He put his hand right around it and didn't want to let go. Earl asked him did he want to hold it and he said no, not that night."

The prosecutor drew out the story till the judge told him to move on.

"Can you describe what happened the following night?"

The prosecutor led DX through an explanation of a "brush arbor" and the "homecoming" gathering, which was attended by people coming all the way from West Virginia to East Tennessee. Probably two hundred people.

"We sang some hymns and then Earl preached a while and then we sang some more, and Professor Jones, he was wailing pretty good on his mouth harp, and then Punkin Bates preached, and then some of the men got covered by the Spirit and started going to the serpent boxes, and Professor Jones, he come up to Earl and wanted to handle my two-headed snake, and Earl gave it to him, and then after a minute he got bit, and Earl and me come to him right away and asked him did he want medical attention, and he said no he didn't. We got him back to Earl's and then gathered around to pray for him."

"You didn't call an ambulance?"

"No. He was exercising his freedom of religion. He didn't want no medical attention."

I could see that the prosecutor had coached him to say "exercising his freedom of religion," but I guess that's part of the game.

DX hadn't been in the room when I shot Earl, but he'd heard us fussing at each other in the hallway, and he'd heard the shot and rushed into the bedroom.

The prosecutor asked his paralegal to bring a large diagram, mounted on some kind of Styrofoam, to the witness stand and placed it on an easel and asked DX if this was an accurate representation of the floor plan of Earl's trailer. He said it was, and the prosecutor moved it into evidence as People's Exhibit 3. Let the record show that Exhibit 3 is a diagram of the victim's—Mr. Cochrane's—trailer. He walked DX through the shooting, from the kitchen, where he'd heard us fussing at each other, into the hallway, past the bathroom, into the bedroom at the end of the trailer. Earl was on the floor, he said, and I was still holding the pistol.

"She was still holding the pistol," he said. "She pointed it at me and told me to call nine-one-one."

"So you were afraid she might have shot you too?"

Stella objected. Leading question.

The prosecutor withdrew the question and asked DX to describe the scene, which he did: Earl lying in a pool of blood with a big hole in his chest. The judge finally cut him off. The jury had already seen photographs of the crime scene.

Stella tore DX apart on the cross-examination. I was glad to see some fireworks. She always dressed down for the trial and looked kind of frumpy, but that was part of her strategy. I was dressed down too in a white blouse and pleated skirt that Claire had picked out for me. None of the fancy clothes from Field's. My "look" was "modest," "nonthreatening." Stella had advised me to look the jury members right in the eye without challenging them. I did my best.

"Everything was perfectly normal? You didn't see any reason to call an ambulance?"

"It was in the hands of the Lord."

"Professor Jones was bitten on a Sunday night, is that correct?"

"Yes."

"And he became violently ill?"

"Yes."

"Vomiting and diarrhea? Swelling?"

"Yes."

"Instead of calling an ambulance, you put him in the cab of Mr. Cochrane's truck and took him to Mr. Cochrane's trailer, is that correct?"

"Yes. We put him in the cab of Earl's truck."

"It didn't occur to you to call an ambulance?"

"Truck was a lot quicker. Besides, there wasn't no telephone in the arbor."

"And members of the church gathered at Mr. Cochrane's trailer to pray for him?"

"Yes, there was about ten of us at first and then more come after the brush arbor."

"You're familiar with the symptoms of snake bite?"

"Yes . . ." He started to say more but Stella cut him off.

"You've been bitten yourself?"

"Yes."

"And did you seek medical attention?"

"No."

"Has anyone in your family ever been bitten?"

The prosecutor objected. "Irrelevant."

Stella rephrased the question: "Has there ever been an occasion when you thought it was appropriate to call for medical attention when someone who'd been bitten by a rattlesnake declined medical attention?"

"My wife got bit once by a copperhead."

"And your wife declined medical assistance, isn't that true?"

"Yes."

"But you took her to the hospital in Rosiclare?"

"Yes."

"You didn't trust the Lord in this case?"

"It was my wife."

"I see." Stella paused to let this answer sink in. "Have you ever seen anyone go into a coma before?"

The prosecutor objected. DX wasn't a medical expert. He couldn't say whether or not Jackson was in a coma.

The judge sustained the objection and Stella rephrased the question: "Have you ever seen anyone become totally unconscious after being bitten by a rattlesnake?"

"No."

"So this was a new type of situation for you?"

"Yes."

"At any point did you think that it might be appropriate to call for medical assistance for Professor Jones?"

"He said he didn't want no medical attention."

"After your wife was bitten by a copperhead, a bite that's much less dangerous than a rattlesnake bite, she declined medical attention. But you used your own judgment and took her to the hospital in Rosiclare. Did it occur to you after Professor Jones slipped into a coma—became unconscious—that it might be time to use your own judgment?"

"Earl said he didn't want medical attention. It was in the hands of the Lord."

"Do you know of any reason Mr. Cochrane might have had to want to harm Professor Jones?"

"Objection. Calls for speculation."

"Sustained."

Stella asked a different question: "Would it be fair to say that on Monday, June nineteenth, the day after Professor Jones was bitten, at two forty-nine p.m. you were concerned enough about Professor

Jones's condition to call Sunny in order to warn her that he'd been serpent bit?"

DX looked at the prosecutor. He mumbled something, and Stella waited for the court reporter, who sat near the witnesses with her stenograph machine, to say that she couldn't hear the witness. The judge asked him to speak into the microphone.

"Yes."

Stella introduced the answering-machine tape, which Julie played on a small but expensive tape recorder: "Your boyfriend's been serpent bit. You better get down here."

"Is that your voice on the tape?"

DX hesitated. "Yes."

Stella moved to enter the tape as Defense Exhibit 1. Julie handed the tape to the clerk of the court.

"So, Mr. Wilson. You were on the spot. You saw what was happening. Would it be fair to say that you thought that the time had come to call for medical attention?"

"I suppose."

"You said, 'Your boyfriend's been serpent bit. You better get down here.' Don't those words suggest that you were worried about Professor Jones?"

"I suppose. But she said he couldn't of been serpent bit because he was in Paris."

"Let's stay focused, Mr. Wilson. You knew something was wrong, but instead of calling for an ambulance, you called Sunny?"

"You mean Willa Fern?"

"She calls herself 'Sunny' now."

"All right."

"Was there any reason not to pick up the phone and dial 911?"

"Earl said Professor Jones didn't need no medical attention."

"Was Earl a doctor?"

"He was a preacher."

"Would it be fair to say that you believed that Sunny would call for medical attention when you informed her of the situation?"

The prosecutor objected: "Can't testify to the defendant's state of mind."

"I'm only asking him what he believed himself."

But the judge wasn't buying it. "Objection sustained."

"No further questions." But Stella reserved the right to recall DX "in our case in chief."

The state rested its case.

On Thursday night I didn't try to play Scrabble. I just watched TV and went to bed early. Jackson and Claire stayed in my room with me, as they did every night after the panic attack, till I fell asleep.

Our turn came on Friday morning. Stella began by spending a lot of time with the two paramedics, who testified that Earl had sent them away, wouldn't allow them to see Jackson. One of them had called the sheriff's office.

On the cross-examination the prosecutor had asked if Mr. Cochrane had had a weapon, if he had threatened them, if he had physically prevented them from entering the trailer.

No, but Stella had made her point. As soon as they got back to the hospital in Rosiclare one of them called the sheriff's office.

The sheriff was our next witness. Stella asked permission to treat him as hostile, and Judge Macklin granted it. Stella showed him no mercy, asking him to read aloud the provision in the Illinois Dangerous Animals Act pertaining to venomous snakes.

The prosecutor objected on the grounds that the Dangerous Animals Act was irrelevant to the present murder trial even if

Mr. Cochrane *had* been doing something illegal. Stella said she wanted to establish that Mr. Cochrane was a dangerous man.

The judge overruled the objection.

"It's just a misdemeanor," the sheriff said, getting himself all puffed up. This was the sheriff that would have served the divorce papers on Earl.

Stella kept asking him to read the provision that she had marked, and he kept stalling, till the judge threatened to hold him in contempt. This is what he finally read:

Sec. 1. No person shall have a right of property in, keep, harbor, care for, act as custodian of or maintain in his possession any dangerous animal except at a properly maintained zoological park, federally licensed exhibit, circus, scientific or educational institution, research laboratory, veterinary hospital, hound running area, or animal refuge in an escape-proof enclosure.

"We don't bother them snake-handling people too much," the sheriff said without being asked. "We let them mind their own business."

"In other words, you simply ignore the law?"

"We don't look on it like that," he said.

"On Tuesday, June twentieth at two o'clock," Stella said, without commenting further, "your office received a call from George Barlow"—Stella pointed to Barlow, the paramedic who had testified earlier that he'd called the sheriff's office—"saying that someone had been bitten by a rattlesnake and needed immediate assistance. Why didn't you respond?"

"No one was available at the time. There's only three of us."

"But your office was notified by a paramedic from the hospital in Rosiclare that a man had been bitten by a rattlesnake and that they—the two paramedics—had not been allowed to take the man to the hospital, or even to see him."

"It was on the machine. We just didn't get to it."

"What would it take to get you to intervene?" And so on.

The prosecutor did his best to clean up the mess by focusing on the fact that the sheriff's office got a certain number of crank calls every day and didn't have enough deputies to answer every call, and by giving the sheriff a chance to say that he wasn't so much ignoring the law as upholding the freedom of religion.

"It wasn't a call for help. It was just somebody'd got serpent bit. And like I said, we let these folks worship in their own way, however they want."

The prosecutor thanked him profusely, as if he'd just driven a nail in my coffin.

Our next witness was the doctor from Memorial Hospital in Carbondale, who described the envenomation in some detail.

The venom of the North American rattlesnake is hemorrhagic. It breaks down the lining of the smaller blood vessels and permits blood to diffuse through the tissues. The swelling then spreads to the heart and, in severe cases, like this one, may rupture the skin. Without medical intervention the swelling—depending on the quantity of venom and the location of the bite—may reach the trunk within twenty-four hours. The victim will experience confusion and extreme nervousness and—again without medical intervention—may lapse into a coma.

Stella showed the doctor a photograph of Jackson's arm, bigger than his thigh and purple-black, and moved it into evidence. The prosecutor objected again, on the grounds that the seriousness of the envenomation was not at issue, and offered to stipulate that the bite had been serious, but the judge reminded him that the death of Mr. Cochrane had not been at issue either.

The doctor testified that the photo was an accurate representation of the condition of Jackson's arm, and the photo was marked and passed around to the jury.

The doctor described the fasciotomy performed to remove necrotic tissue. He had cut open the arm from the palm up to the middle of Jackson's biceps to relieve the pressure that had built up in the arm from the rattlesnake venom. Professor Jones had spent the next three and a half weeks in Memorial Hospital in Carbondale and had undergone four more surgeries to clean out the dead tissue from his arm. Finally, the doctor had performed a skin graft, with skin from Jackson's leg, to close up the arm. He'd been released from the hospital on July 14th with instructions to undergo a course of intensive physiotherapy.

The doctor emphasized the seriousness of the bite and that Jackson was lucky to be alive. That he was near death when he arrived at the hospital. Lucky to have the arm. He had, in fact, lost a finger.

On his cross-examination, which lasted only two minutes, the prosecutor pointed out that the seriousness of the injury was not in question. The issue was that the defendant shot her husband—former husband—at close range.

The judge told him to ask a question or save it for his closing argument. It was time to quit for the week. The lawyers stood up as the jury filed out.

"It's a good way for us to end the week," Stella said later. But it was an agonizing weekend for me. Jackson stayed right with me, morning, noon, and night.

Stella and I went over my testimony, but we didn't rehearse it to death because she wanted it to keep some spontaneity. There were two stories she wanted me to get in front of the jury: the story of Earl forcing me to put my arm in a box of rattlesnakes, and the story of how I shot Earl the second time. She'd hold the door open for me;

all I had to do was walk through it. On Sunday night, in my room, Jackson and Claire and I were like three people out on the river in a johnboat in rough weather. You can't talk much. You don't feel like talking anyway. You just want to get back to the marina.

My alarm went off at six o'clock Monday morning. It was a very complicated clock with two separate alarms and two snooze buttons. I hit one snooze button, then another, and wondered what would happen if I just stayed in bed all day. Would the trial go on without me? I'd been determined to take the stand—to tell my own story in my own words. But when the time came, I was nervous. Stella and I had been over my testimony a hundred times, and Stella's assistant had cross-examined me from every possible angle, anticipating everything the prosecutor could throw at me, including Earl's version of the snake-shed story—his sworn testimony from the first trial. Stella had objected on the grounds that she would have no opportunity to cross-examine the witness; but the judge had said that Ms. Cochrane's attorney at the time of the trial would have had an opportunity to cross-examine Mr. Cochrane, and that therefore she would admit the evidence. Stella could call it into question in her closing jury argument.

"I can't do it," I said to Jackson.

It was hard for us to talk. It was six ten. Jackson was looking out the window. There were still a lot of complex feelings simmering on the back burner—Paris, Mexico, his risking his life by handling, me risking prison to save it by shooting Earl. But it was as if we didn't know what any of these things meant, as if we wouldn't know how to think about them till the trial was over.

He sat down on the edge of the bed and ran his fingers through my hair. It was getting late. He rubbed my back and tickled my arm and we went over the schedule for the trial.

It was late, but he didn't rush me.

"I wish you could get up on the stand with me," I said. "At least you'll be in the courtroom, you and Claire. Along with a lot of folks from the Church of the Burning Bush who'd like to see me fry in Hell."

But nobody wanted Jackson on the stand. Stella didn't want him on the stand because she didn't want the jury to hear him tell how he'd bought the gun for Sunny and how he'd said he didn't want medical attention, and the prosecutor—this was Stella's explanation—didn't want him on the stand because he didn't need Jackson's testimony to make his points about buying the gun and about declining medical attention, and because Jackson would be a hostile witness, a wild card who might say anything.

I couldn't eat anything at breakfast. Stella ordered her usual poached eggs and ham with real Kentucky red-eye gravy.

I sat at the defense table with Peter Franklin while Stella made a few introductory remarks before asking me to introduce myself to the jury. I kept reminding myself that my assignment was to establish two stories clearly in the imaginations of the jury: the snake shed and the shooting. The one thing I was not to do, until prompted, was mention the trip to Mexico, which the prosecutor had already introduced through the back door, until she prompted me.

I kept it short: "I used to be Willa Fern," I said. "Now I'm Sunny. I grew up in Naqada as a member the Church of the Burning Bush with Signs Following. I married Earl, after my daddy was killed when Number Five blew up, when I was sixteen years old."

"And you've been divorced for over a year?"

"Yes."

"So it would be a mistake to refer to the deceased as 'your husband'?"

"Yes."

"The State's Attorney has laid a lot of stress on the pistol that you brought with you to Naqada. Would it be fair to say that you brought a pistol because you were frightened of your ex-husband?"

The prosecutor objected: "leading question." The judge sustained the objection. Stella wasn't supposed to ask me questions that pointed toward the answer she wanted. But she'd planned this too.

Stella rephrased the question: "Could you tell the court why you wanted a pistol?"

"Because I was afraid of Earl. The prison must have forgot to notify him when I got out, but he found out where I was and then he wrote to me at TF—that's Thomas Ford University—and said he was coming to Colesville to take me home. But there was no way I was going back with Earl. I couldn't live with a man I was afraid of all the time. I never answered his letters and I never signed the permission so he could come and see me."

We were coming up on the snake-shed story, and I was feeling more confident. I told a little bit about Earl's background, about him being a fighter up in Chicago, about his felony convictions, about the way he used to slap me around, and Stella introduced half a dozen digitally enlarged black-and-white shots that the police had taken of the snake shed after I shot Earl the first time and asked that they be admitted into evidence. The pictures were mounted on foam core and laminated. Julie passed them around to the jury members.

The prosecutor objected on the grounds that the existence of the snake shed had no bearing on the second shooting, but Stella pointed out that they demonstrated that I had good reason to fear my ex-husband, and Judge Macklin overruled him. The pictures showed the outside and they showed some of the snakes in their aquariums, including a close-up of the big old diamondback that had bit my thumb out in the snake shed.

"The worst time," I said, giving the jury plenty of time to look at the pictures, "was when he held a gun to my head and made me put my arm in a box of rattlesnakes, just like one of those aquariums in the pictures—the one with that big diamondback in with two copperheads. He wanted to see if the Lord would spare me because he said I'd been going with other men."

"Let me see if I understand this," Stella said. "Mr. Cochrane forced you to undergo a medieval trial by ordeal—a kind of witch trial: If you were innocent, then the snake wouldn't bite you; but if you were guilty, it would bite you?"

The prosecutor objected that Stella was leading the witness. Me. The judge agreed.

"Just tell us what happened."

"He made me get down on my knees and get right with God. I told him to just shoot me, and he said if I didn't put my arm in the box he'd force my head down so I could take the bite in my eye."

Then I went on to the bite, the swelling, the shooting—Earl putting his .22 down on the kitchen table and getting a glass of milk out of the refrigerator and me picking it up and shooting him—and calling Sally, and Sally and DX coming over and calling an ambulance. "We both spent the night in the hospital, but mine must have been a dry bite because I didn't swell up too bad and they only gave me two vials of antivenin.

"But at the trial I never got to tell what happened, and that's why I'm telling my own story this time. Earl was saying I'd got a snake out of the snake shed and was trying to get it to bite him while he was taking a nap only it bit me instead. Which was the craziest thing I ever heard of.

"That's why I had to go to prison. Six years. Because I didn't get to tell my story."

"Can you tell the court what you did in prison?"

"It was real hard at first, but then I got to taking classes from the junior college and it wasn't so bad. Better'n living with Earl."

Stella introduced a copy of my transcript from Henrietta Hill, which was admitted as evidence. Julie passed around copies of the transcript, and Stella pointed out all the classes I had taken: English Composition, American History I, American History II, Intro to Poetry, Biology, Economics, Banking, and so on. I'd taken one class a semester starting in 1994, and I'd gotten all A's.

"And how have you been spending your time since you were released?"

"I'm enrolled in Thomas Ford University. I've already declared a major in biology. That's why I went to Mexico with my professor and another student. The meetings of the American Society of Ichthyologists and Herpetologists. In La Paz, Mexico."

"Can you explain 'herpetologists'?"

"'Herp' means 'crawl' in Greek. 'Herpetologists' are scientists who study things that crawl."

"Like snakes?"

"Yes. I came home in the morning and there was a message on the answering machine."

"Did you recognize the caller?"

"Yes. It was Mr. DX Wilson."

"And then what did you do?"

"I called the hospital in Rosiclare to see how much CroFab antivenin they had, and I called Professor Cramer and he signed for me to get some more antivenin from the herps lab at Thomas Ford University, and then I drove straight to the hospital in Rosiclare."

"How long did it take you?"

"It's a six-hour drive. I got to Rosiclare about six o'clock."

"And when you arrived what did you discover?"

"I discovered that Earl had sent the ambulance away when it came to get Jackson, so Jackson never got to the hospital."

The prosecutor objected: "Hearsay."

"Overruled."

"Did the paramedics talk to Mr. Jones?"

The prosecutor objected because we'd already heard from the paramedic in charge. The judge sustained the objection.

"I thought Jackson must be okay," she said, "or he would have been in the hospital, so I drove over to Earl's trailer and there were people all over, outside and in the living room, drinking coffee and praying for Jackson. I went right to the bedroom and Earl was in there with Jackson. Jackson's eyes were closed and he wasn't moving. I picked up the phone on a little table next to the bed to call nine-one-one and Earl knocked it out of my hands. 'He's in the Lord's hands now,' he said. 'Nothing you can do.'"

"I said I should call nine-one-one. Earl kept saying Jackson didn't want medical attention and that if I didn't believe him I could ask DX or anyone. 'He's in a coma,' I said."

The prosecutor objected. I was not a doctor.

Stella intervened: "She's testifying about what she said."

The judge overruled the objection.

"Could you describe what you saw and heard?"

"He couldn't talk. I couldn't wake him up. I wanted to go out to get help, but Earl wouldn't let me leave the room."

"Were you afraid?"

"Of course I was afraid."

"Did Mr. Cochrane have a gun?"

"He didn't need a gun."

"Did he threaten you?"

"I told you. He knocked the phone out of my hand. He wouldn't let me pick it up. He said if I touched it he'd he was going to whup my tail till it wouldn't hold shucks."

"Do you mean he was going to spank you? Like a little girl?"

"Worse than that."

"I told him I had to go to the bathroom . . ."

Stella asked that the diagram of the trailer, which had already been entered as evidence, be placed on the easel, and used a pointer to refresh the jury's memory while she asked questions: this is the bathroom? this is the hallway? this is the bedroom where Jackson was lying unconscious? Yes yes yes.

"Can you tell us what happened?"

"When I came out of the bathroom, I kept the gun on Earl. I told him not to come near me, I told him I was going to phone the hospital, but he kept coming after me, and I backed into the bedroom, and he kept coming till I was back in a corner."

Stella indicated the corner of the bedroom where I'd been standing when I shot Earl. "There was no place for you to go? You were trapped?"

"I told Earl I'd shoot him if he tried anything, and he lunged at me and I closed my eyes and pulled the trigger."

"Did you intend to kill Mr. Cochrane?"

"I did not. I just wanted to stop him, but he kept coming at me."

Stella asked permission to approach the witness, which Judge Macklin granted, and then approached me. "Would you say he was this close when you started backing down the hallway?"

"A little farther away."

Stella took a couple of small steps backward. "Like this?"

"That's about right."

"The record will so reflect that Mr. Cochrane was about ten feet away from Sunny when she started backing down the hallway."

"And then, as you were backing up, he kept coming closer. Would you say he was about this far away from you when you reached the bedroom door?" Stella came closer.

"Yes."

"Let the record show that by the time Sunny reached the bedroom door, Mr. Cochrane was about six feet away from her. Julie," she said to her assistant, "would you show the bedroom door?" Julie used a laser pointer to indicate the way I backed down the hall. Stella approached closer. "And when you'd backed up as far as you could go, into a corner in the bedroom where your fiancé was lying unconscious . . ." She waited for Julie to point out the bedroom corner on the screen. "Would you say he was *this* far away from you?"

"Yes."

"Let the record show that when Sunny had her back up against the wall, Mr. Cochrane was about four feet away from her"—she paused. "And when he lunged at you . . ." Stella startled everyone by lunging at me, striking out at me with one arm to knock an imaginary pistol out of my hand. I let out a little scream.

"Let the record show," Stella said, before the prosecutor could object, "that Mr. Cochrane lunged at Sunny from a distance of about three feet. No more questions."

The prosecutor took his time getting started on the cross. He fiddled with his papers. He whispered in the ear of his paralegal before stepping up to the lectern.

"You've just heard a pretty fantastic story," he said to the jury. "Let's put aside for now the fact that the defendant was convicted of assault with a deadly weapon in September nineteen ninety-three for shooting her husband and was sent to prison for six years. We'll come back to that later. Right now let's take a look at the events leading up to the second time she shot her husband, this time fatally."

Stella was on her feet. "Is there a question here?"

The judge told the prosecutor to get on with it.

"Besides," Stella said, still on her feet. "He was *not* her husband."

"Sorry," the prosecutor said. "*Former* husband." He turned to me. "You've heard testimony from Mr. DX Wilson that when Professor Jones arrived in Naqada last summer—on June fifteenth—he was in 'pretty bad shape,' and you've heard Mr. Wilson testify that you told him that Professor Jones couldn't have been serpent bit because he was in Paris, France. Could you please explain your answer to the jury?"

"I thought he *was* in Paris."

The prosecutor continued to stare at me. More of a glare than a stare. "You've been living with Mr. Jones for over a year, isn't that true?"

"Yes."

"How is it that you thought he was in Paris when in fact he was right here in southern Illinois?"

"He was planning to go to Paris. He must have changed his mind at the last minute."

"Without telling you?"

"Yes."

"Mr. Jones wasn't just a casual acquaintance, was he?"

"No."

"In fact, several times in the course of this trial he's been described as your *fiancé*. Would you say that's an accurate description of your relationship? That you were engaged to be married?"

"Not officially."

"I see. Or, maybe I don't see. Was Professor Jones your fiancé or not? Yes or no?"

"We didn't use that word."

"What word did you use?"

"We were good friends. We loved each other."

"I see. You loved Professor Jones so much that you'd do anything to protect him, including shooting your former husband?"

"Yes."

"Did he give you an engagement ring?"

"No. We didn't need a ring."

"Isn't it true, Ms. Cochrane, that you and your 'fiancé' were planning a trip to Paris together?"

"Yes."

"And isn't it true that instead of going to Paris with your 'fiancé,' you went to Mexico with another man?"

Stella got to her feet and objected: "Irrelevant. My client is not on trial for attending a professional conference in Mexico."

"Your Honor," the prosecutor protested. I'm trying to clarify the defendant's intentions when she shot her husband. Her *former* husband. If she canceled her plans to go to Paris with one man at the last minute to go off to Mexico with another man . . ."

"I'll allow it."

"And isn't it true that you used your fiancé's injury as an excuse to shoot your husband?"

Stella was on her feet again, but before she could object the judge had silenced the prosecutor. "Enough." But he'd made his point. And in fact in my own inner courtroom I *was* on trial for going to Mexico with another man.

"Did your former husband have a gun?"

"He had lots of guns."

"At the time you shot him was he armed?"

"No, but he didn't need a gun."

I thought the prosecutor had lost his way, because he suddenly turned back to the snake-shed episode.

"Let's go back to the beginning, to the first time you shot your husband. He was your husband at the time, is that correct?"

I nodded and he told me to answer out loud.

"You've told this court today that your husband forced you to put your arm in a box of rattlesnakes."

"Yes."

"And you were very frightened?"

Stella objected: "Leading question."

"Can you tell the court how you felt at this time?"

"I was very frightened."

"But isn't it true that you've been handling rattlesnakes all your life?"

"In church."

"And have you had occasion to handle rattlesnakes recently?"

"Yes."

"Isn't it true that you've been working on a project to move an entire colony of rattlesnakes from one place to another?"

"Yes."

"And you're not afraid to handle these rattlesnakes?"

"My professor doesn't hold a gun to my head, like my husband did."

The prosecutor looked surprised. "Your husband held a gun to your head. No wonder you were frightened. But that's a pretty serious accusation. It seems to me that you would have mentioned it at your first trial. But you didn't mention it, did you? You didn't say a word about it."

"My lawyer didn't want me to take the stand. I kept telling him . . ." The prosecutor cut me off.

"Did he explain why he didn't want you to take the stand?"

"He said a good defense lawyer never lets his client take the stand."

"You could have overruled him. It was your decision, wasn't it? You've taken the stand in this trial."

"I didn't know any better back then. Besides, he was in cahoots with the city council. The public defender was. They didn't want any stuff about serpent handling coming out. It was bad publicity."

"Please answer the question, Ms. Cochrane."

The prosecutor introduced the transcript of Earl's testimony and asked me to read the part that he'd circled, about getting a snake out of the snake shed and trying to get it to bite Earl while he was taking a nap. He passed around copies of Earl's testimony.

"That isn't what happened," I said.

"Please," he said, "just read the passage."

I read it. " 'I was sleeping on the couch, it was about three o'clock in the afternoon and we was watching TV, I don't remember what. I woke up and Fern was shouting that she'd got bit. I didn't know what was going on and I could see she had aholt of a rattlesnake. We'd been fussin at each other for a long while and she got it out of the shed and was trying to get it to bite me, but it bit her instead.' "

"That's the craziest thing I ever heard," I said. "It was crazy then and it's crazy now."

"No further questions."

The prosecutor went back to his table, and Stella asked permission to re-call DX.

DX took the stand. He was still under oath and didn't have to be sworn in again.

"The State's Attorney," she said, "has introduced Mr. Cochrane's sworn testimony to the effect that the defendant had taken a snake out of the snake shed and was trying to get it to bite him while he was taking a nap . . . Now correct me if I'm wrong: You were the first to arrive on the scene after Sunny called your wife?"

"Yes."

"And did Mr. Cochrane tell you what had happened?"

"Objection: hearsay."

"Sustained."

"You've heard Mr. Cochrane's sworn testimony read aloud in this courtroom."

"You mean what Fern read just now?"

"Were you familiar with this story before you heard it today?"

"Yes."

"And you were at the scene?"

"Yes."

"Mr. Cochrane had been shot?"

"Yes."

"And Sunny had been bitten on the thumb, is that correct?"

"Yes."

"According to Mr. Cochrane's sworn testimony—testimony that you heard read aloud in this courtroom—she had brought a snake in the house and was trying to get it to bite him."

"That's what it said."

"Would it be fair to say that you agree with Mr. Cochrane's version of what happened?"

"Yes."

Stella looked through some papers on the lectern and then looked up suddenly: "What happened to the snake?"

"What snake?"

"The snake that Sunny supposedly brought into the house."

"I don't know."

Stella looked at the jury, took off her glasses, rubbed her eyes with the heels of her hands, put her glasses back on. "How is that possible?"

"It could of got away."

"Did you search for the snake?"

"No."

"Did the police search for the snake when they arrived?"

"No."

"Help me understand this situation. You believed that a venomous snake, a diamondback rattlesnake, was loose in the trailer, and you didn't bother to search for it."

"It probably got away. Snakes can get through about anything."

"Wouldn't it be more accurate to say that you didn't search the house for the snake because there was no snake?"

"There was snakes in the snake shed."

"Did the police confirm that a snake was missing from the snake shed?"

"Not that I know."

"No further questions."

The courtroom was silent except for the sound of the court reporter tapping "No further questions" on the stenograph machine.

The prosecutor made a lame attempt to repair the damage, trying to get DX to give a plausible explanation of why they hadn't searched for the snake, but Stella had made her point.

But so had the prosecutor.

In his closing argument the prosecutor drew a picture of me the way others saw me. At least some others: a woman who had shot her husband twice; a woman who had shot and killed a man who was a respected member of the church community; a woman who had killed a man people turned to for help; a woman who posed a much greater threat to him than he posed to her. She shot him twice, after all, on two different occasions, six years apart. A woman who had been convicted by a jury of her peers, seven years earlier, in September 1993, of shooting her husband in the shoulder with his own gun; a woman who got her boyfriend to buy her a gun because she was a convicted felon and couldn't buy it herself; a woman who at the time she shot and killed her former husband had just canceled a long-planned trip to Paris with one man who was not her husband in order to go to Mexico with another man, who also was not her husband; a woman who brought this illegal weapon with her to Naqada intending to shoot her former husband. A woman who did in fact shoot and kill her former husband in his own home, though he was unarmed at the time. It was like one of the Bible stories we used to hear at church, like the stories about Jezebel or Tamar, and the prosecutor sounded just like a preacher, full of righteous indignation.

Stella told a story too, but her story was more like the stories we used to hear the grown-ups tell on the back porch when they got to talking after dark. She talked to the jury as if she were explaining something important to a bunch of friends. She drew a picture of me the way I wanted to see myself. It was the same story she started out with, but now she filled it out with some of the stories the jury had heard. This time she spent a lot of time on my "trial by ordeal" and on Earl's prior testimony.

"Sunny had good reason to be deathly afraid of her former husband. You've heard her story, the story that she didn't get to tell at her first trial. Her former husband forced her at gunpoint to put her arm in a box of rattlesnakes. You've seen pictures of the snake shed; you've seen pictures of some of these snakes, and you have seen evidence of how much damage a rattlesnake bite can do. I want you to put yourselves in Sunny's position. I want you to imagine what it would be like to have your own husband or wife hold a gun to your head and force you to put your arm into a box of rattlesnakes. I want you to imagine what it would be like to have your husband or your wife hold a gun to your head and tell you to get down on your knees and get right with the Lord before he puts you to the test, the rattlesnake test. If the rattlesnake bites you, it's no more than you deserve; and if you don't want to put your arm in the box, he'll shove your head right down in it so the snake can bite you on your face, or in your eye. In the eye, that's right.

"I want you to keep this picture in your mind when you consider the events that took place on the evening of Tuesday, June twentieth. Your flight from Mexico has been canceled and you've had to take a different flight, one that makes two stops, both with long layovers, and arrives in Chicago at four o'clock in the morning. You drive home—a four-hour trip—and when you get there, there's a message on your answering machine. You've heard this message: 'Your boyfriend's been serpent bit. You better get down here.'

"So you call the hospital nearest to Naqada, in Rosiclare, to check on the supply of Crofab antivenin. You get some additional vials of antivenin from your own hospital. And you drive six hours from Colesville to Rosiclare. All this time you're thinking that your fiancé has been taken to the hospital in Rosiclare. But when you get to the hospital you discover that he's not there. You think, maybe it's not so bad. But you drive to your ex-husband's trailer and what do you discover? You discover that your ex-husband, the man who forced you to put your arm in a box of rattlesnakes, has refused to let the paramedics take your fiancé to the hospital. And you discover that your fiancé is in a coma. The prosecutor doesn't want me to use that word because I'm not a doctor, so I'll withdraw it and say, you discover that your fiancé is totally unconscious and that his arm has swelled up so that it's bigger than his thigh, has swelled up so much that the skin is breaking." Stella paused and wiped her face with a handkerchief, and then took a different tack.

"Now, you've heard insinuations that Sunny betrayed her fiancé by going off to Mexico with 'another man.' 'Another man.' As if this were a lovers' tryst. The 'other man' to whom the prosecutor has referred was Sunny's biology professor, who invited her—and another student— to go to a professional conference, the annual meeting of the American Society of Ichthyologists and Herpetologists, in Baja California, in Mexico—because of her research interest in snakes. Both these students have been involved in a long-term project translocating a unique population of rattlesnakes in central Illinois from one location, where they were threatened, to a new denning area. The suggestion that she somehow 'betrayed' her fiancé by attending this conference is one you should put out of your minds.

"But the real crux of the matter is this. Mr. Cochrane, Sunny's ex-husband, was not simply exercising his freedom of religion, as the prosecution has suggested, by preventing Professor Jones from receiving medical attention. He crossed a line when he prevented the paramedics from taking Jackson to the hospital and prevented Sunny from calling for medical assistance. It's hard, isn't it, not to figure that he *wanted* Jackson to die. Wanted him to die because he couldn't bear to see the woman he loved happy with another man. A woman he loved so much he forced her at gunpoint to put her arm in a box of deadly rattlesnakes. We know what kind of love that it. And it's hard, isn't it, not to figure that if Sunny hadn't done what she had to do to protect her fiancé, it would be Mr. Earl Cochrane here in this courtroom on trial for first-degree murder.

"At the beginning of this trial I read to you from section seven-dash-one from Article Seven of the Illinois Penal Code regarding 'Use of force in defense of a person.' I won't read it again, but I will remind you that your job is not to decide whether or not Sunny shot Mr. Cochrane. It's your job to decide whether or not she was *justified* in shooting him. And I'll remind you that the law is perfectly clear. Sunny had the right to shoot her ex-husband 'in order to prevent imminent death or great bodily harm to' Professor Jones, who was in no position to defend himself because he'd been rendered unconscious by a rattlesnake bite.

"If any one of you believes that Sunny was justified in saving the life of her fiancé by shooting a man whose violent behavior is on record, a man she had good reason to fear because he once forced her to put her arm in a box of rattlesnakes, then it is your duty to hang on to that belief and not let anyone bully you into changing it.

"Ladies and Gentlemen, this is the last opportunity I will have to address you. Let me thank you for your time and your patience and the care that you will bring to your deliberations."

Stella sat down.

The prosecutor had a chance to rebut Stella's closing argument. There were no disagreements about the physical evidence, no disagreements about who had done what to whom. What he did was attack my snake-shed story, a story that I had told so many times it had become central to who I was. Where was the evidence? he wanted to know. I had been tried and convicted in a court of law that had accepted Earl's testimony, under oath, that I'd gotten a snake out of the shed and had been trying to get it to bite him . . .

But you know the story. My defense depended on my deathly fear of Earl, and my deathly fear of Earl was based on this story. No story, no deathly fear. No deathly fear, no justification for taking the pistol to Naqada.

The prosecutor stumbled around trying to account for the missing snake that no one had searched for, and I think that was a mistake. He should have left well enough alone.

It really came down to what I believed in my heart of hearts, or what the members of the jury believed in their hearts of hearts about what I believed in mine. And the funny thing was, I knew in my heart of hearts that in some ways the prosecutor was closer to the truth than Stella, and he, the prosecutor, didn't even know the half of it. After DX I'd gone with all kinds of men, and sometimes Earl would slap me around a little, and I'd figure I deserved it, but he always forgave me. He said I had a sex demon, and we'd get down on our knees and pray about it, and he'd lay his hands on me and call that demon to come out, and I'd be all right for a while, but it was like I was caught in a big net, just like a fish in a landing net, and was struggling to escape. Nothing I could do except twist around in the net. Earl told everybody I didn't want to live right anymore. Maybe so. I didn't know what I wanted except that I wanted out of the net, wanted to swim in the river. Wanted to experience everything. Wanted to see everything, feel everything. But there I was caught in the net. And then in prison I pulled myself together, and when I got out I chose to change my name and be a certain kind of person. Happy, hard-working, full of fun, kind, loving, and faithful, not living under any man's thumb. And then Jackson came along, and it didn't take any effort to be with him, to love him, which is what I called it now. I didn't have to be afraid of him, the way I was always afraid of Earl. I thought I'd figured out something about myself, enough so I wouldn't be practicing the same mistakes over and over again, like practicing a drum roll the wrong way over and over again. That's why the worst of the stories about me that I had to listen to was the story of backing out of the trip to Paris. It wasn't that I'd been naughty and deserved a whupping, it wasn't that I'd committed a sin and needed to be forgiven; it was . . . I had trouble figuring out just what it was, and then an old song that Warren used to sing jumped into my mind. I was sitting next to Stella at the defense table, along with Peter Franklin, and the judge was instructing the jury, and it was like somebody switching on the radio:

I could have loved you better, I didn't mean to be unkind,
You know that was the last thing on my mind.

I started to cry. Stella put her arm around me. It was the first time she'd touched me. And I figured maybe everything was going to turn out all right.

23

Paris

In Claire's new novel, *Kiss of Death*, the feisty, spunky, sassy, tough-talking, snake-handling heroine and her lover go to Paris in the last chapter to celebrate a decisive victory over the forces of evil. He proposes to her in the Café Anglais, and she says yes, but it's a difficult yes. She's too independent; they both are; they have too many issues to work out, and so on. But they love each other, and . . .

In real life I went to Paris with Claire, the summer after Jackson left, a month before the ASIH meetings, which were going to be held in University Park, Pennsylvania. Six months after I was found not guilty by a jury of my peers in the courthouse in Allensboro.

This is what happened. After the trial Jackson and Claire and I went back to Colesville and picked up the pieces of our lives. Cramer helped me work out a plan for my classes so that I'd be able to graduate in four years. I threw myself into my studies, preparing to take an overload in the spring semester, and sometimes in the evenings I helped Jackson with Claude's notebooks. I couldn't read the difficult French, but I was better than Jackson at deciphering Claude's handwriting.

Jackson and I spent Christmas Eve with Claire and her family, including Claire's parents, at the rectory. Claire had sold her novel and she and Father Ray were in very high spirits, and their high spirits were contagious. Neither one of them could sit still, and I couldn't either. Claire danced with Ray and she danced with Jackson, and she danced with her father, and she danced with me. I danced with Ray and with Claire's father, and with Jackson, and Claire's father danced with Claire's mother. The children watched wide-eyed. The rectory was truly beautiful, not designer beautiful, but homey beautiful, filled with family photos and pictures drawn by the children, Alan and Natalie, and ornaments and decorations and candles from Ray's parents and some from Claire's. Half-melted snow-people candles skated on a mirror pond. Tarnished bronze angels circled around and around a candle flame, dinging little bells on their way. A beautiful Italian crèche was full of Italian cows and sheep and donkeys and other four-footed animals. All the ornaments on the tree were homemade, some of them dating back to Claire's childhood. Jackson and I went along to midnight mass at Grace Episcopal—it was the first time Claire had gotten me into church—and then we went home. Standing on the church steps after the mass, Claire had begged us to go to dinner the next day. Christmas Day. Her father had brought two butterflied legs of lamb from Gepperth's on North Halsted, so there'd be plenty to eat. She was going to serve them with white beans.

If we'd accepted this invitation, would things have turned out differently? Probably not. But sometimes I wonder.

We spent Christmas Day by ourselves. Jackson had put up a tree, and we'd bought presents for each other. We drank *kir royale* while

I fixed Chicken Marengo with frozen crawfish and little fried eggs, and after dinner, about four o'clock, we went for a walk in the woods, and Jackson told me he was going back to Africa. We walked farther into the woods. His daughter, he said, had come to him while he was in the coma. It was time for her *elima*, time for her to become a woman. She wanted him to be there.

It had started to snow, and we wandered off the path—an old logging road—into the woods and walked all the way to the back of the property, which butted onto a corn field. The wind was blowing from the north and the snow was coming at us almost horizontally, and we kept our heads down and stumbled on into a stand of evergreens that provided a little pocket in the storm where we could almost imagine being warm. This was where we had cut our Christmas tree the year before. This was where I had stuck a shovel into Jackson's Indian burial mound, which was now covered with snow.

He asked me to go with him, and we talked about this possibility for about an hour, standing in the snow, stomping our feet, until it started to get dark. It was an exciting prospect, more exciting than Paris: the Mountains of the Moon, the source of the Nile, the Garden of Eden. But by the time we got back to the house I had realized that Jackson wasn't talking about taking a year off; he wasn't coming back, and I knew I couldn't go with him. I thought I could have followed him to Africa, but he was on another journey too, one that led him not just out of the safe harbor provided by the university, but out beyond the defensive virtues that I was just starting to master: prudence, thrift, caution. He was sailing out into a wider sea of courage, risk, adventure, letting go of the self and of the world. I'd caught a glimpse of this sea in my own life, growing up in the Church of the Burning Bush. And I'd even glimpsed it in Earl, but maybe I hadn't recognized it at the time for what it was: Earl, who gave away all his money, who considered the lilies of the field and never bought insurance. I'd gotten tired of living that way then, and I couldn't live that way now. I didn't want to leave the safe harbor of the university, where I could practice my new virtues, my knowledge of the world: how to manage my time and my money, what was left of it after the collapse of ShoppingKart.com and after I'd paid Stella. (Though I knew now that Claire and Jackson had paid more than half the bill, if not more. Claire said she owed me for sharing my snake stories. I didn't protest too much.) Maybe this was an example of knowledge of the world. I wanted to do well in school. I wanted success. I wanted to go to graduate school. And that's what happened. Not right away, but eventually.

Jackson set to work right after the holidays, resigning his position at TF, making contact with the Forest Peoples Project in England, applying for his visa, donating his books—and Claude's books—to the TF library. He laid in a large supply of Lee Oskar harmonicas, taking them apart one by one and tinkering with the reeds till he had them just right.

Laurent-Désiré Kabila, president of the Democratic Republic of the Congo, was assassinated in January, and though his son Joseph, the new president, was promising to back the Lusaka Agreement, *L'Avenir* predicted nothing but trouble. Even civil war. I thought this might deter Jackson, but at the beginning of March he left for London to "liaise" with the Forest Peoples Project people. He spoke French and Kingwana and could get along in the language that the Mbuti used among themselves, and the Forest Peoples Project was glad to have him on board. As the rain forest was being destroyed by logging, many of the small bands of net hunters were spending more and more time in the Negro villages and plantations along the Epulu River, putting on shows for tourists, exchanging bush meat for tobacco, iron tools, and commercial food. Other were entering into permanent relationships with commercial meat traders, called *bachuzzi*, who promoted intensified net hunting. But some were withdrawing farther and farther into the Forest, and I was sure that this is what Jackson was planning to do. He wasn't going to Africa to save the pygmies. He was going to save himself. He gave the house to me. I tried to protest, but he had me sign a quitclaim deed, and he made me promise to look after Maya.

Claire and I drove him to the airport in Chicago. O'Hare. Claire didn't need a map, but I traced our route on a fold-out roadmap: 74 to 80 to 55 to 294 to 190. It was a clear cold March day. The indoor parking lots were full and we had to leave Claire's BMW in a distant lot and take a shuttle to the international terminal. We took turns carrying Jackson's suitcase, an old-fashioned one without wheels. In those days, before 9/11, you could still accompany passengers to the gates, but we waited in the international terminal for Jackson's British Airways flight to be called. He kissed us both good-bye, and after he left we drove straight home. Claire wanted to spend the night with her parents on Bellevue Place in Chicago, but I was too sad and just wanted to get home.

All that time after I shot Earl I'd put my life on hold. I was waiting till the trial was over for it to begin again. But all that time, all that waiting, was my life too, maybe the best part of it. The part I'd remember when I was old and sad.

I cried most of the way home and let Claire worry out loud about the title of her novel. She wanted to call it *Kiss of Death*. The publisher wanted to call it *My Serpentine Romance*.

Every morning at six thirty Maya and I played Frisbee, and I would shout at her just the way Jackson did: "Big pi-pi girl, big pi-pi girl." And then, if all went well, "Big poopy-girl." I'd gotten pretty good at throwing the Frisbee, and in my imagination I could hear Jackson shouting: "Look at the arm on that woman."

I didn't want to risk damaging the timpani by trying to move them out on the deck—this was after the weather had warmed up—but at night I'd open all the doors and windows and fill the woods with the sound of copper—well, fiberglass—and Mylar.

The word "timpani," I'd learned from Paul, comes from a Greek word meaning a vibrating membrane, like the timpanic membrane in the human ear. They weren't called kettle drums till the time of King Edward VI in England, in the sixteenth century; and as Paul always pointed out, they aren't really drums, because they have a definite pitch that can be varied. They're "membranophones." There are references to kettle drums–timpani–membranophones in ancient Babylonian cuneiform tablets and in ancient Egypt hieroglyphs, and in the earliest literature of Greece and the Middle East. In the fifteenth century the Turks carried them mounted on horses and camels when they attacked Constantinople, and pretty soon the Europeans did the same thing. The players of these drums were held in very high esteem and got to wear ostrich feathers in their hats.

The size of the drums was limited by the size of animal skins, though the heads of the new drums are made of Mylar. You needed a thirty-two-inch skin to get a low D out of a drum, which is what you needed for the low notes in *Carmina Burana*. The drums were hard to tune. You had to be a mechanic, and you still have to be a mechanic, though the adjustments you have to make are smaller. Pretty soon you'll need a computer to tune your timpani, just the way you need a computer to tune up the engine of your car. But the quest for the perfect sound will never end.

Paul didn't like the commercial mallets or "sticks" that had come with the drums and gave me two sets of handcrafted ones, and I could feel the difference they made. Each pair had a different balance and required a slightly different grip, and produced a different sound. "The subject of mallets," he said, "is vast." Not something I would have guessed.

On Thursdays Paul came out, in the late afternoon, for a lesson and to have dinner and spend the night. He had grown up in Colesville, played drums in the Colesville High School band, and then gone to live with an uncle in Amsterdam, where he studied percussion at the Conservatorium van Amsterdam. He offered to take me to Amsterdam in the summer, but I had too much work to do to make up for the semester I'd missed when I was waiting for my trial to begin.

Like Jackson, he was a good cook, and after the lesson he'd remove his coat and tie and we'd cook something together, something simple with lots of butter. Paul never gained any weight, but I had to watch myself.

After supper we'd go back to the timpani and—maybe it was because we were a little tipsy by this time—we'd stick some owl feathers in our hair while we looked for that perfect sound.

Cramer usually came out on Sundays. He was always so serious that I told him he needed to tell me a new joke every time he came or I wouldn't go to bed with him.

I don't know where he got the jokes, maybe the Internet, and I've forgotten most of them. All of them, in fact, except one. One that cheers me up every time I think of it, maybe because it's so unCramerlike.

An elderly Jewish man is unable to bring his wife to orgasm, and Jewish women have the right to sexual pleasure. That's the law. So the husband goes to a rabbi, and the rabbi tells him to hire a young man to wave a towel over him and his wife while they're making love.

The husband hires one of his employees, a handsome athletic type, to come to the house and wave a towel over him and his wife as they're making love. The young man complies, but nothing happens.

The husband returns to the rabbi, who tells him, this time *you* wave the towel and ask the young man to make love to your wife.

So the young man comes to the house again. This time he makes love to the wife while the husband waves the towel over them. Sure enough, the wife comes to a screaming, earth-moving orgasm, and the husband says to the young man, "Now *that's* waving a towel, schmuck."

Every time I came to an orgasm, even a little one, I'd think of that joke and it would make me laugh, and Cramer would ask me to marry him, and I'd say no.

When neither Paul nor Cramer was there, I let Maya sleep on the bed with me. And then in June, I went to Paris with Claire.

What happened was that a New York publisher had bought Claire's novel and we spent her advance on the trip. Claire wanted to check the scenes in Paris before the manuscript went to the copy editor. For authenticity. She wanted to go to all the places she'd written about. She wanted to stay at the residential hotel where Jackson had lived with his parents when his father was lecturing at the Sorbonne. She didn't want to go alone. She said she needed someone who spoke French.

We walked along the Seine, drank coffee at a bar near the Hôtel de Ville where Diana and Alexander—the protagonists of Claire's novel—go ice skating; we walked in the Luxembourg Gardens and up and down the Champs-Élysées and from Nôtre-Dame across to the Île-Saint-Louis for ice cream at Berthillon; we looked in the decorated shop window at Ralph Lauren; and Claire lit a candle at the Church of the Madeleine. She took pictures with her new digital camera and made copious notes in a little notebook made out of moleskin that she carried with her in her purse. She didn't know a word of French, so I was responsible for getting us around. I ordered for us at the Tour d'Argent and in a bistro on boulevard Saint-Germain where we became "regulars." We ate a lot of *poulet rôti* and *steak frites*. No one made fun of my baby French, not even at the Tour d'Argent. In fact, everyone treated us very nicely.

A month was not very long, but it was long enough to pretend that we weren't tourists but were actually living there, doing our own shopping and cooking, sometimes eating at home, sometimes in the neighborhood bistro, walking up and down the boulevard Saint-Germain, me in my spaghetti-strap cami and my pale putty skirt, Claire in beige slacks and a striped shirt.

We were surprised and disappointed to learn that the Café Anglais pictured in Jackson's Time-Life French cookbook had been closed in 1913. According to our concierge it had moved to the Place Vendôme for a few years, but now it was gone for good. Claire would have to find another restaurant for Alexander to propose in (and for Diana to accept), and the concierge came up with another Café Anglais—in Maisons-Laffitte, a suburb about thirty kilometers from the center of Paris. The concierge suggested that we go to the races there, and Claire thought that this was something Alexander and Diana might do, so she asked the concierge to book a hotel for us.

The Café Anglais turned out to be a bar, or maybe a brasserie. Whatever it was, it had prices written on the windows with what looked like whiteout, and it was clear that you could drink beer there. It wasn't much of a place, but we were looking for an adventure, not a restaurant. Too bad it was closed on Thursday afternoons.

We ate at the hotel, and in the morning we toured the racehorse museum in Château de Maisons-Laffitte and the training establishment, with its various tracks for different kinds of races. In the afternoon we went to the races. I was totally at sea. I'd never been to a racetrack before. Claire had been to the races at Arlington Park with her father when she was a little girl, but neither of us had any idea what was going on and we probably would have turned around and left after the first race if Claire hadn't got it into her head that she wanted to add a racetrack scene to *Kiss of Death*.

"Isn't it too late for that?" I asked.

"I guess we'll see," she said.

We didn't panic, but we must have looked lost, because a handsome man in a striped silk suit and a yellow cravat came to our aid and explained, in perfect English, how French racing differed from American. The races are run clockwise, for one thing, and exclusively on grass instead of dirt, so after each race an army of men and boys—*jardiniers*—came out to stomp down the divots that the horses' hooves had kicked up; the track, or *Arc,* is twenty-four hundred meters instead of a mile or a mile and a quarter. He showed us how to place our bets and where to find the odds (on TV monitors inside the building), and explained the pari-mutuel betting system, which the French had invented. Claire and I had our own systems. I bet on black horses and Claire on chestnut. Claire bet *gagnant,* to win, and I bet something called *placé,* which gave you a better chance of winning, but you don't win as much.

The grass track was so big you couldn't see the horses when they were on the back stretch. We bet the minimum—one euro—on each race and lost most of our money, though on the last race Claire won thirty euros. She bought drinks for us at a bar on the second *étage* (floor) where we could watch the divot stompers and grounds crew working on the turf.

Our silk-suited friend bought us a second drink, and Claire asked him questions about racing and about Maisons-Laffitte and about Paris and about France in general, always pushing for the sort of details you couldn't get from a guide book. She jotted everything down in her moleskin notebook. We had another drink, and I got a little tipsy and thought Claire was going to invite the man to have dinner with us, but she didn't. He offered to take *us* to dinner, but I said we had to get back to the hotel.

That night Claire asked if I'd have accepted the invitation if I'd been alone, and I asked her what did she think I was, and it took a while for her to answer. We were drinking beer and eating bar food—prosciutto, salami, cheese, bread. "What about you?" I asked.

"He wasn't interested in me," she said. "He was interested in you."

I wanted to protest, to tell Claire, who was wearing a yellow blazer over a flowery summer dress, how good she looked. She'd lost weight and nothing bulged or pulled, and her strappy shoes and her purse matched her blazer, and she looked, well, French. People smiled at us as we walked down the street. People smiled at us in the Café Anglais, and I explained to the locals that Claire was a novelist who was writing about the races at Maisons-Lafitte.

I was thinking about my first night in the garage apartment, coming down to the big house and peeking in the window and seeing Claire and Jackson on the davenport.

"When I first came to TF," Claire said, "I had a manuscript, and I had a New York agent. I gave a big party and put the manuscript in the middle of the table with candles around it. *The Sins of the World.* Everybody got drunk and we went up on the roof—I had a big apartment on State Street, next to Ulrich's Bookstore—and we made so much noise the police finally came and told us to keep it down. The policeman shouted up from the street with a mega-phone. Later that night I fucked Jackson up on the roof."

I had heard some of the story from Jackson, but not all of it.

"We used to take a blanket up on the roof all the time. I've never been so happy. But after my novel was turned down thirty-nine times and my agent had called it quits, and I had to start sending it out to contests . . . I started thinking seriously about suicide. Jackson was afraid I was going to throw myself off the roof onto the sidewalk. After a year no one said a word about the novel. Everyone pretended it had never existed.

"I started going to church, and I started praying. And then I stopped screwing Jackson. It didn't feel right until I had a publisher. This was at the Episcopal church. I turned to Father Ray for help. He would tell me about God's love, and I would tell Jackson about it. Finally, after I submitted the manuscript to the Donner competition, which I read about in *Poets & Writers,* Father Ray set up a prayer vigil. All these people in the church who hardly knew me were praying for me, and then the news came. I got a phone call. I'd won the Donner Prize. I sat on the news for quite a while. I didn't tell anyone except Father Ray and Jackson. Jackson wanted to have a party, but I just wanted to be quiet for a while. Quiet and thankful, prayerful.

"Jackson thought I'd go to bed with him now that my prayers had been answered and the novel was going to be published, but I didn't."

"God didn't write the novel," I said. "You did."

"I wasn't so sure about that back then, and I'm not so sure of it now. I used to think that I did it all myself, but now I've learned—I think I've learned—differently."

"What about the new novel?" I asked. "Did God write *Kiss of Death* too? It looks to me like you're the one doing the work."

Claire signaled the *garçon* for two more beers. "I'm sorry," she said. "I had to unload on someone. I'm glad it was you."

I was glad too, but in a funny way. I was pretty drunk by this time, but the kind of drunk where you suddenly see things clearly. What I saw clearly was that in spite of her encounters with rattlesnakes, the feisty, spunky, sassy, tough-talking, snake-handling protagonist of *Kiss of Death* wasn't me. It was Claire. I'd been thinking all along that I'd come to Paris with the wrong person; I'd been thinking all day long, right up to that moment, that I was here in Maisons-Laffitte with the wrong person in the wrong Café Anglais. But now I saw clearly that it was Claire who had come to Paris with the wrong person, Claire who was sitting here in the wrong Café Anglais with the wrong person. *I* was the wrong person. She should have been here with Jackson.

"Did you make the right choice?"

"For a long time I didn't think so."

"And now."

"Right now?"

"Right now. This very minute."

"It all worked out."

We walked down to the river, holding hands—like the French schoolgirls we'd see sometimes in the Luxembourg Gardens. Like sisters. We didn't say anything because there wasn't anything more to say.

24

Joie de Vivre

I've graduated—or "been graduated," as Claire would say—Phi Beta Kappa, and with high honors. I'm still throwing the Frisbee to Maya, who will be going with me. I'm not sure how much she knows, though I've tried hard enough to explain. What can I say? How can I explain what had happened, why Jackson left us?

Uncle Warren blamed me for going off to Mexico with Cramer. Claire blamed me for not saying yes in the first place when Jackson asked me to marry him at Christmas. Jackson himself said it was because his daughter had appeared to him in his dreams, and wanted him to go to her *elima*.

What did I think? I thought he'd used up his life here at Thomas Ford, his life with Maya and me, and needed to move on. There wasn't anything here that he needed.

I've sold the house and property to TF for $150,000, a lot of money for me but significantly below market value. TF is going to turn the property into a biological field station. A crew is already at work, measuring the house, which will be converted to a dormitory. I have a full ride at UF (University of Florida), and now I have a cushion.

I'm leaving on the thirtieth of June. I'm anxious to get the last few days over with, but I'm an adult now and I try not to wish my life away.

My honors project turned into an article that's going to be published in *Copeia*; Cramer's name should appear on the paper too, but he's left it off, just the way Harold Urey left his name off the Stanley Miller paper on amino acids. This kind of altruism has always posed a problem for evolutionary biologists. Though not an insuperable problem.

It turns out that Illinois ground squirrels (*Spermophilus tridecemlineatus*) exhibit the same signaling behavior that Aaron Matthews had observed in California ground squirrels (*Spermophilus beecheyi*). Matthews was the guy who gave the paper on rattlesnakes at La Paz, the guy who told me that no one knew quite what to make of squirrel "flagging."

What happens is this: When confronting a rattlesnake—especially when defending its pups—the squirrel will raise its tail and wave it back and forth (flagging). I discovered that it's also emitting an infrared signal by pumping more blood into its tail. It's this signal that discourages the snake from attacking. How did I figure this out? With a lot of help from Cramer, I'd be the first to admit. Cramer and I trapped a lot of ground squirrels and caught a few rattlesnakes—some of the same ones we'd translocated—and got them together in the lab in a setup where the rattlesnakes could threaten the squirrels but couldn't really get at them. Everyone knows that pit vipers are sensitive to infrared light—which is really radiant heat—but what no one knew was that squirrels were capable of sending out infrared signals. We tried this and that, and then I asked, "What if we used an infrared imaging camera to record each encounter?" That's what we did, and we discovered that the squirrels were in fact emitting infrared signals. We still didn't know why this particular infrared signal deters rattlesnakes, but we knew we were on to something, and we started generating hypotheses: We know, for example, that California ground squirrels will in fact harass rattlesnakes, kicking dirt at them and nipping at the snakes' tails and moving their own tails erratically. We hadn't observed this behavior in *Spermophilus tridecemlineatus,* but it was still early days. Our initial thinking was that the erratic movement of the tails causes them to heat up and give off more infrared radiation—possibly so much radiation that it overwhelms the rattlesnake's infrared sensor. The problem with this hypothesis was that confronted with gopher snakes, the squirrels flag their tales *without* emitting an infrared signal. There's no need for an infrared signal because gopher snakes are not pit vipers and therefore wouldn't register the signal. How do the squirrels distinguish between the different kinds of snakes? What causes them to emit infrared signals in one case and not the other? And on and on, one question leading to another. And maybe that's all you need to know for now.

My three rented timpani, which I kept till the last minute, have been returned to Thompson's Music. This time I had a bottle of scotch on hand for Mr. Thompson's men. The books—Claude's and Jackson's—have been carted off to the TF library; I have canceled Jackson's subscriptions to the *New Yorker* and *L'Avenir;* the truck is packed, my route has been plotted by the Chicago Motor Club; my last suitcase is open on Jackson's big library table, which I sold with the house.

I walk out to get the mail for the last time. Tomorrow's mail will be forwarded to me care of the Department of Wildlife Ecology and Conservation at the University of Florida in Gainesville. Maya races through the young corn, off leash, but when we get close to the road, I call her and put the leash on. Just in case. It's been more than two years since Jackson left. I've tried to keep up with the news in *L'Avenir*, and you don't have to know French very well to understand none of it has been very good. Where is Jackson now? Does he know how our world has changed? Does he know about the attack on the World Trade Center? About the war in Iraq? About the capture of Saddam Hussein? Has he survived the violence of the Second Congo War? Has he made his way into the depths of the Forest? Has he found his old girlfriend, Sibaku? Or his daughter?

I pause for just a moment before opening the mailbox. I'm still hoping for a letter. Some word from Jackson. I can't help myself. But the mailbox is empty. I turn back and let Maya run free.

Joie de vivre.

Acknowledgments

I would like to thank my first three readers for their support and encouragement: Virginia (my wife), Henry Dunow (my agent), and Nancy Miller (my editor).

Special thanks to the following for reading the manuscript and offering suggestions: Larry Breitborde (anthropologist), Carol Chase (French professor), Jeremy Karlin (attorney), Mathys Meyer (herpetologist), Joanna Tweedy (writer and native of Little Egypt). And to the following for sharing their expertise: Ken Cramer, Dr. Robert Currie, Steve Gardiner, Joan Killion, Stephen Kotler, Nikki Whitaker Malley, Esther Pennick, and Jennifer Templeton.

The two stories that are intertwined (like two snakes) in *Snakewoman of Little Egypt* were prompted, or perhaps inspired, by Colin Turnbull's *The Forest People* and Dennis Covington's *Salvation on Sand Mountain*.

Sunny's work on Illinois ground squirrels relied heavily on "Ground Squirrels Use an Infrared Signal to Deter Rattlesnake Predation" by Aaron S. Rundus, Donald H. Owings, Sanjay S. Joshi, Erin Chinn, and Nicholas Gianni. *Proceedings of the National Academy of Sciences of the United States of America* 104, no. 36 (September 4, 2007).

"'Fieldwork,' Claude used to say, 'is to anthropology what the blood of the martyrs is to the church.'" It was actually C. G. Seligman who proposed this striking analogy in a pamphlet published by the Department of Anthropology 1972–73 (London School of Economics, 1972): 4; quoted by I. M. Lewis in *Religion in Context: Cults and Charisma* (Cambridge: Cambridge University Press, 1986): 1.

The lesson that Sunny learned from Cramer—"that we share the room, that taking turns is important"—was adapted from Lisa Ress's "Setting the Table, Eating What is Served," which won the Word Works Washington Prize in 1987 and appeared in the March/April 1988 issue of *Poets & Writers*. The epitaph that Warren proposes for his own tombstone was prompted by a passage on page 11 of Thomas Nagel's *Mortal Questions* (Cambridge: Cambridge University Press, 1979.).

A Note on the Author

Robert Hellenga was educated at the University of Michigan, the Queen's University of Belfast, the University of North Carolina, and Princeton University. He is a professor at Knox College in Galesburg, Illinois, and the author of the novels *The Sixteen Pleasures*, *The Fall of a Sparrow*, *Blues Lessons*, *Philosophy Made Simple*, and *The Italian Lover*.